D1156289

Originally published in Slovenian as *Menuet za kitaro* by Cankarjeva založba, 1975
Copyright © 2011 by Copyright Agency of Slovenia
Translation copyright © 1988 by Harry Leeming

First edition, 2011

Library of Congress Cataloging-in-Publication Data

Zupan, Vitomil.
[Menuet za kitaro. English]
Minuet for guitar (in twenty-five shots) / Vitomil Zupan ; translated by Harry Leeming. -- 1st ed.
    p. cm.
ISBN 978-1-56478-689-0 (cloth : acid-free paper)
1. World War, 1939-1945--Fiction. I. Leeming, Henry, 1920-2004. II. Title.
PG1918.Z78M413 2011
891.8'435--dc23
                                2011035024

Partially funded by a grant from the Illinois Arts Council, a state agency, and by the University of Illinois at Urbana-Champaign

The Slovenian Literature Series is made possible by support from the Slovenian Book Agency

www.dalkeyarchive.com

Cover: design and composition by Danielle Dutton, illustration by Nicholas Motte
Printed on permanent/durable acid-free paper and bound in the United States of America

MINUET FOR GUITAR
(IN TWENTY-FIVE SHOTS)

Vitomil Zupan
translated by Harry Leeming

DALKEY ARCHIVE PRESS
CHAMPAIGN / DUBLIN / LONDON

MUST MAKE THE TOP

This phrase recurs like a motto in the mass of papers lying here in front of me, handwritten in inks and pencils of various colors.

The compilation is based on daily notes that run for a few pages, then peter out to reemerge later in a plethora of minute details, odd words, sketches of a storyline, all recovered from a soldier's green canvas rucksack: dog-eared exercise books, leaflets, bits of cardboard, scraps of paper covered with an untidy scrawl. There had been a purpose in all this. The material was not particularly legible. Some names had been abbreviated to their initial letters while certain other personal and geographical names had been copied out in full, at the writer's whim. Initial "A" could stand for Albin or Anton and several other names and nicknames. "G" could stand for Goriče or Grosuplje or some other place. The reader had to decide for himself. The writer's own name occurred on most pages: Jakob Bergant, sometimes written Jakob Bergant-Berk. In an eyewitness account of the fighting at Jelenov Žleb, by one who took part, we find: "Charge! make for the top!" cried the partisan commander. "Alla montagna!" yelled the officer commanding the Italian Macerata Brigade. There was only a matter of five or ten yards in it but it was a partisan machine gun that first opened fire from the top. A description of this victory follows, together with the note: MUST MAKE THE TOP.

At one point we read how Bergant, perched high up in the fork of a tree, watches German tanks on the road below, rumbling by with open turrets. In one stands the tank commander. Sensing the hidden partisan's gaze fixed on the nape of his neck, he turns and begins to look up into the trees. To break the unwelcome link, the partisan repeats to himself that isolated phrase: must make the top. The German drives on.

Somewhere near the end, there is a note written in a careful hand: "The road matters, not the goal; the goal alters like the setting sun."

There are several selected sayings, quotations, maxims, entered in the notes, sometimes for no apparent reason, and sometimes as an integral part of them. I could hardly include in this book even a quarter of the accumulated hodgepodge. For example, a good half of one exercise book contains thoughts on the relations between subjects and authority, brought to a close by a quotation from Machiavelli's The Prince: "Happy the man who operates in harmony with the spirit of the age—and unhappy the man who is opposed to it."

The notes were obviously made at different times and later bound together. The ink is faded, for example, where we read: "The night we call cherry blossom night. A tree—stars like the petals of the white blossom, shooting stars. Over Suha Krajina. A minuet. Dogs barking, a mule braying, strict silence, the stones in the wood." There are at least twenty papers appended to this page, describing many details, characters, events, and these probably belong to the time both preceding and following that night. The paper is whiter, the writing more even.

"A spoon stuck in a puddle of congealed blood. The battle at S." And a bundle of new pages. There are many such examples.

A nostalgia for human society and a passionate yearning for lasting solitude rub shoulders on the road from V. to R. G.

Empty offices. Memoirs of a clerk who loved his documents.

Eighty fascists. Blood flowing down the hillside. Shirts that don't fit.

A massive hulk, idly rolling in an oily fluid; cold, cruel, dim, devoid of feeling, awash in the foaming surge. Might and a faint glimmer through the clouds.

A sack of hand grenades instead of a pillow for your head.

Short notes like these are followed by additions and afterthoughts but through it all runs one thread, one road. The diarist tried to keep to his line and the copyist has tried to do the same. It goes without saying that he also drew on the fruit of his own experience. His chief aim was continuity; to engage the reader's interest was his least concern.

Ljubljana - Barcelona 1973/74

"I saw God dead but laughing."
Jose Garcia Villa

"The whole land is made desolate, because no man layeth it to heart."
Jeremiah 12:11

"Nothing really belongs to us but time, which even he has who has nothing else."
Baltasar Gracián, 1653

"In man's world beauty was linked with suffering and suffering with
salvation. Nothing of the sort obtained in Nature."
Henry Miller, *Nexus, p. 130*

"Each marches gaily to crime, under the banner of his own saint."
Voltaire, *Dictionary of Philosophy*

"Character fashions fate."
Cornelius Nepos

"Don't talk like that. Hide your face in your hands; let time answer for
you. How much love were you capable of, my brother?"
Giannini, *The Strangers*

1

Slowly the tram ground to a halt. Green and white, the municipal livery of Ljubljana. From the second-floor window of a house on the other side of the street hung a flag, violent, provocative, red with a black swastika on a white field.

Must head for the hills.

The cool golden October of 1943. Pastel colors of the suburb glowing in the warm sunlight. People, cars, horses harnessed to a heavy cart, all moving gently on their way. As if any undue haste might arouse suspicion. No unseemly noise disturbed the pleasant peace of the afternoon. Even the German soldiers in their dark green uniforms sauntered unhurriedly along the pavement. Among them, I noticed an officer wearing a jauntily aggressive cap with a gleaming black peak. What was there about that blend of green, black, and silver? As we clambered aboard he glanced at Mariana, before favoring me with a look of noble disdain. He would have turned the scales at about sixty-five kilos, I guess. One of my left hooks would have floored him like a straw doll. He had a semiautomatic in a well polished black leather holster, a Mauser Reiterpistole 7.35 no doubt, judging by the long protruding barrel. Range one thousand meters. What on earth had made him turn around? *Must head for the hills.*

Mariana's fingers brushed my face as we climbed the two steps into the tram. She had not even noticed the German. Everyone seemed to have time to spare. I looked out at a sandy yellow house with the sunlight reflected in its closed windows. Three men in overalls passed by, pushing a handcart with a piece of stage scenery several feet high, a balcony or something similar, with creepers on the wall.

The tram jerked into motion. Mariana glanced at me, eyes wide open, bright blue eyes clouded with grief or foreboding.

I could not stand that look. On the road I was taking, there would be no time for grievous sorrow, baleful forebodings, harrowing memories, tender feelings. I had been wrong to let her join me on this journey. From now on I would be singing a different tune. As I observed the roads, the houses, the people on the pavements, the uniforms, the stage scenery receding into the distance, I was witnessing a legend. A legend I had to escape from, and Mariana was part of it. It all reminded me of a painting, by a Dutch artist, I think: a road, trees, a procession with a banner, and even a dog like the one that watched us go by.

Did I really hear the echo of a wailing siren, or was it only my imagination?

"When shall I see you again?" Mariana asked in a low voice. A close-fitting blue costume. A white collar. A legend.

The whole place was full of folk walking, talking, coming, going, appearing, disappearing, bound on their various errands: men, women, angels, robots, orphans, beasts—the righteous, the victims, the executioners. The noise of the siren and the sight of this parade were enough to drive anyone crazy.

"Look," I said, trying to keep the excitement out of my voice, "this is the same road the Roman legions took when they advanced on Emona from the south and the Asian nomads rode this way when they invaded Italy."

"When will you be back?"

"Traders drove their caravans this way . . ."

"Perhaps I'll never see you again."

"In the '14–'18 war too, there were troops marching along this road."

The tram stopped. In the crowded car, Mariana's firm breasts and strong thighs were pressed close against me. The memory of her whole body from tip to toe flashed through my mind. Part of a legend if not part of that Dutch painting.

We moved off again with a jolt that threw me against her. "And this road," I said quietly, "is an ancient route for birds of passage . . ."

She probably did not like that. One more stop to go. I saw no reason why I should cling to the past. The present would begin out there, among the fences, bunkers, and barbed-wire barricades. We shall relive these moments in the past.

Butterflies in the stomach. Just like before a big match.

"Mariana, let's say good-bye now. And leave me without a backward glance. Just turn away and go. So as not to give anyone any ideas. Let's just pretend I'm off on a trip to the primeval forests. Exploring the rapids on the River of No Return. None of these characters in uniform would understand that. But if the Krauts do catch me, I'll do my best to defend myself. I'll explain in my best

German how interested I am in the relativity of all phenomena. Dear Mariana, when we get off at the next stop, each of us must go his own way without another word—that is, if you care at all about birds of passage."

Something ludicrous occurred to me at this most inappropriate moment. For some reason I could have exploded in a belly laugh.

"Maybe I ought to reconsider my nationality, once at least. The Italian call us Schiavi, the Austrians Windish swine, the rest of Europe thinks we belong to the Balkans, Balkan peoples think we're part of the old Austrian Empire, while for the rest of the world, we're just somewhere tucked away between Turkey and Czechoslovakia . . ."

As we got off the tram, I stroked Mariana's blonde locks for the last time, then alighted on the pavement, turned right, and walked off without looking back. Every step brought me closer to the present reality, until it confronted me, eye to eye. It had a face, a face with foxy, beady eyes. In the background stood a fat man with rubbery lips. Beyond him a sentry. Barbed wire. Pillboxes. The barricades of barbed wire on wooden frames— we called them Spanish horsemen—had been moved to one side. The leaves of a spreading oak tree on the other side of the barricade were turning a gentle yellow. The official glanced at my forged pass and then fixed his piercing gaze on me.

Must make for the hills.

Elegantly attired in my fine tweed jacket made to measure, dark blue trousers, soft shoes, bright corn-gold necktie, which in those days would rouse the envy of all who saw it, with my nails polished and manicured (I enjoyed a game of poker), I walked on past the barbed wire toward the shaggy oak tree. Must control my breathing. Good-bye, Ljubljana!

About ten yards farther along the main road, I came to a left-hand turning, the side road that would bring me to our rendezvous. I felt as if the chains had fallen from my body, but the cool hand of prudence checked my high spirits. I kept my eyes on the road ahead, while trying to be aware of all my surroundings.

In front of me, a horse and cart were drawing closer in the western sunlight. To my right, there was a woman with a rucksack on her back returning from town. In front of one house, some children were playing as if they had never heard of the war. Then three girls with baskets. A fellow with an unbuttoned overcoat. Two young German soldiers with gun slung carelessly over their right shoulders were telling each other jokes. One of them burst into a peal of laughter. His neck was sunburned but immediately above the collar a band of white flesh could be seen. He had not done much swimming or sunbathing during the summer. Neither of them glanced at me as I walked by. Judging by their accent, I guessed they were from Northern Germany. I walked steadily on, apparently without a care in the world. But I was listening for every sound, keeping my eye on every blade of grass. I heard something clink in one of the soldiers' pockets, a clipped, metallic sound, as if his penknife had struck some other metal object, a cartridge perhaps, or a cigarette lighter. I saw a plume of blue smoke rising straight as a poker from the chimney of a low cottage. Dust on the leaves of a low apple tree by the roadside. A few yards from where the children, a couple of little boys, were flinging their stones in an improvised game of bowls, a scraggy little boy stood motionless, gazing at a horse harnessed to a cart. The carter was bent almost double in his perch. A long track of smoke drifted past the gentle slopes of a hill. An old man was burning weeds and rubbish in his garden. From behind the wall I could hear the strokes of a hammer. No doubt there was a workshop at the back of the house.

How little I knew of my surroundings. And how little I knew of the planet I lived on. Far off in the primeval forests, life followed its usual course, nature's struggle for existence. Out in the ocean, plankton flow into the maw of the swimming whale. Air raids on cities and railway junctions. Convoys torpedoed by submarines. Sandstorms whip the English and German tanks as they exchange cannon fire. In a park laid waste, the birds still sing. Soldiers fall in a hail of machine-gun bullets. Others go on leave and the birth rate soars. Telephones, telegraphs, communication networks, radio stations. Cries of the wounded. Community singing. White icy mountains in the faint Arctic sunshine. A desert oasis. Horsemen in the savannah. Raucous voices of the victors. Roadblocks. Concentration camps hidden from public view. The notes of a guitar. Songbird dead in trap. Hand grenades. Bulletproof waistcoats. Washerwomen on a riverbank. Factories. Roads. Rain on a hill farm. Someone praying in a dark, empty church. An abandoned child dying of hunger in the cradle. All at the same moment.

By his enormous efforts and exploiting his knowledge and imagination, man bursts out of his narrow environment in every direction. First the Earth.

Then even farther, to explore all time and space, to explore the universe. Later, he may have to return home at any moment. Back to his own insecure environment. Then again he takes to the air, the water, of some earthly labyrinth. To an erupting volcano, to the stars. Are these the thoughts that flash through a man's mind when he faces the firing squad? Maybe in that split second he perceives and is aware of everything that ever happened anywhere at any time, of all the thoughts, emotions, and movements of man, of all the flow of sap in plants, of all the stirrings of tiny creatures under the tree bark, of pebbles on the bed of the river in spate—then suddenly comes back to earth, to his immediate surroundings and imminent fate. But what is the use of all this escapism and introspection? We are absorbed in our own knowledge of what is to come. The infants slain at Herod's orders did not try to escape. They do say a horse can smell death on its way to the knacker's yard. But mankind is given the highest awareness of his fate and the terrible torments and wasted struggles this entails. Consciousness, knowledge, cognition, perception. To see, hear, touch, smell, taste, feel, think. All this originally helped man to hunt, fight, gather food, and stay alive. Later, he branched out into fresh fields of culture. Philosophy, ideas. Conflicts of ideas. Wars of ideas. The invention of gunpowder. Guns. Cannons. Bombs. The steam engine.

All life in a drop of hazy perception.

At this moment of time, a man must be committed. No escaping to the Hanging Gardens of Babylon. This is a war to the death between different kinds of people. And I belong to an army too. Our side is right, theirs is wrong. For their part, often they repeat the same slogan. A man must be committed to this hatred of the enemy. This is no expedition to the unknown rapids of some river in Central Africa. Things are hardest for someone who is not integrated with his community. Deliver him to the firing squad, and he will be wondering whether his executioners are in a state of grace. Torture him, and he will feel the absurdity of his position seen from way out in the galaxy. He is condemned to be at all times and in all places the victim, never the conqueror, never the victor. Maybe there are some periods when such people are properly appreciated, but this is not one of them. Wise Machiavelli ponders such questions in the last chapters of *The Prince*. "Happy the man," he wrote somewhere, "who operates in harmony with the spirit of the age—and unhappy the man who is opposed to it."

If I do not master and control my feelings, if I do not learn to think as the times demand, I shall probably experience the truth of Machiavelli's formulation. Niccolò also said, very wisely, that destiny favors the zealot rather than the cool-headed calculator. Could a ball player play well if he stopped to consider what he was up to—that he was one of a herd chasing after a piece of leather? What is the sense of it, viewed against the unplumbed depths of time and the infinity of space? I must not forget how like an idiot I threw my bout with a German boxer before the war. He was packing everything into each punch, while I was dreaming about the difference between the eight hundred meters and a boxing match and God knows what else. I performed like a robot, and lost on points. Why had I floored so many people in tavern brawls? Then, I was acting on instinct.

There was a heap of rubbish by the roadside and a swarm of flies buzzing over it, settling and rooting in it. Besides the fly family, you have the ants, the bees, the termites. In my imagination, I ran through the various kinds of creatures. Their life is the same at all times, only man's way of life changes. At any moment he should comprehend everything but concentrate only on that morsel of experience which will assist him on the road ahead.

> *Allons enfants de la Patrie,*
> *Le jour de gloire est arrivé . . .*
> Onward, sons of the Fatherland,
> The day of glory has arrived . . .

Softly now! Not far away there are those who prefer Lili Marlene.

Pianissimo! Arise, ye toilers from your bondage . . .

There was a fly buzzing by my ear. Soldiers in green uniform do not chase flies. They despise flies, weak-kneed Italians, their own Quislings, non-Aryans. They are the Herrenvolk, a people with one idea, personified in the Führer.

> Blow, gentle breeze,
> over the rugged crags
> where gallant lads
> fight for the Slovene land.

The house was stripped to its ribs; the plaster had fallen away in patches, exposing the light red brickwork. The gate was closed, the windows broken, and there was no sign of life.

> High up in the mountains, the machine guns sing their song.
> Don't worry, Jerry, now it can't be long.
> How he had hoped for an iron cross
> An iron cross, an iron cross
> And now he has a wooden one
> For you, Lili Marlene . . .
> For you, Lili Marlene . . .

At our French lessons, we had to read stories about Napoleon. I do not know which river it was, but he was out in a boat when, in his usual way, he startled a young officer in his entourage with the question, "How many eagles are there on this river?" The young officer responded, with no hesitation, "One only, Your Majesty." "Un seul, Sire." A soldier must be brisk, prompt, loyal. Hurrah! That lieutenant was a professional soldier.

"We are going to win this war," said the good soldier Švejk. And he was a conscript.

And here I was, volunteering for the second time. The first time had been after the German invasion and it had come to a sorry end. Yes, we were a laughingstock in Zagreb for those pale German youths, perched on the tanks in their dark uniforms, eating biscuits with margarine and jam. On the main street of the capital of Croatia. They came rolling in, the children of the Vater-land, to occupy yet another country. We just looked on and wondered how we were going to get back home.

Yes, indeed, death to Fascism. That should be our only thought.

The bees were still full of life. I could see them on the rosebushes, their wings gleaming in the sunshine. I could sense a call, a summons, or perhaps an ur-gency in that false calm. Why should I be going along this particular path to arrive at some already predestined goal? Behind me lay the past among the barbed-wire barricades, ahead lay the future and something was stirring, or so it seemed to me. What was happening on that fine day? Down there in the south, a whirlwind was blowing in the forests, in the misty mountains. This evening too, night would fall. How would I return to this spot? In fetters? As once before? Or mounted on horseback? Winter would come. Snow would cover everything. One's memories too. The girl in front of me had a nice pair of legs, a fine head of hair too. Her hips swayed as she walked on, looking straight ahead. She was a real beauty but I can't say my mind was on her at that moment. A piece of newspaper on the ground beside the path. *THE SLOVENE.* Its title in capital letters. There is the river. There is the bridge. We must cross the bridge, then turn left toward the Frog Inn. How clear and innocent some moments in life are. And yet you can feel the tension in the air. Balance between past and future. Strange, but everything is just as if preordained.

And nevertheless, here we are, marching off to war. Once it was the custom to perform some spiritual exercises before departure on a campaign, or drink and be merry. How was it that we had set off with no previous spiritual or physical exercises? We had left so quietly, with our forged documents and a pass for our own forces, a little card sewn into our clothes. A secret that could have cost us our lives. But there have always been wars and our ancestors, our grandfathers and our fathers have fallen in battle. Homer tells stories of war, and the epics of India, the songs and legends of China, the oldest documents of every civilization tell of strife, rebellion, encounter, battle. The prophet Isaiah says of Lucifer, "Bright star of Morning, how thou art cast down . . ." And Lucifer said, we are told, "I shall rise to the Heavens . . . I shall set my throne among the stars of the Almighty and hold sway on the Mountain of the Lord." In the Book of Revelations we read how Michael and the angels waged war against the serpent and how the serpent fought. The Titans rebelled against the established order, against Zeus, the king of the gods, and attacked Olympus, their abode. Seven centuries before Christ, the poet Hesiod told the story of Prometheus stealing fire from Olympus and bringing it to mankind. I remembered fairy tales from the islands of the Pacific Ocean, telling of a revolt which broke out in heaven after God had set the stars in the sky and how he quelled the rebels with his thunderbolts and cast them down to the earth, and how ever since there has been strife between man and man, people and people, animal and animal, fish and fish. Homo homini lupus—man preys on man. That old expression had already frequently come back to mind. Jehovah, the God of the ancient Hebrews, is somewhere called Lord of Sabaoth, Lord of Hosts. Some philosophers maintain that war is the natural state of mankind. So here I am, assuming my natural state. I am off to war. And these thoughts of mine seem to be my first real spiritual exercises, although the war has been going on for some time.

I had done my bit in the city, just as I would now serve outside it. True, instead of a uniform, I wore the neatly pressed trousers that I now examine with a critical eye, suede shoes, and a trilby hat worn at a rakish angle. All the same, we changed into soldiers when night fell. We were off to join the forces, a real army, newly forming out there in the mountains to the south. I walked across the bridge and looked at the stream. "Here the stream flows free of the barbed wire," I thought.

Once across the bridge, I saw a building, a sign for "The Frog Inn," grapes. The woman in front of me paused at the gate and looked over at me. Her eyes were a grayish blue. She seemed to be afraid of me. I went into the barroom. A stout barmaid was leaning against the bar, slowly pouring a glass for a customer who was propped up there with a newspaper in his left pocket, just like me. I transferred my paper to another pocket, the agreed signal. At that moment, two bored elderly Germans came in and ordered some wine. There was a man sitting in a corner, reading a newspaper. All of those present, except the Germans, could have been candidates for departure, maybe more of us would be leaving. We had no idea. Someone came in from the toilet and ordered a glass. So did I, as nonchalantly as possible. The two soldiers ignored me. I slowly sipped my wine and continued my spiritual exercises, since I had nothing else to do. I inspected the hands of all present. The Germans, I could see, were simple working men. They drank up quickly and left.

That moment, and that place smelling of sour wine, are stamped into my memory. You never know where a surprise is waiting for you. Who was the man with the keen eyes, who had just come in? There are times when someone takes a dislike to your nose, your jacket, your glance, or maybe your walk, step movements, or the way you light a cigarette. I was no longer responsible for my own actions. When and where I should go, how and with whom, others would decide. Control of my destiny had slipped from my hands.

Our path led across the Ljubljana moors. A path, soft and pleasant to the feet on this afternoon. Five of us had chosen this road. Our guide, Janez, walked in front, with Vesna behind and Mishko at her side. I came next, and last of all, that strange man in the black suit. He never spoke a word, his face betrayed no emotion, he seemed completely withdrawn. Five of us had chosen this road, three men carrying baskets and a woman with milk cans in a string bag.

Janez turned around and said, "You must keep on talking out loud naturally, in your ordinary voices. Talking like people who are going to the village to buy milk." A moment later he repeated, "Talk, I said!"

Formless and shapeless are hardly terms we would apply to trees, woods, a landscape. Every oak has its shape, every roadside pine tree its form. Every bush has its shape, so that we call one a hazel, another a hawthorn, another a juniper. But slices of life do not have clear features. A mass of things seen, and a greater number of things unobserved. What shape does this moment have? Is it like the setting sun? Is it like the strong tang of the country air? The noise of birds' wings? Close by, a bird fluttered out of a bush and flew away from the path into the depths of the wood. Man's senses try to grasp his environment, but they are locked in his journeying body as it walks, shifts, and marches forward toward its goal. If it really has a goal. The gun is aimed at the target, whether it hits or not. We do say that a man's life is on the right track, or goes astray. An arrow is usually directed at a target. Is man an arrow with a target, or without one? I see a cloud of arrows shooting up into the sky and youth bearing them up toward the sun. Then they turn, stop, fall to the ground. First they were aimed at the sun, then came the turn—and what followed? The descent. The ever quickening fall. What else is there?

We had now left the suburb, the roadblock, the guards, and the barbed wire barricades far behind. We had crossed our Rubicon. But the pace of events was altogether too slow for me in my present buoyant mood. How could I describe or define my attitude to the immediate future? It had been different when I had gone skiing or globe-trotting, or stepped into the boxing ring, or gone climbing, or walked to school for those lectures on literature, or set out on my bicycle for the sea. Then, I could have always turned back. But not this time. There was no return. Before me stretched the unknown, harsh, rough, predetermined. Any freedom of choice I had had was now gone. Somewhere over there lay nervous Germany. The terrors of the front line. In the south, Italy had already capitulated. Still farther away were the Americans, the Russians, the English, and of course the Japanese. And here we were, on a tree-lined path. A ditch, overgrown with marsh swamp grass, ran alongside. We walked on, the sky above us, an occasional shot ringing out in the distance, a dead beetle trampled underfoot. But we did not stop talking the whole time. Janez, our guide, had told us that our things were waiting in a village where they had been taken a few days previously. I felt weak and defenseless without a gun in my pocket. I had taken nothing with me. I had sent it all on ahead. Now I was all that was left, and here I found myself, at the mercy of coming events over which I had no control. Well, I had to get used to it.

My imagination wanted to operate as usual. However, this was not a school trip for bright pupils. I lit a cigarette and offered some to the pair in front of me, but they both refused. I turned to the strange fellow behind me but he simply shook his head, as if wondering what had given me that idea. In his old black suit, he seemed somehow out of place, here with us in the countryside, though he provided an ideal camouflage. Funny old pale-faced owl. Looked more like a sexton than a budding soldier.

The trio ahead of me were deep in talk. When the path widened, I drew level on the girl's left, but then dropped back again. The man behind me had not the least intention of making contact with us. Mishko tried hard to engage the girl beside him in conversation but she had eyes only for our guide. She kept leaning forward, as if straining to comprehend everything he had to say. Janez seemed to know this road very well. How many others before us had he taken "to the woods"?

Vesna tripped lightly along. With her graceful hips, long neat legs, and trim figure, she would have attracted my attention wherever I had met her, and we would have got on well together, I'm sure. But here she had no eyes for anyone except the man in charge, the leader of our troop, by comparison with whom I was a mere cipher. I felt the self-pity of a lonely male in the herd. She had no idea that I had been active in the city. Here I was just a beginner, a recruit, a novice of no account. If she had only known how we used to disarm those Ities at night! *Alto le mani!* Hand over your gun. Take it easy. And now just walk straight on quietly. A German would not be so ready to obey. And you would not find it so easy to steal up behind him and stick a revolver in his back, no sir! But after all, the Italians do not regard this as their war.

A local squire, that's what she took me for. She could have had no idea why I kept my nails polished. My dear girl, if you only knew how much black market money has slipped through these fingers into the coffers of our organization! Poker is a fine game, but a bit tedious when the only object is to relieve someone of his money and locate it elsewhere. Your victim does not understand the game. He is apprehensive, reluctant, surprised, does not know how to postpone the inevitable. Who ever won a game of chance, once a couple of experts got their clutches on him?

The soft, sun-tanned flesh at the nape of her neck was a constant shameless provocation. The long hair swinging loose over her shoulder exposed a triangle of skin, which appeared and disappeared again at every step.

Our path widened and wound under spreading branches by a dense coppice. I drew level with the girl, on her left, and made some remark. She took no notice of me and Mishko also pretended he could neither see nor hear me. I dropped back again. I cast a glance at the man in the black suit, the one who seemed to have returned from the next world. Did nothing interest him? Perhaps he was scared stiff.

There was no way of killing time. I seemed to be conscious of every single step, of driving myself over every inch of ground, as minute after minute followed its predetermined course.

A metallic voice rang out.

"Halt!"

A German soldier stepped out of the bushes, his automatic leveled at us. There were two more standing behind him. All three were wearing camouflage capes.

We halted, a little too abruptly. I took another step forward, so that I was now level with the girl and Mishko.

"Your passes!"

"Where are you off to?"

Janez answered in his halting German, "Milch holen, ins Dorf."

I butted in here, since I spoke a little more fluently. "There is no milk in town, and we could do with some eggs too."

The leader of the patrol examined our forged papers, scrutinized each of us, handed them back, and gently waved us on.

I felt a wave of elation.

Vesna began to tell us about how she had been arrested, interrogated, and beaten. She had been released only a couple of days ago. They had not been able to prove a thing.

"But how is it they let you go?" asked Janez.

"They simply had no idea who had fallen into their hands."

Well, how important we are, to be sure!

"All night long they horse-whipped me," she continued. "I'm black and blue all over. But I didn't breathe a word, so they had to give up. None of the others gave way either."

She spoke like a seasoned campaigner.

"Was it the Gestapo?" Mishko asked.

"No, the Whites. The police. Someone in the house denounced me. We know who it was. We've got him on our list. Bloody swine."

Nobody was particularly impressed. However, she went on.

"He's a pensioner. Such a nice old gentleman. Sanctimonious prig!"

I lit another cigarette but did not hand them around this time. Mishko told us how he had been picked up. A few months ago, it had been. They were holding him somewhere in a cellar when the news of the Italian capitulation came through. One morning they threw him out on the street. On the walls, he had seen written in blood what they had done to people. The names, and even some slogans. We were not particularly interested in his story either. We were all loyal fighters, we had all done our bit. Now we were on our way to collect our bright, shiny decorations. A nice castle for each of us. Somewhere to await the triumphant conclusion of hostilities. Anyway, the end could not be far off now. The Italians had already capitulated.

From somewhere in the distance, we could hear the sound of rifle fire: the crackle of single shots, a burst of fire, a few more shots, then silence. More crashes, more explosions of bombs and bullets, another fusillade, silence.

I picked a leaf from the bushes. A hazel leaf, fresh, living still. How clearly each segment, each vein, each cell stood out. Was there anywhere on God's earth at that moment another human being similarly engrossed in another hazel leaf? Such simplicity, and yet so much to ponder.

We came to a clearing.

Beyond it we saw a village. Not a sign of life. Just cornfields, meadows, lines of willow trees. Houses among the trees.

We were made welcome in a farmhouse. Three of us were sitting at the table, while the man in black was in a chair by the window, hands in his pockets, gazing out into space. Janez had indicated to us that we were to wait here and had then gone off somewhere with the farmer. Two women in working clothes looked us over and withdrew from the room. We had no idea where we were, why we had to wait, what was going to happen, or when it would happen. These people did not seem to care whether we needed to eat or drink or relieve ourselves.

Only Mishko and the girl went on chatting. They seemed to be old acquaintances. At least, they had a mutual friend called Boris. Boris was coming this week; Boris had said he'd been in Dolenjska; according to him, we were mopping up down there, we had captured masses of arms and ammunition, cannons from the Italians, and tanks too.

I got up to go out. Vesna looked around and told me off.

"We're not to show ourselves outside. Janez said so!"

Well, well!

"Did he really say we couldn't leave the room?"

I met some hens in the yard.

A complete stranger, an orphan of the storm, in this benighted farmyard. Last but one in the chain of command, with only the man in the black suit after me. Even the hens ignored me. Outside the fence, the trees too had no time for me. Away beyond them was the city I had left behind, together with all the past.

Why had I taken such care over my bath last night? Why had I changed into fresh underclothes? The sense of a break, a farewell, had been very strong. Next day, a new life was beginning, a free life, open warfare.

How many false starts had I made to join the partisans during the Italian occupation? And how unpleasant it had been to reenter the nightmare of our occupied city!

Two or three times I had taken off in the evening, after curfew. We used to foregather at an inn on the outskirts of town, drink and play cards till curfew, when Marta, the innkeeper's wife, would let us into her kitchen to wait for Stoyan. He would always check up on the roadblocks and let us know how the land lay. I knew every garden in that part of town, every shadow, every inch of the road between the gardens. The tall oak trees in the moorland copses, the thickets, the ditches. We used to creep along a dry ditch to the barbed-wire perimeter that encircled the town. The Italians had pillboxes every hundred meters and the spaces in between were patrolled by sentries. Empty cans suspended on the barbed wire jingled if anyone touched the fence.

The rest was a matter of technique. We would start the cans jingling. The sentries would make a dash for the pillboxes. Then came wild bursts of machine-gun fire. This uproar made our task much easier. We had a plank concealed in the ditch. This would be hurled onto the barbed wire so that our people could crawl through. Then we would return it to its hiding place in the ditch and make our way back to Marta's, where a nice hot cup of coffee was waiting for us. Needless to say, we gave up such forays when the Germans took over the roadblocks.

Why had I not been allowed to take to the woods then?

Our patrol was waiting on the other side. They had all heard about me. Jakob! Here I am, a stranger in Jerusalem.

What was biting me after all? Injured vanity? Or perhaps I was simply scared. After all this time, I had placed my fate in the hands of others. I was unarmed, carrying forged papers, and had a partisan pass sewn into my jacket. What the devil was getting me down? Normally my nerves were quite sound, as anybody who knew me would testify. It is true that I was used to being in charge—and here we had Janez at our head, after him Vesna, then Mishko, followed by a long, long interval, after which, the two of us brought up the rear, myself and the silent pallbearer in the black suit. And who came below us? Only the peasant women and the hens! If we were to be surrounded here, all I could possibly do would be to make a break for it across the common, always assuming they gave me a start. I had enough of this.

I went back inside with a lit cigarette drooping from the corner of my mouth. Judging by their scowls, Mishko and the girl were not amused.

Janez followed me in almost immediately afterward.

"You'll have to wait here a bit," he said. "I'm on my way back to town. You'll be hearing soon from Cyril. He'll put you in the picture."

Cyril? Who is Cyril? Who is he?

"Don't go wandering about," he ordered.

"'Most of us don't," said Vesna and shot a venomous glance at me.

"When do we move on?" I asked. Janez was not ready to reply.

"You haven't got a boat," he mumbled.

"Well, let's swim across," I quipped. Janez, however, was deadly serious as he left.

"Just stop worrying. Wait here. Cyril will tell you all you need to know. Right?"

Vesna nodded briskly. Janez left. I turned to follow him out. While I was slowly making for the door, Vesna spoke in an angry voice. "And where do you think you're off to this time?"

I turned to face her. She explained in all seriousness:

"Look, the Whites have posted a lookout in the church tower. He can see the whole village from up there."

Who was she trying to kid? As if they would be coming down from the tower every time they spotted some suspicious visitor from town! They'd be hiding under the bed, more likely!

I was only making fun of the girl, but she dropped all the charm immediately and took on the role of commander. She was right, but could not know I needed no instruction in such matters. Discipline was nothing new to me. When I was a boy, I had been in the Scouts. Later, as a sportsman, I learned all about team spirit. No, it was not the need for discipline that dismayed me. It was something else I found repulsive. I could not stand individuals in the mob continually battling for power; wolves fighting for the leadership of the pack. From the playground, through school, the Scouts, sporting organizations, barracks, prisons, hospitals, the same fight goes on for the rungs of the ladder. Every man is a potential slave or despot, victim or oppressor. Only the harsh fact that we cannot all be oppressors causes our division into those who grin and bear it and those who hand it out. It is a well-known fact that a hen-pecked husband makes the most tyrannical boss. Everyone is a victim in one context and the oppressor in another, whether he is aware of this or not. Women have an uncanny gift of recognizing who does and doesn't have the edge in any group. They all love a winner, someone who can guarantee their security.

We waited and waited.

Cyril, the farmer who had gone out with Janez, came back later to tell us we would have to spend the night there, since our boat would not be crossing the river to pick us up till morning.

The farmer's wife gave us bread and milk.

We settled down for the night in the barn.

There I took my shoes off, put them at my feet, and covered my head with my jacket. The others bedded down too. Before I dropped off, I heard some other people coming in and flopping down on the hay.

The smell of fresh hay.

Moorland hay has a special juicy tang.

In the darkness someone began to snore.

Two people went on murmuring. God knows what they were talking about.

I was restless and could not get to sleep. I tossed from side to side, turned over on my back, put my hand under my cheek to keep the hay off my skin and ears. I was dying for a smoke but everyone would have been at me: "You'll set the hay on fire!" How could they know I had never gone to sleep with a lit cigarette in my hand? I would have been careful to put it out in a matchbox. I would have smothered the butt in it with an unerring hand. Prohibitions are for undisciplined, feckless people, for the absentminded and the high-strung. But because of them, everybody else has to suffer too, like me for example, someone who never upsets a glass of red wine on a tablecloth, who never drops his cigarette ash on a clean floor, and who does not belong to an army occupying a foreign country. I once lent somebody a copy of Tolstoy's *Resurrection*. When I got it back, I found a thin slice of salami in the book, with great oily stains on either side. We all know there are some types who couldn't care less if they have soup stains on the lapels of their jackets.

I thought of a number of little details, important nonetheless, that divide people into categories and groups, constitute connections and differences. For example, pleasure or carelessness in washing the feet, wearing clean socks, cleaning the fingernails, brushing the teeth, looking after the hair or genitalia. Then it takes in our view of the world. Our attitude to nature. When the sun goes down, I am always afraid that someone will give a passionate—or melancholy—or ecstatic—or raucous shriek: "O my! What a wonderful—or beautiful—or magnificent—or unbelievably fine—sunset!" and spoil my quiet pleasure.

Pondering such things in my mind, I eventually dropped off, though my sleep was restless and disturbed by most disagreeable dreams. I was crawling on the ground, in some place unknown to me, and on all sides I could hear the voices of my pursuers; then I was in town, taking a stroll in my socks, having presumably forgotten to put my shoes on. Once or twice I woke up, and then relapsed into those tiresome dreams. In the end I must have fallen sound asleep.

I jumped up, grabbed my shoes with one hand and my jacket with the other. I was through the barn door before I heard what had really happened.

"It's the Whites!" someone croaked in a tense and urgent voice. I could hear bodies catapulted from the hay, groans, heavy breathing, the tramp of feet, and out in the yard, a few shots and shouts of "Halt!"

When I rushed out into the open I heard a crisp report and a long flame flashed from the barrel of a rifle at uncomfortably close range.

Some running figures. Muffled shouts and ferocious cursing. Another shot, this time farther from me. More shouting. "You bloody bandits! Halt, damn you! Halt!"

I darted behind the hay shed, and ran between the trees of the orchard. There was a short burst of fire. "Halt!" a voice rang out. "It's the Germans!" a woman screamed. I could hear some running behind me, but whether it was one of us trying to escape or one of our hunters I could not determine. In any case I bore to the left. I had a feeling the forest was in that direction. The danger of capture made me fly like the devil. It was some time before I realized I was running in my stocking feet! Well, well. I had my shoes in one hand and jacket in the other. We were now shrouded in darkness and the footsteps behind me had stopped. I tried to get my bearings. That is the meadow before me. Surely the forest must be farther over to the left. Have to be more prudent now. Still, I would like to put my shoes on. My socks were wet and dirty, I must have stepped in the mud. Bushes bigger here, hazels. I can crawl in there, put my shoes on, and await developments.

There were leaves on the ground under the hazel trees: I crouched and listened. All was quiet now, except for some loud voices down by the houses, whether in the village or the nearby road I could not tell.

Close by, there was the sound of something like a human voice. I started up, my fists clenched.

"Anyone on our trail?" a man's voice asked in a whisper.

All was now clear. He was afraid of them, he was also on the run. No danger from him.

"I don't think they're headed this way," I replied, just for something to say. "How did you get here?"

26

"Just like you. A little before you though. I couldn't sleep. I was in the barn. Were you?"

"Yes. But I was sleeping like a log."

He crawled nearer. My eyes had by now gotten used to the dark. But I could only make out a blob of unsettled shape. It seemed to have a beard and a moustache.

"They won't be coming," he said. "A night patrol often calls in at the village, sprays a little lead around and then moves on."

"Are you a local?"

"No. I just got here today from town."

"Me too."

After this exploratory sniffing, he spoke again.

"You know, we arrived together. With Janez. I was walking at the back."

"The man in the black suit?"

"Yes. Anton is my name."

"They call me Berk. I'm also known as Jakob."

"Berk?"

"Yes, Anton! What now?"

"Oh, nothing. They rarely come twice in one night. Let's wait a little, then go and see what's what. It will be harder to get to sleep after all this rushing about. Have you got a spare handkerchief?"

"Yes."

"I caught my foot in something and went flying arse over tip. I have a nasty cut on my palm. It's bleeding."

I gave him my handkerchief and helped him to bandage his hand. The silent man was now talking, and talking a lot of sense. I would not have recognized him as our companion on the road.

"Haven't had a sprint like that since the day I was born," he said and seemed to chuckle quietly to himself. "I've often had to run for my life though."

"But in these conditions . . . Without a gun . . ." I could bellyache too.

"Don't you worry, there'll be more arms and ammo than we can handle." He seemed to be thinking aloud. He struck me as a man who knew what he was talking about, sure of his facts. "There'll be enough twisting too . . . You know what the twist is, do you?" (Twisting is cross-country racing.)

"We'll hold out. Shouldn't have long to go now, you know."

"So you're one of the optimists. I'm afraid the war can last for years yet."

"Years! You must be joking!"

"Glad to hear it . . . Are you really so naïve?"

"Years, you say? Well, that's really bad news. Especially tonight."

We looked down toward the village, where people could be heard running about and shouting. After a short silence, the man beside me spoke again. It was rather like a lecture.

"When the Germans were approaching Moscow, Stalin told his people to hang on for a year or two. He never canceled that forecast, even later. The Western allies are dragging their feet. When will the war end? The Germans are a warlike race. The Japanese too. As far as the West is concerned, it doesn't matter whether German or Russian blood flows. The chief thing for them is that no German soldier should set foot on English or American soil. Her vast territory is the salvation and the ruin of Russia. There are parts of the Soviet Union where the war is regarded as the concern of two or three western republics. After all, for most of Russia the war with Finland was only a matter for the Leningrad Military District."

"Hang on now," I objected. All my instincts rebelled against the thought that I might have whole years of war before me. "Look, the situation has really changed with Stalingrad and the German defeat in North Africa."

"No doubt," he conceded. "Things could have been much worse if the Germans had got through the Caucasus and won in North Africa. Then Turkey would have come in on the side of the Axis. And furthermore, if the Japanese had conquered Burma—and if India had not joined the Allies—and if the Germans had made contact with the Japanese in Asia . . . and reached the oil fields . . . There's a whole legion of 'ifs' in every war."

He stopped. We strained our ears but silence had fallen on the village down below us. No sound came our way. He went on.

"The Germans are a hard nut to crack. The English regard war as a sort of game." With a touch of malice he added, "One would not grudge them a taste of German occupation. The Americans make war in cowboy style. For the Russians it's a real tragedy; they know how to die. The Germans are driven by some primeval passion for war. They still have the old Teutonic belief in their armed might; they have a God of their own and act out a sort of heroic opera. Right up to the end, they will not admit they are defeated. And if 1918 repeats itself, they still won't believe it. After all, what are twenty years in the world's history? For them, defeat in the First World War was only an instructive episode—a lesson they misunderstood, my friend! They think they were within a hair's breadth of victory. At the moment, they're bloody powerful. You've only got to consider the territory they control. It will be some time yet before the war potential of Germany itself can be destroyed. There are reports of immense stocks of poison gas and chemical weapons. Where on earth do they get their self-confidence from? So much faith in the Teutonic God of War? So don't be so naïve. See things as they are, my friend."

My friend, eh? He had dropped the formalities without my noticing it.

"And how long do you think it can last?" I asked him.

"Don't be stupid. I'm no prophet. It's not going to be a Thirty Years' War. Two years, I expect . . . or three . . . who knows? The end will come when all is ripe. I should think you realize yourself that things aren't ripe yet."

I smiled.

"Do you find it funny?" he asked, seemingly offhand.

"Not what you tell me now. I was just remembering you trailing along behind me through the Town Woods. I thought you couldn't count to five. Why were you so quiet?"

"Quiet? Really? Have you ever tried chatting with raw recruits? If I'd told you that the war wouldn't be over tomorrow, you would have beaten me up. Or should I have had something to say about the joys of nature?"

"Could I ask what you do for a living?"

"Let's leave personal matters out of it. At least until we cross the Ljubljanica. Don't you think we ought to go down to the village and see what's happening?"

We clambered out of the undergrowth.

So quiet. So peaceful. As if nothing had happened.

A lamp was burning in a house at the edge of the village. I crawled up to the window, while he of the black suit stayed behind at a safe distance. I could see no one in the room.

We proceeded cautiously, feeling our way step by step toward the back doorway. The darkness has its advantages for both sides; it conceals the fugitive but hides the hunter too.

I could hardly restrain a shriek of terror. I had encountered something soft, something that moved, a human being! One who whispered in a woman's voice.

"Who's that?"

Her terror restored my courage.

"We're back again," I answered.

It was Vesna. A completely different person from the afternoon, now trembling with shock. She did not know if there was anybody in the house. She had run away and come back later. She had no idea what had happened.

I went inside, no longer caring what noise I made. No one in the hall, no one in the room. I picked up the oil lamp, turned up the wick and went around the house. It was empty. I put the lamp on the hall table and went back into the yard. There were three people there: the man in black, Vesna, and someone else, a farmer's wife. Cyril had left word that we were to assemble and wait in the yard. The Whites had taken two prisoners away with them, missing two other men who were still in the barn. They had found our boat concealed by the riverbank and destroyed it. Cyril had gone to get another. Vesna was worried that "they" might be back again before the night was over. Maybe. But they always made a racket and came by the main road. She was easier in her mind at this news. She began to tell us that "our lot" would not let her leave for the woods and she had only just now managed to talk them over . . . She seemed to be making excuses, either for my benefit or her own, that she was joining the army only now that victory was just around the corner. She did not seem to realize that the man in black and I were listening with mute disinterest.

The other two from the barn now joined us. One of them was Mishko. We learned how the bullets whistled past his ears, how he leaped into a ditch right on top of "this chap here," a short fellow we had not seen before. He belonged to another group. Who had been taken prisoner? No one knew. An hour or so later, another of the fugitives crept in, soaked to the skin; he had fallen in a bog and had just managed to drag himself out.

The first light of dawn was on the mountains to the south when Cyril came for us.

Over the dark surface of the slow-flowing river lay a clear whitish mist. The trees on the opposite bank rose into view. Day had broken.

Cyril whistled through his fingers. No response. Silently the tension grew as we stood on that moorland river bank.

Cyril whistled once more. This time there came a short answering whistle from the far bank. Cyril nodded. All was ready. He did not look at us, though he knew all our eyes were fixed on him.

Now we could make out the long, flat-bottomed boat which had quietly crossed from the opposite bank. In it we could see the tall figure of the oarsman.

"Once you're across, you'll be in liberated territory," Cyril told us.

He became gradually more talkative as the boat approached. "Both the Whites and the Germans patrol this side of the river during the day, but the opposite bank is in the hands of the Partisans. Sometimes they shoot it out. Everyone finds a bit of cover, settles down, and takes a potshot at the other side."

"Some people have all the luck," he said. "You're away now, but I'm being kept back here."

What had happened during the night? Nothing special. They occasionally came to the village to check up. Had they taken two prisoners? Only one, apparently. He flared up. "Who told you to curl up like a flea in a dog's fur? Don't you know there's a war on? These days you need to always keep one eye open and one ear open too. Myself, I camp out on the common. That way I don't need to run for it."

"We'd have done the same, only no one told us to," said Mishko.

In the early morning light, Cyril gave him a look of disdain but then smiled and observed casually, "Can be a bloody nuisance in the army—all that waiting for orders . . ."

The boat drew in to the bank.

We embarked. Cyril stood motionless on the high bank, watching us. The oarsman was a slim country lad.

Only the river now separated us from liberated territory. Over there, our forces were in control. That was our land over there. A land with no Germans or Whites. How slowly our rotten, sodden hulk crawled through the water! Think of it! A land with no occupying army, no police. And our own things were waiting there, the things we had sent on ahead and were going to pick up any moment now. In my case, I had packed my skiing outfit, ski boots, wool socks, a warm pullover, a fur cap, and a whole load of things that would no doubt come in useful. I had also packed a revolver, my trusty Walter.

The river was flowing very slowly, almost without a sound in the early morning.

Now I surveyed the other bank. As soon as we pulled in, I leaped into the water, to see two Italians with automatics! Two tall, broad-shouldered, jack-booted, menacing types.

A couple of partisans on patrol. Our own troops. Us.

Vesna could not wait. She threw herself into their arms.

I must admit that I too felt a certain exhilaration at that moment.

A last look back at the shore we had left. No sign of Cyril now.

The partisans had five-cornered stars of felt crudely sewn onto their caps.

A short river crossing on a shallow, worm-eaten boat, had brought us to a new world. We had left Hitler's empire of Herrenvolk and slaves for our own land. Over a border that appeared in no atlas.

Some years after the war, I stood again at approximately the same spot beside the river and tried to remember what it had meant to me to cross the great divide. I had many memories of the bank I had left, of the territory occupied by the Germans; memories that resembled scenes in a prewar German film: high-stepping jackboots of the victorious army of the swastika, Stuka dive-bombers screaming down out of the sky, the roar of field guns, speeches of a man with a square moustache, some poor creature stumbling along in rags, a board around his neck with the words "*Ich bin Bandit,*" military bands, cheering, banners.

On this side the future was hazy. Confidence. High spirits. Curiosity. Two ordinary lads in Italian uniforms with partisan badges in their caps, now fending off, with difficulty, Vesna's kisses and embraces while tears poured down her cheeks. Anton, the man in black, scanning the scene with an air of disapproval.

How many things are hidden from us when we make such a crossing.

I did not know that I would survive the war.

I did not know how she would end up. That she would get a bullet in the plumpest part of her frame while trying to escape from an attack on head-quarters. That she would be captured alive. By the Whites. That she would be tortured and beaten to death.

I did not know that I would myself witness the sudden death of Anton, the cool, quiet man in black.

I did not know that some time, long after the war was over, I would visit Spain, without a thought for General Franco, and would then remember this journey, the cart track, the willows, the hay fields, this conversation on an early morning in October, with the cocks crowing in the distance, in the village of Kot.

CON SUPERIOR PERMISO	With the permission of the authorities
Y SI EL TIEMPO NO LO IMPIDE	weather permitting
SE PICARÁN, BANDERILLEARÁN	there will be lanced, flagged,
Y SERÁN MUERTOS	and killed
7 HERMOSOS Y BRAVOS TOROS	seven fine, brave bulls
DOMINGO, TARDE 5.30	on Sunday at 5:30 P.M.
Manuel Benitez "El Cordobes"	Manuel Benitez "The Cordoban"
con sus correspondientes cuadrillas.	with his troupe.
7 hermosos y bravos toros	7 fine, brave bulls
de la ganadería de herederos	from the stock farm of the heirs
de Don Carlos Nuñez	of Don Carlos Nuñez.

Would you like to have your name in capitals printed on a card with the bull-fighters? On a special card, 54 by 97 centimeters?

MY NAME IS
MON NOM EST
MEIN NAME IST
IL MIO NOME E
TUDTTAKAA MIELLYTÄVÄ YLLÄTYS YSTÄVILLENNE PAINATTA-MALLA
HEIDÄN NIMENSÄ TODELLISEEN HÄRKÄTAI—STELUJULISTEESEEN!
DONNEZ A VOS AMIS LA SURPRISE EN IMPRIMANT VOTRE NOM
SUR UNE AFFICHE VERITABLE DE COURSE DE TAUREAUX!

Nor that after the war I would have my own children, who would never be able to imagine what it had really been like.

I too do not know what happened to my father, who went to war in 1914. Not so far from here, he had served on the famous Isonzo front under the command of von Paulus, a young man then. Ernest "Farewell to Arms" Hemingway had been on the opposite side. How many months was it since von Paulus, a field marshal now, had signed the act of capitulation at Stalingrad, surrendering a German army, a million strong, decimated, and surrounded? Yes, a child born this day would have been conceived more or less at the time of that surrender.

About eight miles from here, or a little more, Shvabich, a Serbian officer, had resisted an Italian attack in 1918, and thereby established with his modest resources our western frontier, some way beyond Vrhnika. My father had died two years before. He had fallen somewhere in Bessarabia, in command of a battalion of Bosnian storm troops. For six generations past, no men in our family have died in bed. They were all soldiers but won no military decorations.

I feel ashamed to admit it but at that first moment I set foot on our liberated territory, I felt only a passionate desire that the war should not end too abruptly, should last another month or so.

Once again, Vesna was devoting all her attention to the most promising gallants, in this case the two young armed partisans, who were now chatting with Mishko. Mishko was not walking but fluttering around the freedom fighters, eagerly putting questions to them, chuckling and taking a childish glee in our adventures. Vesna was in a pretty poor mood; she could not get in a word edgewise. Two or three times, she started to tell us how she had been ill-treated in prison but no one paid any attention.

I did not know that my own notes would present such a wicked caricature of the girl. Nor that she would be posted to headquarters, put on weight, and get duck's disease.

Give a pleasant surprise to your friends by printing your name . . .

The solid figure of a gray-haired German in shorts appeared on the road, accompanied by his wife. I guessed he must have been an officer in the German army. There was a hefty scar on his right thigh. Thin hair covered another on his head.

I did not yet know his name was Joseph Bitter.

He walked and I walked after him, as if we belonged together.

Bathers on sandy beaches that stretch for miles and miles, packed so close that you can hardly put your palm on the ground without touching human skin.

I contrived to make Joseph Bitter's acquaintance at a hacienda where one could see "expert riders and the finest horses in Andalusia."

The moon was going down behind the mountain just as the show with the Andalusian stallions was about to start.

Joseph Bitter was now wearing long linen trousers and his wife was in a turquoise-green outfit.

I had noticed him by the entrance, where visitors were being offered hamburgers on iron spits and finely sliced bread in a basket.

A little farther on, there were barbecues where we could grill sausages.

Drinks were to be had at the bar.

While waiting for the appearance of the finest stallions in Andalusia, I leaned on the concrete wall beside Joseph. I began to converse with him in my still reasonably fluent German. On quite trivial topics such as the Spanish tourist industry, the fairly cheap prices, the weather.

A real solid fellow. Wife hardly ever butts into the conversation. When she does, it is usually to agree with her husband.

After the show we went to one of the pavilions for supper. There was a prize for the most uproarious company at the long tables.

Pollo con ensalada? (Chicken salad?) *Lomo de cerdo?* (Pork chop?)

This was no place to discuss the future of our planet, here in the grips of the gigantic tourist industry.

Open every day! *Oppt varje dag!*

I was curious to know the name of this chance acquaintance who, without knowing it, had stirred in me a nostalgia for a war now long past.

But he was reticent. Ready to talk about everything except himself.

More and more, I felt he would have been at home in a World War II uniform.

I dared not pester him too much. His wife was smiling politely and occasionally interposing, "*Ja, ja freilich.*"

What do you think about poetry? Poetry? "*Auch das muss sein, damit Mann komplett ist.*"

An aperitif? Sangria? *Bevanda? Patatillas?* (Chips?) *Aceitunas rellenas?* (Olives?)

Stable, unflappable—that was Joseph Bitter. He informed us that the *corrida* was a very old national custom for the Spaniards.

I was glad to meet him the following day. It was a marvelous morning. Sunshine and a refreshing southwest breeze. A lively café called *La Paz* (Peace), with little tables on the pavement. I sat down beside him as if I had known him for years, asked him how he had slept, and together we remarked on how well the fine weather was holding. I tried hard to amuse him. Earlier, I had bought some newspapers which were on sale in various languages and read the most recent news. He and his wife only had a German magazine to read, so I had plenty to tell them.

Dishonest official robs suicide. Americans worried by shortage of beef for their steaks. Ulbricht dies. No one mourns him—except the directors of films about sport.

Did he know English? Well, only a little. In 1945 he had spent a few months in an American prisoner-of-war camp. What could you do in the camp? Learn foreign languages, maybe. His brother had been a prisoner of the Russians. Mrs. Bitter chipped in: Two years, almost! The food had been terrible. They themselves had been bombed out during the war. Her uncle had been captured at Stalingrad and they had had news from him for some time afterward, till he fell ill and died.

"Well, that's war," she said. "What more can you expect?"

Barcelona Football Club offers Ajax a million dollars for their soccer star Johan Cruyff.

I insisted on paying the bill. We went out together.

I got to know his name when I suggested he order one of those fake visiting cards. "*Na, das ist aber toll!*" he laughed and produced one. Joseph Bitter, *el toreador con sus cuadrillas.*

Where was I from? Trst. Trieste. (I lied about this; it was about sixty-four miles out.) An Italian? No. I was Czech on my mother's side and Austrian on my father's. *Schön, schön.* "Spain is so beautiful," declared his wife.

They invited me for a glass of "real Bavarian beer" at the Deutsche Brauerei on the Arenal coast road.

Joseph Bitter did not like modern art. That fellow Picasso, for example. Mere caricatures. Often you couldn't tell which was the right way up.

How was it then, that I had been at war with Joseph Bitter?

First of all, in ignorance. I did not know that the Allies had bombed him out of house and home, that the Russians had taken his brother prisoner at Stalingrad, where the food had been so bad.

I had acted in ignorance. Also I had been internally disoriented. I could not distinguish the important from the trivial. I was politically naïve, with anarchistic tendencies. I had been full of hope. I was looking forward to pleasant surprises. I believed I was born lucky. I was lighthearted, strong, and healthy.

But I was not prepared for a long and tedious war. Everything intrigued me. My memory registered, in detail, the shapes of the old willow trees, beside the waters of the moorland ditch. I was troubled by the sight of the tall girl, Vesna, striding out ahead of me. There was nothing I could accept as solemn, serious, official. Banners, for me, were just patches of color.

I had no time for ideological matters. The whole world was throbbing with past, present, and future ideologies. And here I was, about to join an army thoroughly steeped in its ideology while clinging to my childish convictions about good human relations, my Scout's and sportsman's belief in comradeship and loyalty.

Throughout the war, I had only one fear: that I might be captured alive.

At that time, I did not yet have the feeling that my whole war service might be a waste of time. For the West, I was a Communist guerrilla; on my own side, I was a one-time "left-wing Boy Scout," not a party member but a "useful idiot." Even in the first year of the occupation, I had quarreled with Franc, the commissar of our group. He told me I would be shot for my "anti-Soviet propaganda." For Franc had asserted that after the revolution there would be no crime; with the establishment of the new society, the causes of crime would disappear. I pointed out that there had been a remarkable upsurge of crime in Russia after the revolution.

It was not a propitious time for debates on matters of principle.

We had also frequently failed to agree in practical matters too. Franc had ordered us to take a black-market trader we had relieved of several thousand marks at the cards table out to the moors one foggy morning and dispose of him. I took him to the railway station instead, treated him to breakfast and bought him a ticket home, to Maribor. Our principle was: if you have relieved someone of all the contents of his wallet, then at least let him have what he needs for absolutely essential expenses. This was no kindness but good business practice; he would not harbor resentment against you and might try his luck with you again on some future occasion. Franc detested me for my lack of discipline. When he left for the woods he said, "Just you watch out in case I meet you out there!" "Don't talk crap!" I told him.

Bloodthirsty Franc, as some people called him, was shot by his own side. He had been transferred but fell somewhere on the way to his new unit. A real commander, he had ordered several executions for "lack of discipline." But one of those insubordinates turned out to be the daughter of a well-known party member. And the blood he had shed now fell on his own head.

Which is not to say that I had right on my side.

Sometimes I think it is nothing short of a miracle that I survived the war.

In fact, a couple of years after the war, I did stray for some reason into our jails (something to do with the ZKLD, the law on the nation and state). But once again I survived.

Viewed from the Deutsche Brauerei on the Spanish coast, it all looked a little ridiculous. On the table in front of me, I have some journals and three books I bought this morning: Salinger's short stories, Solzhenitsyn's novel about the First World War, and a collection of poems by Mao Tse-tung (the American edition for 120 pesetas).

Bitter is decidedly thin on top. My own mane is ruffled by the air from the ventilator. Sensible people lose their hair, fools have to keep it trim.

Who can establish the relative worth of a human being? Bitter is an insurance representative; I work in broadcasting. He drives a Mercedes (three years old, by the way); I drive a DRW (seven years old)! And here we both are, on holiday in Spain. Well, it's some time since we arrived on this earth. Last winter Joseph had a heart attack. "*Der Mensch muss immer wieder ruiniert werden. Aber—nie kaputt bleiben, nee, nee, kaputt nicht! Besiegt? Ja, das kommt vor. Auch die Niederlage ist ein Teil der Lebensschlacht. Ja, ja.*" His wife says: "*Na, freilich.*"

It was pretty hard to get anything after the war, yes, hm. Never mind, all is well now. Joseph's speech is slow, monotonous, grave.

I glance at my paper and happen to see: The Mexican poet and Marxist, Octavio Paz, has called Jean-Paul Sartre "a Sunday proletarian" and "the Diogenes of the sixth arrondissement."

The dollar is slipping, the mark is gaining.

Kidnappers send parents child's left hand.

Bitter says there will never be any order in this world.

Somewhere here in Spain there are white marble steps celebrated by a hundred poets.

The jukebox starts to play "Lili Marlene."

Another beer? No, no, not now.

Vesna turned toward me as if she had something for my ears only. This looked promising.

Anton walks like an automaton.

Mishko was still gabbing away, unaware that the two partisans had given up listening to him.

Vesna leaned over confidentially and said: "Heaven help me, I don't know what to do."

What was wrong?

Her mumbling was inaudible. "What's that? Oh, yes."

". . . dying for a pee since we got into the boat." (Naturally we had no potty on board.)

Why should this come back to me on a Spanish beach?

Autocares sin chauffeur! Rent a car! Calle Berlin 17.

Lili Marlene.

I cannot sort out the important from the trivial. But maybe it is all important?

You are about to see black bulls from Salamanca.

I halt the squad. Off she runs to a clump of trees nearby.

Time stood still.

I imagined the touch of that skin, smooth as silk, and shuddered with lust. But what was the point? Only men from the top of the ladder would have a chance with her.

She reappeared, face a little flushed.

Off we set.

"Well, that did me a world of good," she said, in a serious tone.

"Pity I didn't join you," I retorted shamelessly.

"Filthy beast!"

After this coquettish rebuke, we began to talk. Janez had left. Mishko had deserted her. The two partisans were showing no interest. Now I was good enough. How long would this last? She was hungry. Very hungry. As hungry as a wolf.

We were not far from the village. Beyond the fields to our left, a band of armed men in motley garb were approaching; this was the first troop of partisans we had seen in liberated Slovenia, in the heart of the German war zone, a hundred and four kilometers from Trieste, or even less, ninety-five kilometers, say. There was one man in a hunting outfit of green tweed, wearing a hat, another in the green uniform of the Gebirgsjäger, a third in a gray anorak, while some were wearing Italian uniforms and others civilian clothes. There were ten or twelve of them, armed with firearms of various sizes from long Austrian repeating rifles to short Italian carbines. One was in a railwayman's uniform; another, in civilian clothes, shouldered a double-barreled shotgun. Only one carried a tommy gun, one of those large-caliber weapons of Italian or German make. This oddly assorted company was proceeding in untidy single file, with two men abreast at front and rear, moving easily, at a medium pace.

Since the time when, like the ancient peoples, I got the idea that the earth was round, not flat, like a blob of fat on a plate of soup, I have not been able to rid myself of the illusion which bothers me at times, that I am standing on the top of the ever-spinning ball. To the east lie vast lands and seas; to the west, the Atlantic Ocean; to the north, the cold regions; to the south, the seas, the continent of Africa, and beyond. Here, before this village, we stand on the peak of the Earth, the iron waves of the Wehrmacht pounding our shores, flooding all the surrounding territories, down to the Atlantic, up as far as Norway, and pushing farther and farther along the Russian fronts. Romania, Bulgaria, Greece . . . Crete . . . the islands . . . Italy . . . There is no way of sneaking out, or breaking through the giant ring . . . we shall be here to the end . . . Because, at the proper time to read, we neglected a rather fat book written by Adolf Hitler, a chap from Austria or somewhere, called *Mein Kampf*. It is nicely written. The German sword will soon move into action, it says, to clear the way for the German plow. Adolf foresaw that not everyone would be happy about this. And now, somewhere to the north of us, he was standing bent over a map. He too imagined that he was standing on top of the terrestrial globe, shunting about those armies of his that were going to conquer the world. Over there, a little to the right, sat another man, a man with whiskers, our friend Stalin, listening to news of the battles and movements of his armies. To the West, on the English island, wreathed in cigar smoke, sat Winston Churchill, who had his own ideas about all these happenings. And finally there was Uncle Sam and the Japanese Mikado, far off on the other side of the globe, and a host of minor characters and onlookers. When it is all over, they will write books about these events and each will try to explain things in his own way, so that in the end we shall never know what really happened. Just like Napoleon. A little chap, four feet ten he was, appeared from nowhere, stirred up any number of wars, and went off to die on an island in a distant sea. Afterward, hundreds of writers assessed the man and his deeds, some of them praising him to the skies, others branding him an adventurer and criminal. And even today, we do not really know what he was and why he started all that. Certainly, paper can stand anything. If Napoleon had never existed, would Hitler perhaps have been more modest in his plans? These gentlemen will never learn from each other. It is the same with criminals. A villain knows that nearly all his predecessors have been caught but he still goes on thinking, "He was within an inch of getting away with it, if he hadn't bungled one or two things; but they won't catch me, I'll get away with it."

All these mighty aggressions have left nothing but chaos, and solved no problems, except for somewhat reducing the world population. Eras that favored romanticism have produced portraits of celebrated butchers, on the model of those idiotic tales of the ancient heroes. Heroes of India, Babylonia, Assyria. Achilles. Alexander of Macedon. Hannibal. Scipio. Caesar. Frederick the Great. Napoleon. Adolf. The list will probably never end. Human weakness and stupidity create the conditions for moving the poverty-stricken masses to action. If, in our "enlightened" century, a house painter, a sergeant off a street corner, can form an army a million strong, take charge of tank battles, and have dreams of world conquest, what hopes can we have for the future?

But war is by no means the worst thing. We can see the worst if we take a closer look at the state of what is called human society.

A tree grows, a bush lives. An oak is an oak, a lime tree a lime tree, and so with the hazel, the cornel. They grow if they can, they mature, produce, bear fruit, die off. They are never equal, never unequal. They have no dreams of becoming animals, human beings, or gods.

In human society, however, all the more powerful individuals and their cliques exploit the existence of inequality and the theory of happiness in equality. Along comes some neurotic manic-depressive and makes a name for himself in history on the basis of legends. Men of history share the acknowledgments, honors, glory; they mold people's careers, grant prizes, award sinecures and titles; they apportion blame, dispense penalties, condemn to death and confiscation of property, accuse, abuse, confer testimonials, categorize people as good and evil.

This is how they begin in their own lands. They then introduce the same regime in the foreign lands they have conquered by fire and sword.

Acting on such principles in February, 1942, the Italian troops went from door to door, rounding up the male inhabitants. They drove us to an assembly point, then loaded us onto trucks and took us away to a barracks. There we waited in the yard and afterward passed in single file by a cell, where some of our own compatriots inspected us. They had a magic word for each of us. *Destra* (right) meant back home, *sinistra* (left) meant prison. They kept us stewing a few weeks, confined in the barracks and then, early one morning, they put each of us in fetters, secured us six at a time with cattle chains, bundled us into Red Cross vans and removed us to a camp in Italy.

Benito Mussolini, the Italian Duce, friend and ally of the German Führer, was creating his own legend.

All these leaders enjoy waging war; they are masters of the "barbarian art." They "thump the table with their fists," declare war, take parades, deliver speeches, gamble with the lives of millions of people. They cast the dice, they cross the Rubicon. They stand on the banks of the Neman and plan the conquest of the East. They organize campaigns, discover plots against themselves, march with their armies across mountain ranges, force rivers; they hang, shoot, arrest, torture, award honors and promotion. They start by reading about heroes when they are young. Later they themselves make history. By cunning, deceit, fraud, murder, treachery, and plunder, they win their fame. Above all, they always have plenty to say.

Napoleon loved war. "War is the natural state (*l'état naturel*), liberty and release from the leaden cloak of civilization." To Metternich he declared, "A man such as I cares naught for the lives of a million people."

Hitler must make war to find a place in the sun. And millions will die to fulfill his purpose. Once, in the Austrian town of Linz, he used to see Wagner at the opera house. Now he has composed his own opera and here I was, caught up in it, with a nonspeaking role, on the fringe of the action.

When Napoleon took Spain, dumb fellows like me were walking the rocky paths of Sierra Morena. Of them he said, "We can inflict defeats on them, but we cannot conquer them, because a real battle with them is impossible."

In human organization, you will find nothing like bird flocks, beehives, ant heaps. Any herd of elephants can get on with the business of living but human herds in search of "the right way" blunder on through self-inflicted disasters, plague, famine, war. And there is always someone else who comes along and once again claims to have the secret of *happiness*. Some follow him, some wonder whether they should not do so too, while others resist and object. The most convincing arguments are then used: the cudgel, the axe, the sword, the rifle, the cannon, the tank, the bomb.

I had time enough to think all this over in the camp at Gonars. A fenced-in area in the middle of a plain, with sheds, a barbed-wire perimeter, watchtowers, guards, rifles, machine guns. On parade! Roll call. Their drill. Forename, surname, father's name, address, nationality. To think that Caesar passed close by this place on his advance to the north. Napoleon also came this way on his campaign to conquer our lands. When shall we see our homes again? *Domani o dopodomani.* The *buoni* will go back, the *cattivi* will not. Escape is strictly forbidden. They will fire at you. Il Duce has eight million *baionetti.*

Then Italy capitulated and the Germans occupied the Apennine peninsula. The opera went on and the program did not say when it was due to end. The stage managers could not be seen but everything was in motion, everyone rushing from pillar to post, the whole world a seething mass, with tank battles here, naval encounters there, air raids, troop movements, dances, prisons, camps, inns, meadows and fields, mines, cart tracks, idle chatter, birth and death.

We had now reached the village, alive with the early-morning bustle; the locals—mostly women—the partisans, two horse-drawn carts, some baggage on the carts, a partisan saddling a horse in a courtyard, a couple of children squatting on a doorstep, a wounded man in a hay cart lying on a bundle of straw, dirty white bandage around his head, calmly smoking a cigarette, the tobacco rolled up in a piece of newspaper, one group of partisans leaving the village, a cat, hens . . .

"Are we going to get anything to eat?" Vesna asked one of our escorts.

"Of course."

"But where?"

"At your hotel," the partisan retorted. "Everything you require."

The command post. Wait here!

Vesna could not stand it. She went inside. She soon came out, disappointed and in a bad humor. "They're eating polenta," she said.

Oh dear. She rushed off.

The short-term program for taming this pretty girl was: steer her clear of anywhere where she might meet the upper ranks, commandeer some reasonable food, and maybe find a drop of brandy.

Vesna wondered if I had sent "any pants on ahead." Sure, there were my hunting breeches and skier's jacket. Why?

Could I give her those pants afterward? She would make herself some *Spitzhosen*.

Why not, indeed.

Perhaps she could get hold of a sewing machine. "They're made of good material. Worsted."

A partisan in a well-made Italian officer's uniform appeared in the doorway of the house. He was still chewing his last mouthful and wiping his moustache.

"You're bound for Ribnica," he said. "You can travel with those carts. They will be moving off in about an hour."

Our baggage? The stuff we sent on ahead? "Oh, that's in Ribnica. You'll pick it up there."

And that was all.

Was nobody going to ask for our passes? Janez had handed us over to Cyril, Cyril to the ferryman, the ferryman to the patrol, and the patrol had brought us to the command post. And now we were off to Ribnica? Without telling anybody who we were, without anybody asking for our papers?

Vesna could stand it no longer. "Where can we get something to eat?" she asked.

Our informant was just about to go back into the house but stopped, glanced at her, looked us over, and spoke as seriously as before. "A meal will be served at noon," he told us. "They'll have something for you too, somewhere." With that we were dismissed. We stood there like orphaned children. Adolf Hitler would have rejoiced to see such adversaries.

"Let's go prospecting," I said to Vesna and went back through the village. In this way I became, without knowing it, the leader of half a dozen future guerillas. We dropped in at one or two houses and asked if we could have a bite to eat. Naturally, wherever we asked, the woman of the house took fright when she saw how many guests had appeared. They would all crowd after me into

44

the hall, then follow me out again. "We'll have to break up," I told them. "We'll probably get something if we operate in pairs."

When I was left alone with Vesna, things sorted themselves out with no trouble at all. I quietly let it be known that I would pay. Before long, we were sitting down to fried eggs at a pleasant kitchen table; a bottle of brandy appeared from nowhere. I now discovered that Vesna liked a cigarette.

A well laundered cloth hung on the wall, bearing the motto in red letters and a schoolboy's best handwriting: "Home is best, for those who have one." The strong white homemade brandy smelled of smoke. The woman who was ladling fat into the frying pan with a wooden spoon wanted to know how things were in town; she had not been to Ljubljana for a couple of weeks. She had a married daughter there—whose husband was a clerk in the town hall.

I stroked Vesna's back. Waiting for the eggs to appear, she didn't seem to notice me at all. She wasn't wearing a corset. My admiration for her figure grew.

"Any chance of a shave while I'm waiting? I have my own gear, thank you."

"Warm water?"

"Fine. A towel, too."

"The Italians weren't so bad," the woman told us. "They fixed the prices themselves, but they did pay up. The partisans took a pig and left us this bit of paper, a receipt it's supposed to be . . . The *tenente* used to sit right here at this table, drinking coffee and gin. He came from Videm—Udine." The *tenente* admitted to her that resistance was only natural; any nation would resist occupation by foreign troops. But there was no sense in attacking a stronger opponent with a regular army. And matters would not be decided in this or that village but on the world front and at large green tables. When Italy capitulated, there was utter pandemonium. The soldiers just wanted to be shown the way home to Italy. They handed their arms over to the partisans and departed. The *tenente* from Udine had such a nice grayish green uniform. That day, he had gone out in the morning and he came back two hours or so later . . . but what a state he was in, dressed in rags and tatters with nothing on his feet . . . and he'd had such nice red riding boots . . . "I gave him my late husband's suit, socks, and shoes. The tears came into his eyes, he handed me a whole bunch of those lire of theirs and then he left. Our house was full of partisans and he said he would have liked to join the struggle against the Germans himself, but he was too worried about his poor mother back home."

I finished my shave just in time to join Vesna as the woman brought our fried eggs and bread, and two enormous forks to the table. Before reaching out for the food, I ran both my hands over Vesna's body, like a pianist over a keyboard. "The picnic's a success," I said, feeling in a particularly good mood after my shave. She laughed and dug firmly into the frying pan.

"Married, are you?" the woman asked as she set a basket of apples on the table.

"Not yet," I explained and winked at Vesna.

"You do make a handsome couple," she told us, and surveyed us with obvious approval.

Hardly had we finished our meal when Mishko came in. He stood in the doorway, contemplating our blissful state and the remains of the meal with unconcealed envy. "Shouldn't we be moving?" he asked. "Don't you worry about us, Mishko," she retorted. She had plumped for me, or rather, for the omelet and pleasant kitchen.

Mishko scowled and tried again. "The carts are moving off. If you want a lift . . ." He turned and went off. Vesna laughed, raised her glass briskly and clinked with mine.

Sometimes, nonsense becomes an everyday reality.

There were four of our group waiting for us in front of the house. I met the calm, penetrating glance of the man in the black suit. We live our lives, my dear fellow, as we best know how. Why then make of it a complex tragedy, fraught with dramatic conflict and the sufferings of the unfortunate, even if we still have time for that?

Two more hay carts had now joined the first pair. We could have easily split up and shared them. But no. They all clambered onto the first cart, where Vesna and I had already snuggled down.

Off we went. Two carters, the older ones, were perched in their driving seats, while the two younger ones were walking along beside the horses. There were sacks full of varied contents. There were also several rucksacks. Vesna and I settled down on some sacks of hay, hay for the horses. What a way to go to war! Vesna's eyes were shining after the brandy she had sipped and a pleasant warmth flooded my veins. Her body squirmed deep into the sacking as she laid her head on my shoulder. She smiled and gazed far away, between the hilly horizon and the low-lying clouds to the south, glowing in the limpid lemon-yellow sunlight.

I met Anton's eyes gazing at me. What did that look mean? Envy? Surely not. Enmity? No. Condemnation? Hardly. Banal curiosity? Never. Suddenly it struck me: he was comparing his own life with mine.

Slowly, as if without thinking, I took hold of Vesna's hair; my fist played with those smooth, thick locks.

Time passed like the road beneath the horses' hooves. Our goals were probably already fixed, predestined. At the thought of the future, of tomorrow, a mild curiosity came over me, and I also felt a strange apprehension; I suppressed both feelings immediately and contemplated the immediate reality: the great swinging rump of the horse, the white road with its potholes, those three birch trees in a roadside clump, the rumble of the carts, the smell of horses' dung, the apple I was slowly munching.

At the next village, we might discover that Germany had capitulated and the war was over. Or else, that the Germans had made an attack with bacteria (or gas, or secret weapons), had thrown the Russians back, had made a surprise cross-channel invasion and occupied England. Of course, nothing special might have happened and we would find ourselves once more caught up in a succession of trivial and perplexing events.

The chief thing was that I knew no precedent for my present situation. This was neither peace nor war.

My surroundings roused specters in my imagination. I was lost in thought and faraway.

I was walking along the sandy track by the Jakopich pavilion in Tivoli Park, Ljubljana, with Vida and Joseph. Ljubljana Castle was on the other side of the town. It was a clear bright Sunday morning.

The shrubs, woods, fields, and lawns were coming back to life again.

I was standing on the embankment by the Ljubljanica.

Marigolds among the grass. Vesna's soft warm flesh at the nape of her neck.

No more comfortable bathrooms, no showers, no more strolling around the streets of your hometown, no more arrogant German officers in sight. The streets around the closed university, the houses, the people, their movements—these were still, silent pictures, with the faint alkaline taste of soap.

A small village. A white rabbit in a farmyard raised his head and gazed at us, wondering whether to take flight.

No more sleeping in our own bed. No more winding up the alarm clock at night. Cycling, verboten. Possession of skis, verboten. Listening to the wireless, verboten. Curfew. Excursions to the hills, verboten.

47

A partisan on horseback, rifle slung over his shoulder, appeared from a side road, caught up to us, gave us a cursory wave of the hand, and cantered past.

The Italians had gone. The Germans were so far away, they seemed to have disappeared. Here, "we" were in control.

Cartloads of arms and ammunition boxes, with Italian markings.

Groups of men, armed and unarmed, wearing every possible sort of get-up. We passed through a burned-out village.

The driver told us how our forces took Turjak Castle. The Whites had been forced to surrender. The Italian artillery fire was accurate but then we mounted a surprise attack. What an onslaught! A partisan asked one of the White officers, "Did you expect the Germans to come and help you?" He said, "No, the English." The driver laughed. "Churchill couldn't make it." (He pronounced the name Whorehill.) How far does our liberated territory extend? Who knows! They say we are in action against the Germans on the Kolpa River.

Now the roads are more crowded than ever, with people and traffic on the move in all directions.

A heavy Italian Breda machine gun on its mounting.

All kinds of field guns. A case of Italian hand grenades, so-called red tomatoes. Women and children.

Horse-drawn cannons, Italians, and our forces in attendance. The sound of Italian voices.

I hopped off the cart to stretch my legs. It was a real pleasure to take a few steps. Vesna preferred to ride. Mishko jumped off but kept to the other side of the cart. He was clearly fed up with me.

The deep ruts left by a tank's tracks in the muddy ground beside the road; it had stopped here, driven off and left its mark.

We came to a bigger place, swarming with troops and civilians, with carts, horses, mules, stacks of arms, cannons, machine guns, a mine thrower; the market square was littered with hay and straw.

We watered the horses. The carters arranged a meal for us; we were to eat at the field kitchen over there. What about mess tins? "You can borrow them off somebody. But haven't you lot even got spoons?" It turned out that only Anton had one.

I set off with Vesna through the square.

Another four of "our group" followed behind us. Two Slovenes make a duet, three a choir, four a procession.

A Bosnian pony was headed our way, pulling a small cart. The partisan sitting in it recognized me. This was the first old acquaintance I had met—Stane, a fellow in his early forties, an old soldier by now. He had been a student of technology at the university. What was he carrying? A radio transmitter. It had fallen off an armored train.

"Where are the Germans?" Mishko asked.

"At the moment, they're still far, far away," Stane replied with a smile.

"Nobody knows where they are," Mishko remarked. This put Stane in a good mood.

"Really? Don't you fret. They don't move so quietly they can't be heard." He laughed.

Stane was on his way "to the division." He gave us a pear each from a sack. "What's the weather like hereabouts?" one of us wanted to know. "The weather? Great," said Stane. "It's always fine here except when the Beat's on. But the swallows were very early this year." He shook his head. "That means an early winter, and a hard one too, damn it!" The expletive expressed bitter memories of harsh winters already spent in the woods. He flicked his whip and disappeared as suddenly as he had appeared.

A troop marched by singing a folk song: "Time to whet the scythe blade, now the ears of corn are ripe . . ."

Two officers with automatics on well-saddled horses. Red badges on their sleeves.

Some partisans, complete strangers, lent us dented mess tins and unwashed bowls of Italian make. They offered us spoons too and we cleaned them at the fountain.

"Look out, you'll wash all the vitamins away," a young soldier in an outsize Italian uniform warned us. Without a word from the servers or the served we were given a meal of bean broth, boiled beef, and a hunk of bread. In front of one of the houses a young lad was perched on a stone bench, rendering a plaintive sea shanty on his mouth organ.

When we moved off again, we were so full you could have honed a scythe on our bellies, as the saying goes.

Sunlight. Bushes. Trees. A church on a hill. The road: swarming with carts, horses, mules, civilians, soldiers; a farmer taking a cow out to graze; the sound of singing from a house by the road.

We all lit up an after-dinner cigarette, all, that is, except Anton. Vesna started showing off, blowing smoke in my face. With a good meal under her belt, she had other pleasures in mind.

A breeze stirred the bulrushes in the ditch.

Anton seemed to be constantly lost in thought, gazing down from the cart at the road with a permanent frown on his forehead. The bluish white of his hands stood out in stark contrast to the black material of his trousers. That skin had not seen the sun all summer.

I felt an urgent, irrepressible desire, but for what I could not decide. For a woman? For Vesna? That would come in due course, without desperation or compulsion. I was well fed, warm, snug, happy. Our road was free from danger. The past was behind me and the future was yet to appear on the horizon. What was I hankering for? Enlightenment? Explication? Understanding? Or maybe just a decent uniform, proper weapons, a saddled horse, a posting to a good unit? Rowdy, garrulous company? I did not know myself.

Beneath us the road receded, yard by yard, mile by mile. We passed houses, trees, lawns. I was happy that the rumbling of the cart smothered our voices and made conversation impossible. Eyes half closed, I surrendered to the swaying of the hay cart. I was drifting into that pleasant state between wakefulness and slumber, when words and thoughts dissolve into images and emotions.

Emotions that come or tarry—remnants of words and ideas floated up from the memory and sank again, merging transfused among images and sensations of what was and what had been yes now *ben nota* that's your quota—sketches descriptions oil paintings museums curtains knife trying to meet cannot approaching nearer running into the background colors woodcuts gnarled trees caricature novel picture war engravings chronicles of campaign films all quiet on the western front pen drawings plans of war rainfall frescoes colored wagons photographs toy swords shields lances javelins helmets Ilium ponies printed page hamlet tree tents knife fight man with helmet perched naked in tree and it was all settled white cloth trimmed with lace ribbon coat-of-arms cannon.

The Battle of Agincourt. One evening, two armies camp facing each other preparing for the life-and-death struggle on the battlefield at nine in the morning. Heraclitus says life is eternity and eternity a child playing dice whose throw decides whether you live or die. Sumptuous tents, knights merrymaking, squires and vassals drinking, pennants, silken ribbons, lace, coats-of-arms. Paramours, banquets, carousals. Steeds, swords, brightly lit tents. Night. Heavy slumber. Overloaded stomachs, nightmares. Morning. Preparations. Conflict. And after the battle, a fall of rain. It always rains after a battle. Only at Waterloo it had been raining beforehand and a downpour hampered Napoleon. Rather an unusual throw of the dice for him.

Švejk, barracks, military hospitals, brothels for other ranks, brothels for officers, whores, latrines, garrisons, prisons, chaplains, trains, transports, beer, police, trenches, supplies held up. "We're going to win this war," said Švejk.

Every battle is an almighty muddle; hardly anyone can get a decent view of the action.

Mud, shells, bombs, blood. An airman mows down recruits who have just arrived at the front, straight from school. Instead of scattering, they huddle together. Comradeship, lines of trenches, bomb craters. Wounds, corpses, bayonet charges, death. Abominable rations. Not a spark of life in his eyes. All quiet on the western front. We used to think the Emperor was a taller, stronger man. The serried ranks are gently disillusioned. Pinning-on of medals. Then back to the front again. Mud, shells that moan, shells that arrive hissing, that explode overhead, shattered legs, torn bellies. Lost his legs but kept on running and dived into a trench.

The Franco-Prussian War. An orchard, trees, soldiers; soldiers, fruit trees, a farmyard; shooting, soldiers, trees. *The Quiet Don*, the battery in the blizzard, horses, an old White Guardsman, a sergeant, saves the battery. Horses, horses, Budyonny's mounted army. Sholokhov, Isaac Babel, Lidin, Ivanov. The steppe.

The steppe under snow. Advance and withdrawal. Kutuzov and Napoleon's chess match. A Cossack charge. The French camp. The court ballroom. A villa converted into a field hospital. Wide rivers. Moscow in flames. Lev Niko-layevich. It all happened once, but how it really was, what it was like for those closely involved, no one knows. What was the look on the Tsar's face? Had the Frenchmen really lit a campfire in an open wood when the Cossacks attacked them? A white plain, blotched with dark stains where the corpses lay; snow falling on military greatcoats.

Nearer to waking and farther from it. Back to words and thoughts and away from them. I doubt whether I could pronounce a name. Christopher Columbus. Stph . . . mumbu . . . Sword and cross and steed, a sail, the prow of a ship.

"Put right for me this German land," the German said. The taste of tinfoil, an aerial battle.

All things move along their own course, flow along some channel. The light goes on and off.

Through an orchard (fruit trees again) I float to a place where I had been before, though this was another village.

I see a commander on a hilltop, standing in a hail of enemy bullets, pointing to a map, giving orders. A real hero, that commander. "But a cow could have stood there just as well. Only requires the same lack of imagination," thinks soldier Robinson. Journey to the end of night. Battle.

Men in skins, brandishing cudgels, sticks, stone axes. The attack. Cave dwellers. We had our own too, didn't we, in the Kras country, by the mountain wall. They used to devour their enemies after a victory. The Crusaders set out to free the Holy Land. The Conquistadores conquered America. Submarine attack on convoy. Cowboys and Indians. Hitler liked reading Karl May. Bandits and cowboys. The Thirty Years' War. Swords, muskets, cannons, the Battle of Trafalgar. Nelson's death on his flagship in the hour of triumph. Victory for one side, disaster for the other. He who spends the night on the battlefield is the victor. Homer's *Iliad*. Xenophon's *Anabasis*. Shortages. Clash of arms. City walls. Siege machines. Desert march. Japanese in the Burma jungles. The Russo-Japanese War. The campaigns of Cyrus. Barbarians from the north. Wars in India, in China. Portuguese from Angola invade the Congo. The Spanish Civil War. The Battle of Custoza. The American Civil War. Pope Julius II attacks at the head of his troops. Cowboy shoot-out. Caesar's *De Bello Gallico*. "Soldiers, each of you has a marshal's baton in his rucksack." On St. Helena, Napoleon seduced the wife of his aide-de-camp and had a child by her. He died of cancer. Alexander the Great died of pneumonia. Caesar was stabbed to death. How is Hitler going to die? Shall I survive this war? Every battle is a toss of the coin between man and death, heads or tails, with no third possibility. In one museum, I saw a fine collection of weapons of all ages. "Man should enjoy life and know how to die." The hands that wielded them were nowhere to be seen.

"Woe to the general who arrives at the battlefield with a preconceived plan."

Preparing for combat brings an ecstasy of its own.

They say my father was happy when he left for the front. Two and a half years later, a parcel arrived at our home with his shako, saber, decorations, and some other trifles. In the nineties, his father, my grandfather, tried to stop a runaway horse, was trampled to death, and that was the end of him. His father fell in battle. Odd men out. On the seniority lists of foreign armies.

When I was a little boy, I used to like playing with my father's war medals, till on some occasion, when and where I do not remember, I lost them. He fell for Emperor and Fatherland. Now where did I lose them? Was I playing in a sandpit?

My father's saber had a golden tassel. When the Italians ordered the townspeople to hand over all weapons, my aunt, without my knowledge, carried it down to the river, fatuous old crone. Wrapped it up in paper. Dropped it from a bridge into the water. Of my father nothing remained. He was a stranger, a silent lodger, a shadowy figure in my life. Maybe there was something of him in me? Maybe I too was happy to go to war? Listening in town to the chatter of machine guns on the other side of the barbed-wire perimeter, I was so tormented I dug my nails into my palms. I yearned for the day when I would be allowed to leave the town and its oppressors.

Hostages. Arrests. Raids. Rumors about Gestapo methods, about German concentration camps. Hangings at Celje . . . hangings at Kranj . . . Shootings . . . The Gestapo came around asking for you. They are planning a purge. Barbed-wire barricades in the streets. Black automobiles. Informers, White-Guardsmen, Quislings, the political police. Long live Christ the King. Long live King Peter II.

Keep your head down and bide your time. Things were never easy. All power is from God. The English are coming. The Americans are coming. The Russians are coming. Whose war is this, anyway? Is it between the Axis Powers and the Allies? Or is it the Liberation Front against the Germans and their collaborators? Between Fascists and Communists? Is it a war of liberation or a revolution under the guise of resistance to occupation? What if Hitler had not quarreled with Stalin? Forget it! Why? Don't spread propaganda. Russia's tactics are not your concern. Yes, but what about those two bewhiskered gentlemen, General von Krebs and Stalin, embracing each other in Moscow, although they represent such different regimes? Well, did they—or didn't they? And didn't Stalin later complain bitterly that Hitler had let him down? You'd better forget all that old crap! Only the present moment matters. Politicians do forget, little people do not. Oh, sure, sure. We all forget, otherwise we couldn't go on living.

What were we taught?

To read, to write, to count; not to think—that was left to each of us, to learn, or not, for himself, as the case might be. They injected us with a whole lot of great ideas, which afterward developed, faded, rotted away, fermented inside us, sometimes latent, then suddenly erupting with great force. Justice and honesty were in order as long as they remained vague abstractions. Liberation of the poor blacks (give generously) was a more complicated matter; here, those of us who are on the Pope's side are set against those who are not. The idea of liberty is very dangerous and can be exploited in widely differing ways. Belief in progress also has enormous consequences. Are you a progressive? Or are you a reactionary?

They also swamped us with fairy tales in which, inevitably, good triumphed over evil. They taught us history; that is, the dates of wars and massacres. The geography of frontiers, confines, blockades, iron barriers over brooks, woods, and thoughts, passport geography.

I grew up in an anticlerical household, in the period dominated by two terrorist organizations, the Yugoslav National Party and the Yugoslav Radical Union, the hotbeds for the White and Blue Quislings, people I should not like to be closely acquainted with. Church, God, nation, king, and country, all those holy ideals in whose name you can hang the conscientious objector.

Then came the Italians, who had begun to relate all events from the birth of Fascism. And later the Germans, who have a really poor opinion of the Slavs.

So that serving in this war was, for the ordinary man, something quite different from anything we had read in novels or seen in films. At this moment, all knowledge about previous wars is dead and useless. Every movement fights to increase its membership and must therefore spread its propaganda, ignore the facts, exaggerate, conceal, lie; must have its own high-sounding phraseology—must not concede even a mite of human feeling to the enemy. The enemy is a monster, a criminal, the scum of the earth; our own soldier is a hero, a saint, a gallant and self-sacrificing champion of a just cause, a Man with a capital letter. And so there are few prisoners taken in a small war, when everyone knows what it means to be captured alive. You do not trust the enemy; you do not even trust your own side completely; you have a couple of half-baked ideas buzzing around inside you, as you hurry to meet your fate in a maze of a thousand snares. God stands at the crossroads, and his image is a man nailed to a cross. No one marvels at the sight, neither the Italians nor the Germans, neither the White nor the Blue Quislings, nor the Partisans.

In the 1914 war, there were no lightning offensives, no tank or air battles, no ideological warfare. There were mobilizations, muddy trenches, hand-to-hand fighting, leave passes, latrines, and military brothels. Hospitals with Red-Cross sisters and front-line brothels help to embellish a vision of war, which the pacifists find so sordid, stupid, and above all, incomprehensible.

We must forget all such qualms, if we want to survive. Imagine I have been appointed commander of a battalion. I am leading my men in an attack on an enemy position. I am glad to see they are all fighting mad against the other side. Then along comes some moaner and starts talking the sort of nonsense which has just been running through my head. Would I be happy? If I gave him the go-ahead, he would ruin my men's morale in half an hour or less, for after all, he would only be mentioning things that, deep down, they too would understand. (How could I lead a demoralized mob through barbed-wire entanglements, in an assault on a machine-gun nest, after that?) They would be dropping like autumn flies. Defeatist, alarmist, great thinker. You have caused the death of so many of your comrades! But in fact it was my fault, for not choking you off. The attack fails, the retreat turns into a rout; what remains? Only surrender! We shall be taken alive by an enemy who has no defeatists, panic-spreading philosophers, barrack-room lawyers in his ranks.

It is not universally true that an officer must be a war-crazy blockhead. What happens to them when they go into action? They adapt. They must adapt. Time enough for arguing when the war's over, they used to say. There must be a quiet, unspoken agreement among the soldiers, that they will be soldiers, pure and simple, that they will have only one aim, victory; only one road, the campaign as planned; only one thought, to carry out orders, to do as they are told, to concentrate on following instructions. Therefore, they must accept restrictions, hew, knead, reshape themselves, foster hatred and rage against the enemy, summon up all their strength, common sense, and guile to destroy him. The enemy is not human. He is neither an animal nor an object; he is a robot in the hands of Anti-Man, a detestable criminal, bereft of human features; we must wipe him "off the face of the earth." Amen. This must be our malediction.

It was quite different back in town. There, each group had its allotted task and fighting role. One collected money, another arms. One distributed the propaganda printed by an underground press, while informants gathered information. Another group organized the dissemination of leaflets, wrote slogans on walls. A special group collected medicines and bandages for the partisan hospitals; another took over and brought it to assembly points; a third conveyed the goods from the city to the theater of operations. There was an organization for the assistance of prisoners and their families, another for the concealment of men on the run, a security service, hit men. No one harboring a wanted man could simultaneously take on any other role. All this was going on under the harsh oppression of the occupier's armed forces and police, in constant danger from traitors, the Quisling political police and a network of informers. Death came at the hands of experts, specialists in this line.

Here, for example, we have Franz Böhm, a German conscript on sentry duty. He must be quietly disposed of, without alarming the unit we are about to attack. Franz Böhm is a cobbler with a wife and three children, a good-natured chap, who likes his drop of beer on a Saturday night. And so on. But are we going to worry about man's destiny, about the injustice Franz Böhm is going to suffer, about our own blood-stained hands? No. We are going to kill a sentry at his post. And we need the special knack. We must be able to creep up behind him, without being heard, as the Italians do. We must know how to pounce on and pin him, and where to plunge the knife so that he will not have time to utter a sound. After special training, commandos do not need to use a knife. They can kill a sentry by breaking his neck.

So let's forget about Franz Böhm. The important thing is to be ready to kill, before we go into action, otherwise we shall be killed ourselves. And we have to learn this in an army which has no time for teaching military skills, a collection of people without training, without knowledge of weapons or strategy. And we are pitted against the best army in the world, equipped with the best weapons, led by the finest officer corps, with units specially trained for guerrilla warfare.

We need to know all that, if we wish to survive.

A woman: a creature, whose body I know in principle and detail, since there is not a point on it that does not interest me. Vesna herself had a body of high quality, inhabited by a rather mean spirit. The jolting of the cart had made her hungry again. After a meal, she would feel like a drink. Then she would be tired and drowsy or might also want to make love. All this, including the last item, she was now expecting from me; to ply her with food and drink and in general to see to her physical well-being. She was a flirt with no prejudices.

Proud of her bravery in the hands of the police, proud she had given nothing away, she could not understand why we were not more impressed. She was getting on my nerves now, running over the good things she would like to eat. A lovely plate of homemade polenta with scraps of pork fat, scrumptious scraps of fat, juicy pork. Sometimes she would wake up during the night, dying for a slice of apple strudel and she would not be able to fall sleep again for the thought of it. Lovely crunchy strudel, with finely rolled pastry and a thick layer of filling.

During this recital, Anton gazed at her with a dull, codfish eye and then scowled at me, as if to say, "How on earth can you stand such drivel?" On the other hand, Mishko was deeply moved by this culinary rhapsody. His mouth started to water. When he had got back from the Italian internment camp (he had been in Reniccio), the first thing his mama had to do was to cook him liver in sour cream. I glanced at the two of them. They were deep in an unending conversation about their favorite foods.

I jumped off the cart to stretch my legs. Shortly afterward Anton got down too. He walked alongside me.

"Berk!" He called me by name, as if we were old acquaintances. I started. After all, I had only mentioned my name casually the evening before. "Give me an apple." How did he know about the three small apples in my jacket pocket? I gave him one. He accepted it without any fuss, said nothing, but bit into it with no apparent enjoyment. I saw that Mishko had moved closer to Vesna and looked happier now. She, however, was playing hard to get, sometimes looking my way with a pleasant smile. Dear Mishko, you had better change your tactics!

"I am surprised you remember my name," I said.

"I have an excellent memory." The answer was almost a cool rebuff. I decided I would say nothing and leave the next cue for conversation entirely to him. With wrinkled forehead, he gazed at the ground in front of him. When he had finished the apple, he flipped the core into the ditch and spoke again.

"I've learned to converse without words."

"I thought so. I sometimes hear you, I mean, without always understanding you."

"Yes, you're quite receptive, it's true."

And now we had a silent "talk." He (more or less): Often been on my own . . . my life is so different from your . . . God knows who is right . . .

Now I: You have too little time for the good things in life . . . you should really let yourself go, lad . . . if you enjoy an apple you'll get twice the benefit from it . . .

He: If you can't be handsome and strong, better avoid the limelight . . . repress your emotions . . . but you attract attention without trying . . .

I: Do you believe, Anton, that in spite of this gulf between us, we are basically compatible?

He: I don't envy you, you know . . . I know I intrigue you . . . of course, there have been two possibilities right from the start: either that we should hate each other because of these differences, or be drawn to each other . . . It's true that sheer chance helped us, but that was not essential . . .

I: I really find it hard to hate people . . . Even when I'm furious with someone, it soon evaporates . . .

He: But I heartily detest shallowness, superficiality, infatuation with trivial desires . . . You do too, only you don't show it.

I: Probably you're right . . .

Here he spoke aloud. "It's better to have no set habits. It's easier to conform. If you've had one set of habits until today, and with the change of environment you're forced to accept a completely different mode of behavior . . . it makes you nervous . . . you can crack . . ."

Mentally, I replied: You're going to suffer too, when we have to get used to front-line combat.

He waved his hand as if to say, "We'll manage somehow."

We both bristled when Vesna slipped off the cart and joined us with some trite, hollow remark about her aching bones. We were walking past a completely gutted wayside chapel, where our muddy road ran into a highway. Here we saw the tracks of a cart, which had driven out of the field some time before.

The doors of the chapel were lying in the grass. The inside was a small cavern, painted a sky-blue color.

"As vacant as this woman's head." I caught Anton's unspoken thought.

"Quite empty," I agreed in a low voice.

"No doubt our boys cleaned it out," Vesna blabbed on. "My, how I could do with a good dinner."

The early twilight was beginning to thicken in the shadow of the hills.

We were approaching some houses.

Vesna and I were sitting on the biggest baker's oven I had ever seen, in the main room of a farmer's cottage. A thick, red quilt was spread beneath us. Its cover was torn in places, exposing a grayish white stuffing. We sat there, dangling our legs over a bulky bench. There was a bed in the room, occupied by an ancient man who lay deaf and decrepit, a green blanket drawn up to his neck, staring up at the ceiling, motionless, half asleep. The wick of the oil lamp on his bedside table had been turned down, so that it cast only a faint light in the room. Somewhere in the vicinity, a wheezy accordion was playing a polka. The player had not much musical talent. We could hear raucous voices, stamping heels, shouts, clinking glasses. The windows were shrouded by thick curtains of a striped pattern and faded pink color.

Vesna had ruffled her hair as a sign that she was happy, skittish, and not yet inclined to call a halt to proceedings on this pleasant evening.

Suddenly, the past came back to mind in a flash, as if a sword had swung and cleft through what I had thought the present.

"What's wrong?" she asked.

I could have thumped her.

"Just a moment," I said instead. "I felt sick . . . Probably it was that sour wine."

She felt my forehead. She was afraid she might not get what she had been promised.

"Leave me alone! Just for a moment!"

She moved away from me.

A stage, red curtains in the windows, subdued lighting from outside, accordion playing in the distance.

Raskolnikov pacing up and down. In a moment he will murder the old crone. Russian actors in Ljubljana.

For a long time he continues to pace up and down and in the silence all that can be heard is the sound of his footsteps and the accordion in the distance. He walks as if he were alone in the world, as if we were not there with him in the darkness, as if no one were watching him, as if he had not infected anyone with a strange weariness of the world, with self-pity and perplexity at the world of these people, me, you, us, all of us crammed into this great vaulted space, where we breathe, pant, and smell. Accordion music. Footsteps. Pink lighting. Murder.

Or not quite murder. Rather a war with the world. An idea. A play. A theater with stage and audience. With bar serving coffee and drink, wardrobes, scenery store, offices.

No. Here is a bed, an old man asleep, an oil lamp. Nothing is going to happen. The present belongs to this warm stove. To something pleasant. To contentment, comfort, security, and a certain expectancy.

We had stopped our cart at a house where we heard the raucous singing accompanied by an accordion. Two of the carters had driven in front and the third had started out some time later, after waiting to take us along with him.

We drank some glasses of a sourish, young red wine. The party comprised some civilians, some partisans, including two girls, one wearing a skirt, the other in riding breeches, with a belt and small revolver in a green holster, and a young country lad playing the accordion, in black working knee boots, gray and black striped trousers tucked into his boots and a green shirt. The landlady was a strapping woman of about forty and she was helped by a trim, pretty waitress, the daughter of the house as we heard later, a girl with sturdy legs, lusty breasts and hips, in a skirt that was rather too short for her.

I contrived, with a little exaggeration, to let Vesna see how attracted I was by this bonny lass. The flirtation suited my game. I still had a few thousand Italian lire left and had decided to invest the lot in this evening. This is what led to a proper supper in the kitchen and a bunk on the stove.

But first we had had to get rid of our "company." I fixed things so that they got bean salad, a crust of homemade bread, and a good measure of wine. Afterward we danced; I took the waitress, and Mishko partnered Vesna. All his canoodling was doomed to failure. She was watching me and my partner like a hawk. I tried hard to be flippant and amusing and this appealed to Marichka.

60

She asked whether Vesna and I were married. I admitted as much but with a casual wave of the hand, indicated that neither of us was jealous of the other. I arranged that the others were to go on ahead while "the wife" and I would have supper and spend the night here, continuing our journey next day.

Polenta! Sure, you'll love it! Pickled cabbage too, sure, cooked with diced pork, just the thing to make your mouth water.

Would we mind spending the night on the stove? No, that should be all right. You'll have Dad in there with you. He's been bedridden for ages.

The carter had helped us. He had been keen to get away. He even said that he would be glad to come back that night and pick us up, but the horses would need a rest and some fodder in Ribnica. Mishko organized another liter of wine and danced once again with Vesna. In the meantime, I had told her she was my wife, that we were going to have supper together; exactly what was on the menu, I did not say; that was to be a surprise; she entered into the spirit of the plot.

Getting rid of the others was the difficult part, as I had foreseen. They were all ready for setting off, watching and waiting for me to get up and lead the way. The only one who understood the position was Anton and he discovered an appropriate maneuver. He signaled to me that we should all go outside. We did so, although Vesna was very unhappy, taken aback, disappointed and bewildered, until I winked at her, and she then began, a little too eagerly, urging the others to get a move on. Whose business is it, anyway, I thought, whether I go now or stay here, and yet . . . If it had not been for Anton, they would have all stayed with me, without any of them knowing the reason why.

I could understand Mishko. He liked Vesna and the poor fish even had some vain hopes in that direction. Anton was ready to help me because the whole business was getting on his nerves. Vesna now began to complain of a headache. Mishko twice jumped off the cart and twice climbed back on again, inviting Vesna to join him. Altogether, it was enough to turn your stomach, but the carter whipped up the horses. The cart slowly jerked into motion and Mishko yet again jumped off and approached us.

"I'm staying too," he told us obstinately.

At this, Vesna turned into a real hellcat, though she did not physically sink her claws into him. I did not bother to watch how she got rid of him. I went into the porch and then into the reception room where I leaned against the bar.

"Your polenta is cooking," the daughter of the house told me.

By now Vesna was standing beside me. "Well, that's a good one," she snorted indignantly. "The idea of him staying behind! Meddling louse!"

God knows why she called Mishko a louse. And there was no law preventing him from staying here.

She came up close and eyed me suspiciously, "Have you been making up to her?" She indicated Marichka. I could not help laughing. So we were really a loving couple after all!

Polenta, big juicy pieces of diced pork, tasty pickled cabbage. All this had its effect on the emotions and evened out all the mountains and valleys into the fair, smooth prospect of this evening in a one-time wayside inn.

Anton and the rest were off now into the night!

Now Mishko would not be able to butt in any more.

Anton, who needs himself, but cannot love himself; those two, whose presence one does not notice because they are empty masks without source or echo; the carter, cut off from the other two carts because of us; he would soon rejoin them but would never meet us again; good old, lumbering cart-horse, completely unsuited to war service, and four cart-wheels, of a type known five thousand years ago in Mesopotamia.

The struggle to escape from "our lot" had brought Vesna and me close together. The supper, much to her taste, had made for even greater intimacy. She was also amused to take on the role of my lawful wife.

And here we were, sitting on the stove. A number of factors had combined to spoil my enjoyment of sex. And these were now joined by a ghost from the past—Raskolnikov, preparing for the umpteenth time to murder an old woman.

Vesna had spread a blanket over the red quilt. It was a fine thick horse blanket with black, green, and yellow squares. This was to be our cover. She took off her skirt, folded it and put it under the bolster which was to serve us both as a pillow. Large and white, smelling of fresh linen, it had been brought out especially for us from the cupboard. She covered herself up to her waist. Obviously, she was thinking that everything would go as smoothly as our supper. If only my head would stop spinning.

"The wine wasn't really a good idea," she said. The old man lay there, motionless. He did not even seem to be breathing. The frame of the gas lamp threw a shadow across his emaciated face and the cavernous hollows of his eyes. Perhaps he had already passed on?

Vesna snuggled down, joined her hands beneath her head and stared up at the low ceiling. My own shadow fell on the wall. What if the old man should choose to die tonight and we conceive a child? Santa Madonna! I could not be very sure about Mariana; last time I had gone the whole way with her. Was there some unknown secret design in all this? My fight against death? To hell with such thoughts! Why could I not meet a woman like Anton, with whom I could reach an understanding without any idiotic, artificial chatter? Of course Anton was self-centered, feckless, mercurial, touchy, and aggressive, but he had the knack of easy relationships. Imagine that character, housed in a beautiful woman's body! That would be something! A body like Vesna's, for instance; I was now lying at her side and she was finding it hard to believe I had a stomach ache. She waited; *che sarà, sarà*; the supper had been worth days of waiting; perhaps we should go to sleep. Her leg moved against me. She was wearing stockings, a suspender belt, panties, and a lilac-colored slip. It was hot and she had not washed herself, apart from face and hands, since leaving home.

Did I really want her? Or was I simply carrying out a task I had set myself? Hell, no, I had been mighty taken with her when I saw her walking in front of me. Surely I could make up to her, chat her up and not let that bloody stupid wedge come between us. We know all about that.

But there was something that repelled me. Nothing to do with personal hygiene or the like. Between Vesna and me, I felt a barrier, chilly, resistant, and I had to break through that barrier. Otherwise I would be sulky and downbeat tomorrow, and I would feel she had used me for her own pleasure after a good supper, without asking who I was, what I was, how I felt. Now I would have to look after her in every way. I could just see it; I would have to make sure she had plenty to eat and drink, had nothing to complain of, and after carrying out all these duties, tuck her in bed and get a good-night kiss. There, there darling, go to bye-byes, pussy, give Daddums a big kiss.

Maybe, after all, this was better than the brutish approach: come on, what are you waiting for? She was the one who was rude, raw, simple, though beautifully lacquered with the veneer of our civilization. Still, there had been no mistaking her intent when she took hold of my thigh a few times after supper and pressed it gently. Yes, there was something else I had to bear in mind: if I did not take her now, I would run the risk of mortally offending her. At the very least she would think me impotent, or even a homosexual. She was proud and jealous of her power to turn men's heads and rouse the most violent passions. When she had been sitting on the wagon, she had been careful to reveal what lay under her skirt, in moderation of course, not too little, not too much. Anton had been so unpleasant; he had been the only one who would not gaze at the proffered bait. Vesna, bless her simple heart, did not realize that Anton knew exactly why she was parading her thighs, and wanted none of it.

I turned to face her and groped beneath the blanket. I slid my hand up her stocking leg, found the clasp of her suspender belt and undid it. "Are you feeling better now?" she asked with an air of concern. She helped me to unbuckle her stockings and then slid them down herself. Her skin was smooth and warm, her flesh tight and firm. This was even better than I had expected. Now her panties went the same way. The arch and sweep of her rump left me breathless, thunderstruck. A tide of lust engulfed me, turning my body into a jangling mass of raw nerves. A shudder ran down my spine, something I experience only when anticipating the utmost peak of pleasure. I stripped off my trousers and trunks and tossed them against the wall, taking care that nothing should fall out of the pockets. An old knack of mine. If a man cannot remove his trousers swiftly, in such an emergency, things can go very wrong. She surveyed me with interest and reached for me rather hastily, so that I felt the scrape of her nails. Her hair was pleasantly soft to the touch, her moist lips were spread and slightly parted. Fine. Now I turned to her breasts. I drew her pullover and blouse up over her head. When they were removed, her full breasts seemed to grow beneath the flimsy slip, two firm, soaring hills, each one designed to fit a real man-sized palm. She wanted to take her slip off but I held back her willing hand. The gentle, lilac-colored silk went so well with her golden-brown skin. Apart from that, I am a little afraid of stark nudity. Maybe my eyesight is too keen, or something else. But I do not think it is only that. Sheer nakedness is never so naked as that which is still partially concealed, as that which promises more joys to come. And when all is shown, the explorer's journey is over, and there remains only the road back to concealment. Moreover, our Eastern gurus are right when they insist that we should not rush into pleasure, or press on too rapidly or come to a sudden end, but adopt an unhurried approach, then gradually increase the pace of events, and after reaching the peak, once more, without haste, conclude the endgame. They are right, I say, although I frequently do not follow their advice, since I find other things, and maybe profounder things, of greater importance. To ask yourself what you are after, what you really want from this or that particular woman—that is the most difficult thing of all. No one in this world has a completely open and frank sex life. Even the tactics and strategy of approach demand much pretense. Then there is modesty. The customs and lifestyle of the day. Poor briefing as to the actual possibilities. Someone might find himself with a power station beside him, when all he wants is a sip of water. Furthermore we each have, frequently without realizing it, a particular ideal which we seek throughout our erotic quest; we try to deceive ourselves, we strain our imaginations, we distort our memories, we cheat our partners and ourselves. Relations on the mental plane can powerfully affect those on the physical plane, and the natural act of sexual union can become extremely complicated.

I kissed her limbs, as my palms grew to know her and she to know them. I was annoyed by the steely grip she took on my rudder, as if she was afraid it might escape. "Gently there," I told her. She released me hastily, too hastily; I saw she was submissive and a little unsure of herself. Her features took on that beautiful fecund expression, when the eyes become a little wild and tipsy, with fire in their murky depths, when the lips swell and lightly part as if in pain, when the teeth gleam behind the lips, ready to bite you, when in her pallor, the cheeks flare red, when two furrows appear beside the nose, suggestive of fatigue, when the hair is ruffled in a special way, when the photographic persona disappears to reveal the aboriginal mask of an expectant female . . . She was staring at me as if she could not see me. I felt myself drowning in the expression of her face, beginning to forget who she was and how I had met her; trapped and intoxicated by her charms, I began, despite myself, to fall in love with her . . . the fragrance of her flesh, the scent of her sex, electrified me . . . Just another short moment and I shall bend over her . . . lean on her . . . fall on her . . . and it will happen.

"Show me where you were beaten," I said. She looked bewildered, as if I had woken her from a dream. I had thought that she had made it all up. She turned on her side and showed me her rump. I could see the bruises down her back, darker and lighter spots, all the colors of the rainbow from light blue to yellow. I fondled her. No point in holding back any more.

"Kneel down. On all fours," I directed and helped her into this position.

"What for?" she asked.

"Don't ask questions."

"Is the old chap asleep?"

"Yes."

Somehow I managed to spin her over on the stove and assailed her with all my might, without thinking, without knowing what I was doing, in a sort of mist. I kissed her. Her mouth opened, our tongues met and we sucked at each other as I drove into her till we finished our wild ride together. I remained there, my head resting in her tresses while she whispered in my ear, not bothering to keep her voice too low, or so it seemed to me. A husky note crept into her voice, as she shuddered beneath me and I felt the clasp and spasm of her core.

For some time, I must have been miles away, till I heard her calling me back to the here and now, back to a strange perch on this farmhouse stove.

"If you only knew what a funny chap I thought you were! I never thought you'd have any time for me . . . I even had the impression you couldn't stand the sight of me . . ."

I felt I might give her another run, if only she would stop chattering. I took off. She gasped and tenderly kissed me, on the ear and the cheek.

Then she stopped me in my tracks with a question I had not expected, least of all at that moment.

"What's your name?"

Right enough. She did not know my name. But this was not the time for such enquiries. I knew her name, though I had never called her by it. I had had enough of Mishko bandying it around, with his "Vesna this" and "Vesna that."

So I did not respond, but she went on gabbling.

"Ooh, it's lovely . . . It's lovely, darling . . ."

"Look, let's drop the wishy-washy stuff," I retorted. "Face facts if you really must talk. Go on, tell me, what are we doing?"

"We're making love," she replied, after a short pause. I thought she was going to swallow her tongue in embarrassment at the unseemly expression.

I forced her, slowly and clearly, to repeat the appropriate terminology in its homely, obscene version. "Does it turn you on?" she asked.

"No, but I can't stand these sugary evasions."

She told me I was a hard man. She loved nice words for nice things. She soon gave way to the pleasure of the moment and began to mingle her own and my style, though the end product was rather ludicrous. "Ooh, darling, you're marvelous . . . stick it in your whore . . . oh, you're marvelous . . . dig harder, my golden ramrod . . . strange, I don't even know your name . . . and your fingers are poking my arse . . . and I never thought you cared . . ."

Afterward, we slept like dormice. She held me close and snored gently.

Shortly before dawn, I woke up, ready again for action, and went at it immediately. I doubt she really woke up.

Throughout our whispering, sighing, and panting, the old man lay motionless and the lamp burned evenly, with its wick turned down, while the windows showed, behind the curtains, the light of approaching day.

I turned away from her and fell into a dreamless sleep.

I washed and dressed before Vesna woke up.

She watched me with a smile as she dressed under the blanket, while I sat at the big maplewood table and picked up an old almanac.

The old man looked out with interest, from under his bedclothes.

Vesna slid down off the stove, approached, and kissed me on the cheek before going out of the room. Hardly had she closed the door behind her, than the invalid poked a hand out and beckoned me over. "Come here, lad!" He tried to keep his face straight. I went over to him. In a whisper, he asked me to bend down.

"What a lark!" he gurgled. "I saw it all, you know . . . only you needn't tell her . . . lord help us, they say there's nothing new under the sun . . . but never before, in all my born days, have I seen such a performance . . . always used to put the light out first, the missus and me—you know what it was like in those days . . ."

He choked with laughter.

The two women brought our breakfast, white coffee, soft-boiled eggs, and tasty homemade bread.

When we were leaving, the old man summoned me once again with a wave of his hand. I approached, leaned over him, and heard him whisper.

"You know, now I'll die a happy man . . ."

He was quite serious.

We set off along the high road. It was sunny and the morning air was fresh.

"What did the old chap say?"

"He asked me for a cigarette. He's not allowed to smoke."

"Did you give him one?"

"Yes."

"You shouldn't have." We walked on.

Now she was back to yesterday's form. That vision of the night had disappeared.

There were some logs stripped of bark and stacked by the roadside. They looked inviting. We sat down. We were in no particular hurry. High up in an oak tree, a blackbird was singing. There was something heavenly in that timeless calm. Has anyone ever set off for the wars like this before? Probably, Vesna thought. After all, there's nothing new under the sun.

In the daytime I found her insufferable. We watched the people passing by.

I remembered a French song, "*Sur la plus haute branche chante le rossignol,*" and softly crooned:

> On the highest branch
> The blackbird sings;
> Sing on, swarthy singer,
> Bless your joyful heart.

The bird sang out as if he understood me. For once, thank Heaven, Vesna kept quiet. I was afraid she would blurt out something about it being high time for lunch.

> By the white rocks
> I washed my hands
> And there I bathed
> In the swift stream.

We had already started off again when a cart going in the same direction caught up with us. The driver, a lad with a blade of grass between his teeth, let us sit on a bench across the back. The horse was young and frisky.

We covered a few more kilometers.

Carts, men on foot, mules, detachments, civilians.

68

Her fair hair, unbound, was tossed by the wind. She was relaxed and happy. She teased my crown, as if suddenly remembering the night before. But surely she was not thinking that I would be doting on her from now on. I am exaggerating a little. I give the impression of great certainty, self-confidence and even self-conceit. I really ought to think this over seriously. In the armed forces you should merge with the crowd, not stick out like a sore thumb. All communal life is based on education toward that end. Most people divide their companions, be it in schools, hospitals, prisons, barracks, or offices, into two categories: the sub-normal and the super-normal. I would be a natural target for comment if I did not pull myself together; especially if I were posted to a unit commanded by an officer of below-average height. I had had that sort of trouble before. Very well: I should have to bear that problem in mind too. But for the moment, I could just enjoy the landscape, the weather, my own high spirits, the clip of the horse's hooves, and this timeless interval, which would soon end. Vesna, give us a song; go on, anything you know!

"Where are those paths of yesteryear?" As her clear voice rang out, all doubts receded into the background. We must love life. And be prepared to die. The carter liked her singing too. If only this pleasant jaunt could continue forever. Why am I not a horse? Perhaps in one sense, I am a sort of horse. If a horse breaks his leg he must be shot, since the bone will not knit. If my unbounded imagination is broken, they might as well shoot me too. How could I go on living in the here and now, no longer able to flit away to other places, other times?

"Why did you want us to use such filthy language last night?" Her question came out of the blue, unexpectedly.

"Didn't you like it?"

"No."

"Oh. Well, how should I put it?" (Indeed. Here was an occasion for dropping all self-consciousness, all self-regard. Try to explain why you wanted the girl to use foul words.)

You see, there are obstacles, gulfs, brick walls separating people from one another, and these prevent us touching, making contact, merging. (No, that would not do.)

There is something primeval about sex. All the clutter of civilization simply prevents us from achieving true sexual union. (This would not do either.)

"Would you like me to tell you?" she asked. By all means, I said.

"It must have been some woman you once knew who put you up to it."

(There was not a word of truth in this but I was not going to admit it.)

"I'm right, aren't I?"

I suddenly decided to tell her. What a face she pulled!

"It's the sheer sound that's at the root of it. Sight, smell, touch, and taste play their role, and so does sound."

"But sound without sense, without meaning. You mean that turns you on too?"

"Sure. Look, I was in Greece, Cyprus, Rhodes. At the height of the crisis. I was working on an English vessel and I was paid in pounds sterling. The pound was worth 250 dinars. It didn't mean much to us to spend a pound. And you could have a woman for one or two drachmas, that meant at the time, half a dinar or a dinar. Meanwhile, in Yugoslavia a professor was earning a thousand dinars a month. And we could have five hundred women for a pound. Can you imagine a year?"

"Yes. But we were talking about sounds."

"Well, I was coming to that. I don't know Greek. And those Greek girls don't know any foreign language. All the same, one voice was different from another."

"Why, you're just a bumptious whoromaniac!" I never heard this expression before or have ever since. Obviously she had lost any respect she had had for me. I had imagined that I had made my mark in her eyes as an expert lover, and now I realized, to my surprise, that I was just an ordinary, dirty, little "whoromaniac." I tried to explain. I strove hard to remain affable and polite.

"It's no use," she told me. "A sort of sadism, I call it. Just like you going crazy when you saw the bruises on my arse." (So that was why I "went crazy"? Makes you think.)

She laughed and looked at me. Suddenly our eyes met. Her hand seemed to drop accidentally to my pants. She scored a direct hit. "What about it?" she whispered.

A man can never boast that he knows women. The lowliest goose-girl could astonish Casanova.

A lot she cared for Greece, Cyprus, Rhodes! A lot she cared for the psychological roots of obscenity! Off the wagon and into the trees! And she was not too bothered about the proximity of the busy road. When she bent down and proffered that finely fashioned rump, what words came tripping off her tongue! No inhibitions there, only the warmth and fluency of experience!

When we returned to the road, she was holding me around the waist, as if I were the girl and she the boy.

Nothing in the world gives me more pleasure than a nice surprise. And they come in series, or not at all.

We wandered off the road and found a deserted hayloft.

A barefoot boy with a basket of ripe pears met us and told us to help ourselves.

Well, we would reach the village soon and probably find that we were too late, that the war was just over.

We took a soft path through the grass to the main road, where we could see partisans and civilians moving in either direction.

Like ranks of multicolored, lightly embroidered banners, flapping in the wind

like flocks of starlings, wheeling in a clear, rain-washed sky, over fresh green fields

like a great blue-and-gold image of the Almighty, set high over the soft, downy white clouds

as if from depths unknown

arose a joy supreme

of just being

in a paradise

not for losing

but lasting only a second split

between an eternity of loss

and

an eternity of anguished expectation.

"All about us are thousands of lives unknown to us, whose secrets are unfathomable. A child feels some awareness of them, hence his timid susceptibility. Every sound you hear is a sound from beyond.
A yearning, unconsoled and inconsolable, to understand the tiniest gnat which has settled on your bald head and to understand God who cradles you in the palm of his hand, this is your lifelong suffering, your struggle, the essence and significance of your whole being."
Ivan Cankar, *Cockatoo*

"Mother is putting my new secondhand clothes in order. She prays now, she says, that I may learn in my own life and away from home and friends what the heart is and what it feels. Amen. So be it. Welcome, O life! I go to encounter for the millionth time the reality of experience and to forge in the smithy of my soul the uncreated conscience of my race."
James Joyce, *A Portrait of the Artist as a Young Man*

"The marquis is not in the least inclined to return to faith, to hope, or to God, who could rejoin in one whole the split halves of his world, but remains in the skin of a devaluated human being and in his name, loses the certainty of things."
Marjan Rožanc, *The Marquises' Diabolical Rationalism*

2

What first struck me about Ribnica was the straggling length of the place. I have been there often since, but the main road that runs down from the upper to the lower village has never seemed such a drag as it did then. With swarms of people everywhere, it reminded me of the Ljubljana market. People dressed in clothes of every color and all styles, civilian suits, military uniforms, combinations of both. Slowly, the eye grew accustomed to this motley. The predominant hues were black, navy blue to light blue, and every possible shade of green. There was an equal variety of firearms. There were wagons, horses, mules, a field kitchen for troops in transit, long convoys on the move in either direction, serious faces, happy ones, people singing, people lost in thought, people deep in conversation. Caps of various colors, with red five-pointed stars, large and small, sewn on to them. A detachment headed by a strapping young fellow carrying a flag on a thick staff.

Credere, obbedire, combattere; believe, obey, fight! This slogan, in capital letters, had been daubed in thick black paint on a cottage wall. Beneath it someone had added in red paint: "Death to Fascism, liberty to the people!"

Three songs could be heard, in counterpoint and contention.

Some of our lads were singing a Slovene folk song as they marched by: "Whet the scythe, the crop is ready . . ."

In front of one of the houses, a group of Italians were sitting on the ground. One of them was giving a pleasant rendering of "*Solo me ne vo per la città . . . passo tra la folla che non sa . . . che non vede il mio dolore . . . cercando te . . . sognando te . . . che più non ho . . .*" They had the sun in their faces. They were dreaming of home.

In the background somewhere, an accordion was playing a sentimental Russian tune.

The smell of smoke and horses.

I was directed by the people at the command post to a requisitioned hotel. There I recovered the suitcase with my things. Everything was there—except for my pistol. Complaints got me nowhere. Where should I make enquiries? Try the armored tram corps.

I put on my blue riding breeches, long black wool socks, and ski boots. At least my lower half was in order. I then donned my dark blue ski jacket. Around it, I fastened a thick prewar Yugoslav army belt. One of the household, a girl who used to be a waitress or something, promised to sew a star on my cap.

"Let me take care of that. You'll come back sometime in the morning, right?"

An old wireless, set in what had been the lounge, was being switched on and off all the time. On when music was being broadcast and off as soon as a German voice started to gabble. I was told I would be eating here and I was shown my sleeping quarters, in a capacious room on the first floor. I noticed another bed there. Whose? Osip's, of course.

What's that? Didn't find your revolver in your baggage? Don't you worry, there's plenty of that gear to be had. Where? On the Germans, of course. You'll get a revolver from a dead Kraut. And where can I find a dead Kraut? So far, I've seen no sign of them, dead or alive. Not to worry, they'll soon catch up with us. Our last engagement was on the Kolpa riverfront. Nine days the battle lasted. They're pushing through the mountains now. Heading this way? Of course.

I had no idea who had fixed me up with board and lodging in this one-time inn, or allotted me a bed in a neat, comfortable room, which still had the fresh, clean smell of decent hotel accommodation.

Vesna saw to it that she got my wool pants.

No sooner had we arrived in Ribnica, than she met an old friend from town. He was properly outfitted and armed with a revolver and a Schmeisser. In a word, a much more attractive catch.

When I met her the following day, she was already wearing the *Spitzhosen* she had sewn from my pants, and a very good job she had done with them.

She had very little to say, because she was off to her "new post." She told me only that a German offensive was imminent.

The castle. Once our men had been confined within its walls, now the Whites languished there.

Vinceremo! said a notice on a fence: *We Shall Conquer*.

"We're going to win this war," said the good soldier Švejk.

A wall-newspaper; news on duplicated sheets. Russia is winning, we are winning.

To the Italian slogan *Evviva* someone had added *Thievery*.

I had discovered that I could get excellent pear brandy at the old inn; cigarettes, too, could be bought for Italian lire. It's hard luck on anyone who can't stock up now, they tell me. Soldiers stocking up?

I met Katerina, a young girl I had known while at university. She was very surprised to see me here. She had a brown leather bag and a Biretta, an Italian carbine pistol, at her belt. She asked me about this and that but did not offer me her hand either at meeting or parting.

So far not a living soul had asked to see my pass.

I wandered around. I lounged in my billet. I chatted with old acquaintances. There was no sign of Anton. I met some people whose faces I seemed to recognize but somehow could not place. One such fellow took a close look at me and walked on. I turned to see if I could remember him and he turned around too. I had the impression he did not like me.

My first meal was not at all bad. Rather tasty goulash with polenta.

Afterward, I lit a cigarette and stepped outside. In the street I soon encountered a face I knew. It was Anton! I looked him over and exchanged a few pleasantries with him. He was dressed in a prewar Yugoslav gendarme's uniform, with belt and gaiters. The whole outfit was a little too big on him.

I now learned that, as an illegal immigrant, he had been harbored and kept out of sight in Ljubljana by an officer in the gendarmes. That was how he had acquired the uniform, which he had sent on ahead to the front. We were walking along the narrow village street. He was now off to his "post." What was that precisely, his "post"? He looked at me incredulously. "Some of us are assigned to units, others to posts. And where are you going?"

"How should I know? Not a living soul is taking the least bit of interest in me."

"Really! You're getting the cold shoulder?" He laughed.

So Anton could laugh too. What a pity I could not see the joke.

Some of Anton's mates appeared, men in uniform, real soldiers, properly armed. He joined them, gave me a desultory wave of the arm, and disappeared.

While I was still standing there, gazing after them, a crowd of people was headed my way, including Vesna with her latest friend. She hardly even noticed me. She had a leather bag too. It was hanging by a strap from her shoulder, stuffed and bulging. What with, I wondered. Had she been stocking up? At that point I was nearly bowled over by a great trundle wagon hauled by two horses. It was carrying ammunition boxes with Italian markings.

Leaping out of the way, I almost flattened a chap from the same street in Ljubljana. He recognized me and called out my name. When had I arrived? Where was I bound for? Had anyone else we knew turned up? At least here was someone I could chat to.

Not to worry, he told me. Things were properly organized here, not like that almighty foul-up back in town, with everybody at each other's throat. You get your grub, your bunk and everything else in due course. Just wait for orders and take it easy. It had been up to me to make my way there; now the rest was out of my hands. There's only two rules in the service: don't ask questions, and don't go poking your nose in where you're not wanted; your orders will come soon enough. I was grateful to him for the advice. Watching him go, I was so conscious of my own Švejk-like image, odd man out, in ski jacket and old army belt, in the turmoil of that busy street, that I could not help laughing.

I had a very palatable broth for supper and drank a few glasses of rather sour Dolenjska wine with some strangers before going to bed. Some unknown benefactor's hand had brought a long white candle to my bedside table. It fell off twice before I had stripped to my underwear and turned in. I dowsed it and tried to get to sleep. I was kept awake, first by people walking up and down the street below my window, and later by the sound of singing. There was a flurry of thoughts in my fevered head, as imagination molded the events of the day into a motley procession, and I was overcome by an uneasy feeling. Here I was neither fish, flesh, nor fowl. It was as if the sea had cast me up on a lonely shore, where all around were strangers and I myself did not know whether I was soldier or civilian, whether I belonged to any group or was on my own, whether I was secure or in danger. In this state of mental confusion, it was some time before I could get to sleep.

I was awakened by a beam of strong light directed straight at me. I opened my eyes at once without at first being able to get my bearings. The light moved away from me and settled on a bedside table. I raised myself up on my elbows. Someone approached my bed and gave me a friendly greeting.

"Hello there, Berk."

He was in uniform and had not yet removed his cap. The face seemed familiar. He explained that his duties sometimes kept him out all night. He spoke as if we had last met at supper. It was a fellow called Depolo, someone I had met ages ago, at the sports club. Half awake, I listened to what he had to tell me.

"You know who was talking about you the other day? That painter, Kerzhan."

What could Kerzhan have told him about me? And why had he come to give me this news in the middle of the night, if it was not yet early morning? He had a fine uniform and a large pistol in a red leather holster. The light came from a carbide lamp. He was wearing soft brown leather knee boots. I gladly accepted one of his cigarettes, a poor Italian brand but slightly above average. He gave me a light from an Italian wax match, which he struck on the sole of his boot. I now heard the story of how they had disposed of some Whites, either that night or a couple of nights earlier. The poor bastards had holed up in a sort of dip in the ground and had to make a break for it, one at a time . . .

"Took them all prisoners, did you?"

"You must be joking! There was a white horse lying there, not far from where they were being picked off . . . Strange thing . . . They all seemed to want to get their hands on that horse . . . Raced through the dark, covering their heads with their hands . . . But none of them uttered a word . . . And none of them tried to stop in the hole . . . Only, when they realized what was waiting for them outside, one of them even started saying his prayers . . . Something like that can give you a nasty turn, you know . . . upsets your nerves . . . I can't get that horse's head out of my mind . . . that blue and purple tongue sticking out of its mouth . . . There was only one of them didn't go down immediately . . . lurched on toward us . . . mouth gaping . . . still alive . . . tongue sticking out . . . thick, red . . . Afterward you can't get to sleep . . . Anyway, you've had a good rest, haven't you? How do you find the food?"

"What time is it?" We had a cup of tea with schnapps. "Have you seen Kerzhan quite recently?"

It turned out that Depolo was that very Osip who slept in the other bed. He groaned with pain as he took his boots off. He was a chain smoker. A nonstop talker too. The Germans had made a breakthrough and would reach Kočevje any time now, if they weren't there already. They were coming in strong. Things were really heating up. Crack units were arriving. The Prinz Eugen Division, so they say. There's a lot of activity in Kočevje. A meeting of delegates from all regions of Slovenia. Rallies, food, drink, dancing, the lot! Whites and Blues on trial too; some condemned to death, others let off. Speaking for himself, he would have seen the whole bunch of them shot. "How can we afford to waste time on that trash when we have the Krauts on our tail? Who's going to feed the bastards anyway, when our own bellies think our throats have been cut? Don't imagine you'll always have plenty to eat. Raw mule meat has been on the menu before now and we've had to survive like hermits on roots we've dug up from the ground." He had not tried locusts yet but had tasted everything else. Anyway, I would soon see for myself.

He turned in and put out the lamp.

He went on talking for some time still. I would have liked to ask some questions about my own future but controlled myself, remembering my recent lesson: ask no questions, and don't be nosy.

He was still asleep when I got up in the morning, dressed and went quietly downstairs. His knee boots were lying apart like an estranged couple.

La Tarde de Domingo (Sunday afternoon). El Arenal, August 3.

It is no hyperbole when people say a man can see the whole of his life in an instant on his own internal projector.

The millionth part of a hundred-thousandth of a second equals, in a certain perspective, a couple of billion years.

This is because of pressure on the spiral in which life takes its course.

The awe and fear of passing time surrounds us, as long as we conceive infinity as a line connecting an unseen past with an immeasurable future.

If we begin to think of infinity as a circle, without beginning or end, and look at it from below with a frog's perspective, or take a bird's-eye view, we shall see only repetition in the running circle. In reality, it's a moving circumference, a helical curve. At times it is compressed and then becomes for an instant a simple circle, although this comprises many circles, imposed one on another at intervals of time.

A Sunday afternoon at Ribnica fuses with another on the shores of Majorca.

I was leaning on a farmyard wall, watching a cat move across the sand from the house to the sheds.

With all its internal and external sensors, the animal was gathering information from its surroundings. Its intricate mechanisms were selecting from the enormous multitude of echoes, those which were more important, quickly judging and considering these, then choosing the most important, and on this basis, determining its future course of action. I scraped the sand with my heel. This sound from close by, contending with all the rest (footsteps in the road, music from the house, people talking, sparrows chirping, car in the distance, horses' hooves in the stable), made her glance at me but, realizing the insignificance of my slouching figure, she went on.

Ear-piercing bark close by; halt! Beyond the fence; dog not too near. Fresh information at every fraction of a step, new choices, new decisions; at a jolt of the gate that leads from farmyard to road, she moves lightly to one side, to be closer to a tree in case of need . . . Her body moves into the future, while her steps recede into the past. The cat has her own news to deliver too: there is a lot going on; all that agitation spells some important event.

That was in the yard of the old inn at Ribnica; here at El Arenal, the curve of memory touches the circle of events, and perhaps only now, things become integral, complete, actual. When an upper circle bears down on the present, we recall the future and are struck with sudden astonishment. How often have we had the feeling that we already know what someone is about to say, or that we have been in this marketplace before, perhaps not in this lifetime, or that we already know what we are going to find around that corner—and so it turned out. For what we call time does not flow as we imagine it to and in reality is quite different form our concept of it. Time as a process does not exist. But we experience events in time.

Thus in the yard at Ribnica I felt a memory of Spain, of something yet to be. In Spain, I would remember Osip's boots, thrown untidily on the bedroom floor, and a cat in the farmyard.

And all this because of my meeting with Joseph Bitter.

Someone had told me, in great confidence, that the Prinz Eugen Division and the Death's Head Division were on their way, and with them Pavelich's Ustaše and Mihajlovich's Chetniks, together with Vlasov's German and Russian SS units. Their tanks were advancing along the roads, their infantry were combing the woods. They were slaughtering, burning, spreading ruin, leaving a black and bloody trail of corpses, hanged men, gutted buildings.

We had captured prisoners: Whites at Turjak, Blues at Grčarice.

The offensive was getting nearer.

Meanwhile I, not a cat but an unarmed soldier, stood there in the yard, picking up information, true or false, which echoed inside me and cried out for clarification, while curiosity waned in the boredom of waiting.

"Just wait and see. They'll forget all about you. They've got enough on their plate at this moment. Afterward, you'll be making a last-minute dash for the woods. You'll be captured alive."

"Who by?" Those ghosts who leave a winding black and bloody trail behind them. I shall be interrogated by some Joseph Bitter. Or Franz Böhm. And he will be faceless, without any distinguishing features.

I didn't know how to pray. I had only leafed through the Scriptures out of sheer curiosity. I knew that Baden-Powell had founded the Scouts and Tyrš, a Czech, had started the Sokol movement. I knew very little about Marx, only what was in the air at the time; I had not read his works. As for Hitler and Mussolini, I shared the general attitude of our intellectuals. The war had really flared up before I got started on a copy of *Mein Kampf* I borrowed from Professor Smolichki. And since I have the bad habit of first looking at the beginning and end of any book, I read in the conclusion: "The nation which, during a period of racial contamination, devotes itself to breeding its noblest racial elements, must some day become master of the earth." Obviously Chamberlain, the gentleman with the umbrella, and Daladier, that stocky gourmet, had never read that far.

The Herrenvolk had started out to become masters of the earth. And here we were, making a bloody nuisance of ourselves in Ribnica and its districts. They would be justifiably angry if they took me alive.

I asked Joseph Bitter, "What do you think of Hitlerism?"

He looked away.

"*Grössenwahn eines Österreichers.*" He produced this rather like a mathematical formula, then, remembering I had told him my father was Austrian, he added politely, "*Entschuldigen sie.*"

"Hardly. No one had any time to think then." He smiled, and his wife smiled too.

La tarde de domingo.

For a second, each of us, Bitter and I, relived a war, the whole of that war which lasted years and years, in a single, fleeting moment.

La tarde de domingo.

The message came while I was out. I was to see the Ribnica district secretary the following day. I was to go to house number twenty-eight or some such at nine o'clock and ask for Stefan. Who had brought the message? Oh, someone. What had he said? Who had he been looking for? Don't know, didn't talk to me. Why do you want to know? Oh, it doesn't matter, thanks.

That evening, Osip got in early. He said he was worn out; some people rest while others are slaving away. I told him I was to have a word with Stefan in the morning. "A posting," he said, not particularly interested. I was happy to see that things were moving. Sensing my exhilaration, he snuffed it out immediately.

"Look here, Berk, you want to watch it."

"Watch it? Why?"

"Yes. Mind what you're saying. You're in the army now."

"Haven't the faintest idea what you're on about."

"Why are you going around gabbing about the Prinz Eugen Division, scaring everybody?"

"So what if I am?"

"No excuses. No explanations. Just mind what you say, if you have to keep up this blathering to strangers about troop movements."

"Well, I like that. Someone down below was just telling *me* about the offensive."

"Okay, okay, let's drop it."

"No. Let's work this out. You're being childish."

"Knock it off. In the army, we're not concerned with who said what or what was really said. We've no time for chewing the fat."

"Just in case anyone reports us."

"Yes. You must be prepared for that. Understand?"

"I still don't get it."

"Don't worry, you will. You've seen nothing so far."

Here he stopped and shot a keen glance at me.

"Not a word about this to Stefan. That would be a bad mistake."

I still wanted to clear up this "business" which had really surprised me. I was not at all frightened but more than somewhat aggrieved. I remembered the conversation very well. Others had been talking about the German forces and I had asked whether there were, in fact, whole divisions.

"Forget it, Berk! Look, I'm only trying to help you. Here you are, under close scrutiny and you go around blurting out complaints about being fed up waiting . . . and so on . . ."

Well, well. This must be little Katerina, no one else.

The sooner I get away from here to some unit or other, the better.

Come on, Adolf; come out of your corner fighting!

If there is anything utter in this world, I must admit that the following day I behaved like an utter idiot.

It was with mixed feelings (hope of a posting but uneasy forebodings) that I reported at the appointed hour to Stefan, the district secretary. He received me himself, in a large room where several maps and sheets of paper were spread on a table. He was wearing an elegant Italian officer's uniform and only the badges on his sleeve and cap showed he belonged to the National Liberation Army. He was cool, polite, taciturn. He asked for my pass. I had it ready. He invited me to take a seat.

What jobs had I been given in town? Some active service and various minor tasks (collecting funds and weapons) and of course giving a hand with the propaganda. Yes? I had been recruited in July, 1941. Hauser had enrolled me. I had been arrested by the Italians and sent first to a camp at Čiginj near Tolmin and later to the Gonars CC (*campo di concentrazione*). I had joined the liberation front during my internment. Yes? I had not been allowed to leave town before now. How was it that my pass was issued by the cultural section? Oh, that had nothing to do with me? I see. Very well.

He gave a sign that the interview was over. Could I ask a favor? What would that be? Could you please let Hauser know I've arrived? We're old acquaintances, you know. Indeed. It's not going to be so easy. We've other things on our mind. Still, if it's at all possible. Good-bye.

I didn't seem to have gotten much from this fairly high-level conversation. Come to think of it, what had it really been all about? Was it because I knew Hauser? I had told Depolo he was a close acquaintance and I would be glad to have a word with him. I had mentioned it to little Katerina too. Or was it something to do with the "cultural section"?

There were seven of us for dinner, in what had been the hotel reception room. We had been joined by a teacher from Gorenjska, Pochivalnik by name, a Styrian by birth. There was also a boisterous, corpulent figure with the curious name of Tujchko. He had a flask of homemade fruit brandy and offered us all a sip from a tin cup. We also got wine with our dinner of thick soup, beef, and potatoes.

Pochivalnik's contribution to the after-dinner talk was a report on the situation in Gorenjska and Styria. Things were heating up everywhere. The partisans had set up a network covering all the villages. More and more men were taking to the forests to continue the struggle. Isolated farmhouses and mountain villages were being burned down. Hostages were being executed. Notices with the names of those shot or hanged were posted everywhere. The prisons were bursting at the seams. There had been shooting in the Drava valley; anyone caught was bound to the stake. We were executing informers and carrying out attacks on police stations. The woods were continually echoing with gunfire. The Germans were at their wits' end. Etc.

I must say we were as well, if not better informed on such matters back in town. News that is no longer new, pressed into a few hackneyed molds: our beloved, steadfast folk; German swine; Quisling swine; long live the fast approaching day of victory—try keeping up your morale with that guff. Tujchko had already had a bellyful of it and this latest dose of martyred solemnity stuck in his throat.

"Has there ever been a more distressful country?" Pochivalnik sighed.

Enthusiastically Tujchko agreed. "Nowhere, but the buggers are used to it by now. The harder you hit them, the more they like it." He had a genius for finding the softest spot and a childish glee in pressing hard on it.

The schoolteacher, completely put off, could only descend to the same level. "What a bloody idiot you are, Tujchko!"

"The world needs idiots like me," Tujchko retorted. "It's you clever people that have gotten us all into this shit."

While the drink and the talk flowed, Tujchko occasionally let out a loud yell, often complete nonsense, but sometimes to the point: "As the farmer said to the barn-door!" Or: "The whore can't help it!"—"Death to Fascism!"—"To the fence, lads!"—"He told his mama!"—"Crap and grease the oven!" He liked me because I could not help laughing at his free association of ideas.

There was a meeting on at the hay frame. Should we go? Sure. "The fuckers will leave us in peace," Tujchko shouted, "they've got other things on their mind!"

A small improvised stage with no curtains. Combatants and civilians, women and children. A girl of about fourteen, reciting in a high voice Prešeren's "Sonnets of Adversity." A partisan quartet, singing to the accompaniment of an accordion. They sang in unison, "A partisan high in the mountains stands" and "For homeland, for Stalin to battle we march." The most vigorous applause greeted a Slovene folk song, "This night, this morn, the dew did fall." At the words of the chorus, ". . . shall light sweet freedom's torch," Tujchko joined in and echoed them in his deep, resonant bass.

Someone came on with a Hitler moustache and a Hitler hairdo, giving a raucous imitation of his oratorical style: ". . . *ich werde die englischen Städte ausradieren . . . ausradieren . . .*" adding in halting German, "*ich werde zu Weihnachten in Moskau . . .*"

Tujchko kept up a running commentary, much to our amusement. Pochivalnik said, "You'll come to a bad end, Tujchko."

"Sure enough, I made a bad beginning and I'll make a bad end. Meanwhile no one gives a bloody toss. They've got other fish to fry."

We joined in the dancing, whirling around in polka and waltz, kicking up our heels in a quickstep. One of the local wenches had a really nimble pair of feet. I also danced with the partisan girl who had sewn me a cap from some blue material. Little Katerina asked to be excused, as she was feeling far too tired. Our stout friend Tujchko, about as elegant as a bull in a china shop, stamped his heels and let out the occasional shriek.

On the way back, Pochivalnik buttonholed me and bent my ear with his domestic misfortunes. They had three children already and when he left, his wife was expecting a fourth. He told me life would be something new after the war, something completely different. Society would be reborn, for the first time in our history, the small man would be the master of his own fate. He stopped in front of one house where a slogan had been painted in enormous letters. He pointed to this and cried out with deep feeling, "These things shall be!" I read the slogan: "Once a Nation of Slaves—Now a Nation of Heroes."

"We are witness to a great age," he instructed me. "The new man is being born, in pains and convulsions."

I asked him whether he really believed what he was saying. It was as if he had been anticipating my objections. Completely carried away, he began to ply me with a barrage of questions. I answered but felt my spirits declining as he went on and on. No, I told him, I had not seen the new man yet, And was it not the case that the higher we hang the slogan and the bigger the letters we write it in, the greater the gulf between slogan and achievement, between ideal theory and daily practice? Moreover, nothing in this world was ever achieved overnight. Everything takes time to prepare, to develop, and to take shape.

"But revolution is a great leap forward," Pochivalnik asserted. "We're not talking about evolution now!"

We now began, God help us, to discuss history and plunged back in time, to the culture of Crete. "Gentle civilizations did not collapse internally," I argued, "They were destroyed by barbarians. And the barbarians have taken over now. The essence of barbarism is the suppression of all joy, all hope, by fear, terror, violence; the cultivation of envy as a motive force, the concept of love as a conspiracy . . ."

He argued, objected, spoke of the class nature of the struggle, as if this were not a conversation but a contentious oral exam in political theory. He had two hundred million Russians to back him up, while all I had was the bewilderment of this unusual night and the sporadic objections that occurred to me. All this left me with an unpleasant aftertaste when we parted and I went to my own billet.

Up in my room, I flung the window wide open and leaned on the sill. I took a deep breath in the night air and cooled my poor head, still reeling from the drink and the confused jumble of words and impressions. The village was quiet, asleep, except for some occasional passerby walking along the street.

Between the houses, from the direction of the castle, came the sound of slithering feet and voices, at first indistinct, muffled, then loud cursing as the footsteps approached.

The noise grew louder, closer. It still remained muffled and mysterious. Two partisans with rifles at the ready. A column of men in Indian file. The escort was urging them to get a move on. Were these captured prisoners? Their guards marched beside them in ones and twos, some with automatics, others with rifles slung over their shoulders, hunter-style.

The Indian file in between was moving slowly, hands unusually contorted. The guards urged them on with short, quiet orders, delivered in sharp tones. A rifle butt for someone in the ribs. One of the men turned toward a guard, who pushed him away.

Each of these prisoners had his hands bound in front of him and they were all strung together on a long wire, a telephone wire, as I learned later.

Right in front of my window, one of the prisoners let out a loud yell: "Down with Communism!" The nearest guard swung his rifle butt into the face of the protester. There was a dull crunch, as if it had dropped on a ripe pumpkin and squashed it. The prisoner staggered but could not fall to the ground as he was tied to the men in front of and behind him. They both took hold of him and supported him. "Forward!" For a moment the column halted, then again moved on. Those in front of and behind the man who had been struck hauled his motionless body along. They disappeared. Shadows in the dark. A slithering sound. A smothered scream. Hoarse cries of "Move it!"

It was almost morning before I fell into a light sleep, from which I woke soon after, or so it seemed. I opened my eyes; Depolo had come in. He flung his cap on the bed and drew a deep breath, watching me without a word. I lit a cigarette. He sat on the chair beside his bed and pulled off his tight boots, panting as usual.

"Woken up, have you?" he asked meanwhile. He seemed sullen, worn out, in a bad humor. After getting his boots off, he approached the window in his socks and lit a cigarette himself. "What a bloody life," he cursed, without raising his voice.

"Been to see Stefan, have you?" he asked me a moment later. Yes. "Well then?" Nothing in particular to report. "Nothing in particular? You're making a big mistake, Berk. Everyone here in Ribnica is fed up with you." Fed up? With me? What's all this about now?

"Look here, Depolo, I came here to see some action, not to waste my time sitting around in this flaming village."

"Maybe you'd better take off for Berlin or London if you've had enough of Ribnica."

"So boredom's a crime now?"

"Just you watch it, Berk."

A gentle warning, eh? He took off his jacket and flopped down on the creaking bed with all his weight. "Sleep it over," he said and turned onto his side. The mattress groaned beneath him as he tossed and turned nervously. He seemed so charged with electricity, I could feel it flashing in my direction. I was as tense and wide-awake as a wild cat. I felt my nerves jangling as his irritation infected me. Sparks flew between us. Obviously we were not going to get much sleep.

"What a bloody life," he repeated. The early morning sunlight came in slanting beams through the window to blotch the greenish paint of the bedroom wall. My mouth felt like the inside of an oven with the continual chain-smoking. All the same, I had to light up again. So did Depolo, without a word. The only sound was the inhaling of cigarette smoke.

"Why are you so jumpy?" he asked after a while.

"What, me? Jumpy? Take a good look at yourself."

"I have good reason," he said with a brief, dry smile. "But you're in clover."

"In clover?"

"Sure. You're having a real holiday. Not a care in the world. Nothing to do except eat, drink, wander around, argue, go dancing, frig yourself . . . You're as free as a bird . . . The only thing that's lacking is the Black Death and that's getting you down . . ."

"Does it bother you, Depolo?"

"No, Berk. That's not what bothers me. It's something else about you."

"Such as what?"

"It's hard to say. If it hadn't been for Kerzhan in Ljubljana having so much to say about you, I wouldn't be talking here and now. Kerzhan said you were a real philosopher . . . a really bright fellow . . . He thought the world of you. You could be very useful to us. Only you're making a very big mistake."

"Am I? Why?"

"Well, take yesterday with Stefan, for example."

"Did something go wrong then?"

"What?" he gave a short laugh. Tensed up, I began to wonder whether I was getting on everybody's nerves. I quickly ran back in my memory over my interview with Stefan. What on earth was wrong with that? I raised myself up on my elbows and looked at Depolo who was shaking his head and muttering, "No, no, Berk. It's a very bad start." I waited in silence.

"Do you know what it means to be received by the district secretary?"

I did not say a word. Maybe I really did not know.

"Look, chum, around here you pull as much weight as a battered old umbrella . . . But you, of course, couldn't grasp that . . ."

The blood rushed to my head. One of them tells you, don't speak till you're spoken to, don't ask questions, don't go poking your nose in, leave it to the army. Someone else then calls you "big-head" and says you're too thick to understand. Do we really need a course in good manners before joining the army? You're off to the North Pole, but don't forget to chop the firewood first. You're off on an expedition from which you may never return, but before you go out, remember to tidy up the room.

"Took you long enough to get here from town," he said.

Sure, I mentally retorted, and yesterday I went three times for a crap.

He went on. "Whoring . . . They've come down pretty hard on it here sometimes . . . a transfer was the least you could expect . . . it could mean a court-martial . . . and the thirteenth battalion . . . Know what that means, do you? You've had it, mate. Only now there's no more thirteenth battalion; it's the thirteenth brigade, if not the thirteenth division . . ."

Well, well. But Vesna would not have complained herself. It must have been Mishko! Wonder where the bastard is now!

"And the way you've behaved since you got here has been getting on everyone's nerves . . . Maybe you were a gentleman in town . . . bloody persiflage, mimicry . . . we'll have none of that here. You're one of us now, only you seem to be keeping aloof . . . Can't you be like the rest of us? Must you always be a loner?"

"Do you think I should pack up and go home?"

"Of course not." He was furious. "You wouldn't get far anyway, you can be sure of that. You've seen too much already."

"What? What have I seen, for God's sake?"

"Look, you're wandering around all day long, poking your nose in everywhere. Why were you standing in the yard for two hours on Sunday afternoon? I don't suppose you were watching the hens?"

I did not understand.

Sunday afternoon? A cat, walking through the yard . . . Receiving . . . transmitting . . . stopping . . . sparrows . . . a dog . . .

"I don't understand." I said.

"I hope you don't."

(It was only years and years later that Depolo told me I had fallen under suspicion because I was hanging around the yard while they were fixing up, in a stable, a bunker for the underground press. The enemy advance was getting close.)

"Did anyone walk through the yard?

"Did anyone go in or out of the stable?"

"I don't really know. I can't remember. Why?"

(Just like Charlie Chaplin in *The Gold Rush*. He, walking beside a precipice, with an enormous bear following him but he sees neither the precipice nor the bear, twirls his stick and saunters on as if he was on the safest sidewalk in town.)

How much easier life is if we do not see all the dangers that beset us. And how unlucky the cat that must accurately process all the information it receives from its surroundings.

"Do you imagine you are here with me in this room by chance? Here? Now?"

What did this mean?

"You're an individualist, Berk, and people like you contaminate the whole environment with their individualism and liberal ideas. Oh yes, we get them sometimes, the odd one, who sticks out like a sore thumb—not fit for the thirteenth battalion—not fit for any other unit either. The sort of chap who says he's got three enemies: the Krauts, our lot, and himself too. No bloody wonder he lands in the shit."

The technique of survival is complicated. But was he concerned only with survival?

"Look, I'm not telepathic. I wouldn't stick my hand in the fire for you and you wouldn't do the same for me. There was a Russian here who wormed his way into headquarters. It later turned out he was a German agent. Do you think the Abwehr rests on its laurels? Or maybe you don't know what the Abwehr is? Better if you don't.

"*Nolenti non fit injuria*—I'm a lawyer, you know," he continued. "We've got the lot here, you know, all the world's intelligence services. You must realize that here we've got more than one microscope focused on us.

"Look here, do you think the army is led on a leash? The army is guided by that quiet unseen poison we call the intelligence service, so you think all we have to do is murder, burn, beat people up, and all that crap? No, there are more subtle pastimes, my dear Berk; chess, poker, and so on. One player sits in Berlin, the other in Ribnica, and they play chess by correspondence . . . One in Moscow, another in New York . . . Their pieces cover the globe . . . Understand?"

I understand, but my mind is on something else. Thank God for Charlie and *The Gold Rush*!

"And do you know what's going through your mind, Berk? I know what you're thinking: bugger you, Depolo; you can preach your bloody sermons but I know my own mind. And what do you really know? Maybe you are an expert on Balzac and Aristotle, maybe you really have a brilliant mind as Kerzhan says. But you certainly don't know there are fifteen intelligence agents patrolling Ribnica up and down, up and down."

"Fifteen?"

"If not more."

He jerked upright and sat on the bed. He began to count on his fingers. "The Germans have three at least, then there are the Italians, the English, the French, two Americans, the Russians, the Blues, the Whites, one for Nedich, one for Lyotich, possibly the Hungarians, the Bulgarians, the Rumanians, the Spaniards, probably the Japanese too; and you can bank on it, the Ustaše have their man here too. Do you think I'm exaggerating? Be happy you can't see inside that infernal machine. It would give you a fright.

"We are working for an idea; others for money. For big money, too. Sometimes running a spy system can cost more than equipping an army. Specially trained men, who really know their job, first-rate equipment, elaborate networks, fresh methods all the time . . . you see that and such units of a Kraut division are breaking through at Brod on the Kolpa River, making for Gorjanci. But hell, man! That's just the end product. The man who's running things is sitting somewhere far away, God knows where, bluffing, setting traps, feinting, noting every move and counter-move. Or take a hand grenade. You fling it at a cannon, take aim, crunch! But if you don't know where or why, it's a waste of time and money. Why do you think Napoleon lost his war with the Russians? Okay, there was General Mud, General Winter, the fire of Moscow. But Napoleon couldn't discover what Kutuzov was up to and that was the end of him. People talk about Russian morale, Russian impenetrability. Why didn't Tolstoy write about it? He had no idea. Just like you. Or are you going to go on pretending?

"I advise you not to make yourself out to be a bigger idiot than you really are. It might draw suspicion."

"Got your eyes on me, eh, Depolo?"

"Of course. That's my job. Hell's teeth, I even have to suspect myself. As you see, for me it's no different from rooting out bloody vermin. Let's say for the sake of argument you might be—maybe are—disaffected. You'd be laughing up your sleeve at me now, wouldn't you?

"Aren't you a little confused?"

He got up and began to pace up and down the room. It was a long time before he spoke.

"Look, go to sleep, Berk, and be happy you're not in my skin."

By now, footsteps could be heard outside as people went up or down the street. Fifteen agents, at least. The Japanese one was up first.

After this night, would I be able to experience war and battle in the elementary sense, as a game of life and death, that had broken out here and now? Or was I going to have the feeling that I was nothing but a pawn, about to be wiped off the chess board? I do not know how to pray, they will not let me count, I cannot stop thinking, although I feel an utter idiot. Close your eyes and await orders. At least I am not in Napoleon's shoes.

I had a glass of wine, found an old issue of the St. Mohor Society's almanac and went back to my room. I lay down and read "How to protect your turnips from caterpillars; the best way to grow potatoes."

A partisan, with a rifle slung on his shoulder, came in without knocking. He asked me casually who I was, then informed me I was to go with him. Should I bring all my gear? Sure. I took my old ski bag, crammed some bits and pieces in it, my clothes and greatcoat—and was then ready to go off.

We went along that long road, where the enemy agents patrol up and down, to a school. Sentry at the gate. Into the hall. Up the stairway to a room on the first floor; a classroom with benches and a blackboard. There was someone standing by the window, looking out. He turned around. Another man was lying on a bench. The door closed behind me and the man with the rifle remained outside.

I went up to the man by the window. He glanced at me but said nothing. He was wearing a shabby Italian uniform with no belt and no weapon. The fellow on the bench had a thick grass-green pullover and riding breeches of unknown military provenance, hefty boots, and a leather gaiter, such as our gendarmes wore before the war. I threw my own blanket and the greatcoat I had been carrying down on a bench. I decided I was not going to start up any conversation.

I walked around the room. I went up to the podium, sat down at the teacher's desk, opened a drawer. I found an exercise book, some paper which I put in my pocket right away, and a prayer book. In the exercise book, I read a calligraphic exercise: "Ljubljana is our capital city. Above the city stands an ancient castle."

Just something to rest my eyes on.

The door opened, a tall figure came in, and the door closed behind him.

"Been fed yet?" he asked with some concern. The one by the window simply shook his head. The newcomer slumped down on the front bench and snarled to himself . . . "Bastards! Bloody brown lightning!" Or something similar. At any rate, something Napoleon in Moscow had never heard of. Suddenly he burst into a rage.

"You bring a load of spuds to the garrison command, then lose the lot—horses, cart, every bloody thing, and end up in the nick!"

The nick? Well, well.

"What are you here for?" he asked the man by the window.

"Taking French leave."

Strange, how un-Gallic. (Don't ask questions and don't go poking your nose in.)

I sat at the desk and read the "Intermediate Catechism." Hail to the most holy True Presence. When you pass a church, or enter one, or meet a priest carrying the most holy True Body, say: "Praised and honored be the most Holy Sacrament, now and forever! Amen." If you have more time, add: "Holy, holy, holy, Lord God of Hosts." (And two or three more lines of thanksgiving, praise, and adoration, then.) One hundred days' indulgence once a day—Pius VI, May 24, 1776. Once a day for a whole year would bring thirty-six thousand, five hundred days' indulgence a year. A second, very short ejaculation ("Jesus, mercy!") brings one hundred days' indulgence *each time*—Pius IX, September 14, 1846. I worked it out that, taking it easy, without undue strain, at five ejaculations per ten seconds, this would produce eighteen thousand days' indulgence every ten hours, more than six and a half million per year, that's more than one hundred and sixty millennia. Better then replace the call to the commander of hosts with the short cry for mercy. A pity they do not write and tell you how many days of purgatory a sinner gets for each particular sin or crime. You could work it out which crime pays and which does not. I read on and found an ejaculation which was even more worthwhile: "Sweet heart of Mary, be my salvation"; three hundred days' indulgence each time—Pius IX, September 30, 1852. This would bring forty millennia in ten years.

Mathematical meditations were broken by mealtime. What! No mess tins! Whose bloody army are you anyway?

A very thin potato soup, rich fare if I compared it with what the Italians fed us in their "Campo di concentramento per Prigionieri Civili" at Gonars. Six black, finger-long strings of macaroni in a brown soup was the record for our barrack. This had its compensation. You did not need to go for a crap so often; only once a fortnight did you feel the urge to go and crouch on the latrine boards. Something like a large, bone-dry dumpling would accumulate in the large intestine and we had to pick at it with our fingernails. Those turds did not smell. They looked something like horse droppings. Sometimes, one of us would have a dizzy spell in the bog and topple off his perch into that cast-off human property. All the same, no one blew his top. Then came the fall of Mussolini and the capitulation of Italy. The Germans took over and "we all together suffered under the Prussian jackboot." I don't believe anyone in Rome gave a tinker's curse for those internees, who used to drop their pants and crouch over that stinking ditch. And our poor *tenente* from Udine even lost his uniform. But that could have been for strictly practical reasons.

I went out of the room into the corridor, where a sentry was sitting, reading the Croatian magazine *Cinema*. Where you off to? A crap? The bathroom's over there.

When I returned, I asked him if he would lend me the magazine when he had finished. "Get back in there," he said. I offered a cigarette, he took it, and we lit up.

I wanted to know when we would be moving on. "Haven't the faintest idea," he said, in unpleasant but convincing tones.

Leave it to the services.

I had noticed there was a quite feasible escape route through the lavatory window. Not at all an athletic feat. Maybe it would not be a bad idea. I could go and see Stefan and ask him why I was stuck here with deserters and suspicious characters and why I was under guard. Should I make a break for it at dusk? I had not seen any sentries out in the schoolyard and no one seemed to be particularly concerned about us. That also gave me cause for thought. What if I wasn't under arrest? No one has wanted anything from me, no one had looked in my pockets. I would have even had my revolver still, if someone had not earlier removed it from my baggage. Better wait. I was not going to stir from here, at least for the time being. In the last resort, I had strong hands and nimble legs and the windows were not barred.

The tall man who had joined us needed to talk and none of us paid any attention when every quarter of an hour he blurted out something in his local dialect. "Come at nightfall, the bastards, and butchered the whole family." Who it was that had "come," where or when it happened, he did not explain. The wife had tried to protect her husband and got a bullet in the guts, after which they both "snuffed it." Shakespeare without the dialogue; nothing but fatality and a pile of corpses at the end.

Three more had dropped into the room before evening. Two had arrived together and sat at the back, talking quietly. The third, a farmer in his forties, had toured the room and inspected us all as soon as he came in. Lofty found him a grateful listener. We now had the seven dwarfs; Snow White should appear at any moment now.

After the long spell of dry weather, it started to rain at dusk. "We'll have a wet departure from this world," the farmer said. This irritated Lofty.

"What on earth for? I ain't done nothing. Just bringing spuds to headquarters. Then forced to leave the horses and the cart . . ." he repeated his story.

"Confiscated them, did they?"

"They confiscated it all, and then they pulled me in!" It turned out that he hadn't been on his own. His father had driven the cart back home.

"Come off it! You weren't arrested for spuds!" scoffed the man in the green pullover.

"And maybe he was," put in the farmer. "I was arrested because I wouldn't . . . The horses are sick, I told them . . . it's too much for them . . ."

Supper cut short any further discussion of the weighty reasons for our presence in the building. Raindrops were beating on the panes as we ate our bean broth. Soft patter of rain on the windows, warm feeling in the stomach after the broth, conversation livening up in the darkness. The smell of a school classroom. Waiting, killing time.

What had I gotten myself into when I passed that roadblock out of town?

I stretched out on the bench. Is pine a soft wood?

I had the stupid idea that I could remember by heart a poem on the battle of Waterloo I had learned in high school.

Waterloo! Waterloo! Morne plaine!
Comme une onde qui bout dans une urne trop pleine,
Dans ton cirque de bois, de coteaux, de vallons,
La pâle mort mêlait les sombres bataillons.

So as not to fall prey to the timelessness of such a night, I thought I might try my hand at translation.

Waterloo, Waterloo, sullen weary plain!
Like a wave surging in a brimming vase,
here in your circling woods and hills and vales,
pale death did bring the dark battalions face to face.

Never could master that rhythm. I was quite pleased with part of it, unhappy with the rest.

Il dit, "Grouchy!"—c'était Blücher.
Napoleon said, "Grouchy is coming!"—but it was Blücher with his troops.
He shouted, "Grouchy!"—but it was Blücher.

I went back to the second and third line again, chopped, changed, altered, then went back to my first version. I was uncomfortable on the bench, spread the blanket below me, rolled up my greatcoat and used it as a pillow. I heard loud voices in the corridor, a little agitated, footsteps. The door opened and the light of a carbide lamp shone into the room.

Napoleon said, "Someone will arrive soon!"—It was Tujchko.

Yes, Tujchko had arrived. He barged into the room, pissed as usual.

"Quiet, I said," he bawled. "Everyone has his own victim and God has us all."

He made a tour of inspection. "Anybody got a light? Might as well have a cigarette while we still can." I ducked. The farmer gave him a light. Tujchko had a good look around in the flicker of the flame, still jabbering away, pausing only to inhale. Sweat and rainwater were streaming down his round face, his hair was sticking to his forehead, while his cap, a few sizes too small for him, with a star, was pushed right back to the nape of the neck.

"Okay—they say—you're fouling things up, Tujchko!—What, me? I say.—Sure, I started this war—I confess—I've been collaborating *mit der Krauts* all this bloody time—Supplying them with ammunition by the barrel—I confess—If you call that fouling things up—I plead guilty . . ."

He went on yakking till morning, going from one of us to the next. We were all fed up, told him to go to hell, pacified him, cursed him, begged him for a bit of peace. But he continued to expound his theories. The war had been started by German homosexuals with too much time on their hands. Whores don't go to war because the food isn't good enough. A man goes on learning all his life but is still stupid when he kicks it. Then the clover grows out of his arse, a rabbit takes a mouthful and learns sense straight away. How do we know? He keeps well away from men, so that "a skirt never touches his arse."

It was almost morning and the daylight was appearing in the windows before he gave up. He sat down by the wall and went to sleep, snoring thunderously. Now Lofty spoke up: "Come at nightfall the bastards . . . butchered the whole family . . ." We still did not know who were the butchers and who the butchered.

That was one of the longest nights of my life.

Early morning. The road was crowded with men and animals. For most of the time, we made our way northward, mostly meeting small groups proceeding in the opposite direction.

There were ten of us, eight without weapons. One partisan marched ahead, triple-edged bayonet fixed on his Italian carbine, while another, with a wide-barreled Italian automatic, brought up to the rear. Tujchko had recovered from his hangover and was prattling as usual. He seemed happy that he had met me, I don't know why. He said he could see right away that I had "oil in my lamp." Judging by the tone of his voice, this was to be taken as recognition of a praiseworthy characteristic or something of the sort.

Someone we passed called out, "Where are you off to, Tujchko?" He answered, loud and clear: "To the hot pot."

We could all hear it quite well but pretended we each knew his own business. The hot pot? Who was going to cook our goose, the Krauts or our own side? The ones who have time, Tujchko would have said.

I suddenly caught sight of a man wearing a most elegant uniform and polished knee boots, a revolver in a black leather holster, and an automatic slung over his shoulder. He was with two partisans, who were also well armed and equipped. Hauzer! I was rooted to the spot: it was as if some deity had brought him to this encounter. I stopped, smiled, and waited for him to recognize me, halt, and call out, "Well, who have we here? Berk, is it really you, a sight for sore eyes?" Yes, here I am, Hauzer.

He did in fact spot me but walked past with a nod. Was it possible? Hauzer? Didn't he recognize me? Impossible. "Come on, don't dawdle," urged the guard at my tail. We went on.

Hauzer! "Let Hauzer know I've arrived from Ljubljana. Hauzer knows me well." I remembered the district secretary and a wave of shame came over me. Stunned by the blow, I trod the metal highway, washed by the night's rainfall, full of puddles and whitish-gray mud. A valley opened up on either side of the road. Somehow, I was no longer responsive to the sounds and images of my surroundings. After my disappointment, I lurched forward as if my limbs and feet did not belong to me. All the same, I was not angry with myself; why should I be? After all, nothing so dreadful had happened, had it? Some character called Hauzer had cut me dead, and the best of luck to him. He'd had more than one dinner at my expense. My dark brown suit fit him quite well. Sometimes we'd sat up talking into the night. When I had wanted to go into the woods a year ago, he'd held me back. "Don't go," he said. "You'll be court-martialed. We need you here." My aunt's house welcomed all kinds of illegal activities. There we collected arms, sheltered wanted men; there we operated a secret radio station that had to move whenever they were hunting it with special cars; there we held meetings; from there we went out into action; there Hauzer and I had listened to the BBC; written our encouraging news bulletins, registered everything broadcast by the Soviet stations; there too we had joked, eaten, drunk, and kept our spirits up. Why did he not need me around any more? Are you just like those Venetian pigeons, Hauzer? Down on the ground they eat out of your hand, but then they take off and shit on you from a great height? Let Hauzer know I've arrived from Ljubljana! Sounds pretty impressive, eh?

I once took a boat from Krk, Croatia, to the little island of San Vito, where there is a Serbian war cemetery from the First World War. There, I read on tablet, and learned by heart:

> On these mounds in foreign soil
> Serbian blossoms will not flower.
> Pass the news to our dear children;
> Never shall we meet again.
> Let these lowly mounds remind them
> Of their fathers' fight for freedom.

Let Hauzer know I've arrived from Ljubljana.

Meeting old acquaintances is usually a sloppy business. We had arrived at a lively, bustling village. There was a battery of field guns in the market place, horses, hay, people. Our leading escort went into a house, and we leaned against a cart or sat on a bench in front of the house. The whole place was throbbing with action.

Mishko! With a pair of red Italian hand grenades fastened to his belt. He was in a hurry, though he did stop for a moment. He had been appointed a quartermaster's assistant. He went into the house.

And now who should step out but Depolo. He glanced at me. He was in no hurry. Came up and offered me a cigarette. I thought he might tell me something—where I was off to, what was going on, what was it all about? But Tujchko spoiled it all, again feeling the need to produce his interesting theories. Depolo told me that a German offensive from Kočevje was getting closer. Tujchko thrust a finger at his shirt and asked him, did he know what God had made woman from. From the same pith he had drilled out of Adam's arse. Depolo turned and walked off. Mishko came out of the house. This time he completely ignored me.

A sharp, bitter quarrel suddenly broke out between the guard who had stayed behind with us and the farmer, one of our eight. The latter had spotted an acquaintance, who had greeted him loud and clear and invited him to join him for a jar, as he said. The farmer wanted to accept this invitation but the guard stopped him curtly: "Knock it off! We're leaving shortly." The farmer said he would be right back. The guard cocked his automatic. End of argument. But it left an uneasy atmosphere. Tujchko said, "Looks like they've run out of Krauts and we're their target practice."

Soon the other guard reappeared. We set off again. A rather faint, autumn sunlight broke through the clouds. We were walking along the path in ones and twos, making our way along, with the guards fore and aft. Tujchko kept up his chatter. Lofty was scared stiff. "There'll be summat around next corner, you'll see!" And once again, no one knew who it would be around the corner, our lot or the Germans.

"Get a move on! Goddamn slowpokes!" complained our guide.

"But where are we really going?" Lofty asked him.

"You'll see soon enough," the guard replied.

"And even feel it too, if you've got time," Tujchko added with a laugh.

People were scurrying like ants along the road, as if nothing was happening. As if this were any other day. Everything decided beforehand, unknown, inevitable.

Two things ruined any chance of my feeling at ease. One was my own bewilderment, the other was the unattractive nature of the circumstances from which I could not escape. But there was, above all, an upturned transparent dish of horror, of the unspeakable, of fear of the wrong goal. Into the hot pot! They'll be around the corner, you'll see! I'm not telepathic, Depolo said. Would you plunge your hand in the flame for me? I wouldn't for you. Come on, come on! That murky luster in little Katerina's eyes. The glance from that stranger on the road. The connection between all this was still unseen. And we go on, like beasts, consigned to our inevitable fate. Into the boiling kettle.

A high-pitched, quiet buzzing in the head. A landscape, bathed in the clear golden light of the cool autumn sun. Everything seemed so close at hand: clearings, bushes, tree stumps, gently sloping hillsides. Somewhere far off beyond them, are lands where life runs its normal course, where there is no war, where couples stroll along the seashore, where children play with brightly colored balloons. The waves, the breakers. A humming in the ears. Sound of the breakers in a seashell. I should like to be there, but I am here. I straightened up, flexed my limbs and muscles, especially my hands and feet. Breathing regular; heartbeat sound as a clock. I bent down and then straightened up again. I halted and leaned forward gently, like a cat ready to pounce.

"I'm going for a crap," I told our leader nonchalantly. I made my way past the tree stumps into the undergrowth. "Halt!" I looked around but the guard's shout was not directed at me, only the rest of them on the road. If he had been shouting at me, they would have never seen me again, I told myself.

I was all ready to crouch, but went a bit farther on, then a bit farther still. I was a good way off by now but no one on the road was paying any attention to me. That way lay Primorska province, and beyond it Italy . . . then a whole lot of harbors, cities, seas, countries whose languages I knew. And down below there were two guards and eight men bound for the unknown. Was I going to regret it if I didn't slip off that very instant? I had to decide immediately. Were they driving me to slaughter? To the boiling kettle? If so, I don't suppose the guard would have let me disappear into the woods without a second thought. I crouched down and met the healthy air of the plants. I looked up into the sky. A light breeze was driving packs of small clouds. The west wind rustled the leaves of a nearby birch tree.

Afterward, I took my time descending to the road where my escorts were waiting. Tujchko said with deference, "Well you've had a good crap—three goes at once, like the banns for a wedding!"

A concrete bunker facing the forest, remnants of barbed-wire obstacles, once a strong point. A field kitchen under a double hay frame. Grub was ready. The cook, a plump, stubby fellow, wore a white vest, and voluminous Italian breeches tucked into black knee boots with double soles. In front of a large house belonging to some wealthy villager, three saddled horses were tethered. Partisans were in and out all the time; what was going on?

Potato soup, a big piece of boiled beef and a hunk of bread. "What? No mess tins? Whose bloody army are you? No spoons either? A spoon is more important than a gun, you'll see!" said the good-natured cook and threw in something "extra." "Here you are, and none of your airs and graces," he said, when I tried to thank him for the offering. Tujchko also shoved up close and gave me the benefit of his advice. "Never admit you've had enough in the army, even when your guts are bulging. Complaints are what we want, mate—always be on the lookout for something to complain about, that's the drill."

Lofty, the farmer, and the man in the green pullover were escorted into the house by the first guard, who came back alone. Now there were five of us who went off with our two guards, and no one asked where the other three had disappeared to. Tujchko, tight as a drum, slapped his belly, yelled uproariously, and broke into a Croatian song.

No one's better off than we are,
If every day should be like this . . .

He was a bundle of accumulated energy that could have driven a power station. Beside him we were all, armed or unarmed, pale shadows. Hardly a soul passed us by, without Tujchko pressing greetings on him. What I liked most about him was that he was always the same, drunk or sober—always rowdy, voluble, incorrigible.

I had found a spoon, that indispensable requirement in all armies, camps, and prisons in unsettled times. It was lying on the grass by the roadside, ogling me with a rusty glint. I spent a long time cleaning and rubbing it, and it soon became my proud possession. Then I tucked it into my thick sock at the shin, where I had previously seen the implement carried, so that it was always at hand, though on the leg. It is only high functionaries who carry their spoons close to their hearts, in their breast pockets. In my incurable optimism I was now looking forward to a whole series of pleasant adventures.

We caught up to three women with a handcart, in which a child of about three was sitting with a green knit cap on his head. The oldest woman was walking on the left of the cart, which the two younger ones were pulling. The one on the right was quite pretty, with a nicely rounded figure in a skirt a few sizes too small for her. She had the noble profile of many a raven-haired beauty: her long tresses hung down from a yellow head scarf, her hips were full, her legs stood sturdy but trim.

I caught up with her on her left and tried some innocent banter: were they all off to join the army? If it had not been for that business of going for a crap, if I had not been pleasantly full of good food and if I had not been overjoyed at the discovery of the spoon, I would not have been able to relax and enjoy this encounter, her glances half veiled by thick eyelashes, her warm, smooth skin, which had the same intoxicating effect on me as a glass of strong drink. I walked beside her and brushed her hip with my fingers. Her firm young breasts quivered slightly as she moved.

She would not tell me her name, so I christened her Bridka, the bitter one, which she found quite ridiculous.

"Oh, you have bitterly afflicted me, Bridka!"

"You been drinking?" she enquired.

"Sure—sunshine, fresh air, and potato soup! Just let me take off your stockings and kiss you in that smooth hollow below your thigh, behind your knee. I can feel you in my palms, Bridka, you dazzle my eyes, you sear my skin, I'll never forget you."

I was transmitting such powerful waves of lust that soon, she too began to tremble; her cheeks first flushed, then lost their color. I knew what that meant. I was conscious of her whole body, from the pouting lips to stumbling legs which had now lost their steady rhythm. A shudder ran down my spine. Her voice was huskier, her eyes were glazed. I felt a tremor as I touched her. We were lost to our surroundings, aware only of the glow of our own bodies, interrupted by the ghosts of dying, lustful glances and a growing inner need. This is it! I thought. This is basic, stronger than anything else, when all inhibitions and emotional barriers give way. What a serpent in Eden! What an apple! O felix culpa! This is the softly lapping surge of a fluid warmth, joining two bodies in its billows, now dragging them apart and now driving them together, bearing them into a distance where all desires are realized, red, violet, gold, and black . . . The smell of her hair, her skin, her sex . . . The roar of waves . . . I feel you . . .

Coitus interruptus! They turned left, across the highway, and into a side road. I stopped and watched her receding, while some strange chilling force kept me pinned to the white road. She looked back. She seemed to be calling, inviting me: "Come on, where are you, come with me, how could you leave me, part from me, slip away from me?"

"Let's go," said our leader.

I lost contact with her in a moment. My body temperature started to fall. I felt a loathing for the highway and for myself, on my way to God knows where.

We were walking like robots. I looked at the countryside again. What did it mean to me now? Something strange, foreign, oppressive. One cannot live, one cannot die, one must survive. Something I cannot escape from now. Somewhere over there, she was crossing a field, thinking of me. I could distinctly feel her want. Oh, Adolf Hitler, what have you done!

A sudden roar. An aircraft flashed by, flying low overhead. Some of us leaped off the road and dived into the grass but the rest stood staring after the German reconnaissance plane.

My eyes were full of the greenery, the blue sky, the trees, the grass, the corn-fields, the woods. To see the sky and the clouds again after so long among city walls, streets, roofs. I had an ache in my neck despite the slight breeze and the fresh air. Also, my feet were beginning to complain after this long hike.

A large, sturdily built wagon drawn by two strong bay horses rumbled up behind us.

How long did the French Grenadiers take to march from Paris to Moscow? What sort of soles did Alexander the Great's infantry have, those men who tramped through Asia Minor, Palestine, Egypt, Persia and other lands as far as India, and back again? The earth is small, but the roads that cross it are long.

A young carter in farmer's clothes but with a red star in his cap and a rifle slung over his shoulder was perched up on the seat of the cart. Beside him sat a neatly dressed partisan in an officer's uniform. On one sleeve he wore an epaulet, with a red cross on a white field. I knew this face very well. He recognized me too and called out, "Berk! I was just wondering—is it you or isn't it? Where are you off to?" It was Frenk, a medical student.

"No idea. You'll have to ask someone else." I pointed to our guide.

"Where are you bound for?" he enquired with a serious look. I must admit that he knew how to show his authority. Our escort replied, "To division." And so we had now learned that jealously guarded secret.

"Sit up here!" he invited me casually and moved along the seat to make room. I jumped up. He took my hand, shook it, and greeted me warmly. He had no idea how he had raised my spirits. In an instant, all the nightmare of that journey was forgotten. When had I arrived, and why hadn't I arrived earlier? We were soon firing questions at each other.

He had taken to the woods during the previous winter. He was carting hospital supplies. He was now on his way to division. He signaled to my companions: "Get up on the wagon, there's plenty of room. The horses are strong and fresh." They climbed up, three on each side of the wagon. "A good lift is better than a poor hike," Tujchko shouted. It was turning into a fine, sunny day. Tujchko let out a yell and I burst out laughing.

"You're in good spirits," said Frenk.

"We're always in good spirits," Tujchko explained, "when we have time to spare." He broke into song: "My father had two ponies . . ."

I told Frenk how on my own long trek into war, I had been thinking of the long campaigns in the past. *The Anabasis*. Soldiers marching and riding out on distant campaigns since the earliest times; in Egypt, Assyria, Babylonia, China; the Greek expedition to Troy; the military campaigns of Cyrus, Xerxes, Darius, Alexander the Great; barbarian invasions from the north; Roman and Carthaginian campaigns; the incursions of the barbarians and nomad peoples from Asia, horsemen who lived in the saddle; the invasions of America; the Crusades; wars in Europe, in Asia; the campaigns of the Japanese and Chinese armies; French campaigns in Spain, Egypt, and Russia, by desert, river, and sea, through blizzards, on foot, on horseback, in boats; campaigns, campaigns . . . well, and now I myself have embarked on my own . . . through Ljubljana . . . through villages . . . over fields and meadows . . . via a school in Ribnica . . . an open-air kitchen under a hay frame . . . forward along the road . . . advancing to Berlin . . .

We both laughed.

"Well, you're pretty chirpy for someone who's just joined up. Of course, you've always had your own way of looking at things." He nodded.

Before the war, a common interest in sport and in games had brought us together. For the most part, he had been a shy, quiet fellow. He now told me he could not shake off the feeling that things were going to be pretty dangerous this time. It was rather unlikely that our forces could have held the Germans at the Kolpa River for ten days. There was a newly formed brigade, the Ninth, with some of the officers from the old West Dolenjska regiment and apart from that, raw recruits, with no experience for the most part, hardly any military training, and very little artillery. Of course, you can slow down even a regular motorized army for some time by digging up the roads.

In his ear-splitting voice Tujchko was singing:

Then the gibbert creaked beneath him
And his soul went down to hell . . .

"I was speaking to a German prisoner," Frenk told me. "He was quite a sensible chap, from somewhere in the Rhineland. His father keeps a big hotel. He said they had not expected such resistance and their high command is very disappointed the offensive is going so slow."

By now Frenk had had dealings with all types of forces operating in Slovenia. He spoke without passion, as if he stood outside it all.

The Italians had preferred to operate with large forces, playing it safe; they feared nothing more than being transferred to the Eastern front. It was not true they were poor soldiers. Their units were a mixed bag. They had fanatical storm troops: the Arditti, Cravatte Rosse, Blackshirts, Fascists, beside the less bellicose formations, who hated serving in the Balkans, which were for them the ends of the earth. Some Italian officers took their units out on forest patrol, while others simply made a lot of noise and sent back fictitious reports.

Vast numbers of them had been deployed in one offensive. Kočevski Rog was infested with their riflemen . . . "I still don't quite understand how we managed to escape alive when they had us surrounded so closely . . .

"Astounding the way they changed their tune when Italy surrendered . . . Turned out they had always been against the war . . . We let those pacifists go home, after handing over their weapons . . . The language they use about the Germans! The Krauts have had a bellyful of them too . . . Some of them stayed behind and joined us. But I don't envy any Eytic the Germans catch serving with the partisans."

And how much of Slovenia had been already liberated?

"Quite a good deal by now. The Germans are still holding out on the old frontier from Ljubljana down the Sava toward Zagreb, and the Ustaše are along the Kolpa line, though the Germans have taken over there for the present offensive. The Ustaše are real bastards when they have a good numerical advantage, otherwise they avoid engagement. They're quite happy to occupy some Serbian Orthodox settlement and spend their time converting their Orthodox brethren into the Catholic faith. The Croatian territorials are a sort of regular army. We don't come up against them very often. They can't stand those strutting Ustaše. We get a lot of arms from the territorials. We have our supporters among them, don't you worry. Then the line runs to Rijeka and from Rijeka to Ljubljana, forming a sort of triangle, right in the middle of Nazi-occupied Europe.

"The Whites are having a hard time, their morale has hit rock bottom and they'll have to withdraw again. They have some good battalions but many of their strong points are manned by a rabble who are neither fish, flesh, nor fowl; half army, half police. They have no support from the population, though they don't realize it. They fraternize with the Germans in the bars, then tell the cooks and waiters in the kitchen that they're really on the English and American side. No one believes a word they say."

"What about the Blues?"

"For the most part mere wind and water from what I've seen . . ."

"Old members of the Sokol movement like us don't seem to count for much, do we?" I remarked.

"Well, you should know that by now most officers here are ex-Sokols. You'll see how some of them are getting on!" He laughed. "Janez Kershtajn is in command of a brigade." More seriously, he added, "Viki was taken prisoner at Grčarice; arrived fresh as a daisy but soon landed in the shit." Well then? What had happened to him? Always a smart lad he was, a character! "They didn't condemn him to death at Kočevje, that I know. But where he is now, I have no idea." Well, who would have thought it. Viki Krapczh. "That's education for you. Pretty poor arithmetic." How come he missed the bus? "I did have a word with him." Well? What did he have to say for himself? "Oh, nothing much. I said I was ready to answer for him, but they said better wait and see. Well, that's the army, what can you expect?"

And Janez Kershtajn really had his own brigade?

"He was a lieutenant in a prewar Yugoslav Alpine Regiment, remember? A reservist but a good soldier. He was active in Ljubljana for some time, then went to join the partisans in Gorenjska and now he's got his own brigade. I heard he was leading an attack on the old German border. He still loves horses."

Yes, we once rode out to the Kočevje area on Hitler's birthday. There were a few artillery officers and some members of the Sokol riding club. The local Krauts were lighting beacons on the hills and we were putting them out. Janez Kershtajn had the biggest mount, a real giant of a horse. General Rupnik (those days he called himself Lev Rupnik) was chief of staff for fortifications, and then in charge of frontier defenses against Italy and Germany. Later on, he became known as General Leone Rupnik, a great friend of the Italians. Now he was Leon Rupnik, confidant of the Germans. A rare example of adaptability to his environment, a true Slovene lion. He was still lecturing us on the right path, preaching loyalty and perseverance in the fight against evil.

"Tell me, Frenk, what would all this look like, viewed from some other planet?"

". . . as the ant said to the bear," he retorted.

"Has Kershtajn joined the party?"

"Stands to reason. Seeing he's got a brigade."

"Have you joined?"

"Sure. And so will you. Otherwise you're asking for trouble."

"So the left wing of Sokol doesn't exist anymore—not even as a cofounder of the Liberation Front?"

"You can forget it."

"What about the Christian Socialists? Are they still around?"

"Yes, they have their organization still. Until recently, they even had their own commissars. They'll disappear, they won't last out like ours. They aren't much of a party . . . and with their religious affiliations . . . well, you can imagine."

"Tell me then, where does someone fit in, if he's against the occupiers, against the Quislings, isn't a Christian, has no special liking for the English or the Americans or the Russians or for prewar Yugoslavia or the monarchy—and not for the one-party leadership either?"

"Where? In hospital, maybe. There is no place for him really. We have no anarchists like those who fought in the Spanish Civil War. And the Whites and the Blues have made such a bloody mess that none of the Allies want anything to do with them either. There is no compromise. Our great bourgeois politicians have fixed things so that you have no other way except joining us. You're not so much aware of it in the towns as here. But here, you're on a battleground; here, everything takes second place to the war effort and there is no other way but the left, our way, our discipline; take the other road and see where it lands you. And our discipline is in the hands of the party, the only one prepared for war."

"But the party is in the hands of the Russians, the Bolsheviks."

"Not so that you'd notice. God's high above and Stalin's far away. And we have the Germans on our tail . . . You'll see, if you live long enough, what it's like to have a Kraut percussion band rattling their tambourines at your heels. Bastards pissed on me the other day in Gorjanci. You should have been there and seen what happened." He laughed. "When they're after you, you don't give a tinker's curse for politics, philosophy, history, or even tomorrow."

"But that's action. That's war. What are we in for afterward?"

"You might not survive, in which case—grass doesn't grow for a dead donkey. Then again, you might. A live donkey eats thistles too. Look, I'm no politician, and neither are you, so why should we lose any sleep over it?"

"I am a bit worried all the same."

"The sooner you join the party the better, then you'll have a quiet life. If you don't want to join, don't criticize; just say: 'Look here, I'm no use to you, I'm an alcoholic and a lecher; if I do join, you'll only have to throw me out again. Expulsion in wartime means a bullet in the head; better just leave me in peace.' Then you should add; 'All the same, I consider the invitation a great honor.' You wouldn't be the first to take this line. A pity you're not a medic. You'd find things easier. The devil himself knows where they'll send you, especially now that the bastards are getting so close."

"You know, I have a funny feeling . . . very strange . . . deep down inside me . . . I really want to fight the Krauts, but, I don't know how to tell you . . . all this mess, half civilian, half military, is getting on my nerves . . . after all I've heard, read, seen, either in paintings or on the films . . . I want a gun . . . I want action . . ."

"You want to watch what you're saying. In the first place, it's completely different from what you might imagine, far away from the action. Things have never been good and they're only going to get worse. You don't want to meet the Germans, I can tell you that right now. Don't despise them . . . they're real soldiers . . . not bogeymen . . . Fortunately they haven't got any stomach for guerilla warfare. They're too used to good order and military discipline, to battle plans, to formal tactics and strategy . . . advance, pincer movement, breakthrough, encirclement, liquidation of small pockets of resistance . . . they're used to roads and frontal assault. They always try to force the enemy to fight and make war on their terms . . . They can't do that here . . . though they now have units specially trained for guerilla warfare, assault groups of three men, able to move like Indian scouts; they have specially trained dogs, light and efficient equipment, carry only automatics . . . But all the same, they hate guerilla warfare.

"On the other hand, a good partisan commander has the essence of this small war at his fingertips: strike when you can surprise the enemy; when ambushed, avoid engagement and withdraw. Act when you hold the initiative; retreat when the enemy has the initiative. Learn to move your troops speedily, under cover of darkness, improve your reconnaissance, avoid encirclement, and when you are caught—pick the right time to strike and break out. You'll see for yourself soon enough.

"The Whites just creep into their strongholds, install themselves in fortified churches or castles, make occasional forays and then withdraw behind the barbed wire. They've little to show for it but their hemorrhoids. You wouldn't get a partisan retiring behind walls, bunkers, or barbed wire . . . He trusts only the forests and mountains . . ."

One unit we passed was singing a Russian song:

> *Vintovachka bjej, bjej, vintovachka bjej;*
> *Krasnaja vintovachka, fashista ne zhalej . . .*

We arrived at the village where the division had its headquarters.

Frenk gave me a vivid account of a partisan attack on some Whites who had barricaded themselves in a church. They had turned the tower into a machine-gun nest, after hauling a heavy Breda up there. The grassy slopes around the church offered no protection against their fire, except a small shrub here and there. Since nothing would induce the partisans to dig a trench for cover, there were casualties, naturally. As always, the Whites were expecting reinforcements to arrive from Novo Mesto but they didn't materialize. Bullets and insults were flying in both directions. "Commie whores!" from the belfry; "Bloody Whites!" from our side.

"Pick the beans out of that, comrade!"
"Down on your benders, White trash!"

Our bombardiers cleared out the church, but those up in the tower would not surrender. They went on cursing us, laughing and singing to keep up their courage. They ran out of bombs but kept on firing, though they tried to save ammunition. We set fire to the bell tower. The spiral stairway was like tinder, hadn't seen a drop of water for a hundred years. The flames shot straight up to the belfry. The bastards went on singing to the last man. Not one survived. Just went on ringing the bells and howling like lunatics . . .

We had stopped in a wide marketplace.

Men, mules, horses, cattle, hay, straw, sacks, ammunition boxes, mine throwers, machine guns, a mortar, bustle, the smell of smoke.

As a parting gift, Frenk had given me a well preserved Italian mess tin in which someone had notched in capital letters: *TI AMO CARINA, TUO GIACINTO.*

On such a distracted, unsentimental journey into war, a man becomes, to all appearances, an automaton enclosed in a skin, beneath which past, present, and future images sprout, entwine, and shift like algae in a sluggish stream. He himself has no idea what is happening to him, but, without realizing it, he is adapting a completely different response to his surroundings, as a new self gradually takes over. Meanwhile he continues to talk but his own and other people's words have no immediate meaning other than their surface sound. And pass, on a spinning tape, into his memory, to be stored with other information.

In time, the great variety of arms and equipment and the parade of unusual outfits became a familiar sight. One man in a German uniform, with Italian knee boots, another with Italian uniform and German infantry ankle boots. Red, black, brightly shining hand grenades in their belts. Rifles, Schmeissers, tommy guns, revolvers. A shirt of striped camouflage material, black riding breeches, long off-white wool socks, sturdy climbing boots. Green, brown, blue, black caps, each with a red star.

My conversation with Frenk had restored some confidence in the situation. I leaned on a cart and turned my face toward the sun. I lit a cigarette.

I had changed the town for the country. Walls and streets for green fields. City smells for the smell of earth and cattle. A foreign occupier for the forces of liberation.

Is it possible to hold and maintain one single viewpoint on all these events? For example: a lunar point of view? There, down below, is the Earth, crawling with men and animals. Or the view from a Manhattan skyscraper? Or from the top of a Moscow tower? Or from the heights of the Himalayas? From there, everything must be so distant, tiny, blurred.

Or the geographer's point of view? Below me lies the Earth, with layers of soil, rock, minerals, right down to the hot magma at the heart of the great globe; above me, the air and the atmosphere thinning out as it goes higher; the earth has been leveled into gardens with plants, beasts, and mankind; the force of gravity holds the seas in balance.

Somewhere, somewhere, somewhere, I myself am standing, a tiny mite on the planet's crust; for the moment I exist but soon, I shall be no more in this form—and who cares? Am I any different from a blade of grass, a midge buzzing over a watery ditch, a brown shrew scurrying along a furrow, while from the heights where eagles soar, all plunges back upon itself, to the place of tiny pulsing hopes and fears, where thirst and hunger rage, where imagination runs riot, down to the night-black, blood-red depths, where all life bides and throbs in embryo?

In one sudden, terrifying flash, you realize you can never cut loose from your environment and take a cool look back at yourself from the surface of the moon, and you can never plumb the depths of your own being to find your true image. You are always left suspended between extremities, damned to a continuous vacillation between all else and the secret of your own ego. All through your life, you seek that moment when you will stop and comprehend things—in vain, in vain. I felt a pain in my guts. In vain, in vain.

Now I am here, "at division." I, Jakob Bergant (who?), am at divisional headquarters. But our escort had told us, just now, we were going to "brigade."

We used to hear in prewar Yugoslavia about army generals, divisional generals, and brigadiers, a sort of ladder of military honor and authority. Jesus, Mary, Joseph: the hierarchical ladder of the "Holy Family." Corps, division, brigade. Jesus, Mary, Joseph. Battalion, company, platoon, bishop, rector, curate. Voices were singing: "Cornfield, who will care for you? . . ." Moon, Himalayas, brigade. ". . . who will care for you when I go forth to war?"

I slept twice with the girl who fixed my cap for me. I had joked (with heavy emphasis) that I would visit her after dark. She laughed, but I tried her door all the same. She lay quiet, pretending to be asleep, but her quickened breathing gave her away. She had gone to bed in her knickers, I don't know why. She was lying on her left side. I pulled her nightdress up and tugged her knickers down.

Later, I left without a word. During the day, she behaved as if nothing had happened. This really exasperated me. No one could have imagined there had been anything between us. A spotless maid. Why all this annoyed me, I could not say. With deliberate politeness, I enquired whether she would consider sewing a button on my trousers. With equal politeness, she answered that she would by all means. Not a glimmer of recognition, not the ghost of a smile, she might have been a thousand light-years away. I have plumbed your depths and you leave me drifting on the cold surface of your daily life. Keep your secrets then. Slumbering innocent! But she did groan, she did squirm, didn't she? Will you be waiting for me again tonight? Darkness, groping, action, departure.

She gave me a signal that we could have a quiet word together in the hall, then went off, pretending she had something to do in the next room. Two-faced hypocrite! Cunning little vixen! I bet she went to church regularly but might forget to mention our little "transgression" to her confessor; strange things happen in our sleep sometimes. I had forgotten all about Marichka, or whatever her name was, by evening and remembered her only when I happened to be passing her door late at night. I thought I would see if it was open again this time. It was, of course. I approached your bed, Marichka, in the darkness, feeling not the least desire for your body, only a determination to make you sit up this time.

I came down from the moon and I landed with you. Why?

Bridka I shall never forget. But you will evaporate like a short, sharp, crapulous nightmare. With Bridka, I felt the contact of male and female essence. What are you? Merely a bubble in the froth on the surface of a night's frivolity; froth bubbles and vanishes. I shall go on lusting after Bridka but you'll be soon forgotten. Even at this very moment, as I approach your bed, I am not thinking about you, only about myself, breathing the humid air, uncovering you, scenting your sweat and sex, lifting your nightgown right up to your armpits (once again she was on her left side, facing the wall), tugging down your knickers (those bloody knickers again!), joining you in bed, without bothering to remove my clothes or my boots.

Wonder what this would look like from the Himalayas, or from the Eiffel Tower. This body of yours, smooth, naked, warmly straining, will be swallowed up in the earth; this body of mine (unbuttoned pants smelling, even stinking of sour wine; someone else spilled a glass on them) will also (probably quite soon) be devoured by the upper layer of the earth's crust, always assuming it isn't first blown to smithereens somewhere above the surface

Bubbles of froth! But maybe you have the right idea. The whole business isn't worth a second thought. Kiss me, kiss me not . . . I don't care, and neither do you. But we might get a baby like this. With you? Like this? That wouldn't do. Moist blooming rose of poesy . . . Are you moist, eh? She's dumb, too. She hears no sound, she sees no sight, she's like a lifeless thing . . . War, smooth, tight skin, and that soft fur below, down between your thighs (I prized your legs apart; you gave no sign of life; if you meet a bear, pretend to be dead); a hot cleft, breasts straining even more than when I saw them swelling your dress on an ordinary, busy day . . .

Aren't you going to wake up at all? Just like our dear homeland; attractive only in the dark, blind and unfeeling to your lovers, virtuously disloyal, sharing no passion, feeling no real pain. Don't tell me you actually moved then! Perhaps you'll live after all! Did I hear you moan? Go on, groan! Well then? No, it isn't a false alarm. Aren't you going to put your arms around me? Where are you off to now? Let's get a firm hold on these hips. You'll soon see what the world spins on. Its axis, yes. Now you haven't got any escape, you've got your back to the wall. Why has your voice gone so husky? One more second, and in we go. Do you still think it was a false alarm? Would you still say I'm rather short of experience in these matters, eh? Are you seeing stars now? Far away on a silvery, thousand-pointed star, there's someone laughing at the thought that you are thinking I've lost my way.

We were moving on. Thanks to our encounter with Frenk, I now knew our destination from our escort. "To brigade," he confided. A military secret, no doubt.

For a moment, I stood stock still and looked around in amazement.

Only now did I fully appreciate a striking and unusual fact, which I should have noticed before. The whole village was a hive of military activity. There was a continual movement of armed men around all the buildings: rapid movement, as if they were all bound on some urgent errand. There was a constant traffic in and out of all the houses, as men strode into one or left another, not casually sauntering but making for definite goals, with a sense of purpose, each of them engaged on his own peculiar task, some of them well, others poorly equipped or completely unprepared, some high-, others low-ranking. The whole ant heap had its own rules. I was bound for a more distant goal and could not familiarize myself with what was going on here. I had been "at division" almost without realizing it.

One of these houses was the commander's headquarters, no doubt. But what were all these people doing? There must have been a whole legion of them!

Are we moving off now? Sure, we're off.

I happened to notice one soldier, with a bundle of black leather under his arm, entering one of the houses.

Two girl volunteers came into view. The shorter of them was carrying a typewriter. I recognized the other. It was Vesna. She glanced my way and gave me a curt nod. I smiled as I saw my old, well-tailored pants, now refashioned for her needs.

Are we off now? Sure, we're off. From division to brigade.

"Care for a smoke?" I said to the escort with the automatic.

He took a cigarette. At the same time, he seemed to look into my eyes. Fair enough: he was also a human being, a person, with a first name and a surname, with thoughts, feelings, desires, a destiny.

Sure, we're off.

GRANDIOSA CORRIDA DE TOROS.
Plaza de Toros
Domingo, tarde 5.30

Bullfight on Sunday evening at 5:30.

Joseph Bitter says that it would not be possible to stage bullfights in Germany, because there are so many Societies of Friends of Animals and Associations for the Protection of Animals opposed to this blood sport. His wife was, yes, indeed, quite right too. Her indignation was directed not so much against bloodletting, as the time it took to kill them. Once again, today, a bull had not fallen at the first stroke of the sword. It was not the sight of blood that upset them; Mrs. Bitter was a woman and a lady; Mr. Bitter had been through the war. A man must allow his feelings to become blunted; otherwise he would have a nervous breakdown; warfare has been a bloody business for some time, of course.

The bullfighter teases the bull, performs some dance steps, lets the charging animal brush past him, to the thunderous excitement of the spectators. Unexpectedly, the bull does not sweep past but gores a young mule, brakes on his front hooves in the sand and once again launches himself sideways. The bullfighter's body, in its silken finery, flies up into the air and drops with a thud on the sand of the arena. The bull drops its head and turns him over. His assistants come running to the stricken man's aid. A bull is dangerous when he does not follow the usual patterns of behavior of his kind, when he does not keep to the ancient customs of his race.

Into the arena steps El Cordobes himself, to avenge the gored fighter, now being carried off on a stretcher. He also experiences the liveliness of this animal, escaping his horns by a hair's breadth. He wants to finish him off as quickly as possible. The first attempt was not successful, although the sword was planted in the vital spot below the left shoulder. He tries again with a new sword. The bull staggers but has no intention of falling. All his assistants

116

are obviously feeling nervous, as the man in silk strikes a third time. The bull stumbles, sways, staggers to the fence, faces its enemies with lowered head, again attempts to swing its horn.

One of the toreador's troupe stabs him; he takes careful aim and plunges the blade deep. The animal sinks to its knees, rises again, frothing blood at the mouth. Sweat and blood pour down its sides, the flags on the daggers planted in the meat of his back quiver and shake with the quaking of the great black body, doomed to die. Then it collapses as if undermined, and on the bloody sand, no longer seems so great, dangerous, and powerful. The crowd whistles and cheers.

The style of bullfighting as practiced in Andalusia and Salamanca is specially developed at the Cortijo Vista Verde, directed by the manager of bullfighting, Anton Martini. The principle is that the animal should be lively, aggressive—in a word: dangerous. It must be ceaselessly provoked, pricked, teased, while at the same time its blood is being drawn. Long daggers, with flags in the national colors, must be planted in its back. A horseman plunges a lance into the meat of its back. The horse he is riding has stitches in its belly after an earlier goring. The half-drugged nag shows no fear. Stench of sweat and dusty sand, blood, men yelling, horses neighing, music, roars.

In the recesses of the beast's fading consciousness flickers a memory of native pastures, the pain of paradise lost.

Unless we have lost a golden paradise, hell cannot impress with its full power.

Entrance 500 to 2000 pesetas (a peseta is worth 24 to 28 old dinars).

Cloaked figures: Veronica, Farol, Gaonera, Chicuelina, Rebolera . . .

Figures with mule: Estatuario, Redondo, Natural, Pase de Pecho, Molinete, Manoletina . . .

> *Hermosos y Bravos Toros Serán Muertos (Domingo tarde, 5.30)*
> Hamburguesas! Hot dogs! Frankfurter! Danzas! Bailes! Cada día!
> Every day. Tous les jours. Jeden Tag. Comidas y bebidas! Food
> and drink to order!

Bloods spurts down the bull's shoulders, drips onto the filthy sand. His mouth is covered in foam. He stops and glares. His belly rises and falls with his quickened panting. At the same time his testicles swing, his penis rises and falls under his belly. The women see it and men, more punily equipped, look sullen and morose. Shouts and whistling greet the toreador.

> *Gran fiesta en el Cortijo!*
> We offer our honored guests the opportunity to fight a bull.
> Come and try fighting a one-year-old bull!
> Vous pouvez aussi "torear!" Escuela Taurina, School of Bullfighting
> Jeuves, jeudi, Thursday, a las 17,00 horas, at 5 P.M.

Typical show!
Solemn music in the arena. Thunder of bulls' hooves. Olé, olé!
You shall see the black bulls from Salamanca.
The bull's cradle song is stilled; we ask for a moment's silence.
We know all about this already; the kidnappers sent the parents the child's ear and left hand.
Amid the flood of Scandinavian pornography floats a tender craft, the love affair of two Scandinavians, innocents in Spain. In the tempest of violence, a child's voice: Mamma, I want to go home! In the jostling crowd, someone stops. People walk over him, trample him, casually, not intentionally, those at the back push those before them forward.
For service that can't be beat, try the Don Quixote Hotel in Ca'n Pastilla.
Talk of blood brought us back to talk of war. Everything comes to him who waits. "The war was a terrible experience," said Bitter, without real conviction. I admitted that I too had been in the war, only, how should I put it, in a very minor way.
"Where?"
"Oh, in the Italian army. Ljubljana. Yugoslavia."
"Oh? Really? I know those parts. I've been there too."
"There were a lot of insurgents, rebels."
"Sure, sure, the Communists. *Die partisanen.*"
Bitter had been sent in 1942 from France to Greece via Yugoslavia. "*Na, ja, so ein Spaziergang war das, kein Krieg eigentlich.*" After the capitulation of

Italy, he traveled once again through Yugoslavia. "You know, the Italians had every right to surrender. But that was an awkward moment for Germany. We had to scatter our forces, you know. Because of Yugoslavia, our invasion of Russia was delayed, and we really suffered that winter. Italy's surrender forced us to move a lot of units south. It made a great difference, really."

He had to smile when I said that sometimes I felt a nostalgia for the war. "Oh no, not at all, by no means." He shook his head.

I told him that's the sort of person I am. "I feel quite homesick, when I recall the toughest times. After the war I had a spell in jail, we need not go into details but it was somewhere in the East, and now and again I feel a longing for those wretched days. When a man is exposed to danger and attack, he is forced to show what he is worth. He can be pure and clean, he can be mean and filthy, there is no third alternative.

This did not amuse him; war is a terrible thing, however you look at it. Moreover, warfare is a profession of sorts; some have a talent for it, others have not.

In the fall of 1943 he was on his way from Yugoslavia to Italy.

He thought for a moment. "The Germans have always had good soldiers, but poor politicians," he declared, as if delivering some wise pronouncement. "Churchill was a good politician but an unpleasant character, *ein Purzelbaummensch* . . .

Danza de muerte.

Dance of death.

Joseph Bitter brought it all back to me again. How could I possibly record all this? Joseph Bitter had been on his way back from his trip to Greece, when I was on my way from division to brigade.

Remember, remember.

September, October, November.

Ameniza el espectaculo una brillante banda de musica!

A fine military band will accompany the spectacle.

"What was it like on your way back from Greece to Italy?"

"Oh, we were just mopping up."

"In 1943?"

"Yes, in the fall."

"What about the Yugoslav partisans?"

"Hm. What about the partisans? They were up in the woods and the mountains. One lot here, another lot there."

"But didn't they have their divisions and brigades?"

He smiled.

"Sure . . . I'd call them gangs, some bigger, some smaller . . . scattered around, here and there . . . All the same, such units are a hard nut for a regular army to crack . . ."

I still had some more questions to ask but he indicated his wife, reminding me that she did not like hearing about the war. "You're interested, are you?" he asked quietly. I nodded.

Into the arena stormed a fine, powerful, lively Andalusian bull. He scattered clouds of sand with his pounding hooves. He had no idea what awaited him in that noisy circus, stinking of blood and death.

I lit a cigarette from a packet labeled *Suppremos*. It tasted like a cigar, as Spanish cigarettes usually do.

Gangs scattered around . . . gangs, some bigger, some smaller . . . detachments . . .

I too had not known what it meant, to go "to division." At least not then. People walking in and out of houses? Moving up and down the village street?

Could I remember everything that lay concealed in that settlement? It would be difficult. Gangs billeted here and there in the houses?

Somewhere no doubt, the commander of the division was sitting, and with him, probably the divisional commissar; both of these had their deputies; the chief of staff, often a former officer, well read in military theory; a woman staff clerk; the commander's messenger; the commissar's secretary; a party secretary; the SKOJ secretary; the doctor. The quartermaster's store. Sanitation. Divisional politburo. Divisional agitprop. Divisional intelligence. Divisional staff cell. Divisional HQ defense battalion and its cell. The cook, messengers, mule drivers, grooms. Theater company (occasionally); a cultural jack-of-all-trades—writer, poet, composer, singer. Printing shop. Choir. Local peasants coming and going, members of brigade staffs, messengers from Corps and subordinate units. Commanders of town, region, district. Divisional tradesmen, barbers, tailors, cobblers. All working, contacting, planning, executing, receiving, and transmitting orders, instructions, circulars, and supervising their execution, receiving material and information. All this making a honeycomb of smaller centers, billeted out in the houses, an organism with its own rules of operation, accepting orders from above and transmitting them below. Leather was commandeered from an enemy stronghold, and brought by pack mule to the divisional quartermaster's stores; the commander's messenger got a chit from the commander for the quartermaster; he assigned the DR leather for a pair of boots; his assistant issued the leather to the DR, who tucked it under his arm and conveyed it to the boot shop, where Miha, the chief cobbler, measured him for a new pair of knee boots (only get a move on, Miha, the Krauts are getting nearer, they'll be nipping at our heels soon).

Meanwhile the brigades are carrying out their instructions: digging up roads, demolishing bridges, blowing up railway tracks, setting up roadblocks, mobilizing recruits, equipping, organizing, holding propaganda rallies with dancing. One brigade was carrying out offensive operations along the German frontier (the old frontier) on the Litija, giving the border garrisons no rest.

The Germans flooded our liberated territory with their troops. They were combing the woods, mopping up; they overran and swamped divisional headquarters. Some were taken prisoner, others killed, others shot, and their corpses were piled by the roadside like stacks of firewood. They drove the division toward Ljubljana, tried pincer movements, aerial bombardment, raked the hill slopes with salvos from tank guns, wiped out one unit after another, drove the division back on Mount Mokrec, combed through forests where no Italian forces had ever encroached, and, after liquidating the remnants of the division on Mount Krim, announced that the bandits had been exterminated. Ten days of hard battles, withdrawals, pursuit.

One week later, the division, almost intact, reformed in Suha Krajina, where it gathered its forces, reorganized, and prepared for a new campaign. No one asked how you had escaped the offensive. Everybody had his own story to tell. The only ones who kept quiet were those who had taken refuge beneath a rock, in an underground cave, or up a tree. Men from the highlands of Gorenjska in particular had the knack of finding a good hiding place. They had had plenty of practice in the Dolomites, on Mount Jelovica, where there was pretty dense cover.

How many ambushes, how many break-outs, how many escapes, how many wild and desperate assaults, how much luck in the midst of our misfortune—don't bother asking. A twenty-eight-hour march from Bald Mountain to Upper Korinj with the wounded through the rain; we were almost exhausted before the finish.

On the other hand, that night in Suha Krajina, a treacherous place with its whitewashed buildings, had been so weird, in a house with an old man on his deathbed, in a stuffy atmosphere, permeated with the sickly smell of freshly gathered corn, hanging down in bunches from the baker's oven.

The sole of my right ski boot had split lengthwise, so that water seeped in at the front but could not flow out at the heel. In that steaming cauldron of a farmer's front room I slept on the floor, with my bag under my head, and, in a nightmare, recited Župančič's "Duma" ("Hamburg . . . Hamburg . . ."). I thought the lice would eat me alive that night.

Seven fine brave bulls will die . . .
Y serán muertos 7 hermosos y bravos toros.
Once on a Sunday afternoon seven poets
were born in seven different parts of the world.

> Society bred them on special
> pastures for special purposes
> of which the bulls (poets) long
> remained ignorant.

The age was called "the death of
poetry." We all know that young
poets are lovable beasts, shaggy and
trustful, ready to sing of moonlight.
They do not know the moon comes
out to boost the tourist trade.

1973! A time of the greatest
abundance, of deadly famine, of
account books and scandal sheets,
of anxiety and the amusement
industry. Middle-class processions
visit the lands of want. Calcutta
particularly popular.
Mali not bad either.

As he grows up, the poet becomes
a more and more dangerous,
independent beast—his horns
become sharper—he is irritable,
erotically disturbed, reckless. More
and more frequently, he tries to
gore the hand, the culture, that
feeds him. They tease him but now
beware his horns.

The poet acquires habits that his
environment will not tolerate. But
his breeders know what it is all
about. *Danza de muerte.*

Some are castrated and bred as
meat for general consumption;
others must perform their monthly
jump. But the most independent are
teased as before and schooled for
their encounter with the servants of
culture.

Grown-up, he will be a powerful,
aggressive beast, no longer a
plaything. Then comes the special

official inspection and the selection. Again, some go to the beef market, others to stud, but the rest are destined to die to the sound of music some Sunday afternoon.

Then they are driven out on the Saturday before, via the avenue of Black Heroes, to a great festival, from which a silent road leads to the city abattoir.

Ameniza el espectaculo una brillante banda de musica.

"You know, the wife doesn't like hearing about the war. All my friends know this. But now that we're alone, there's nothing to stop us talking about our wartime experiences. And I can take a drop more than usual. She's worried about my heart. Herr Ober! She went through hell during the war, poor girl. Herr Ober!

"Of course I'm no military expert, you know. I can only tell you . . . from my own experience, you might say . . . what I remember . . ."

Some German tourists had crowded around the jukebox.

A Latin-American samba was followed by an old hit: "*Eine Nacht in Monte Carlo . . .*"

"*Die Partisanen . . .* They had their own kind of tactics . . . though these did not really comprise any system at all, since they had no military schools; it was improvisation, rather; yes, improvisation's the word.

"They were no threat to the main body. It was mostly our forward detachments and flanking patrols that came under attack. Direct conflicts or battles were few and far between.

"We would occupy the towns, villages, roads, valleys, mountain passes . . . Then we would close in . . . The area was divided into various sections, squares or triangles . . . We would hold the edges and drive the guerillas back into each other's arms . . .

"At first, I had a completely wrong impression. I thought they were simply suicides . . . Well, I mean . . . teasing a large, powerful, regular army with these little inconveniences—but later, I saw that the guerilla war was a whirling *perpetuum mobile*, a seething cauldron with a lid no one could ever hold down . . .

"I tell you one thing: the partisans were never too tired to retreat. That was their ongoing maneuver . . . A regular army commander sometimes felt he was dealing with a swarm of insects . . .

"Mopping up would have been easier if they had not had the civilian population on their side . . . You can't exterminate them all, you know . . . Then of course, if we'd only had more time. An instruction would come along: 'From the 17th inst. to the 29th inst. your units are to mop up the sector between hill 249 and hill 211 in the direction of . . .' and so on . . . 'The enemy is to be cleared from this area; news of the completion of the operation to be sent on the 29th inst. at 22.00 hours . . . to such and such a place . . .' Maybe, sometimes, you would ask for an extra day or two . . . but you would have to withdraw . . .

"Of course, they had different kinds of formations: some elite, crack troops with more experienced commanders, fanatical young fighting units . . . and others who had no stomach for a fight, unless you caught them by the scruff of the neck . . .

"It was a large territory, mountainous, with forests, and resistance was strong. No prisoners taken, at least, not on their side, certainly. No knowledge of military strategy, no concern for their lines, no taking up fortified positions, reactions frequently so harebrained they drove our regular officers up the wall.

"Then there is always the question of luck in battle and the effect of news from the front lines on morale and fighting spirit.

"Oh sure, there's a world of difference between a regular army and these forest bands. Regulars are well equipped, they get their meals on time, sleep in fairly secure billets, where they can relax; they have a secure base in the towns, they hold the initiative. The other side are poorly equipped; they have no ordnance, no quartermaster's stores, no regular meals, and they are continually on the move. They don't know when or where they'll get any rest. We go to bed in the evening, knowing they are at point A. When we get up in the morning, there's no sign of them . . . In one particular night, we discovered later, they covered forty kilometers over rough country, uphill, downhill, God help us . . . somehow they just kept going . . .

"By the edge of the forest, I saw two corpses: one of our men and one of theirs. What a difference, even after death, I tell you. Ours looked a part, a dead soldier . . . But that wretch was like a pale, damp husk, a mere shell, almost transparent, as thin as a poker, dressed in rags and tatters—God help us . . . I shan't forget him.

"A war like that is terribly costly. Relatively small returns for considerable investment in men and resources . . . aircraft, tanks, armored cars, trucks . . . all engaged in transporting, moving, spoiling, firing . . . cannons aiming into the void, mine throwers, machine guns, automatics . . . rockets . . . all this continually at work, in action, on the move . . . Afterward you review what has been achieved . . . Hardly anything compared with the immense expenditure . . .

"As for those so-called Quislings! Two-timing bastards! They caused us a great deal of harm, gave us a bad name with their cruel atrocities. They weren't all the same, of course. *Die Handjar Division . . . na, das waren schon Soldaten . . . aber die Domobranen . . . nichts!* To tell you the truth, I had no time for them myself. Fair enough, we needed them, okay. But they might at least have behaved themselves. A friend of mine told me how he had defended the Serbs from the Bulgarians who came in with us, yeah . . . *Und die Ustascha . . . dann die Tschetniks . . . na, danke schön!* They were only happy pillaging and murdering in the villages to our rear. Talk about the Balkans! They got ammunition from us, went to their posts, then shot the whole lot into the air; shortly afterward, they were back again: come on, Kraut, let's have some more. As if the war was a game or something."

The jukebox was intoning for at least the fifth time:

> . . . *wie schön das ist,*
> *wenn man eine küsst,*
> *die man nie vergisst . . .*

Herr Ober!

His wife was so sunburned she even had a slight fever. She had gone to sleep, poor dear, in the sun. That Spanish sun, always accompanied by a breeze from the sea, so that you never know when you've had enough. Well, anyway, we can knock back another glass of beer.

We arrived at brigade, just in time for the evening meal. For the first time, I ate with "my own" spoon, from "my own" mess tin. A dish of white polenta with a thick goulash poured over it. Brigade HQ lay in an idyllic little village between two low hills. In the distance could be heard the crackle of machine-gun fire, like the indistinct, erratic rattle of a stick on a revolving wheel. An old farmer was slowly and unconcernedly taking a cartload of manure out to the fields. Once again, I saw the familiar bustle of partisans toing and froing.

Three of us had been issued firearms, namely rifles (Italian carbines with triple-edged bayonets, fairly short and unreliable weapons) and two Italian "tomatoes" (noisy defensive hand grenades). Tujchko and the quiet chap in the tight plus fours got nothing.

"How many clips of ammunition do we get?"

"Let's say three. Why? You'd like four, would you? Look, there's no shortage at battalion."

"So we're off to battalion, are we? Where exactly?"

"You lot! You're joining the Alpine Navy! Sure, you need to test your gun, only shooting's forbidden in the village and on the main road too. Stands to reason, don't it?"

"Well, how can I find out whether the thing works?"

"Stick the barrel in some dirt and pull the trigger."

"Well, well. And if I want to know how well it carries?" It looked to me as if it might well fire around corners. A glance at the barrel was far from reassuring.

"You'll find out when you take a potshot at the Krauts. If you hit one that means it's working properly."

"That so? Thanks for the tip. And what about these hand grenades?"

"You must count, or pull the firing pin and count: . . . twenty-one . . . twenty-two . . . twenty-three . . . then throw. If you throw it too soon, you might get it back in your face, and if you wait too long, you'll find out what you've been hiding under your skin."

"And are we allowed to count eleven, twelve, thirteen? Has it got to be twenty-one?"

"Look mate, you can count one thousand, three hundred, and thirty-three if you like, but don't come back here moaning afterward. Try to get rid of them as soon as possible and find something better. For a bet, the Ities would plant one, primed, under a steel helmet, then sit on it. When it went off, they only got a kick up the arse. Just you try that trick with a Kragujevac grenade or a French fizzer! You'll end up with your head in the ceiling and a harelip on your bloody crotch!"

"And what's the range of this carbine?"

"Farther downhill than up; I'd lay a packet of cigarettes on fifty meters, or two packets on twenty."

I went into a stable and stuck the barrel in a pile of manure. I pressed the trigger and thus fired my first shot as a member of the National Liberation Army and the Partisan Detachments of Slovenia. When I emerged from the stable, Tujchko asked me, "Did you hit the shit?"

Sometimes it's just as well we're not telepathic. How the old partisans would have laughed at me. The feeling of a weapon in my hands was like a great relief after a weird nightmare. A solemn feeling came over me and I felt a quiet but powerful desire to acquire a better weapon as soon as possible. Hitler, come out fighting!

What is happening to me, I wondered. Are my warlike ancestors' instincts reasserting themselves? With some shame, I thought of Remarque's excellent novel, *All Quiet on the Western Front*. Forgive me, Erich; it's not really my fault.

Right at the beginning of your book you say: "This is not meant as accusation nor confession; it is just an attempt to report on a generation destroyed by war, even if they escaped the shells." And in your last chapter, you state your conclusions: "We are not needed, even by ourselves . . . Some of us will come to terms, others will never submit, many will never know what it was all about . . . Months and years will pass and they won't get anything more from me; there is no more to take . . ."

Your book came out in 1929 (at least that was the date of my edition), eleven years after the war. Fourteen years later, here I stand, with a miserable old popgun in my hands that any of your old army mates would have flung on a rubbish dump, and I am overcome with a romantic enthusiasm—ugh! Shall I also be required to render a report of some kind? Who knows? I am full of ardor and trust in my good fortune but have no confidence in the necessity of reports. In any case, I am only a blade of grass, one of the many that grow here by the paddock fence, a blade of grass, carrying a *carabinieri*'s popgun on his shoulder. We'll see what I think about it a year from now. Now we are off to join our battalion, three recruits, and one escort, a new one. We got him at brigade HQ. Tujchko and the chap in plus fours gazed after us. Tujchko gave us a holler but the other seemed to be deep in thought.

Three buxom middle-aged peasant women were walking along in front of us. They paid no attention to us, they were so used to the army by now. Their raucous gossip grated on the ear. A shell had landed in someone's vineyard, smack on the wine cellar and the wine had run out of the barrels; I imagined their skin, their flesh; they revolted me with their bloated self-satisfaction. Outside one house, our guide gave us a sign to stop. The women waddled on, swinging those massive buttocks, without noticing that the men were no longer following them.

Six more lads joined us, four looking more like country boys. They had similar guns to ours. One of them, apparently a real urban namby-pamby, in boots a couple of sizes too large, had something that made my mouth water, a prewar Yugoslav army rifle with a sound butt and a barrel of good steel. How few of those rifles were fired the week of Easter, 1941, when the Germans rumbled through Yugoslavia on their way to Greece and the sources of Hellenic civilization?

Then, we were running around the barracks in Zagreb, asking where the front line was. Was it somewhere south of Zagreb? Or was it in central Bosnia? We had heard both reports.

The Croatian officer was smoking a cigarette, which he held, delicately, in his outstretched fingers.

"Take it easy, you Carniolan bees," he said in Croatian, with an ironic smile. "In an hour or two, the situation will be clear. Time is on your side."

Hardly an hour had passed when we saw what he meant. The German tanks rolled through the wide-open gates of the barracks. Where could we escape to? Over the wall, into the street, along the street, and then? I still have not forgotten one of the worst sights I ever saw in my life: civilians, chasing one of our soldiers in uniform out of a dairy, or was it a buffet? He must have said something to provoke them. They literally tore him apart with their bare hands. While they killed him, they were shouting something about those bloody Serbs. I can see him now, vainly trying to break free of his attackers, then sinking to the ground under the weight of the enraged mob, that first pounded him with fists and feet, then kicked him to death as he lay there.

They chased me too, but I could cover eight hundred meters at quite a brisk pace. They soon grew tired of running after me. Others who tried to block me or head me off were not very nimble either. Once I had shaken off my pursuers, I slipped into a small bar. "Is there a phone?" "Yes, right there." "Hello, hello, is that you, Vojo? Can I come over and see you? It's urgent, okay. Give me your address. Number seven, Grkovič Street? I'll be over right away."

The old waiter behind the bar was able to direct me.

"It's the street you're in at the present moment. This bar is number nine, yes, nine Grkovič Street. Number seven is next door."

I changed into Vojo's civilian suit. He also gave me an overcoat and a bat and we went for a walk through the city. For the first time, I had an opportunity to inspect German tanks and tank crews in their black uniforms close up. They had clearly taken a fancy to the girls of Zagreb and the feeling was reciprocal, judging at least by the way the girls were lining up to talk to them.

This memory brought something else back to mind: how my cup contained at one and the same time a double dose of both the purest, most incredible good fortune—finding that Vojo lived next door to the bar with the telephone—and also of horror and black misfortune—defeat, disgrace, slavery, occupation, and without the least opportunity of resistance, as it then appeared to me. Why had we been fed for twenty-three years on chauvinistic rubbish? Why had we, as children, recited nonsense about "peoples who are invincible if they are loyal to their homeland," about "Slav heroes with hearts of steel, stout bulwark of their country"? Laugh, clown, while your heart breaks with sorrow!

Thank you, Vojo, for the suit I was never able to return to you. And thank you also, gentlemen, Karageorgeviches, Stojadinoviches, Cvetkoviches, Kujoviches, and whatever your names were; thank you for all those fine words, which I can now return to you, unspoiled and just as relevant as before. You will find the words you once vouchsafed me particularly apt. Even now, I still see that soldier, with one hand reaching for his hair, a second ripping at his ear, a third grabbing him by the nose. He would have willingly gone to the front line and I would have gone with him; God knows how many others there were like us. But what was our government doing then? Our generals did not seem unduly perturbed. But where were our leaders? They had fled in confusion—a sorry story. It makes me furious to think of those hulks of lard, cramming their gold and gems into trunks and briefcases, scuttling off to the airport so fast their shirttails did not touch their rumps, then, as soon as they reached a safe haven, ranting and spouting again, even before the chill was off their nether jowls.

Later, in Ljubljana, I was hunted by their agents, now working for the Germans, the gentlemen of the "Black Hand Gang." They would label me a traitor to my country, since, as a one-time member of the Sokols, I had fraternized with the Communists. Could you believe it? They were collaborating with the Gestapo for strictly tactical reasons, but I was a fully committed fellow traveler! The English and the Americans would compensate them for the distress they had suffered as associates of Benito and Adolf. But I would end up on the gallows. (They promised me and other "traitors" a public hanging in Congress Square; some of us were captured, bound with barbed wire and drowned in the Sava. Since I was not present, it would not be fair to repeat what I have heard about the practice of massage before bathing.) I found it easier to put up with outright Quislings like Pavelich and his Ustaše, tearaways with no political talent. Well, we shall see how it turns out in the end.

The fellow whose rifle I envied so warmly had a German grenade in his belt. One of the country lads kept his feet really dry, thanks to a pair of green gaiters. His nether extremities were all the more conspicuous as he walked with a limp. Probably because his feet were giving him hell, he had more to say than the rest of us. I was rather glad of this, as I was beginning to miss Tujchko's raucous chatter.

Two of the new recruits were singing, in soft, harmonious voices, various songs they had learned in the *campo di concentrazione* on the island of Rab. They had been freed by the parish priest, who, after the capitulation, had fled to Ljubljana. Our people on the island were dying of hunger and exhaustion. It was also true that there were internees working in the cookhouse, helping themselves to the camp provisions and gorging themselves like pigs.

On and on we marched.

On to an unknown destiny, no longer masters of our fate. We could stop nothing, we could start nothing; we could not even fire our rifles yet. No doubt there was someone, somewhere, thinking of us, but who, where, what, and with whom, we knew not and we would never learn. But this is how the soldiers of thousands of armies in the world's history marched to war. They joined their units, went into combat, and now schoolboys read that the battle of so-and-so took place in such-and-such a year. Later, Dante and Virgil visited Beatrice in Paradise.

The fellow with the sore feet had no need of an amplifier. He had a really unusual, deep, booming bass voice. The first time he opened his mouth, we stared at him in amazement.

"If only the Krauts would start shooting at us . . ."

He repeated this three times before explaining.

"Makes you get a real move on if you've got those bastards on your tail . . . You soon forget all about aching shins . . . or tight boots . . . or eating and drinking . . . even about your mother and father . . ."

We had to take an occasional break because of him. The road through the forest brought us to a clearing, with huge logs by the roadside stacked long ago and now beginning to go rotten. Like schoolchildren exhausted after a day's ramble, we sat there in the idyllic peace of the forest at evening, some of us perched on the chopped wood, others on a decaying tree trunk. A little way below me, on the log pile, sat the man with the Yugoslav rifle, which he was holding between his knees. The barrel was aimed directly at my head. Its dark mouth did not worry me unduly, until he started fiddling with the trigger. He looked at me and I looked back at him; later I wondered what there had been in that meeting of our eyes. When he turned away from me, I leaned back slightly, so that the barrel was no longer aimed directly at my head. There came a loud report and a bullet shot past my face, just missing me. I could almost claim that I smelled it. Everyone jumped and turned around to see what had happened, the man who had fired the shot included. He seemed genuinely bewildered. I grabbed him by the collar and gently pulled him to his feet . . . We glared at each other, without uttering a word. Our escort told him off. He told us there had been many accidents with firearms in the days immediately after the Italian capitulation, when weapons had fallen into the hands of all and sundry.

An accident? Carelessness, inexperience, pure ignorance? Or was it something else? I probed my memory to discover what had passed between us, the first time our eyes had met. I found no enjoyment now in the sight of the countryside. Again, I felt a sudden chill. This was not fear, not a question of life and death, but a feeling that there was a plot against my life, some unseen, imperceptible, unproven intrigue lurking in the air, regarding me malevolently with murky, expressionless eyes. I gave way for a moment to depression, disappointment, a sense of grievance. This won't do, this just won't do, my boy. This is no way to survive my first days in action.

I felt angry with myself and with someone else, but who? With that twerp who had a good rifle he did not know how to use? With that steel-and-lead missile that had shot straight up into the air, without encountering my flesh and bone on the way, to fall to earth in an arc, dropping through tree branches and ferns to rest on the forest floor? With someone, somewhere, who had made a false calculation? With a pure mistake? With my own destiny? "And the best of luck!" Tujchko would have said, "they're all out to get you, those with the time to spare!" Yes, the old Yugoslav gendarmerie, the Ities, the Krauts, Rupnik, Pavelich, Ljotich, Nedich . . . I could just see those dark figures with fixed bayonets, Schmeissers, automatics, revolvers, and blackjacks . . . All around us . . . Vlasov's Russians, the Moslem Handjar Division, the Hungarians, Bulgarians, Ustaše, Chetniks, the Blues, the Whites . . . The Russians would suspect me of being pro-Western . . . For the English and Americans I was a Russophile . . . Just as well that I didn't know the Japanese . . .

But where was I? Walking along a forest path in liberated Slovenia, bearing arms in our own army, on my way to my front-line unit, and bothered by the thought that this bloody shit had really intended for me to join those who had already fallen for their homeland. I felt all the better for this outburst of indignation. I calmed down and decided to write a friendly letter to the Eskimos in the far north. Not much point in it, though—I am too sensitive to the frost!

I now put the fear of hell into the sickly oaf by carrying my rifle as if I were accidentally pointing it at him. I had it slung over my shoulder in hunter fashion and was fiddling with the trigger. Sometimes our eyes met.

This was my simple sporting instinct, the joy of the game, the risk, the challenge to fate, which had often turned out to my own detriment. Why? A sensible person would have reasoned thus; the whole thing had been an unfortunate accident, all's well that ends well, let's forget it, let's drop it. If in fact there were some ulterior motive, it would be a great mistake to kick up a fuss, and alert those dark forces, lurking in the background, to my intelligence (devil take it!), and readiness to fight (ant against elephant!).

Nightfall almost took us by surprise.

In the darkness we felt more like talking.

The full moon floated up over the valley and lit our path.

The lame man's foot was aching more and more.

Any chance of a kip? You'll be lucky. A short break, then we push on.

Hills, valleys, woods, fields in the moonlight. A white radiance covers the fields, woods, valleys, hills. An uphill road.

"Pity the Krauts don't operate at night." Another complaint from our stentorian friend. "The safer you are, the more your feet ache."

". . . when it's going dark like this, your imagination plays tricks; you think there's more of the enemy about than there really are," our escort told us. For most of the day he had had little to say. "I was in the Gubec Brigade then and we were once out on the road before morning, with rearguard and advance guard . . . We had been told not to expect any Italians . . . Ahead of us we had a two-man patrol with a local guide . . . Suddenly all hell broke loose . . . we were making our way along the road to Jelenov Žleb . . . We were escorting casualties . . . They were way behind us, with the battalion . . . We soon forgot it was a cold night . . . We dived for cover, off the road, into the bushes on the hillside to our right . . . Couldn't see a thing . . . but the sound of those guns was simply deafening . . . one hell of a racket . . . Then the yelling started . . . couldn't make out a bloody word . . . We blazed away though it was dark all around us . . .

"Then I heard a shriek that almost burst my left eardrum: 'Get those flaming machine guns up the hill! Up to the top!' I leaped to my feet, rushed past some rocks, tripped, fell down a hole, picked myself up again, fired, watched one of my mates taking a rock in his stride; we were deafened by the grenades and the rifle fire; I couldn't feel my arms or legs but everything seemed to be in working order . . . One of our men let loose a volley from an automatic . . . at a moving target somewhere to our front . . . I stumbled over the tree stumps, got tangled up in the dry branches of a fallen tree . . . at last I made it . . .

"We, in the Gubec Brigade, had the Italians to our front and the Cankar Brigade had taken up a commanding position above them . . . That was at Mala Bela Stena. We were all mixed up together, staff and all, but we kept on driving uphill, higher, and higher! Charge! Through the grenades and machine-gun fire . . . The whole forest reeked of Italian explosives . . . cartridges stuffed with bloody macaroni . . . How long it went on, I've no idea. Time has no meaning at moments like that.

"We still had another hundred meters or so to cover up a pretty steep slope to a sharp ridge on our right . . . Might even have been high as the castle hill in

Ljubljana, I'm not sure; it was mighty rough going anyway . . . The Italians were screaming, 'Alla montagna! Alla montagna!' And we were yelling, 'Charge! Take that bloody hilltop!

"We were shrieking and cursing, that I remember. Madonna! What if the Italians made it before we did!

"However, it was one of our gunners with a light Breda who first made it to the top. And did he let them have it! . . . I can still hear them screaming . . . Wouldn't like to have been in their shoes . . . Well, the whole operation went like clockwork after that . . .

"During that action, I thought the whole place was swarming with Italians. After the Italian capitulation I heard they also imagined there were thousands of us, although in fact, taking the Gubec and Cankar Brigades together, there can't have been more than four hundred of us, probably more like three hundred and fifty. There were a few more of them . . . but they were not used to operating in such bloody awful terrain . . .

"They took to their heels and stumbled through the trees, one after another, to a timber slide which got more and more slippery as they plunged headlong down . . . About a hundred of them, I guess . . . They must have fallen more than fifty meters . . .

"The mules were braying, stampeding along the road and through the forest.

"The road was littered with Italian equipment, weapons, mine throwers, ammunition, helmets, tenting, bags, brand-new red leather boots, dead and wounded Italians, a mule shot through the knees. A toothbrush, an illustrated magazine, soap, a book, holy pictures . . . a full-fledged garage sale . . . God knows why, I picked up some hair oil. It was in a very nice tube."

Must make the hilltop.

"It was only when I was picking up the brilliantine that I noticed my right sleeve was torn and blood was dripping from it—my blood."

"Halt!"

(We halt).

"Who goes there?"

"Yozhe with the recruits!"

"Forward the leader of the patrol! The rest of you halt!"

We had arrived at battalion headquarters, a small village on a hillside. Cottages, surrounded by fruit trees; in the middle of them a small church protected by a stone wall, a one-time fortress, a stronghold in the days of the Turkish invasions. There were lights in some of the houses. In the distance, we could hear the dull, steady echo of machine-gun fire, silence, then once again rat-a-tat, rat-a-tat. There were just a few hills between us and the old German-Italian frontier on the river Sava.

Our escort went into a house where a sentry stood on guard. He returned and showed us where we were billeted for the night.

I was directed to a house where there were already about a dozen bodies stretched out on the floor of the main room, with another pair occupying the bed. The moonlight poured in through the closed windows. Couldn't I sleep in the hayloft? You've got your orders. I learned I had joined my unit. So now at long last I had arrived. Three other new recruits had joined with me, including our friend with the mighty voice.

We lay down on the floor.

The great orator spoke.

"Now get those boots off. God knows when you'll have your next chance."

"What others find unusual I find quite simple, what others find interesting,
I find boring."
Josip Murn, letter (1898)

"To have a complete, European, all-embracing human consciousness, and
yet have so little choice, such a limited field of action: what torment, my brother."
Giannini

"A way must be opened to the human understanding entirely distinct from that
known to our predecessors . . ."
Bacon, *Novum Organum*

"Let us now examine the history of the Counter-Reformation. Half of
the decent people in our lands were then killed and the other half fled. Only
the foul rabble remained. And we are the sons of our ancestors."
Jerman in Cankar's *Servants*

"From a nation of lackeys to a nation of heroes."
Wall slogan in liberated Slovenia

"Man is condemned to be free. Condemned, because he did not
create himself, yet is nevertheless at liberty . . . thrown into this world, he is
responsible for everything he does."
J. P. Sartre

"Believe in liberty, my brother; do you know how much harder slavery
would be? The blind have a better world than ours. Without light they
cannot see the dark."
Giannini

"Conversation with a German N.C.O. on a forest road at night:
I (brusquely): *Halt! Wer da?*
He (amiably): *Hier Feldwebel Swoboda . . .*
I (automatically): Trrrr . . ."

"And so we see that our comprehension or failure to comprehend is
dependent on such minute factors that we have no right to express doubts
in what we cannot imagine."
M. Maeterlinck, *The Intelligence of Flowers*

3

A man should avoid becoming a creature of habit. When times change, the most trivial and convenient habits begin to ruin your enjoyment of life. What thoughts, what vivid memories, echoed in my mind all through that night! This, I felt, marked the beginning of a new stage in my life. I got up when the first faint light of dawn appeared in the windows. I carefully picked my way over the snoring, sleeping, recumbent figures of those who were my companions for that night and would be, no doubt, for the days to come. I crept along by the wall, where I found a bookshelf. I selected a book at random and took it with me. At the doorway, I looked back; I had forgotten my rifle. There is a saying, when we leave something important or essential behind, that it is like a soldier forgetting his rifle. This simply will not do, I thought, and retraced my steps to recover the old blunderbuss. I felt slightly ashamed of myself.

Out in the yard, I climbed up and took a seat in a cart. Some people were already up and about. I started to read. It was a German book, neatly bound in light-colored linen, entitled *Four Thousand Years of the German Reich*. I would have preferred to pick up the almanac which stood beside it on the shelf, but I had no intention of going back now. A horse whinnied in the stable. He was hungry, no doubt, and had heard me moving about the yard. I coughed, so that he might recognize the voice of a stranger, from whom he could expect no food. Somewhere in the distance, a dog barked. In the dim light of the approaching day, I tried to read the tedious tome which destiny, for reasons known only to herself, had brought me from far-off Berlin.

My life is full of strange happenings, or perhaps I am myself rather strange in interpreting so many coincidences as a fatefully significant chain of events. Here, probably, also lies the source of my rather naïve faith in my own good fortune. In Zagreb, Vojo had happened to be living next door to the bar from which I rang him: pure chance. He would be a prime witness to my good luck. And now, in this book which was beginning to engross me more and more,

I had a valuable introduction to the character of the enemy I was about to confront.

What did I know about Nazism? About National Socialism? About Hitlerism? Almost nothing. Yet this regime now dominated a vast area, from the Atlantic to the Caucasus, from Narvik to North Africa. It took some mental effort to imagine that expanse. Suddenly, in that yard, I could see all the armies of Germany, stationed worldwide, advancing like specters, occupying first the territories, then the souls of men. I read avidly and tried to grasp the essence of this ideology of German lordship over the Earth.

"What our forefathers strove for whole centuries to bring about, has now been achieved in a few short weeks by the German army under the leadership of its only Führer, Adolf Hitler: the face of Europe is transformed!"

". . . has taken the German people as the source of its power . . ."

"Nordic man has freed art and science from the tutelage of the church . . ."

". . . has sent the cattle merchants packing, with their privileges and estates . . ."

". . . has given liberty its true meaning: not freedom from anything, but freedom to act, to serve the community; true community knows no pressure, since its inner legitimacy is understood; this community educates by example and leadership . . ."

". . . Freedom, from whatever it may be, has led to the dismemberment of the state and the dissipation of human effort . . ."

"The German people has risen against all those forces foreign to it and has rejected the clauses of the Weimar constitution which were dictated by the Liberals' conception of freedom."

"Thought can be expressed only by those who have it . . . Only the awareness of a sense of community, only thought gives strength . . . There can be no thinking divorced from the service of the community . . ."

"High politics have always been in the hands of lords, princes, and sovereigns, but the people have always conducted their own popular policy."

"For centuries, the so-called fine arts have been in the hands of the churches, royal courts, and high society, but alongside it, popular art has lived on, among the peasants and small craftsmen."

"Our people are the eternal source of that power which has preserved the German Reich for four millennia . . . They will bring this war to a victorious conclusion . . . They will ensure the existence of the Reich for further millennia . . ."

"The appended chronological table shows that, in the millennia preceding our era, and throughout our era, German history is no less rich in occurrences and events than the history of Egypt, Asia Minor, Greece, and Rome."

In the table I read: "At the time of the Trojan War, about 1,300 years before our era, the Germans acquired Central and Eastern Pomerania (Pommern). At the time of Spartacus's rebellion in Rome, Ariovistus the German crossed the Rhine."

"Adolf Hitler's creation comprises all the Greater German area, an area in which our predecessors once lived for hundreds and thousands of years, tilling it with the plow, shedding their blood for it in countless wars. From the Atlantic shores of Scandinavia to the Vistula and Bug, from the Black Sea to the Pyrenees and across the Mediterranean . . . there are millions of people prepared to build the new order . . . united for the construction of a new, greater future . . ."

"(Thus wrote Kurt Pastenaci, Berlin, 1940, dedicating his work to the memory of comrades fallen in the Great War.)"

I went on reading. I did not notice dawn nor sunrise, nor the yard filling with people.

Someone looked over my shoulder and observed, "You see he halted at the Pyrenees, thanks to his good relations with General Franco . . ."

It was the lanky fellow in military uniform with a button missing from his collar. He had a sallow, foxy face and an ironical twist to his lips.

"Remember 1940?" I asked. "And how he then halted at the Bug and Vistula for the sake of good relations with Stalin? Unless my memory fails me, the Germans and Russians partitioned certain European territories after that, didn't they?"

His eyes narrowed and glittered.

"You joking?" His voice was scarcely audible. He turned on his heel and went off, a tall, slightly bent figure, head hunched into his shoulders, hands in pockets. The trousers of his uniform hung wide and loose on his bony buttocks. He went into the house without a backward glance. What a slovenly type, I thought, yet had to admit I quite liked him. Sly, selfish, and self-centered he might be, but he was alert, intelligent, and educated too. However, he hated being teased or provoked.

"Come on, lads, let's see you!" Our escort of the night before was summoning us. "On parade!"

We learned that he was in command of our unit. I half expected him to deliver a speech. We stood there, like an old-fashioned fire brigade. But it all went off very well, without any fuss. He divided us into platoons of ten men, checked whether our weapons were in working order, and told us we would be taking up "our position" after lunch. The lanky fellow with the foxy eyes was the machine gunner in our platoon. His mate was a small, sickly youth, who could hardly carry the ammunition box. Our platoon leader was a quiet fellow of gloomy aspect. I noticed, in particular, a lively young chap from Ljubljana, who showed unusual interest in me: when had I arrived, where was I from, what was my name? "Berk," I told him.

He introduced himself. "I'm Iztok." His quick, dark eyes, restlessly survey-ing his surroundings, did not make a good impression on me. His jerky gossip was shallow and trivial. "We've got a political delegate here . . . and a battalion commissar," he told me in confidence. "It's quite voluntary," he added, "but you new arrivals ought to report to battalion HQ to be registered."

Our friend with the booming bass voice announced slowly, deliberately, "A Gestapo agent is going to be shot, over by the church." Was he a German? No. A Slovene who had insinuated himself into the camp.

He was standing in a blue-and-white striped shirt, dark riding breeches, and polished black knee boots, on a grassy slope in front of the churchyard wall, behind which we could see the silhouettes of the crosses and gravestones. At the entrance to the churchyard, by the half-open gates with their iron rail-ings, stood an elderly man, leaning on a spade.

On the grassy slope below the condemned man and above the cart track which circled the hill, a squad of partisans were waiting, rifles hanging from their shoulders, while in the middle of the ring, a gunner lay on the ground with a light machine gun, black in color, mounted on slender supports and trained on the blue-and-white shirt.

Another man, armed with an automatic, was standing slightly to one side. There were some elderly villagers, men and women, watching from farther off. Children too. Two girls, one of them as swarthy as a Gypsy, with a full bosom, though she could not have been more than fourteen years old. A man with a cart had halted on the road. We were standing quite near his cart. The white church tower, with its red helmet and solitary peephole. The dusky beauty was rubbing one thigh against the other, as if she needed to relieve herself.

"Off with your boots!" the man with the automatic ordered the condemned spy.

Silence, except for the distant chatter of machine guns. The air was sultry, oppressive. The autumn sun shone faintly.

The condemned man removed one boot and slowly placed it on the grass, while keeping his eye on the machine gun, still trained on him. He had socks of thick, probably white, wool.

He had some trouble with his other boot, which did not come off so easily.

Suddenly, up he shot as if propelled by a spring. In his white stockings, he ran full tilt at the machine gunner and his weapon, leaping over them, diving helter-skelter into the bushes on the steep slope beyond the cart track, turned a somersault, tumbled down the slope, launched himself into the air with a mighty leap and was immediately lost to view in the apparently impenetrable thickets of the ravine down below.

A few revolver and rifle shots sounded in his wake. The man with the automatic let out a string of curses; his weapon had seized up. The machine gun joined in, only when the gunner had swung it around to face in the new direction. Some men rushed into the dense thickets but advanced much slower than the fugitive. They were not fleeing for their lives.

"They'll never see him again," said the man with the foxy eyes who was standing beside me. There was no note of regret in his voice. We exchanged a quiet smile.

"Would I recognize that face again?" I mused aloud.

"Did he have a face?"

When we set off to take up our position, my exhilaration was tempered by a small, nagging suspicion.

There were a number of sensations that sustained my good humor. I had eaten a good meal and enjoyed a quiet postprandial smoke. I was getting on well with the rest of the unit and felt no tension. And now there was this pleasant road, leading up over a stony hillside, through a sparse oak wood, with its masses of bilberry bushes and velvety moss on the rocks. The leaves were just beginning to turn yellow in the autumn sunshine. There was a scent of moldering tree bark in the air. Two belated butterflies fluttered by. Strange about that fellow. If he had really been a Gestapo agent, would he have set off to spy on the partisans in a pair of jackboots that stood out a mile? It was hardly my business anyway. In the confusion that followed his escape, I approached the Gypsy girl. There was something about her that attracted me. While I was talking to her and her friend about what had happened, I laid a hand on those swarthy shoulders. In the warmth of her flesh under my palm, I could feel something like the flutter of a bird's feathers. I still carried that tremor in my right palm, like a promise of things to come.

Only the behavior of the hawk-eyed Iztok was causing me annoyance and anxiety. He kept weaving around me, asking questions, and in general, showing altogether too much interest in me. When the path widened, he popped up alongside me; when it narrowed, I had him treading on my heels. I didn't like the careless way he handled his rifle either. Once bitten, twice shy. Or was I developing a persecution complex?

Foxy was bent double under the weight of his "light" machine gun but kept up a steady pace with long, measured strides. His assistant with the ammunition box floundered clumsily after him. Obviously unused to physical exercise, he made no attempt to find a foothold but clambered on as if he had been walking on the level; putting his feet down wherever they chanced to land, whereas every schoolboy knows you need to pick a stone or a root for your heel if you are going up or your toe if you are coming down. I liked our commander Yozhe, a modest but sensible fellow. His whole frame seemed to be perfectly fused with belt, equipment, and rifle into one natural whole. I had the impression he was constantly and fully alert to everything that was going on around him, although he did not bother to show it. We met a patrol on the way down, a couple of country lads. They stopped for a moment and exchanged a few words with Yozhe. Overall, it seemed, there was nothing special to report from our allotted position. We proceeded at an easy pace. I noticed that each of us carefully stepped over a line of ants scurrying across our path, with the solitary exception of the gunner's mate, who trampled on the busy insects in his usual clumsy way. I picked a stag beetle in his bright livery off an oak leaf and put him on my shoulder. He marched on with me. Neither battalion, brigade, division, nor corps headquarters had any idea that, after wiping out a whole column of red ants, our unit strength had increased to eleven with the admission of this well-armed recruit. "We're going to win this war," said Švejk. Iztok heard me whispering this to the stag-beetle and asked, "What did you say?" I repeated it aloud, at the top of my voice. "Of course we're going to win!" Iztok gravely agreed. What a pain in the neck. At that moment I could even have wished the firing might start. Then we'd see what's what, my lad! But the Germans were holed up in their bunkers along the old frontier, occasionally spraying the area with machine-gun fire. That is what we had been told by those who had already been up the line. What was going on behind us, to our rear, either no one knew or no one would say.

A whitish gray rock, partly covered with a low-growing, light green moss, and overhung with bilberry bushes, was such a neat, wholesome, and attractive sight, a man could have simply stopped there, drinking in those surroundings, nibbling a crisp young pine sapling or chewing a piece of white birch bark.

PLAYA DE PALMA (España 1973)

À la nature!
(J. J. Rousseau)

Bluish-golden, airy-sunlit, blessed and breezy,
this Babylonian tower of indolence and slow haste,
of buildings by the channels, the unseen channels,
where money flows by day and night,
where on all sides the music booms,
riot of color, amplifiers, talk, and hum of engines,
close-packed mass of bodies on a beach by the shallow sea,
riders pedaling their white craft over the peaceful surge,
men sporting whiskers of all shapes and styles,
women on double soles and high, higher heels,
the middle class of Mitteleuropa.
It is not true that God in Babylon confused the tongues of men
—from them he fashioned one sole language
well-known even to the cab horse in the red sombrero.
All is at peace
save for the restless breezes off the sea
and a persistent hawker of gold bracelets.

I was reading the French newspaper I had bought that morning on my way through town. Henri Wetch, the bookseller, had spent some years in prison in postwar China. He had studied the ancient Chinese mentality, which had no connection with revolutionary thought.

"*Le but n'a pas d'importance. C'est le chemin pour l'atteindre qui, seul, compte*": the end is not important; the way there is the only thing that matters. (I should have to give this some thought.)

"*L'homme supérieur—l'homme évolué—est toujours content de son sort. Il sait l'accepter*": the more highly evolved man is always content with his lot; he can take it.

"*La vie est un perpétuel changement. Il faut donc admettre tous les avatars, poliment, en souriant, en nuançant les paroles. Tcheou-yi, c'est l'adaptation consentie*": life is continual change; therefore we must accept all vicissitudes, and accept them politely, with a smile, choosing the right words—Cheu-yi, which expresses resignation, agreement. (Revolution, on the other hand, teaches disaffection with the status quo, and the need for reform; but is it possible to forget private troubles and work for social change?)

By now Bitter and I had broken the sound barrier, the barrier of mistrust, that is, and were discussing our day-to-day affairs like a pair of old friends. I noticed that we moved on quite easily and naturally to military topics. He knew I liked hearing about the last war and that I was particularly interested in minor operations, guerilla warfare, and the conduct of partisans. He too seemed to take a growing pleasure in talking about the war, but only in his wife's absence, or when it was so noisy she could not hear us; she was in fact a little hard of hearing and rather ashamed of it. So as not to admit she had not heard us, she would sometimes put in, at a most inappropriate moment, "But of course, of course."

Bitter really appreciated my concern for "Madame." Altogether, he regarded me as a good companion, not realizing I was only a good listener.

He told me in confidence that, ever since the war, he had suffered from frequent headaches, and that he tried to keep this from his wife as far as he could, since otherwise she would be watching his alcohol intake with an even more hawk-like eye. In a certain town (in Yugoslavia), a bomb had been thrown into the officers' mess. Some of those there had been killed, others injured, and the explosion had hurled him against a stove. He had lain unconscious for a long time and had woken up in a hospital. There had been no visible wound but he had been soaked in blood. The blast had caused bleeding through the nose and ears.

Who had thrown the bomb? Of course we knew who was responsible. There were footmen, servants, waiters, attendants. An irresponsible attack. What could you expect in the Balkans? Of course, it was the hostages that paid for it.

Hostages.

The method of every regular army in history. Mental pressure on the population. Subsequent pressure from them on the morale of the resistance movement.

"The mechanics of pressure applied in full, eh?" I remarked.

Deep in thought, he nodded agreement. He too was adrift on a flood of past events. He said nothing but watched some internal flashback. His forehead was creased in a puzzled frown. For his simple soul, the memories of the lost war were like a drink, whose effects were unpredictable. Time and time again, in the postwar years, he had sat down as now, with some acquaintance and had to talk about the war. And he was always unhappy. A man of an orderly and systematic bent, he was forced to discuss that important period in an unsystematic way, as a disorderly series of chance happenings. Without great satisfaction, he recalled sensations, catalogued events, retraced some winding road of the past, and floundered in a welter of haphazard reminiscences. He was constantly plagued by a furious and bitter consciousness that things should not have gone that way. "Why? Why, oh why? *Mein Führer*, Adolf Hitler, the swastika, Minister Goebbels speaking, Air Marshal Hermann Göring, Minister of Police Himmler, waiting for our new secret weapon, *wir marschieren*, a place in the sun. *Herrenvolk*, defeat at Stalingrad, air raids on German cities, collapse of the front, the battle of Berlin, Hitler's death, the occupation of Germany, the prisoner-of-war camps, the Nuremberg trials, reconstruction . . . we went through all that. We didn't lose the first war in our history and probably not the last . . . We don't get excited about all that anymore. It is the memories of those days that split and divide us, exhilarating some, causing others pain; and this has nothing to do with politics."

"Blood is spilled in all wars, atrocities occur, people die, settlements are destroyed, wide-eyed children meet a new way of life. These are clear and well-known facts. Great armies march out on long campaigns and occupy foreign territory, find ways of persuading stubborn spirits, despise the enemy, hope for a victory which will wipe out all memory of the horrors of war and the persecution of the population; there's nothing new in this. And if you lose, you foot the bill."

Bitter shook his head and I expected him to continue but his wife appeared, wearing her usual friendly smile.

Both of us, my dear Bitter, were mere pawns in the war. The great players will write their war memoirs or have someone write the history of their campaigns. But we are sitting somewhere in Spain, simply wondering what in fact happened. We have left and we shall leave no memorial behind; not even a blade of grass by the monument to the unknown soldier, that curious fabrication, that hardened plaster for the wounded conscience of the cruel bourgeoisie. What do you think, Madame, should we visit the flamenco show this evening?

We were lying in the position we had occupied, just behind the slope of a grassy mound, returning the German rifle fire across a shallow valley. In spite of my schooling and my training in the Scouts, as a sportsman, as a Sokol, and in the army and the navy, I was just an ordinary civilian with no self-discipline, and I knew it. I had always allowed my feelings and imagination full play and wide scope; I had tried to view everything simultaneously in a close and distant perspective, to identify cause and foresee consequence. Some soldier!

The mound, the grass, molehills, and on our right an oak wood, which, farther along the hill, gave way to thickly growing pines and later a shrubbery; to the left, we could see the valley, a cart track running along the hillside and down below, a light brown path winding between neglected, untilled fields, with furrows cut along their whole narrow length; a ditch or stream, some willows growing by it, and beyond it, the grassy slopes of the hill facing us, rocks, a few bushes; above us a string of German concrete bunkers with hardly visible loopholes through which, here and there, poked the barrels of heavy machine guns.

Bullets were whistling around us. The ones you hear have already missed you. The ones that do not miss, you do not hear. We returned their fire without getting carried away. There would not be any point in it and it was hard work carting ammunition about. Maybe it was just to let them know we were here? Or perhaps there was some other idea behind it. No doubt this action would be called an assault on the old German frontier on the Litija. Suddenly I heard a whooshing sound overhead . . . Foxy grabbed me close and we both pressed our heads against the ground. A mine! The Krauts were beginning to probe our position.

"Keep your ears open," said Lofty, "then you'll soon learn to tell when one is going to land on your head."

This one exploded quite close, on the other side of a low rock, and showered the two of us with earth, grass, and torn roots. There were some stones too, mixed up with the rest of the rubbish. The only effective protection against a mine is a layer of concrete above your head. Our own mortar also joined in. About twenty meters from us, it stood like a small cannon, aiming at somewhere high above. Meanwhile, I had taken over as the machine gunner's mate. Our clumsy fat friend had twisted his ankle, even before we arrived at our position.

"Talk about the death of the old gendarme," Foxy remarked, "twisting his leg just before the balloon goes up. He hasn't broken it, mind you, not even sprained it, just twisted it, so that he's neither fit nor sick. You can hardly stagger along yourself and then you find you have to drag some helpless child behind you."

"Should we open up?" I asked, holding out the cartridge belt. He gave me a withering look.

"Do you want a bomb on your thick skull?" He began to edge away leftward tugging the Breda with him. "Never stay glued to the same spot too long. They've got excellent binoculars and plenty of time." We settled down in a smooth hollow between two tree stumps. Lofty lay on his back, looking up at the sky, while I lay on my belly and inspected my carbine.

"I'd like to try it out," I said.

"Well, why not?" he replied without looking my way.

I chose for my target the branch of a young oak tree, above me and about thirty paces to the right. I fired without result; I fired again with no luck. I took very careful aim and pressed the trigger: another miss. The rifles around me were firing away steadily.

I heard a noise behind me and looked around. Iztok was lying in the grass, propped up on his elbows, with a faint smile on his face. Our own machine guns were silent but the German ones on the other side of the valley were firing steadily, crackling, resting, then barking again. I felt angry with myself when I noticed that Iztok's rifle, by some chance, happened to be pointing at me, somewhere on my right side. Why was the sly brute smiling? I moved away and lit a cigarette.

"So you're bird-shooting, are you?" he asked, rather insolently.

"I leave the moles to you," I said dryly. He crawled away toward the mine thrower.

I turned to Foxy. "Any idea what that earwig was on about?" He pretended he had not heard me.

A two-man patrol passed us on their way down the path. One of them called out to the machine gunner and me: "Having a good rest, eh?"

"You can tell them down below that if we miss supper once more, we're off home," Lofty replied without raising his voice.

Don't ask questions: I had made a mental note of this principle of good soldierly conduct. Everyone must decide for himself when to depart from it and judge the right moment. I lay there, chewing a blade of grass. It was almost evening. The smell of the earth, the freshness of young blades among the sallow old grass and the wrinkled plantain. The bitter taste of the blade I was chewing. The gentle breeze blowing down the slope. The firing on both sides had slackened by now. A bright rocket flew up into the air and began to descend in an arc over the valley. It exploded and illuminated a wide expanse of country on all sides. They were just checking up. Tramp of feet, jumbled words, supper from the cooking pot, people, a mule.

At Foxy's suggestion, we lay down together, covering ourselves with both blankets and a tent cloth of a mottled salamander hue. So we were to spend the night at our post. We had hardly settled down, before Iztok crawled out of the hazy gloom and started babbling away as usual: he was on orderly duty till midnight, it was quite chilly that evening and he thought there would be a very bright moon.

"What sort of orderly duty?" I asked and immediately bit my lip for breaking my resolution not to ask questions.

"Oh, they're rounding up the bats." He said this with a completely straight face. I swore a quiet oath never again to ask stupid questions.

The man beside me began to scratch his chest, then groped between his legs, lay quiet for a while, before he was off again. "Scabies or something," I wondered. Just an itch? Or sheer nervousness? What if it is the crabs? I held back for a time, then addressed him in steely tones, thereby once again breaking my resolution. The following dialogue ensued:

I (briskly): Listen, you! Got the crabs, have you?

He (couldn't care less): Don't pretend you haven't.

I: What . . . you mean everyone's got them?

He: (sniffs)

I: What's your name, by the way?

He (very reluctantly): Yosht. Why?

I (feigning unconcern): Oh, you know. I'd like to be able to call my crabs by their proper name when we wake up tomorrow. Also in case someone asks me later whose they are.

He (casually): Stupid idiot.

I decided I would not speak again till morning. Not that I could be really angry with him. But it was indeed a rare event in my life to sleep under the same blanket with someone without guessing, probing, or discovering in some way, who or what he was and what made him tick. It was true that Yozhe, our platoon commander, had appointed me his assistant and it was also perfectly possible he found me in some way repulsive and unattractive. Maybe he still thought, as he had told me in that yard, that I was an agent provocateur, and that it was no accident I had been made his assistant. I rejected the thought. I told myself it was all of a piece with my general mental confusion, although I was not fully convinced of this. Every so often, a rocket soared up on the other side of the valley.

I slept badly, on the installment plan, while he snored away gently like a buzz saw. During the night, we turned over twice, once to the right, once to the left. When he was lying behind me, he kept himself well away and made no contact with arm or leg and I felt only his warm breath on the back of my neck. We were woken about dawn by the sound of shooting. Brisk volleys were being exchanged as play resumed from the previous day. Yosht lay still for a moment, then folded his blanket and tent cloth into a long roll. He munched an old crust of bread that he dug out of his satchel and nibbled an onion at the same time, sharing both with me, quite automatically and with no hint of generosity. In the same way, he took my cigarette after breakfast and accepted a light.

Soon afterward we commenced a real fusillade.

Rat-a-tat, rat-a-tat, rat-a-tat . . .

He settled himself more comfortably and drew on his cigarette.

"Flaming sunshine!" I felt better after this heartfelt curse. He gave me an owlish look and the ghost of a smile flickered on his lips. He rapidly smothered it with his butt, recovered his habitual serious expression and gazed up at the sky.

Our other machine gun opened up below us. It was a longer burst of fire than usual. Our platoon occupied the ground between. There came the sound of rifle fire. The sun was coming up behind the woods to our right. The light haze and thin veils of cloud glowed orange and red, hardly a sign of good weather. I attempted an affirmative statement: "It's going to rain today."

"Better today than tomorrow," he said, and fell silent again.

"I'll try to find myself a more entertaining colleague for the next war," I declared and looked away from him at the spreading fan of the sunrise. No response. As if he had not heard.

Later, Iztok the gabbler came to visit us. Funny how different people get on your nerves, one with his never-ending stupid prattle, another with his silence. Iztok wondered whether I knew German. Yes, why? He just wanted to know. Yosht lay there as if Iztok simply did not exist, and who could blame him?

I kept on testing my rifle. I decided it was completely unreliable, one of those that shoot around corners, as they say. Absolute rubbish for a good shot, such as I believed myself to be.

The man with the voice like a foghorn was somewhere in the vicinity but so far off that I could only hear the sound without distinguishing the words.

By noon it had clouded over and started to drizzle. Yosht opened his roll and spread the tent cloth over both of us, leaving a space for our heads. Now we were living cheek by jowl in our tiny dwelling, hearing and feeling every single breath but not exchanging a word. But I was used to it by now. Every half an hour, we fired a short burst, then relapsed into our previous inactivity. A wounded man was carried past on a stretcher. "Poor clumsy bastard, couldn't dodge it, eh?" I spoke in a low voice, to myself really. He had been hit in the head, you could tell by his blood-soaked bandage.

The rain stopped almost completely but after a short interval, began to fall again, this time more heavily, unpleasant, chilly, fine drops in the still air. A meal of warm potato soup with bits of beef and suet did us a world of good. We ate slowly, in silence. Afterward, Yosht put his mess tin upside down on the grass to let it drain off, licked his spoon carefully and wedged it by the handle inside his gaiter. He tore a long square of newspaper, rolled it and worked it into the shape of a sort of gutter, into which he poured tobacco dust from his breast pocket, nibbled the edge and, with a deft, practiced movement, produced a cigarette. It flared up when lit, then subsided into a dull glow. He did not offer me a smoke but then, I still had a box of factory cigarettes. I deliberately hung back a while and only then lit up. Yosht's cigarette smelled of burned newsprint. He started scratching under his left armpit. If it itches even in the cold, that means whole squadrons of the gray tanks. Heaven help me, I've been itching myself all morning. Is it my imagination? Or have I got them now?

"Don't worry, you've got them too," Yosht said coolly. "You were bound to get them sooner or later. At least mine haven't got the Red Cross." What this meant, I did not know and did not want to ask. Typhus.

To liven things up for us, the Krauts now began to open up with their mine throwers. Yosht listened for both of us. They dropped close only once or twice. I tried not to betray the hot tension I felt inside. You don't hear the bullet that hits you, I repeated to myself, but you do hear a mine coming. And your ear must be trained to tell. I saw what mincemeat it made of a low cone of rock when one exploded. For the moment our itching stopped.

We went to relieve ourselves against a hazel tree below the path. Such a walk was always welcome. I flexed my limbs, surveyed the landscape, which seemed to be swarming with soldiery. A copse of small oak saplings a little farther down gave good cover for a crap.

I had just crouched down and was listening to the bird song, when I felt someone was looking at me from behind. I turned around. Iztok was perched on a rock above, observing me. I was furious. The man gave me no peace even at such a moment. What did this weasel want of me? He disappeared as quickly as he had arrived.

It is hard to analyze your surroundings correctly when there are two conflicting emotions at war within you: one, cut to your choice, in accord with your inner spirit, your imagination, yearning for warmth, security, and good company; the other, originating in warnings of danger, cool calculation, attack, and perceived by some inner instinct over some wavelength where neither the senses nor the imagination have any say. You have a feeling of imminent danger but try to smother it with the bland assumption that all is well. War is the best school for eradicating these mistakes.

Down in the valley, someone was practicing the trumpet. The rain had stopped.

Movement on the hill. Our relief had arrived. Yozhe collected his men and we marched away to the village. There we lined up in the village street. Someone I did not know was taking drill, giving the orders in a keen young voice.

"At ease! Number off in twos! One, two, one, two . . . Line up in two ranks! Jump to it now! By the left, dress. Close up on the right. At ease! Mark time! At ease! Mark time! Halt! What do you think this is? The bloody fire brigade? I want to hear one foot, not a hundred. And no yakking in the ranks. You're not in your backyard now. Attention! Dress by the right! At ease!"

He took a mimeographed sheet of paper from his pocket and read us the news from the Eastern Front in a slow, clear voice. The enormous successes of the Red Army . . .

I was a "number two." Yosht was in front of me, with his tight machine gun before him on the ground. We were only half listening to the news.

The children of a nearby house were gazing at us. A very young partisan was leading a mule past. Dismiss! We split up and went to our billets in the houses and farmyards. I dumped the heavy ammunition on a bench behind the house. I had seen my dusky maiden hanging out the washing next door.

Gran festival de cante y baile
Flamenco
Fandangos
Sevillanas
Seguidillas
Tarantas

Fiesta hasta la madrugada! Entertainment right through till dawn!
Con el concurso de los mejores cantaores y bailaores!
Had he met cases of troops being scared?

"Fear?" Bitter said. "Terror? That's the most avoided topic in the army. But it stands to reason that a soldier is only human . . . Yes, yes, of course . . ."

In the fearful racket of music and song, Madame, who had no idea what we were talking about, put in, "*Na, ja freilich . . .*"

A glass of sangria, perhaps? Rather a weird drink. Madame simply took a sip and then left it. Joseph and I did not mind so much. After all, we had tried most things before.

"A man really only begins to wonder whether he was afraid after the war is over," Bitter declared. "You've no time for meditation when all hell's breaking loose around you."

Achtung: fünf Getränke inbegriffen! Look here: five drinks are included!
Un ballet de arte!

"You will never hear a soldier talking about being scared. I was in the army for four years and I never heard anyone mention fear. Once, we were being bombarded by Katyushas—Stalin organ-pipes—and we were in such a weak position that fifty percent of us got hit, if not more . . . why, of course . . . there were only one hundred left alive and fit out of five hundred . . . Our tanks had run out of oil . . . we were short on ammunition . . . we'd had no food supplies for three days . . . it was sheer hell . . . the barrage went on night and day . . . I was half deaf . . . people were changing visibly . . . one man spoke to me . . . I gazed at him and had no idea who he was . . . I took a closer look at the eyes below that helmet, then recognized him as Gerhardt. Yes, Gerhardt, all spattered with mud . . . with blood caked on his sleeve . . . with a sort of dust, like white flour, in the bristles of his beard . . . Where had he got it? He had been eating flour straight from the sack. An officer, a man who had been awarded the Iron Cross, mark you. He later fell in the defense of Berlin.

"Corpses, wounds, blood . . . we soon get used to it, it affects you only at the start. *Der Mensch ist ein Gewohnheitstier,* man is an animal with habits. The most frightening thing is when you don't know what is happening, and you glimpse terror in someone else's face. Then there are the shells, of course . . ."

"*Freilich,*" Madame added parenthetically.

"It's worse when you are bombed and machine-gunned from the air . . . but when it's over, you shake yourself like a wet dog, recover your breath, let out a volley of oaths, exchange glances with someone and then march on.

"Panic-mongers? I can't really remember any cases of panic. I did hear of a case of shell shock, a soldier who climbed out of his dugout and began to make a speech, before he was hit in the back. That sort of thing is quite rare, though. Even madmen learn sense in the army, while the rest of us go crazy. Heart patients are cured, stomach ulcers disappear, rheumatic pains cease."

Bitter's face had taken on the features of a sage. He now smiled quite easily. He had changed from a stiff, officious type into a thoughtful philosopher. I had made this possible as his willing audience. He therefore began to like me and need me. He had forgotten what was happening on the stage. He had a new attitude to his excursions into the distant past, a new resolve to explain things to his own satisfaction . . . and all because of me.

Flamenco show!

How to fit five people into each square meter of space in a pavilion, seat them on long benches and serve them drinks? This is the Spanish tourist industry. In Yugoslavia, tourism is only a minor trade, with enormous investments and mediocre achievements.

On the stage, three women dancers sit at each of two tables on the left and right while the men stand; there are solo dances, turns by the whole group, songs, guitar music, colorful costumes.

"In reality, it's a question of the initiative. If a soldier has the impression that his 'all-seeing and all-knowing' commanders hold the initiative, then he is calm, loyal, optimistic. He can be induced to undertake any action and all sacrifices are regarded as normal and necessary. He hates the adversary and believes in victory. It's harder for him when he sees that the enemy has the initiative . . . especially if this lasts for any time. Then his morale begins to waver. Now the officers, and particularly the N.C.O.s, must provide a good example. A soldier should never see the slightest hint of indecision in a man giving orders. Our trained non-commissioned officers were really excellent, you know.

"But what when the main strategy has not been worked out by generals, by military men? It sometimes nearly drove us frantic. Plans would arrive from the offices of politicians who paid no attention to the position at the front . . . the actual state of affairs . . . and demanded victory at any price . . . What does that mean in the army? It means human lives. If our politicians had had as much military talent as our generals and field marshals, and if these had had as much as our N.C.O.s, how often things would have been different? How much voice did a front-line general have? What influence could he bring to bear on the course of an action, with his reports, analyses, recommendations, submitted daily to the OKW (*Oberkommando der Wehrmacht*)? Frequently, the OKW would not even dare to pass his reports on to Hitler's office. In the first year of the war, Hitler was expecting to be in Moscow and there was going to be no repeat of the Napoleonic story. Everything that accorded with this plan was right and good and made welcome, but whoever disagreed was on the verge of high treason, my dear sir . . . yes, indeed . . . The invention of good news was rewarded, while hard fact was condemned. And how much time passed before the truth dawned on us? Even today, nobody can accurately say what our losses were. You can persuade your troops to make a breakthrough here, a breakthrough there, you can persuade the remnants of a shot-up division to undertake a new offensive, you can even get a unit to fight to the last man . . . but your transport won't move without gas, you can't shoot without ammunition, you can't survive without food, you can't run when the mud is up to your knees, you can't march when your feet are frozen . . . All this is beyond the understanding of people safe in a heated office in a deep shelter. Along comes the order: tomorrow you will occupy Kursk, and you are actually bogged down God knows where, hardly able to withdraw from encirclement. These are problems but do not necessarily induce fear.

"What is fear? Nature has given it to every creature in varying degrees. A rabbit needs more, a lion less. The French and the Americans write about it; the English, Germans, and Russians don't. Neither do the Japanese. The French rather like such slimy sides of our nature, the Americans understand the book market, in the torrent of books and films about the brave heroes of the Wild West, a story of fear and the horrors of war could become a best seller."

"Do you read a lot?"

"About the war, sure. We have translations of everything. Sometimes, when I can't get to sleep, I read, but what of it? I read a very fine Japanese book, about the Kamikaze pilots. And another about the air battles over the Pacific, a very good one, clear, written by an expert."

"Is there a difference between the German and Japanese military spirit?"

"Military spirit, you say? Well, first of all, what do we mean by this? Is it tactics or morale you have in mind? Right. The Japanese are good tacticians and their morale, meaning their courage and dedication, is on a high level. But there is a certain difference between the German and the Japanese armies, yes, there certainly is. They have a rather religious attitude, we have a more professional attitude . . . perhaps that sums it up. A Japanese believes in a paradise beyond this world and in the divine origin of his Emperor, while a German believes in the victory of superior arms. Doubts do occur on both sides, of course. On the clasps of our belts, we had inscribed *Gott mit uns*, God with us, but that was the only contact we had with religion. Any one of us could doubt the existence of God, but no one dared to admit even a moment's doubt of victory . . .

"Fear? A regular army, officially at least, does not admit the concept. But every good commander must recognize it. A man must fear his superior. The colonel must fear his general, the major his colonel, the captain his major, and so on, right down to the private soldier, who must—in due degree—fear all those appointed above him, the military police and the court-martial. No one should fear his subordinate. And one way or another, the enemy is a filthy coward and a blockhead until he wins. Then he is a monster, a criminal, a fool, who will come to no good in the end—for God is with us . . ."

With his eyes half closed, he smiled a cunning smile. In this serious, simple man, cunning was something new. Bitter was becoming a soldier again, remembering how much terror he could impose on those below him and how much he had to show to those above. The game had its own carefully defined conventions, its unwritten but pervasive laws. I had to laugh. He regarded me with gentle indulgence.

Típico Espectaculo Flamenco!

Some activity at our position: new units were arriving, the firing was more intense, there was evidence of increased activity on their side too; a howitzer launched some shells in our direction.

We're moving against the German bunkers tonight. What?

"Our" bunker was the corner one . . . the one above the rocks . . .

But don't ask any questions! Just as well we have those rocks up there.

Yozhe, our commander, is calm and serious.

There is the sack with the grenades.

Bombers needed! Any volunteers? We want two, three at the most in any case. I volunteered first, without too much thought. The second to volunteer was Gartner, a student from Ljubljana, not really an athletic type, a scraggly fellow in spectacles. What a pair we were to take on Hitler with our bombs, old chum! I had been hoping to get more reliable partners, with some experience, so that I could watch what they did and follow them; not the sort who would be relying on me to give a lead. What did the Serbian mother say? Don't go first or last, my son, it's always a Slovene who goes first, with his snout or arse for sale.

Angry with myself, I rummaged in the sack of grenades. Most of them were Italian tomatoes; after the reports I had heard, I did not trust them very much. The German Stillers seemed clumsy. With joy, I discovered three Yugoslav prewar grenades and appropriated them. I also found a smaller black one. And what was this? A good Ustaše grenade. I slipped it into my pocket: you'll be my darling, my dusky little friend, just like the one I seduced last night. Someone interrupted my train of thought. Who? Iztok. I might have guessed. He had not volunteered. He was standing to one side, looking at me as if he could not get me off his mind. Gartner helped himself to some Stillers. I would have to take care that he would not drop any on my head.

One of us was holding an enormous pair of scissors for cutting tinplate; God knows where he had got them from. For slitting the barbed wire, of course. Everybody got something. A whole laundry basket full of ammunition; the domestic touch.

Yozhe was talking, without noticing whether we were listening or not.

The frontier is weakly defended . . . sometimes you get Krauts only in every other bunker . . . reservists and roughnecks . . . we're moving off at nightfall . . . last week, some of our men were "up there" . . . they came back with their pockets and bags full of cigarettes, margarine, and biscuits . . . two revolvers, a Schmeisser . . . brand new . . .

My mouth was watering, not at the thought of margarine and biscuits, but a revolver and a Schmeisser; "behold . . . it is I myself," says Saint Luke.

I was quite excited by the new atmosphere. Yosht was not smiling, however, as he regarded me with a flash of resentment in his yellow eyes. He had lost his assistant and would have to take on another. But why should he hold it against me? Maybe he was right; times beyond number, I had been very dissatisfied with myself. Beneath my apparently hard skin, I was too easily affected by the course of events. I found it hard to ignore my ups and downs.

. . . we'll be going through the proceeding as far as the road down there . . . then on into the furrows . . . slowly, cautiously forward . . . mustn't move a finger if they fire any rockets up over the valley . . . if they sniff us out, press on . . . find cover . . . if you can only squeeze through to those rocks . . . you'll have good cover there . . . beyond the machine gunner's angle of fire . . . then just see that you get up to the blind spot beneath the bunker . . . pull the firing pin . . . and shove it through the slot!

. . . the slot? The slot is so wide . . . you can't see it from this distance . . . take care it goes right in . . . and get your timing right . . . otherwise the Krauts will fling it out again . . . and you might get it on your head . . .

"See you all in Berlin," remarked the man with the voice like a foghorn. No one laughed.

On our way down through the wood, I had a brush with Iztok, who was constantly dogging my heels and swinging his weapon with reckless abandon. I stopped for a moment and threw my arm around his shoulders as if I wanted to embrace him tenderly. As we walked on, I spoke to him quietly but persuasively.

"Now listen here, Iztok, and mark what I say. If I catch you behind me when the Krauts open fire, you'll regret it, understand! Never carry a firearm so clumsily it might go off by accident, understand! Walk where you like but stop treading on my heels, if you know what's good for you. Got the message?"

He just looked at me and his eyes seemed to be very wide open. He hurried forward. Yes, lad; I may be in the right, I may be in the wrong, but I don't care. I'm feeling better now, that's the main thing.

We were down in the valley, lying in the marshy grass beside the ditch, when a rocket soared up high in the sky, then curved back in an arc, giving such a bright light you could have read fine print by it. The Krauts started firing and I thought they had already discovered us, a most disturbing thought. It was quite a dark night, with a cloudy sky, made to order for our venture. The light haze which lay over the marshy meadow covered us gently and hid us from questing binoculars. Of course, the bad weather of the preceding day had its bad side too. While we were crawling along that ditch or brook or whatever it was, our arms and legs were sinking in the squelching morass, our clothing was soaked through, and once my knee went almost a foot down in the mire . . . but nothing better awaited us when we arrived at the field . . . what had looked from above like a cornfield with fairly deep cut furrows, now turned out to be a sea of mud and clay. We were as filthy as pigs when we rushed up the grassy slope, between the low bushes. Only a little, only a little farther now . . . Let's hope they don't fire a rocket now! One shot up immediately, as if in answer to my thought. Now all hell broke loose, bullets were whistling about our ears, earth and grass were flying through the air. I heard the man with the booming voice say, "I've had it." He spoke in a tone of melancholy resignation that only struck me as ludicrous very much later. Some of us were returning their fire but that thought had not occurred to me. Yosht was directing his fire upward and their guns were booming out all around us. For a moment, darkness, utter, blinding, darkness fell. Then the next rocket flared out, followed by two more at least, and a light as strong as high noon flooded the valley. I gave a mighty sigh of relief when I hurled myself under the cover of those rocks. Where on earth was Gartner? Yozhe rushed up to join me, then someone else. What the hell? Was I the first of the lot to get up here? Sport, lads, helps you to keep fit! I wanted to catch Yozhe's eye. Out of the question. He was staring up and down all the time and shouting, what and to whom I had no idea and could not hear. He did not even notice me. Another moment of darkness—I rushed upward around the rock, by sheer good luck grabbed a handful of some wild plant and dragged myself up . . . there was such a volley of firing that I could hear nothing else, apart from an obbligato of human screaming . . . I felt the earth quaking below me, but whether it really was so, I did not know . . . explosions, fire, thunder-clap . . . were they also throwing grenades? Surely it was not our men . . . we were up here at the bunker . . . why should our lot be firing at us? Here we are! In the blind spot. Quickly now . . . I strike the percussion cap of my grenade against the jagged rock . . . twenty-one . . . not too soon, not too late . . . a long tongue of flame flickers over my head and lights up our surroundings . . . What, was Gartner here too? And Yozhe? How was that?

I do not know whose missile exploded in the bunker first: my own, Yozhe's or Gartner's. One more! Things had altered. While firing continued to my right and left, there was no sound from above me. I was only the fourth or fifth to push through the opening in the barbed wire . . . Yozhe was standing at the entry to the bunker, holding a long bright strip of newspaper in his hands like a torch. Yosht had set up his machine gun on the narrow platform behind the bunker.

The whole thing seemed outrageously simple.

Iztok also came crawling up. I had the impression he was avoiding my eye. The sound of furious barking! Where from?

A fine German sheepdog had hauled itself up to the entrance to the bunker. Evidently its back was broken as it had no control over its hind parts, but the loyal creature bared its teeth at us, foaming with fury. Yozhe put it out of its misery with a shot between the eyes; it jerked and lay still. There were three figures lying in the bunker. We could hardly make anything out in the flicker-ing light, not even the color of their uniforms. They seemed to be covered with dust or plaster. They were lying one across the other. One man's hand stuck out, open, white, twisted around behind his back.

We heard a burst of fire, quite close; it was Yosht.

Where were those Schmeissers and revolvers? I turned a corpse over, taking hold of its outstretched arm. This was no lightweight. No weapon in his belt. The head drooped, close cropped, with a smoothly shaven bull neck.

Soon we were on our way down, making better time than on the way up, and the enemy was firing at us from all angles. One of us was hit, I had no idea what by, a single bullet or a volley. The flares were floating overhead, lighting our way down into the valley. The air was full of flying grass. Seeing a whole line of eddies of earth and debris spinning around me, I took a dive, rolled over and felt something strike my cheekbone . . . Is this it? I dully wondered. Then I was across the brook and into the bushes on the other side. There were scurrying figures all around me.

We did not stop until we dropped behind the slope on our side.

What had really happened? Had they caught us by surprise? I behaved just like everybody else. I was back now, I would not ask questions but wait for someone to tell us. But not a word. Yozhe sent some men out on patrol, God knows where, Yosht was firing his machine gun again, Iztok was lying on his stomach, breathing heavily. I felt something running down my cheek. Blood. I explored the wound on my cheekbone with my fingers. It was a short, shallow cut. I must have banged my head somewhere. I tried to remember. Hell's teeth, had I been so clumsy as to catch myself a blow with that rifle I would have been happy to throw away? No excitement. The action was over. The platoon were to meet down by the hayloft.

Some people had lit a fire down there and were sitting around it. One man took a potato from a bag, skewered it on a twig, and was baking it in the flames. The army has a different way of doing everything compared to the scouts.

I learned we had destroyed three Kraut bunkers and escaped in the nick of time. Help had arrived instantly from the valley. Their white rockets acted as flares but the red one had been a call for reinforcements. The red one? Had I not even seen it? I would never know what had really happened that night. They were still firing up there. I dried myself and peeled off the clay and mud. Yozhe was standing by the fire, waiting for the mud to fall off on its own. Yosht smiled at my ardent efforts to clean my clothing.

"You've got another assistant now," I said, taking care to make it sound like a statement, not a question.

"Aye."

"You won't miss me, I imagine," I asserted.

"Miss you, eh?" Not a wisp of a smile. "You're always exaggerating," he added, and I now realized what had upset him about me.

Yozhe had a word with someone who, judging from the state of his clothes, had not been with us. He had joined us from our side of the valley.

And what about Gartner? Where on earth was Gartner? He was a medical student, he had gone down the valley with the casualties. Then why had he volunteered for the bombing party, immediately after I did? War is a string of questions, unframed and unanswered.

If I compare two short excerpts from the whole action, I told myself, for instance, when I was lying motionless in the marsh by the brook, in the light of the first rocket, and then that moment, when I rushed from the secure cover of the rocks up to the bunker: what happened then, what were my feelings, and what could I discover about myself?

I was lying there and my only chance at that moment was that the Krauts would not spot me. I was a mass of gooseflesh, I could feel something draining, circling, and working within me. I was as tense as a coiled spring. I waited and listened and that moment seemed as long as any bloody Monday. I seemed to have a cramp in the region of my stomach. The light grew brighter. Now I was dying for a crap. No definite feeling or emotion; just a gentle, chilly tide—this must be what they call horror. Somewhere, eyes were peering into binoculars, raking the valley. There was nothing you could do. You dared not even move. I gritted my teeth. Yes, I could still remember it.

But it had been different when I had chosen my moment, rushed up around the rock and climbed that beetling slope, with machine-gun fire hissing around me. There was not the slightest trace of bodily reaction, such as the urge to crap or a twinge in the stomach or a chill on the skin. I did feel a fury against those Krauts in their pillbox, faceless goons, filthy reservists, behind their safe concrete walls, against those bastards who had come from so far away, to make us their slaves . . . and so on, and so on. Strange but necessary. And I had an overwhelming desire to own a Schmeisser; in all innocence, I had set my heart on this. But if I now looked at the rather gloomy expression on our commander Yozhe's face, I had to smile at myself. Easy on, lad—but what about my ambitions? I liked to be first, I liked to put on a show. There were two elements at play here: the sporting instinct and the craving for glory. A whole host of ingredients really, many of them not at all pretty.

Yosht was right, I did exaggerate. But so what? A man cannot change his nature. Both the experienced Yozhe and the inexperienced Gartner had done well. And yet no doubt they each had a completely different scale of emotions and desires. As for Yosht, he had got up there almost as soon as I did, in spite of his heavy and awkward firearm. Now he was sitting beside the fire without a trace of pride; for him, everything that had happened was normal and necessary. For that reason, he had no need to talk about his inner feelings nor any interest in learning the experiences of others. Was I wrong?

Our political delegate, Loize by name, was giving us a general review of the position at the fronts and the approaching end of the German armies. He spoke in a loud voice, as he had been trained, without expecting confirmation or contradiction of his words. The National Liberation Army had been transformed from smaller units, detachments, and companies into a large, well-organized army, into corps, division brigades, and battalions. We now had also heavy armor and artillery. Soon, we should also have an air force. The population was with us to a man. Now the time had come to deal the wounded beast his final deathblow. The morale of the German troops was sinking lower and lower, and the invader's lackeys, the Blues and the Whites, were quaking in their shoes, terrified by the just punishment which awaited them.

He paused for breath. His speech did not arouse any particular interest among the partisans.

"This is all very fine," one of the men remarked, "but how much longer is all this going to last? I joined up over two years ago."

"Give somebody else a chance to win some credit," replied the man who had been conferring with Yozhe. "Just think how many have joined us since the Italians surrendered."

There was a note of self-congratulation about all this, and we all felt it. Probably something a little less abstract would have been more suitable, after what we had gone through during our raid on the bunkers.

When we moved off down the valley the sky was turning gray with the first light of dawn.

Inside the house some lay down for a rest, while the rest of us sat around the table. I persuaded the lady of the house to make us a drink of lime tea.

Through the latticed windows, the gray light of morning lit up one side of our faces, leaving the other half in gloom. What would it have revealed if one could have seen through those foreheads? Weariness, questions, hopes, forebodings. No one spoke aloud about the forthcoming German offensive, although we all knew about it.

"The Germans are carting slave workers to Germany from all parts of Europe, yes, even at this very moment," I said, to divert the thoughts of those present who were still awake toward wider horizons. This got the ball rolling. I told them what I had learned about the German concentration camps.

"On the Volga, the Germans have bitten off more than they can chew."

I reported what I had heard over the radio. In Stalingrad, there was not simply house-to-house fighting, but even floor-to-floor and room-to-room. "The myth of the invincibility of the German armies has been destroyed and that is of the greatest importance for the further course of the war."

Why, they are beginning to talk in Berlin? The serpent bites its tail, the serpent dies, but its head keeps on hissing.

I saw that some of them enjoyed listening to what I had to say. They had livened up. In the main, I was repeating what Loize had been telling them by the bonfire but I was putting it to them in a different way.

"The war has passed its turning point, the climax is behind us. Now we shall see how the drama is played out, until the final defeat of those bastards. Every day, every night, there are air raids on Germany. It's getting harder and harder to keep the front supplied."

"But how much longer is it going to go on?"

"And what's going to happen meanwhile?"

"It can't be too long but it can't end overnight either. The German serpent has to be dissected, segment by segment. When the axe reaches its head, that will be the end. And it will never be whole again. In fact we're even well-off. At this moment, there are many parts of Europe where people are much worse off."

I launched into a vivid account of German prisons, of investigations, of the shooting of hostages, of sudden raids in the towns, of torture by the Gestapo.

Meanwhile, we march out and one fine evening liquidate some German rein-forced-concrete pillboxes, after which we pop into this attractive village for a cup of tea. We were not so badly off really.

This idea appealed especially to one young partisan, who burst out laugh-ing and thumped the table with his fist. "Sure, you're dead right," he said with conviction. "Go on, tell us some more. You're taking a load off my mind."

Iztok had been lying in bed. He now got up, joined us, and sat down beside me. His expression had changed completely, his eyes were bright with confi-dence. He said nothing but listened intently, as if he wanted to pluck the words off my lips.

Hitler went raving mad when he did not reach Moscow and the battle of Stalingrad came later. Some people believe that the war was decided on the outskirts of Moscow. Young lads flung themselves and their bombs beneath the tank trucks. They only had ten or fifteen kilos to go.

Imagine what it meant for Hitler, not to be able to read the speech he had prepared in Moscow. Napoleon had reached Moscow just as the capital started to burn, and he had to retreat in the depths of a cold Russian winter. Hitler had calculated that he would reach Moscow in time to make it his winter quarters. But there had been one or two minor errors in his calculations.

The Russians had just issued the last of the flour to the population when German aircraft appeared over the capital. They did not drop bombs, they did not strafe the town; they dropped leaflets. Take your flour home, the message went, and bake your bread; tomorrow we shall be along to eat it!

But they did not come. Nasty of them, wasn't it?

The lads enjoyed the joke.

And the tea was very much to our taste.

Such major and minor trifles determine a human being's mood. A sort of family warmth now prevailed among us. Iztok's enthusiasm for my sto-rytelling had smothered all my black suspicions concerning him. In my unusual surge of love for these ordinary beings, I had to curb my tongue, so as not to betray my emotion. No one will ever know all the hopes and fears these boys feel, I told myself. I can go on prattling about myself, if I survive, but they'll never be able to express themselves. Long after the war is over, they'll meet somewhere, argue about whose round it is, laugh, curse, and tell their anecdotes about the incidents they saw, a jumble of reminiscences, with no head nor tail to it, as they say, and afterward they'll split up again, each with his own inner void. They will not be able to tell each other what it was really like.

That morning, we seemed to have brought victory already within our grasp.

"And what about afterward? What will life be like after the war, after our victory?" some people wanted to know.

If we were now to sketch some golden dawn for them, would they not then want to know what to expect later and later still, after death even? Mere dreams, castles in the clouds? Ah no, dear friends, it is a little early to talk about that. Should I mention the fact that, in the whole course of our history, I have not observed a single sensible politician (with the exception of Henrik Tuma)? Nothing but vile subservience and, more or less, treacherous self-seeking greed and pride. Slovenes and politics!

"Will we be in charge afterward?" a country boy asked.

"Who else?" another put in.

(Spirits, once conjured up, never desert you.)

I directed our conversation to another topic: What does a man need? Health, money, some said. Others suggested peace, justice, pleasure.

"It's best if we consider the unborn child," I said. "He has everything he needs, neither too little nor too much. He's in paradise in his mother's womb. Food on tap, warmth, security, settled relations with the whole, no worries; there, a man is still a part of the whole. Later, he is born and his exile begins. The most unhappy man is the most isolated. And who is that?"

"A hermit, of course!"

"Come off it! What about a prisoner doing solitary?"

"Lunatics?"

They produced an odd collection of examples. Sick people, criminals, those with a contagious disease, lepers for example? Old folks? Castaways? Scholars?

"No," I told them. "The loneliest people are the leaders, the generals, the tyrants who sit quite alone, at the peak of the pyramid they have built themselves."

Our talk became more perfunctory but the lively atmosphere persisted.

Gartner came in and told us that our friend with the booming voice was dead.

In one morning, I had experienced, at least four times, a sense of inferiority, and I was feeling rather perplexed.

That voice amidst the uproar, that strange stentorian roar and the words, "I've had it." If he had only just died, as Gartner had said, that meant that someone had looked after him, had halted in that rain of bullets, had picked him up and carried him down the valley and up the other slope or to our side. And I had merely been amused by the tone of those words. By his call for help, by his dying cry. Poor show, Berk! Sit down.

Next, how wrong I had been about "scraggly" Gartner, whom I had taken for an unfit urban weakling. He had reached the bunker no later than I did, he tossed a clumsy German Stiller through the narrow slot, crawled through an opening in the barbed wire to the bunker, then came out and saw the casualties back safely before rejoining us, looking exactly as he had before the commencement of the action. He was a medical student too, but he didn't make a song and dance about it. Healthy and honest to the core. Not at first sight attractive to the girls. His talents lay elsewhere. I looked at him with respect and discerned truly fine features in his face. Poor show, Berk! Be seated. Alternatively: reexamination in subject with title "Gartner."

Furthermore, if I consider very carefully what I saw of my surroundings during my climb uphill to the bunkers, and later on during our rush downhill, how much time did I have to glance at another man's face? Very little, almost none at all. I was too wrapped up in myself, too concerned with my own skin, my rotten ambitions, my thirst for glory, my desire to show off. No, no, I never sought perfection, why should I? And one should try to reconcile military efficiency with one's character and principles hidden deep below the skin. But, without going deeply into military theory, it is clear that you cannot acquit yourself efficiently in battle unless you pay regard to the course of events, which even so, in the heat of the moment, is likely to be obscure enough, and also to the actions and reactions of the men around you.

Finally: what else did I give the men in my pep talk but hope of imminent victory (although Anton was probably right in his prediction that the whole thing would drag on much longer), wrapped up in the most senseless trifles? Altogether, it smacked too much of egoism, demagoguery, and low cunning: how useful it is to endear yourself to those around you; to improve your position; to remove possible doubts and suspicions; to win over someone like

Iztok, for example; to secure yourself a good name; to have your importance recognized in the group? Season to taste with a discreet touch of emotion. How shoddy can you get? Marks for style: unsatisfactory, Berk!

To apply, in life's strategy, the proper measure of solemnity and pleasantry with your fellow man and to remain utterly genuine and express yourself with inexorable honesty: that is the hardest task. Sometimes the naked truth is as lethal as a dirty lie. To decide at any moment the right dose of reality to be blended with (benign or necessary) deceit is impossible. This matter requires a great deal more thought.

I retired to my dusky chamber.

Iztok was the unit scout; I did not know this, nor had I any idea what his duties were. So I could have hardly known that he had now been detailed for a job and that he had been told to take another man along.

He came looking for me and asked, "Coming with me, Berk?"

Why not? But where? Oh, down to take a look at Vishnya Vas. Fine, but oughtn't we to let someone know about it? Don't worry, it's all fixed up. Okay, let's go. But how are we going to slip through? I then learned that we were off on a "recon patrol." Good show, what!

It was a pleasant day in spite of the bulky clouds scudding across the sky in whole convoys. We sauntered slowly down the highway, chattering away without a care in the world. Iztok said not a word about our quarrel in the wood and neither did I. What was the point anyway?

We dropped in at a house in one village, where Iztok was already well known. They dished us up some leftovers from lunch: polenta with fried pork and milk. Meanwhile, they reported on the Germans' movements. They told us they were worried and expected them to turn up here in a day or two. There had apparently been fighting in Ribnica and the Cankar Brigade had suffered heavy losses.

Iztok said that not only a scorpion had a sting in its tail. We had a large army and even our own artillery now. He reported, at length, the story of our attack on the old German frontier, how we had demolished the machine-gun nests and thrashed the Krauts in their bunkers . . . I just watched him. If I had not been in that action myself, I would still have believed at least a quarter, if not all he said. How we pounded, pulverized, and generally played havoc with the Krauts . . . But he did stop short of claiming that we drove them, living or dead, back to the suburbs of Berlin. The worst thing for me was to observe that quietly ironic smile on the lips of some of those country folk. They knew exactly what had happened—but Iztok was not aware of this. Oh boy, you should have been there!

We took our leave and moved off. He looked at me.

"You've got to keep their spirits up." There was a wicked smile on his lips.

"Wouldn't it have been enough to tell them the truth? Surely that was good enough, wasn't it?"

"Truth is something you tell your friends." This was imparted like a gem of wisdom.

"You mean they aren't our friends? I haven't had a meal like that since I joined the army."

"Keep in with me and you'll do even better than that, Berk. These folks are scared of me; they have no idea how much I have on them. I drop a hint, then change the subject, so they're never really sure what I'm on about."

"They're on our side, aren't they?"

"Well, yes and no. In this village, they're regarded as well off. If the Germans come, they'll soon be in there scarfing down sausage and omelets. We'll pop in again for a short while on our way back. The old man's got a stock of tobacco."

All quiet in the valleys.

We halted at the odd house, had a word with the folks, chewed an apple, drank a glass of brandy, smoked a cigarette, and moved on. We heard that people were fleeing along the road toward Ljubljana. That the Western Dolenjska unit had suffered heavy casualties. That the road had been dug up here and there. That someone had seen German tanks only eight or ten kilometers to the south. We packed our rucksacks with apples, pears, dried fruit, bread. "Have you any salt?" Iztok asked me. No. Why? "Here take some, wrap it up in paper, you never know when it will come in handy." And a bag of flour, too. For pasta. You never know what tomorrow will bring. Hang on—why did you throw that butt away? Are you mad? Stick it in your pocket. You'll thank yourself for it later. Have you any paper? Look, Berk, you mustn't only think about today. See, I have a needle and a bit of thread too. And a flint. That time in the Dolomites taught me a thing or two. Yes, we've had to bloody well rough it sometimes.

I was slowly beginning to understand him. A prematurely grown-up child, who had suddenly attached himself to me.

"You know," he said while we sat chewing our dried fruit on a thick, recently felled tree trunk, "I get really scared when everything is quiet and peaceful like this. The calm before the bloody storm. Ever since the Whites caught us in that nice, quiet cottage . . . We were having a mug of sour milk and cooling our poor feet . . . chatting with the farmer's daughter . . . meanwhile, her old woman had gone off to fetch the Whites . . . suddenly the whole place was swarming with them, in the doorways, at the windows, all around the house . . . a hail of bullets . . . then they were holding the man beside me . . . I can still remember the face of the one who grabbed him from behind . . . Since then I've always been suspicious when things are quiet . . ."

He scanned the vicinity.

"And didn't they capture you?"

"No. I got away. God knows how. I left my boots there, my blanket, my kit . . . my rifle too . . . What my idea was, I don't know . . . I threw myself to one side. Like this . . . down on the ground . . . then on all fours . . . leaping and skipping like a bloody rabbit . . . shot through the legs of the man in the doorway, into the hall . . . something flashed over my back . . . I was hit on the head too . . . I howled . . . flew through the door and landed on my snout . . . One of them had tripped me up . . . and maybe he saved my life, for I heard something whistle overhead at that moment . . . Anyway, I escaped. Sometimes it pays to be on the short side."

So that irked him too.

He was gazing at somewhere in the distance.

"The Whites murdered my mama, you know."

Poor little chap . . . "My mama"—how tender, how intimate it sounded. Neither of us spoke.

I stole a glance at him, expecting to see brooding and self-pity. But he was sitting there, with lips pressed together and eyes half closed, as if he could see something unpleasant in the distance.

"I made them pay for it." He gritted his teeth.

So the child could also be a little beast. A scout. And not without reason.

171

"So you've seen the firing squads at work?"

He nodded. Suddenly his face cleared, as he stopped reminiscing and returned to the here and now. A partisan unit was marching by.

"Would you like to be in the reconnaissance?"

"Well, to start with . . . not at the moment, probably . . ."

"You wouldn't regret it . . ."

"But I'm all right as I am."

"That's what I like about you, Berk. I don't find this with others but you're like a knife—straight and to the point."

I was beginning to think that this war would be one continual hike for me.

We had a few words with a farmer in his yard. Lads, lads, he repeated, deep in thought, what will come of it, what will come of it?

What's going to happen? What next?

Can't you hear?

From far away came the dull intermittent boom of cannon fire.

The Germans.

We walked on along the country road. On and on we hiked. Where is this Vishnya Vas? Just over this hill. "I know the very spot for us," Iztok told me with pleasure. The butcher's. Smoked shoulder of pork, we'll stuff ourselves with it. And a bit of cabbage wouldn't be amiss.

There was a cart in a cornfield. Two sturdy horses were cropping the grassy verge, beating off the flies with their tails. A farmer was standing beside them, motionless, looking in our direction, with a hand on the neck of a chestnut horse. He was in his shirtsleeves, with an open waistcoat and a rough hat turned inside out on his head. Iztok waved to him but got no response. "How are things?" The farmer pretended not to hear. "Bloody fascist swine," Iztok muttered to himself.

The tepid atmosphere, the faint breath of air in the foliage of the tall alders by the stream and beyond the fields, a grassy slope and then the trees, a beech wood apparently. Over the gentle hillside, the clouds were creeping westward.

We walked beside the stream and came out on the narrow high road. We had set out along it when Iztok changed his mind. "Let's take a shortcut," he proposed. At a small bridge carrying the road over the stream we turned aside and made our way through the grass, which here grew thick and high on the marshy ground and rustled as we plowed through it.

"They'll have more to tell us at Vishnya Vas," Iztok said.

"What about?"

He gave me a rather mocking glance.

"Don't you know why we're out on patrol?"

"No, I don't."

"Some people say the Germans are already in Bukovec and others say they've avoided this valley. Maybe you haven't had a chance to talk with partisans from this area?"

"No, I haven't."

"Well, I have."

There was little joy for me in all this riddle-me-ree. I had no idea where Bukovec or Vishnya Vas were situated, or which partisans had joined us from where—and anyway, what had all this to do with me? I was a mere ranker now. I did what I was told. And that was that. I started to whistle an Italian melody I had learned in the internment camp.

With my rifle slung over my shoulder and both hands in my pockets, and with a full stomach, I was enjoying this outing in the sunny weather. And it all counts as service.

A beautiful large moth was perched on a blade of the marsh grass.

The air was suddenly filled with the hiss, crackle, and whistle of bullets from a nearby wood. Iztok dived for the ground. For a moment I stood transfixed. Then we were both running like bats out of hell. He was in front and I could hardly keep up with him while the bullets flew past our ears. Again, I ought to point out that I had a good time for the eight hundred meters but in escaping from that hail of fire, I could not catch up with the lad in front until we were back over the bridge and across the road.

He looked around. There were the trees, the grass in front of them, but no sign of any human being. Iztok's face was flushed, his cheeks were on fire, his mouth was hanging open. As soon as we had slackened our pace, he started gasping and cursing.

Who had been shooting at us?

The Germans! You'll learn in time to recognize the enemy by his fire. And up there, they've no idea the Krauts are here already.

We hurried back to the farmer who was turning his horses around.

"Unharness them!"

In vain the farmer tried to argue with Iztok's order. "What about my horses?" wailed the peasant, a man of about fifty.

"You'll get them back in the village."

We threw the harness straps over the horses' backs and rode off without bothering to remove the collars. We rode along the country road, between grassy verges, at the heavy trot of our requisitioned steeds. I had taken the piebald, Iztok the chestnut. Mine was more docile; the chestnut wanted to get back to his master. Iztok was a poor rider. I took his mount by the bridle and we ambled on.

"God help us," moaned Iztok, "to think that up top they've no idea the Krauts have got this far."

The chestnut was playing up. When we reached the first house, it began to buck and turn and there was no way of driving it forward. Iztok decided we should continue on foot. We dismounted, left the horses at a farmhouse and rapidly set off up the road. We made no farther stops, either at farmhouses or partisan units. We both stank of horse sweat.

Why had not the Krauts let us get nearer before opening fire? They could have had a sitting target.

Or they could have let us advance into the wood and attacked us with their bare hands. I felt terrified at the thought of it. Why has a human being such an imagination? To feel those hands which could have closed around his throat? To hear the words and shouts of those unseen assailants? To see those grinning faces thrust into his own? To feel the blows that might have fallen? Death is probably a mercy by comparison with the sort of things that can happen to a captured bandit. Never again will I approach a wood with my hands in my pockets and my rifle slung over my shoulder. Okay, it's one experience more. But what sort of an army is this where a unit has to send a couple of characters like us out on reconnaissance? To discover the enemy's whereabouts? Or maybe there was some hidden motive behind it all? Something that even the canny Iztok knew nothing about? But let's have none of these reflections, let's put no awkward questions, let's not exaggerate. Let's simply say it's been an interesting day. But I had committed another military blunder. I had not thrown myself to the ground when they opened fire. I had better make a mental note of that. How we got away with it, I shall never know. Maybe the Germans in that wood belonged to the anti-Hitler movement we hear so much about!

Back at our station, we found a hive of activity, some men drilling on the road, others cleaning their rifles, some moving at the double, others mounted, while the locals were worried sick. Obviously everyone knew the enemy was advancing. Our higher ranks knew more, our lower ranks knew less, but the farmers knew all there was to know. The higher-ups talked things over, the tankers pretended not to listen, the farmers said nothing. The boom of cannons could be heard in the distance. An aircraft flew low over the valley, so low we could clearly see its German markings, a menacing cross on a white background. A reconnaissance plane. Meanwhile we ate, walked, carried out our bodily functions, and awaited the inevitable.

"Take shelter! What's the meaning of all this?" yelled the commander of the second unit. "I don't want to see anyone on the road!" And a moment later: "Can't you see he's taking photographs?"

Iztok had decided we should sleep on the bed and the rest on either the floor or the benches. The lads crouched on the bread oven and watched us with bright eyes. On the great, solid, maplewood table from the last century, flickered the tiny flame of a votive lamp, the sort that burns before a saint's picture, in a little green vessel.

"Get some sleep," he told me. "We'll be on the move soon enough."

"Where to?"

"How do I know?"

"Maybe across the old frontier and over the Sava into Styria?"

"I've no idea. The Krauts are pressing on from all sides. The brigade staff were here yesterday. Everything's fully prepared. They've brought up considerable forces. We won't have time to be bored." Then he stifled a laugh. "Crossing the Sava? You must be stoned out of your mind. Go to sleep. We'll be on the move as soon as we get our boots on."

We were the only ones who had taken their boots off. Iztok had commandeered some *shufechne* for me, strips of white linen; these were far better for a long march than ordinary socks. There was the sound of footsteps outside. Who's that wandering around the house? "They're from the Cankar and Gubec battalions," Iztok told me. "The Krauts are driving them all up into the hills."

"Can't you two shut up?" Yosht, who was parked on the floorboards by the bed, had had enough.

Iztok dropped his voice to a whisper. "The morning the Germans came, we were out in the yard playing ball. Mama called to me from the window: 'Stan, put your pullover on, you'll catch your death of cold.'" He was shaken by a short, spasmodic shudder, possibly a laugh. Then he added: "Yes, they sure pissed on us from a great height, those bloody Krauts!"

When the firing started . . . It was like a blow to the central nervous system . . . a split second of immobility . . . then spin around . . . and get away, as quickly as possible . . . I had looked around, it was true. But when? Straight away? Shortly afterward? That, I could not fathom. Once again, I saw that strip of grass on the edge of the forest . . . not a soul in sight.

Drop it. You must sleep, rest. Calm down. Iztok had been playing ball in the yard, a child still, a sentimental teenager, a bit of a mother's pet, but keen to get on in life. Unhappy he would not be growing any taller.

In a gentle daze after the efforts of the day, with my lungs full of the healthy country air, I started to dose, woke up again, and then fell asleep.

You wake from a torrent of vivid colorful dreams and think they have some important meaning for your life; you go back over them immediately, and put them into words, so that they will not fade from your memory.

I was standing on the brink of a dry riverbed. Grooved sandbanks ran its whole length. Down and past me flowed a long line of cattle, brown, black, beating out a brisk, even tread, their heads lowered, black with white horns. None of the beasts looked my way. It was as if I had not been there. I knew this long procession was heading straight for the slaughter and I knew they realized it too. On the high bank opposite me stood a tall, thin man with his very long arms raised aloft. At the same time, in a voice that seemed to come from a loudspeaker, he was intoning: "I have eaten his body and drunk his blood . . ." Beside me, someone said in a perfectly normal voice: "And very tasty too." Are we cannibals then? I wanted to ask the question but the words would not come. And there, on the spot, I began to eat the tasty river sand, with the running herd of cattle trampling me, for I too must eat his body and drink his blood . . . And I that he was I . . . I myself, who was translating from some Romance language (not Latin, nor Spanish, nor French, nor Italian either) the lines of an ancient poet . . . I could not make any sense of the poem and yet I had to hurry, for the waters of the rising river could be heard thundering in the distance . . . and only the lines of this incomprehensible poem could stem the cataclysmic flood . . . Desperately I ate the sands, that is those lines in a foreign language, and from them composed words in my own . . . weak and frail, they fell on the ground . . . and I knew they should grow, should become strong and mighty . . . should stop the advancing surge . . . Verses like these: "Aim for the heights . . . the heights be your aim . . ." It was no use; I could not do it in the time . . . I sweated with the strain . . . hurried . . . tried to pull it together . . . and now the task was done:

> Aim for the heights,
> for the fresh blue of the morning sky,
> then bend low
> red black into her body
> live in desire
> perish in love
> be reborn in fire
> shun the eyes of the dead.

I woke up and without realizing where I was, I hurried to put my dream into words. This was all very important, a matter of life and death; why, I should discover later. In my fitful drowsing I knew it. Soon I was asleep again.

"Get a move on!"

"Let's be having you!"

Cries, shouts, odd words, bustle, footsteps, the clank of a mess tin on some other metal object. Iztok and I tugged our boots on.

We assembled on the village street. It was still night. The machine guns were parked on the deck in front of the company. Mules, the field kitchen, horses . . . We were off. As the command was given, we all moved quietly and smoothly.

We made our way down the road in Indian file. The heads of some of the locals peered out through the windows, one woman, tightly wrapped up in a shawl, came out onto the doorstep. The light went on in one house. Dogs barked, a horse neighed. In one cattle shed, the animals started lowing uneasily. A man on horseback trotted past us briskly, on the way down. The smell of smoke indicated that the wind was bearing downward; bad weather was on the way. Iztok was ahead of me and Yosht behind me with a light machine gun on his shoulder. We were in a long line . . . both the head and the tail were out of sight.

What was it in my dream that seemed so important, such a matter of life and death? Does some damned oracle dwell in a man's insides, keeping him alive? Under the influence of my dream, this march struck me as a most solemn occasion, almost a ritual.

On and on we hiked . . . nothing happened . . . not an interesting word was spoken . . . Gradually it became lighter . . . these surroundings seemed familiar . . . off the high road on to a country road . . . then back again . . . uphill . . . past the houses . . . past the church, past the well-barred vicarage and down again . . . From somewhere ahead came the order to halt. It had been passed on from mouth to mouth, God knows from where . . . I too passed it on . . . We halted . . . in an untidy line that disappeared behind the next bend . . . we stood there, the mules stood there . . . the machine gunners laid their weapons beside them on the ground . . . no one spoke, we didn't feel like talking. Again the word was passed down the line and this time I could watch its progress and make it out clearer and clearer . . . advance . . . advance . . . advance . . . The line started to move off again . . . "Advance." I passed the word on. Yosht swung his Breda up on to his shoulder again.

This sort of thing was frequently repeated. Sometimes our halts were long, sometimes quite short. Some of us sat down, others remained standing. We went through a small village where there was not a living soul. The shutters were closed, the doors too, and there was not a living creature in sight. We took a forest track. After negotiating some mud at puddles we returned to the main road. Here was a lonely house. Down the line came the word: "Halt!" Behind us, the line disappeared into the forest and ahead, was lost to sight, behind a bend in the road. A messenger rode past us on the way back. I lit a cigarette and offered Iztok and Yosht one too. They did not refuse. "Waste not, want not," said Yosht, as he broke the cigarette in half, putting one half in his breast pocket and lighting the other from mine. "Advance!"

Among the bushes I saw a demolished signpost. It read *Muljava*.

"There was a well-known writer born not far from here," I told Yosht.

"Fuck him," came the answer, without the trace of a smile.

Suddenly, there came the sound of heavy gunfire not far to our left. We quickened our pace as the shooting drew nearer. From a walk we broke into a gentle run, a dogtrot as it is called by the Indians, who prefer running to walking. One mule brayed, then another. We hurried down to the river, on to the bridge which had been blown up in midstream and over the planks which covered the open space. I could hear the crackle of rifle fire on all sides—but no bullets whistling by. Somewhere a cannon boomed, three shots in rapid succession. The machine guns opened up and we scurried over the bridge . . . A mule dug its feet in, its driver struck it on the muzzle with a branch, the animal bared its yellow teeth . . .

Uphill, on a rather steep path.

What the hell's going on?

Below us shells exploded. Earth, leaves, and stones flew through the air. Some men threw themselves to the ground but got up again immediately. A mule was trying to break away from its driver, tugging at its halter, backing away, its haunches colliding with a thick beech tree.

We arrived at a well shaded cart track. From down below came roar, crackle, and thud. "It's the tanks," Iztok told me. "They're pushing straight up the hillside." A salvo of three cannon shells, then the hollow sound of machine-gun fire . . . Like the others in front of us we lay down behind the rim of the cart track, thinking ourselves secure here against any fire from below. Then we heard a noise overhead; that was the tank shells exploding. An aircraft came thundering in low, with its machine guns chattering. Leaves fluttered in the air. One of our gunners fired a volley at the departing plane, holding the Breda in his hands. Some men fired their rifles into the air. Suddenly I noticed one chap writhing on the ground, clutching his leg. I could hardly believe my eyes. His thigh was cut open, cloth and flesh, all its length, so that the white of the bone could be seen, where the blood gushed from the wound. Someone approached him on hands and knees. It was Gartner, who was now wearing a white band with a red cross on his left sleeve. Meat. Just like the butcher's.

Hamacas, 20 pts. Todo el día.

Deck chairs, twenty pesetas. For the whole day.

That's a little less than one German mark, Bitter said. Quite cheap, really. In Ostend, it costs one mark an hour. His wife asked us what we were talking about (that evening, that noise). Then she contradicted him; Joseph was mistaken, she said. Her husband soon gave in.

Out on the choppy waves of the bay, there were a lot of pedal-driven blue and white catamarans. What about taking one and going out for an hour or so? His wife told us to go by all means; she had a magazine to read. She was sitting in the shade of a conical parasol made of bulrushes, mounted on a stake of some gray wood. Gaily colored towels and bathing wraps hung there. She was happy her husband had found such a quiet, polite companion, whose conversation she also enjoyed.

We rode a good way out. The motorboats taking people on excursions were passing us by when we, as if by prior agreement, stopped pedaling. In spite of the scorching sun, we did not feel the heat, with the gentle southern breeze fanning us and slowly driving us back toward the sandy shore covered with bathers and dotted with shelters roofed with some creeper, rather like bamboo, that gave them a very African aspect. We sat on our high white plastic perches, enjoying our isolation from time and space, suspended somewhere between sky and water.

I knew he would be the first to start.

"Last night you said that since the last war, all the military skills of previous conflicts have become outdated. We now have the blitzkrieg, enclosures, the dynamic front . . . Later, I was thinking it over. No doubt there is a great deal that is new. But there is something that all armies have had since time immemorial, and that will remain too, no matter what innovations are made in tank armor, ballistic missiles, aerial warfare, or even atomic weapons; that is the ordinary soldier and his fighting spirit. Hitler used to have a lot to say about it but didn't know what he was talking about. It is something that only the really great commanders understand and there aren't so many of them. Rommel, for example. And you saw what they did with him. We used to wonder how the war would have gone if the Russians had not killed Tukhachevsky. After his death, it was a principle of instruction in the Frunze Academy that the Red Army knows no retreat. You realize what that meant? The Russian marshals had to relearn the technique of withdrawal before a rapidly advancing enemy, at a time when they were already in full retreat."

I waited for him to draw breath. Then I told him I was interested in two other questions, namely:

What goes on in the mind of a man, a soldier, when he is stretched out on the ground, with the enemy firing at him from all sides?

And secondly: what does he feel during an attack, be it man-to-man fighting, or an assault on a fortified line, on concrete bunkers and barbed wire?

180

"Once again, please. Would you repeat that?" I did so.

Well. Hm, I'll have to think that over. Wait. They're both difficult questions . . . You're lying there . . . caught in the enemy cross fire . . . and you can't escape . . .

Let's say you can't even raise your head. Hm.

In an attack? Well, that's a bit easier . . .

Joseph Bitter's forehead creased as he tried to think. He was delving deep into the past.

"About the attack . . . That Japanese pilot, whose book I was reading this spring, puts it quite well . . . rather like this. When you're waiting to see what happens, you're all tensed up, but when the attack is launched, you're as light as air, you feel no pain . . . You're like a machine wound up by some external agency . . . yet you know perfectly whether you should be worried only about yourself . . . or whether you should be keeping an eye on your subordinates . . . whether you have only one pair of legs or have become a centipede . . . this is all hard in the beginning, but a man gets used to it. And of course, some are more gifted in this way than others. I dare not lead a regiment but I could always take a company into battle. If I were offered an army I'd rather face a firing squad . . . Of course that's easy to say; after one year at the front, probably nothing could induce you to say 'no' . . .

"Troops normally hold up better in attack than in the first example you quoted to me. There's nothing worse than lying out in the open and realizing that *che sarà, sarà*; that game of chance simply eats up your nerves. Mines, shells, bombs, bullets, shrapnel, stones, wood . . . and you're lying there, lying there waiting . . . A raw recruit shits himself too, and not because he's a coward . . . After such a battering of a man's senses . . . his nerves give way . . . sometimes the reaction comes when it's all over . . . We were once pinned down three days and nights by a barrage of Katyushas . . . every square inch of earth had been turned over by the shelling . . . not a single tree was left standing . . . there were dead and wounded everywhere . . . medical orderlies too. You begin to think you're a stiff too but once again feel a sudden tremor . . . right up into your brain . . . I tell you, at that moment I wanted nothing more than a bullet between the eyes . . . like the chap on my right . . . not in the guts like the one on the left a small way ahead of me . . . I saw him . . . it seemed an eternity before I managed to crawl up to him . . . and what could I do then? I had no painkillers, I wasn't a padre. There was no let-up in the barrage, I could see a stretcher but it was useless, torn to shreds, with two medics sprawled one over the other beside it, as if poleaxed . . . Along comes a messenger, crawling on all fours, leg bleeding, covered in mud, hardly able to get a word out . . . 'Charge!' He passed on the order and crept on. I looked around me . . . for a moment I thought I was the only survivor . . . then I noticed one face gazing at me, and then another . . . How could I rouse these half-dead creatures and urge them to make a bayonet charge? . . . I felt like weeping . . . Then I heard a rumble on our left. I looked in that direction and saw our tanks on the move. Forward! After the tanks! We didn't get very far. That attack had been thought up by some idiot in the security of an office chair.

"But what really goes on inside a man at such times? That's a very difficult question. Maybe nothing at all. You probably imagine a soldier suffers agonies at such a time. But he has no time, not even to think about his family; he's too concerned with himself. Everything within, a man's whole insides, are kneaded into one small ball . . . and the longer you are at the front, the harder that ball becomes . . . There are some who say, 'They've missed me three times . . . now I'm for it!' Others feel there's no reason they shouldn't come through safely a fourth time. You understand? Pessimists, melancholics, and pacifists have a hard time on active service. You can see it in the staging areas behind the front. Some men seem able to forget it all, to sing, joke, and let off steam . . . Others just watch them, baffled."

"And what do you think about guerilla warfare, Mr. Bitter?"

"Now that's something quite different. An army of occupation holds the initiative. It may decide to clean up the territory or not to bother . . . Let's not talk about minor skirmishes. You have the initiative, everything should go according to plan, you have superiority in firepower, numbers, intelligence, everything . . ."

"But I've read that Napoleon's army cursed the Spanish guerillas."

"Every regular army curses the guerillas. There's no clear picture, no settled front . . . and no glory either. A swarm of insects attacks a horse . . . the horse twitches its tail, kicks out, fidgets . . . it drives them off with its hind legs and they settle on its neck . . . There's only one successful method of dealing with guerillas and that's to send in counterguerillas, not regular troops. That was how the Americans overcame large-scale, organized gangsterism, a real guerilla force you must agree, since Al Capone was much better armed than any of these resistance movements. When we were on our way through

Yugoslavia, I told my subordinates we were going straight through, with no individual initiatives. I wondered whether it was really my job to teach Berlin counterguerilla tactics. Some of my commanders did drive into the forests and tackled those inaccessible hills. Have you any idea what it means to arrive in formation where two carefully located machine-gun nests have you at their mercy? To be caught in their cross fire?"

Our eyes met.

Then we surveyed the swimmers, the boatmen, the yachts with their billowing white sails, a couple on a yellow inflatable mattress, seagulls, a great steamer in the distance.

"You know, Mr. Bitter," I said, "I get the impression you rather like war."

He looked at me, perplexed. He could not make out whether I was angry or amused.

"What, me? Like war?"

"Just a moment," I continued. "I know you went through a great deal. Your home was bombed, your wife had a very hard time, to say nothing of the sufferings of your other relatives. I take all that into account. But I am talking about that faint, almost imperceptible, hankering for those stormy days, full of action, adventure, surprise, exhilaration, and disappointment, comradeship, appreciation of real men, real characters, intoxication with the male ethos, when you got to know yourself, and those around you wore no masks . . . you told me, you remember, that a man then has no time to think about either his sufferings or his family . . . leaving aside the question of war in its wider aspect and its consequences?"

"You must give me time to think it over," he answered slowly.

We drew near to the shore.

The probing shellfire from the tanks was a welcome relief from the mortars. It was nearly always possible to find adequate cover against the trajectory. I lay by the roots of a mighty beech which had been growing so long that even the cart track had to give way to it. Even so we had another casualty. Someone was clutching his shoulder, with a look of hurt surprise.

Three field guns were being hauled uphill. The drivers were urging the horses into the trees.

On both sides of us, down below and in the thickets over the ridge, machine guns were chattering. From the other side of the ridge, came the sound of rifle fire too. Were we surrounded? The firing grew louder and faster, drew nearer, then faded away again. Who was firing? What was going on? Why were we lying here, waiting? In the army you don't ask questions.

Advance! Advance!

Now we were off again. Up through the woods, by the winding cart track. We saw marks in the mud—no doubt the man on the motorcycle. There was no talking. All the faces, at least as far as I could see, were serious, calm, and without tension, unless they were concealing it. After all, each of us was asking himself the same question: "What's going on? What's that? Where? What next?" We were moving forward steadily, with each man treading in the footsteps of the man in front, eyes glued to his back as if nothing else now existed in the whole world. Our pace occasionally quickened, then slowed down again, driven by some unseen motor. Most of us had Italian arms and equipment and were wearing a compromise of sporting, hunting, and military apparel. We were indebted to that Mussolini for a whole load of free gifts, from bulging mess tins to mules and heavy machine guns like the Breda, to say nothing of a heavy Fiat and mortars we simply called "launchers." These were not bad at all; heavy and light, they were now marching with us. Benito his name was, I believe, though he liked them to call him "il Duce." He had locked me up and almost finished me off, and I myself had caused him some trouble. Even so, I didn't know who he was or what he was, except that he was bald and had been a schoolteacher. When the war was over, I should have to find out more about him.

"Halt!" From mouth to mouth, the order came back down the line. We stopped.

"Machine gunners, forward!" The message was delivered as calmly as any "halt" and I passed it on like a stage aside.

With his machine gun on his shoulder, Yosht broke out of the line and rushed forward, followed by his mate with the ammunition. One by one, the other machine gunners all raced forward. Soft footsteps in the quiet, which had suddenly—but when?—descended on the woods.

Ce . . . ce . . . (back it comes along the line) . . . nce . . . ence . . . lence . . . silence . . . I pass the word on: silence . . . ence . . . ce . . . departing to the rear of the line.

We stood there in silence, motionless, straining our ears. It seemed to me that our minds were blank.

Cannon. Machine guns . . . down below and not very far away. What was going on? No face betrayed either expectation or tension. Nothing, nothing but petrified and immobile shapes in the darkness of the woods.

Advance!

We move off like automata. We march on.

The forest thins to shrubbery, yellowing grass, bracken. Through the branches, we glimpse the white glimmer of the high road. At a slight rise in the hillside, the machine gunners lay with their guns already fixed and trained, and a number of men with automatics stood among them, Yosht included.

I passed quite close to Yosht. His long legs were sprawled out over the mossy stones and his head was propped on the weapon in front of him, as if he were trying to get some sleep. His new assistant lay on his side beside him. Our eyes met without him giving the least sign of recognition.

There was a bend in the highroad at this point. The two in front of me ran down and disappeared in the trees on the other side.

We made the road crossing. Two at a time, with sometimes one man on his own, and occasionally three at once. Three men stood by a clump of hazels and directed the traffic. Quick! Quick! Come on! Come on! Why are you dawdling? Hey, you there!

We could now hear the sound of car engines, no doubt somewhere down the road.

Get a move on! Don't dawdle!

Once on the other side of the road, I joined the line which was slowly climbing up the bank. We found ourselves in a sea of low undergrowth, a meshwork of roots. Silence!

The noise of the engines drew nearer and nearer. There was no firing so far.

Soon all hell would break loose!

The noise of the vehicles was far below us. We could see nothing. We could not distinguish the sounds. No firing so far. Any minute now!

From behind came the order: "Advance!"

Shortly afterward we were joined by Yosht, who came up along the line behind us.

The din of the car engines faded and was lost in the landscape, somewhere over the ridge to our right. On and on we plodded, with no end or stop in sight.

Perhaps they were tanks, or maybe armored cars and trucks with troops, or motorized cannons, or a combination of all these, ready for battle. Some of our side do know but we do not. We shall never know and there is no good reason why we should ever know. At any rate, this was the German army which had come a long way to root us out. We reached our field kitchen, in the narrowest part of a small V-shaped valley. The cook had a hot meal ready for us. The supply mules were grazing on oak saplings.

There was no time to finish an after-dinner cigarette before we were on the move again. I saw that everyone else had dowsed his cigarette and put the butt in his pocket. I did the same.

For some time, our path wound over hill and dale, till we came back once again to the cart track. It was quiet all around us but there was a dull drone in the distance.

I had had a good meal, a pleasant smoke, and was now enjoying a quiet walk. The Gypsy girl came back to mind. That had been a pleasant surprise. The Montenegrins have a very apt saying, that woman was born three days before the devil. Simple she may have been, untrained and inexperienced, but she knew all there was to know about the tactics and strategy of love: challenge, retreat, provocation, teasing the victim . . . For quite a time, she managed to elude me or let me only go so far . . . and then ran away. She would stand somewhere, watching me, till I felt her eyes on me, then she would rush off and wait for me to follow. She was herself well aware of the seductive power of her full hips and breasts . . . I must admit I underrated her at first. Afterward, I could not forget her smooth skin or hot breath. She had in fact little to say, though I found her low, husky voice attractive. It was due to her that I was determined to return to that village.

Each of us gazed only at the back of his leader. Probably I would become his carbon copy, if this were to go on very much longer. We reached the edge of the forest and yet another valley opened up before us, though from what I could see, no one was inclined to admire the view. We were only interested to know whether it was empty or whether it held some unpleasant surprise. I myself noticed nothing there, but then I was still thinking about the Gypsy girl and how she had shuddered when I slid my hand into the sleeve of her blouse and kissed the soft down of her armpit. In each of these apparent robots, there was something that lived, burgeoned, grew, knew both joy and pain, longing and despair, a spark that flared, a bubble that swelled, something rising from the mists. And the whole world belonged to it, its own world, a world, a life of boundless frontiers, enclosed yet evanescent, elusive, incomprehensible, silent phantoms, hidden in the weft of matter, enough to populate the whole planet. Was it really so? And what power drove this mysterious engine?

I fingered the boughs of an oak . . . and it became a book . . . for me the most attractive thing on this earth, next to a woman . . . Strictly speaking, I mean not the book itself, but the written and printed word that draws the veil and reveals the heart of the matter—the charm of recognition, that delusive draft. Recognition is a game like love; challenge, retreat, provocation, escape, assault, encirclement, possession, loss. That is how I think, read, talk, chain-read: hope, enchantment, idea, deliberation, loss, oblivion, recollection. I once discovered in a certain magazine the thoughts of some faraway thinker . . . and he made something clear to me . . . In one book, I found an article I could have consumed . . . like the most tasty food . . . Yes, indeed! This is how the truth is revealed, to inspire and intoxicate . . . till the whole world glows with a new light . . . and we are on the very threshold of the ultimate revelation . . . but a moment later we are back at square one . . . Of course, there are words or books that can revolt me, provoke mockery or irritation . . . An overblown book is like a plump, wealthy matron with no sex appeal . . . But the book written here, in the boughs of this oak wood, that I have never seen before and shall probably never see again, contains all our half-hidden secrets . . . I can sense them, I know they are here, and for the moment, that is enough. I shall never have the chance to discuss this with anyone.

We spent the night in the shallow valley, not far from the main road through the forest. I had intended to take off my jacket and fold it into a pillow for my head as usual but Iztok delivered a weighty reprimand.

"Don't be an idiot all your life, Berk! A fine pickle you'll be in without a coat. You're on the march now. Keep your boots and your clothes on."

He was right. We were awakened at dawn by a rain of bullets. The noise was shrill and deafening and came from close by.

I never discovered what had really happened. Later on, someone told me that the Whites had driven a truck along the main road and opened fire with automatics. Maybe. I have absolutely no recollection of waking, getting to my feet, or recognizing those around me. My first impressions of that morning were blurred: trampling feet, whistling bullets, bursts of automatic fire, racing hell for leather up the hill. The sparse trees gave little cover. There was someone racing ahead of me and someone running behind me. I heard the bullets hissing past my ears . . . then an unknown voice yelling, "You bloody idiot, halt and return their fire!" The man running alongside me, by some rapid contortion, swung his rifle around and opened fire. I did the same, though I could detect no target in the early-morning mist . . . I was afraid of hitting one of our own men, so I aimed high. I could hardly hear the crack of my own rifle in the general melee . . . I fired twice in rapid succession . . . I felt something like a gentle tap on my right thumb, as if it had been struck by a piece of wood . . . I looked down and saw to my surprise that the thumb of my right hand, which was gripping the rifle was red with blood. The skin behind the index finger was torn, where a tiny tube was poking out, spurting blood, pulsing gently . . . I took hold of it with my left hand and pressed it back into the tissue . . .

I rushed after the man who had been crouching beside me, firing. He was now streaking upward toward the cover of the bushes . . . The whole place was swarming with people . . . We hurried up the steep slope and down the other side . . . In an upland clearing, we joined forces. Someone said we ought to veer left. There was a shot from down below but the firing was slowly receding into the distance. At the same time our pace slackened, until those in the lead came to a halt. I saw that I was the only one from our unit. These were complete strangers. There was a gray overcoat lying there in the grass. Someone quickly grabbed it and put it on. Any abandoned gear belongs to the one who finds it first. By now it was day and the early sunlight was breaking through the mist. On a high meadow, we saw another group of partisans. My hand was bleeding badly. I bandaged it up with a spare handkerchief that someone near me helped to fasten firmly on my wrist. I felt an itch in my armpits. The lice were multiplying fast and Yosht's brood were particularly productive.

A partisan in a leather jacket detailed someone to take charge of a platoon and I was allotted to it. We moved off. Should I not try to find my own unit? You don't ask questions in the army. We pressed on uphill. We had two light machine guns and were joined by a muleteer with his animal and a whole load of ammunition boxes. On the way, we encountered a long, stationary hay cart, with a single horse. There were three wounded men lying on straw, one of them either unconscious or asleep. A young nurse, wearing a Red Cross armband, was hoisting some bags up onto the back of the wagon and three partisans were standing by. Suddenly we heard a wild fusillade on the other side of the hill. Our leader turned left, off the path where bilberry bushes grew among tree stumps and young oaks. We blundered into a jungle of brambles that clawed our clothing with their long thorny branches, rustling and scratching, while the brushwood crackled beneath our feet. A couple of men armed with automatics appeared from somewhere, either from the side or up above. They stopped for a few brief whispered words with our leader before plunging downward in the direction of the firing. Our leader changed course and we soon arrived at the cart track. This brought us to the three field guns we had seen pass us the day before. The horses were still hauling away. Shortly afterward, I just happened to hear that I was now in an artillery defense unit. I learned some very useful tips from the rosy-cheeked lad in front of me: pluck a few blackberries here, pick a leaf of sorrel there . . . and pop it into your mouth. Fresh gray mushrooms were also very tasty. "See what gifts fond nature offers, haste to gather all she offers." I recalled these words of Valentin Vodnik, the first Slovene poet, who "despite the monkish robes he wore, song and the wineglass ne'er forswore," as Prešeren, our greatest bard, wrote of him. And now Prešeren had a brigade named after him while Valentin did not. Maybe because of those monkish robes. Our culture, our art, our history . . . Nothing particularly exciting about them, eh? "Blaise and Nezhitsa at Sunday school," with some (my word, how daring) highfalutin endearments but no action. Kept a discreet silence about the swarthy wenches they fumbled with, and celebrated some incorporeal Laura.

We arrived at the top of the gentle slope and took up position between some low rocks and the sparse, mighty beech trees. Now firing broke out on the other side, below us. A long burst of machine-gun fire, yelping of rifles, explosion of hand grenades. By now I was beginning to distinguish the sounds of the various weapons. My chubby young friend whispered the names to me; I listened carefully and remembered. But what next? In the army you don't ask questions. It will all come out in the wash.

They unharnessed the horses, threw their bridles over their backs, and released them to graze in the mountain grass and shrubbery.

The firing pins were removed from the cannon.

Chubby sat beside me on a flat stone overgrown with low, soft moss. We each lit up—I a whole cigarette, he a miserable butt. We watched one of the gunners carefully raise the moss between two rocks, slide a firing pin into the interstice and painstakingly replace the moss over the metal, so that no one could have possibly guessed where it had been hidden.

"We're going to have snow," Chubby said.

What the devil was all this about snow? Autumn had only just started. Of course, it had been getting a little colder and some quite enormous banks of clouds had been coming in from the north for the last few days and drifting west. But did this really mean snow?

"I can smell it in the air," he added. He did not seem to care what I thought.

The firing was coming closer from the front, from the valley before us.

The Germans did not believe in wasting ammunition and neither did we. That meant that somewhere out in front, men were fighting, while we had a quiet smoke and listened in. I had to get used to this new outfit. I had a heavy bag of ammunition. Also some salt, a bag of flour, some bread crusts too, dry but tasty. Little Iztok had taken good care of me. Where was he now? And how on earth had we lost each other?

The firing was now nearer but on our right flank, as if we had been by-passed. Two men came running and out of breath. They had a word with the gunners.

Advance!

We swiftly made off in a new direction. One more look back at the cannon waiting there on the forest path, yawning blindly at us. We left the horses there too, taking only the mules. One of the horses neighed. Ponderous creatures, not designed for riding. The bullets started whistling past our ears. We broke into a run, skirting the forest but keeping well inside and out of view.

Suddenly the ground ahead was swarming with our men, firing, running, stopping. Our machine gun joined in. We joined the wave surging through the wood. I saw Chubby aiming at some target to his right . . . There were some green figures there, also running and stopping. Our machine gunner sang out. We joined the others. I heard some orders but could not make out the words . . . I too began firing at those figures to our right. They were Germans, I realized, this was combat, and we would soon meet in a life-and-death struggle . . . Anyway there were not so many of them . . . But now they were firing at us from the ridge . . . while we pressed on down the valley, over the stream, onto the opposite bank . . . The bullets had stopped flying . . . One man clung to another's shoulders and was hauled to safety . . . disappeared into the undergrowth . . . We found a clearing where the grass grew very high . . . Here we stopped and regrouped . . . in patrols, in groups of ten . . . with the minimum of talk . . . The firing was by now far behind us . . . But which act of today's performance had we reached now? Once again I had changed units and had no idea whether I now belonged to group or company or something else. We now had a new leader, a partisan with a German Schmeisser in his hands and two leather bags hanging at his side. And now we were off again . . . It was much later that I learned the song: "Forward, forward march, with your rifle at the ready, into battle for your freedom, for your bread . . ."

I was wondering how I was ever going to pick up a better weapon if we went on like this. Not that I particularly wanted to get to close quarters with the Krauts either. The whole business seemed rather haphazard.

Three times more that day, we "approached" the Germans and broke contact again. I myself had two more changes of unit, once when I had chosen my own route and three others had followed me. It looked like an easier path but we almost finished up in the wilderness. I finally landed up in the bracken alongside Yosht. I was overjoyed to see him but he kept his dignity.

"I haven't the faintest idea where this chase is leading us," I said, just in order to make some affirmative statement.

I rewound the bandage on my right hand. The handkerchief was already crawling with lice.

We sat or lay in the bracken, listening to the rumble of the German armored cars on the road down below.

"This is only the beginning." Yosht seemed unconcerned. "But it's one hell of a mess with all you rookies around since the Italian surrender . . . At least we used to know who could be relied on . . . But bloody hell! . . . With this new lot, you'd think every shot was the crack of doom . . . They're off and up the first bloody bank they see . . ."

We spent the night in the bracken. Or rather we slept, or dozed, or simply lay there, for a few hours. We made our way down the valley while it was still dark, quickly crossed the main road and turned right, westward, with the

191

rays of the weak, reddish, faint sun on our backs. We were joined by another unit, including some Italians. They disappeared at the first sound of firing. God knows where they got to.

The village we came to, Gabrije or some other name beginning with G, consisted of some five or six houses, a few cottages, and a church. Some of the houses had been burned down and were still smoldering. In the ruins could be seen the frame of a heavy machine gun, charred and black. In the little churchyard, an ox lay flat on its back, with a taut belly and four legs jutting up into the air. We made ourselves a meal here. There were only some women, old men, and children left in the village and even they did not emerge from the houses.

We had not yet properly finished eating before the firing started again. There were some short, sharp bursts and two partisans appeared from nowhere.

"Look out! The Germans!"

From the cover of the house Yosht sprayed the hillside opposite. I lay beside him and tried to give some support with my weapon that hardly deserved the name of rifle. We had to move off pretty quickly when they started firing on our other flank. Fortunately we were not far from a thicket. We reassembled there and the Germans did not come after us but remained behind in the village. Our commander was wearing a green shirt, with sweat-soaked back and armpits. He was talking with a couple of civilians in farmer's clothes, but whether they were locals or not, we had no idea.

"We're going back there, lads," he said. Back where? To the village? One patrol had rushed off in an unknown direction. But we retraced our steps. We lay behind the raised brink of the country road and opened fire. There were only a handful of Germans in the village returning our fire.

"Charge!"

As we raced through an orchard, I saw someone hurl a grenade that exploded beside the house. In the shelter of a tree, I got out my own "tomato," drew the pin and started counting . . . Unfortunately, by this time our own men had rushed past me . . . so that I had to throw the grenade carefully to one side, making sure that none of ours were about . . . I felt ashamed of myself as I ran up to the house . . .

Yosht was now lying on his belly in the middle of the village street, his legs splayed out behind him firing in the direction of the church, whence we were being sprayed with hails of bullets . . . Some two hundred meters ahead, a German in a steel helmet lay on his belly where his legs had given way under him, head pointing in our direction . . . Beside him lay a black Schmeisser . . . What an opportunity! I hurried past the house toward him . . . but arrived a bit late . . . Someone brisker than me had already reached the German and relieved him of that firearm . . . Intensified firing from the church suggested that the Germans had received reinforcements . . . A whole line of infantry was advancing toward us, skillfully leaping walls, sheltering behind corners, firing all the time . . . I saw Yosht pick up his Breda and make a dash for the end house, with his assistant at his heels. In the middle of the road, one of our men clutched his stomach and pitched forward, landing with his head on the ground.

We took up position on the edge of a copse and reopened fire on the village and the scurrying figures of the Germans. And what's so special about this place? I could not suppress the idiotic question. New units joined us from our right and left. Our numbers were growing all the time, bringing more and more firepower. A stray mule trotted through the village at the height of the fusillade, without being hit. Now our mortar joined in.

Hand grenades at the ready! Charge! Once again we were storming toward the village. I had my Yugoslav grenade at the ready but it seemed as if the moment to throw it would never arrive. Eventually I did hurl it, when I caught sight of some steel helmets in a courtyard. We took up a position behind the end house, with the Germans behind the next. Bullets were flying from all sides. Yosht and another machine gunner beside him were keeping up a steady bombardment of the village. The second gunner, with a slight shudder, released his grip on the weapon and his head slumped to one side. Our commander in his sweat-soaked shirt pushed the dead man's body to one side, grabbed the gun, and continued firing. Then he too was hit in the right hand . . . Again we withdrew . . . to the back of the orchard . . . taking cover by the roadside . . . Yosht was there . . . and so was the man in the damp, green shirt, who now had his bleeding right hand tucked into it . . .

We kept up the struggle for that village till evening. An unusually bright night followed. We rested in a clearing under a sky full of stars. Only with difficulty could I now recall the separate movements, the minor incidents, the figures of men on both sides, attacking, retreating. So this was what they called close combat, an assault on a village, house-to-house fighting, Someone gets a bullet in the chest. He falls, you think he's dead, but next moment he's up on his feet again, still firing. Did I hit anyone? I had no idea. You cannot hear the sound of your own gun in the midst of a deafening fusillade. I wondered whether I should ever be able to make any sense of the confused events of the day. That ox with its legs up in the air. That rank of German infantry advancing inexorably toward the village. Who decided when to advance, when to retire? Or how long we should hang on and when to give way? And what was the purpose of it all? Someone told me we had been covering the departure of some high-powered political committee. Someone else said the culture section had been moving out. There certainly had been some movement to our rear. But can a man think clearly in the heat of battle? The situation had been continually changing. By morning, my mind was a blank and my headache returned only when firing broke out all around us. I had used up my grenades, except for a small black one that I had no intention of wasting. I remembered how my throat had been . . . though I had only realized it when I was lying by the roadside. My head was on fire. I felt terrified—if my memory was accurate—only at intervals, and then not when the action was at its fiercest . . . How he had flung the dead gunner to one side and seized the machine gun. That had filled me with enthusiasm . . . But when he was himself hit immediately afterward, I felt a sense of foreboding. The Germans must look on all this much as we do, except that some of them have no idea where they are on the map. It must be an equal strain on them. A savage attack. A reckless charge into a hail of bullets. Halt. Regroup. Back again! Will it succeed or not? Forward! Back! Take care! Look out! Action! Stand firm! On guard! Take cover! Attack! Nothing but a constant violent assault on the nerve ends. No wonder my ears were still ringing, my eyes full of the things I had seen. No wonder I had pins and needles in my legs; no wonder my guts were quaking . . . and I still had no clear picture of the day's events. I hated the enemy of course. There was that insolent fellow who had taken a deliberate pot shot at me. But I made out no one's features and they might well have been creatures from another planet. Encounter of men in caps, with men in steel helmets. One helmet had come rolling down the path between the cemetery and the village street. Where had the civilians hidden during the fighting? In the cellars? There was not a living soul to be seen. Whose was the cap with the star, on that doorstep?

Advance! Again, so soon? In the army, give your brains a rest.

Wipe your head clear of all past impressions. It is all utter chaos to the innocent novice. It is all a blur, with no scenario, no direction, no rhyme or reason. I had not chickened out but I could hardly be pleased with my performance. I had been caught up in the crowd and my huffing and puffing had done nothing to shorten the war in Europe. Anyone who likes watching westerns should keep out of the army. What was my deepest impression of that day? Probably the hobnails on Yosht's boots, when he was lying on his stomach, with his legs spread wide, on the village street.

I already felt I would not make a good soldier. Why the devil did I have such a feverish imagination?

While we were on the march that bright night, I merged for the first time with that moving line. A bitter and profound sense of disappointment with myself came over me as I fused with the mass. Moreover, I was unable to identify the cause of my disappointment. Maybe it was simply that I was accustomed to search for a meaning behind any event.

The night sky was full of stars. Without halting, I looked up. It seemed to me that the trees had shed their foliage during the last few days. Was it really so or was it only an illusion of my weary spirit? However it was, I had never in my whole life seen so many shooting stars. In the dark, twisting network of bare branches, they drifted like white cherry blossoms, reminding me of a Japanese painting I had once seen. The slim, lithe fellow immediately ahead of me was following a nurse; the two of them seemed to be moving in a stately measure, dancing an old-fashioned minuet.

Absolute silence!

We were on a forest path. Dogs were barking in the village down below. Those innocent traitors would alert the Krauts to our presence.

The clink of a mess tin on a rifle sounded to our ears like the peal of a tocsin.

We halted abruptly. A muleteer seized the jowls of his braying animal too late to stop her having her say. Now we heard shouting and the rifles opened up.

Slowly but surely, I was losing all sense of time, for hours as well as days and nights. I could no longer reckon when it was that we left that village, where now no doubt my swarthy girlfriend was entertaining some strapping German trooper.

Sometimes there was food and sometimes there was none. When the firing started, you soon forgot your hunger.

Fording the main road, night marches, skirmishes, flight, regrouping, breakthrough, charge, hurry, shoot: all this was now the order of the day. There was such a continual strain on the nerves that days and nights passed like a dream, with occasional flashes of clarity. Shortly after the red sunrise, we were lashed by icy cold raindrops. The nights were getting colder and colder. I noticed that others too seemed to be living in a dream. Yerney, who had been in the partisans virtually from the outset, was sleepwalking, hanging on to the mule's harness. There was a trick I had not learned yet.

When we were lying down, huddled up close together, trying to keep warm, he said, more to himself than to me, "I'd still like to go on living. At first I didn't give it a thought. I've been losing my memory. Now that the end of the whole business is in sight, I know there's a nasty surprise waiting for me. All this time, I've had only a month in dock, though I got one through the rungs at Rog. Sometimes I try to remember what it was like at home. Was there a bookcase in the corner of the room or not? I've completely forgotten, believe it or not." He had a smell of pine resin.

My arm had begun to ache, first in the crook of my elbow and later the glands in my armpit were swollen. Was this an infection? Sometimes I got the shivers. I wanted nothing more then than a bed in a warm room, so that I could cover my head, drop off, and forget all these strange dreams. A medical orderly gave me some aspirins and dressed my wound. I threw that foul handkerchief away. In an unbroken line, the lice had laid siege to the oblong, festering wound, and flocked around the purulent blisters. Yerney regarded the sight with contempt. He had seen worse cases before, and after all, so had I.

"I learned to write," he told me, "after seeing a trick some jokers pulled on a chap who couldn't. He was dictating a letter to his girlfriend but you can't imagine the filth they put in it."

He gave me such a nice piece of bacon that I looked at him in astonishment. "Dry fruit is the best fattener," he said, by way of excuse.

We could still hear the thunder of artillery in the next valley but we lost contact with the Germans for a whole day. We cooked a hot meal and enjoyed the brief respite in our long march toward the mountains south of Ljubljana. The mighty bulk of Mokrec, with its virgin forests, was the object of our dreams. The occupying forces had not yet set foot there, so we heard.

Three of us were detailed to keep an eye on the road to Notrjansko. Yerney and I had been joined by an older man from Bela Krajina, a quiet, steady family man. We were on the lookout for deserters. Conscripts from Primorje were slipping off home. We had orders to capture them and bring them back to base. In fact, we relieved them of all their military equipment and allowed them to proceed. "Go where your heart dictates," said the man from Bela Krajina. In his opinion, people from wine-growing districts had no stomach for fighting in the mountains. They were not carrying arms. We exchanged their blankets, kit bags, greatcoats, belts, and other things for our own, but left them their mess tins. In this way, I acquired a gendarme's raincoat and a leather kit bag.

The rain thickened and it began to snow. Snow at the beginning of November! Our voices sounded different in the wintry landscape and there was a scent of scorched hay in the air. Yerney told us how eighty fascists had been machine-gunned on a hilly road and the blood had poured down the slope. My other companion said he would like to go home and rejoin the forces in spring. "What's the point in wandering around the hills and woods all winter? You'll be afflicted with rheumatism for the rest of your life. And you won't bring the end of the war a day nearer." Yerney tried to tell him off for these sentiments but could not find the right words. We cooked up some white corn mush in the shelter of a dense pine tree. A man on horseback appeared. We called him over. He dismounted and we loaded the gear we had captured onto his horse's back and carried it to our unit. Was the snow going to settle? More and more was falling. It would melt into slush, then another layer would drop.

By night we pushed uphill toward the villages. I was now a lot better informed than I had been at the beginning. I heard we were going to spend the night in a village. I now really began to feel that I was in the forces, that I had my training behind me and my regular service was now commencing. We had a pretty girl with us. She wore an Italian uniform and had taken the name of Sonja when she joined the partisans. She came from Rijeka and later on, I discovered she was a Jewess and liked singing beautiful old plaintive Hebrew melodies. In spite of her good looks, I could never think of her as a woman. In any case, we were both lousy, weary, unwashed. We did, it is true, share the same bed that night in the village but we kept our clothes and our boots on, pressed close together in the confines of that narrow bunk. I cannot believe she was unhappy that I kept my hands to myself. The lice came back to life in the warmth of that room and had us each scraping and scratching in turn. By morning, the snow was knee deep. An older woman had spent the night with two children, perched on top of the baking oven, muttering her prayers till morning came. Parade at dawn? Forward! By now I was utterly indifferent to everything. All my movements were simply mechanical.

For about half an hour, we floundered along a path through the snow, till we came to a road, well worn by horses' hooves and cart wheels. We climbed the gentle gradient and when we came to a bend in the road, turned left into the hills. We negotiated some deep snow, then skirted a low hill. We dropped to the ground, forming a long line in the snow. The machine gunners made sure their guns were set firmly. So we were expecting the Krauts! I was next to Yosht. He tried a couple of shots and noted where he had kicked up the snow. The other gunners also checked their aim and range. The snow was falling quite gently in the icy air but the gray, white, empty landscape dazzled and blinded the eyes.

"Call this an ambush!" Yerney's tone was quietly scathing. According to him, we were too near the road. The Krauts would be up here before you could draw breath. We weren't dealing with the bloody Ities now. There should have been at least two machine guns on the opposite side of the road, to catch them in our cross fire. The man from Bela Krajina, who had kept close to us since our hunt for the deserters, now asked, "Would it really bring the end of the war any nearer, Yerney?"

We fell silent and pressed close to the ground when we heard the roar of car engines down below. The snowflakes whirled in transparent eddies over the land through which the road was cut. I thanked the lucky stars that had presented me with a gendarme's raincoat. All in all, I had reached a high point in my military career, I reflected. In my leather bag, I had a tin of sardines complete with key—acquired in the house of a village shopkeeper—flour, some tobacco, salt, needle and thread, spare socks, a flint, everything the doctor ordered. I also had a Cossack-style fur cap rescued from a deserted house; a time would come when I would tuck my bare feet into it before sleeping. The thought of turning it inside out particularly filled me with glee. My fever had left me, the swellings in my armpit had subsided, so there was no fear of an infection. Best of all, the tables were turned; I was about to ambush the Germans, and not the other way around.

The noise drew nearer as the vehicles approached the gradient and the snow, with their engines racing. The trunk of the first truck shuddered into view at the top of the slope. I could clearly make out one man at the steering wheel, with another beside him, both in steel helmets . . . The back of the truck was covered with a greenish tarpaulin. It was a long, large vehicle with a high roof. Now came the next . . . and a third, slowly wheezing up the slope that was growing steeper all the time . . . The drivers had to change to a lower gear . . . I heard the engines revving . . . "God, you lot are in for a nasty surprise," I thought, with the true enthusiasm of the hunt . . . Between them and us lay a thick layer of virgin snow . . .

Suddenly, the machine guns barked in that snowy waste . . . The first truck got a direct hit in the engine . . . We fired away like mad . . . The convoy halted . . . The road was swarming with figures . . . returning our fire . . . taking cover behind the wheels . . . Then, God knows from where, some were running up the slope . . . others were storming our hill, falling . . . picking themselves up again, rushing forward . . . Now the bullets were whistling around our ears . . . I felt a bit apprehensive . . . this had not been on the program . . . I shot when I had a target . . . Yosht kept on firing . . . They were falling and picking themselves up . . . But some of those on the road showed no sign of life . . . A light snow was still falling but maybe the snow on the ground was not deep enough to cause them any trouble. Now they were firing on us from above . . . Where the devil had they sprung from! They were pushing upward on both our flanks . . . We were in danger of being encircled. The snow was falling denser now, almost by design, it seemed . . . Shouts, orders maybe, were borne and carried off by the wind . . . We kept on pounding away at any movement down below, till we were gradually withdrawn from the position. Yosht picked up his Breda and joined a patrol detailed to our right flank . . . Wading knee-deep in the snow we were under fire as soon as we moved off . . . The air was full of the crackle of rifle fire and the hiss of bullets . . . They must have been right on our heels . . .

Wet through, sweating, out of breath, we halted in a wood deep in snow. What on earth had gone wrong? "I did warn them," Yerney remarked. I heard a voice directing a patrol to a nearby village, without noticing who went where. Yosht lit a cigarette, slimmer than a toothpick. He looked straight at me with a gleam in his eye, as if to say, "Want to make anything of it?" At least he had dropped the high-and-mighty attitude. Maybe he no longer regarded me as a complete greenhorn. With a sudden whoosh, the branches of the tree he was leaning against shrugged off their load of snow and straightened out. Yosht had shuddered violently and now it was my turn to smirk. He knew why, all right. There's no such thing as a man without nerves, my dear chap.

We set off for a remote village, the last one below the vast tree-covered heights.

Here we spent a pleasant evening, an unusual night, and a nasty morning.

First of all I ran into Iztok, who was delighted to see me. He told me we were headed for "Abraham's bosom," in other words, for safety in the wilderness, where the Krauts would not follow us, the green republic of Mount Mokrec. He gave me a pinch of real tea and some Italian saccharine. The Russians were pressing on toward Germany, he told me, Kiev had fallen, and there would be a crack-up any day now. Then we would be heading for Ljubljana. He was brimming over with good news. He was also armed to the teeth, with a whole cluster of grenades around his waist, a knife in an attractively designed hunter's sheath, and a cartridge belt full of ammunition across his chest. I complained about my poor weapon and told the story of the German Schmeisser that I almost captured in that village. He promised to get me some hand grenades. He was working at headquarters now.

We were sitting in an old house, at a great maplewood table with the date 1811 carved on it. There were nine of us: myself, Yosht, Yerney, the man from Bela Krajina, Sonja, a student from Ljubljana, two fellows from Šentvid, and an odd character who was carving a wooden puppet with a neat little pen-knife. We had a meal of boiled lentils and a drink of rose-hip tea. The lady of the house was a garrulous but affable woman who topped off our tea with a powerful homemade brandy that seemed to flow directly into the bloodstream. We could not forget the war completely but we had some relief from the nightmarish experiences of the last few days. The man with the knife, a joker whose jokes kept falling flat, sustained a running commentary while he carved out the eyes and nose on the puppet's head. There were whole settlements of partisans on Mount Mokrec. He would open his puppet theater there and present nothing but comedies. At the moment he was carving the head of the mayor and his next would be a German, Dolfy, who would be playing the part of the wolf in his production of Red Riding Hood.

I found a book in Italian, a biography of Benito Mussolini, with a whole gallery of photographs; so this was the chap! The student, who had got a bullet in the calf, was dressing his wound. He was lucky the missile had spent its force and penetrated to a depth of only an inch after piercing his puttees. He now had it in his breast pocket and intended to wear it on a chain around his neck when the war was over. It was a small-caliber bullet from an automatic. The drink went to Yerney's head. He was as red as a lobster and growing steadily more incoherent; he would start talking about the Italian fascists and end up discussing rheumatism. One of the two from Šentvid told us that half of the lads in his village had joined the partisans and the others were with the Whites. "The landowners' sons are on our side; the poor crofters' boys are with the Krauts." I remembered what Cankar had said about the farmhands.

"Mussolini is not a jocose character nor a man of wit, as the French say. With his icy glance, he quells immediately the merry words on the lips of anyone who dares to jest in his presence. His concept of life is highly dramatic and verges on the tragic," wrote his official biographer.

"He loves contrasts of light and powerful emotions."

"He has a mortal hatred of men in beards."

"He loves cats and white horses."

"Mussolini is a poet in the style of Carducci, writes about government in the style of Machiavelli, writes and translates plays and film scripts. He is producing his own autobiography, has written studies of Napoleon and Jan Hus. He rides, swims, plays tennis, drives his own car, pilots his own plane, goes skiing, pummels a punching bag, plows, reaps, and swings a pickaxe. 'I was an unruly youngster,' he writes of himself, 'and often came home with a crack on the skull from some stone. But I knew how to get my own back. At the age of fifteen, I was a fully grown man.'"

I scanned the photographs: a fourteen-year-old kid with a broad head; a portrait, heavily retouched, that was an evocation of energy, mounted on a tall white horse about to jump a fence, in short-sleeved shirt, diminutive arms like alligators' legs; a skier, bare-chested, in a balletic pose, with a badge in his cap, gripping his skis in a most inexpert manner; a pilot at the controls of a grounded aircraft; a swimmer; with pickaxe raised high (and the motto "Mussolini the worker") surrounded by stuffed shirts and dress uniforms, staring in mute expectation at the magic pick; joining in the threshing, in a sports cap and white slacks; in general's uniform, grimacing at mothers and infants in prams; in a brand-new miner's helmet ("Mussolini visits the mines"); il Duce salutes (with rather short arm and small hand); at work in the Palazzo Venezia (here serious, most important); his birthplace ("King and Emperor on visit to Mussolini's birthplace"); at the Munich conference (with Hitler in the background). "You have created your own myth," D'Annunzio wrote to him.

"He was a wild boy."

"He devoted his attention to the girls."

The new Caesar. Someone who had worked as a bricklayer in Switzerland. A teacher. A socialist. A novelist. A hero.

This mediocrity with outsize ambitions became the megalomaniac leader of an army of eight million bayonets, to use the phrase he repeated in his thunderous speeches. In alliance with a house painter from Austria, who revived the four-thousand-year-old German Reich, he came and carved up the land where I was born, and "with his icy glance he quelled immediately the merry words" on my lips, threw me in chains and carted me off to a camp, where I could study the dramatic and tragic concepts of life. God help us! Next, please!

Iztok came to the house and rooted me out. He had brought me a real rifle, a Yugoslav make. I was as pleased as Punch. "Hand the other one over," he said. I asked him where he had got it. He told me that someone who had been severely wounded was making the swap. The wounded were being taken to hospital. I gave him my old weapon and he left. He had been completely serious throughout this transaction, though he was hardly more than a child. Here the old grow young and the children age. And so we all avoid senility somehow. We are all fairly healthy, somewhat shot up, reasonably confident, though we are mere ciphers for one of these Rubicon-crossing Caesars. I showed the student the book about Mussolini. He was not in the least interested. I was unable to induce him to contemplate the profound importance of the question, who attains power where, how power usually becomes something private, how the private burdens of some ambitious type become historically important and mold the system of government. And what hopes can we have for the future if, here and now, such a coot could be responsible for the life and death of millions of human beings.

Only Sonja was interested in Mussolini; she said she knew a shopkeeper who was the very image of il Duce. She sang a soft, plaintive melody in a language no one understood. She told me what a marvelous little garden they had at home, "two spans wide and three spans long," with a tree, roses, a stone bench and table, all in the cramped space between the walls of the houses, so homely, so peaceful, so old-fashioned. She had a gray cat that weighed more than six kilos, with a long coat, so that the whole apartment was full of her hairs. War was cruel and innocent at the same time. Somewhere, down there in the valley below, the Germans were also no doubt sitting and talking about their homes, their families, and their wives. Tomorrow they would be doing their job and we would be hoping to survive in spite of their efforts. I could not wait to see that partisan stronghold, Mount Mokrec, that everyone seemed to be so happy about. I heard they had been moving casualties up to the hospitals all night through; this bolstered my confidence.

I slept with Sonja, who kept on repeating in my ear unintelligible words in some sonorous tongue. I could sense their warmth and rhythm . . . Belted, booted, fully clothed, we rubbed our rough surfaces together, and a rainbow seemed to form between us, magical, full of longing . . . Half asleep, I heard words like the hues of a pastel drawing. When I awoke in the morning, Sonja was sitting up beside me, leaning against the wall and combing her hair. What were the words she had spoken in the night and what language was she speaking? It was Solomon's *Song of Songs* in Hebrew. She looked through the window and slowly combed her long tresses while declaiming, without another glance at me:

> Thy name is as ointment poured forth . . .
> The king hath brought me into his chamber
> we will remember thy love more than wine . . .
> My beloved is mine and I am his:
> he feedeth among the lilies . . .
> By night on my bed I sought him whom my soul loveth:
> I sought him, but I found him not.

Somewhere I felt a deep, dull pain.
Forward march!

Parade, shortly followed by new dispositions of men, animals, armaments. From the house in front of which we were standing came the sound of a wild altercation, shouts, curses, swearing. A man with bloodshot eyes in civilian clothing shot out over the threshold. He was followed by Iztok, who looked as black as thunder, and three others.

"He's been spying for the Whites," someone said. He was led with kicks and blows along the snow-covered road past our column, as if we did not exist.

We caught up with them up the hill. He was standing in a ravine with the other four around him. Iztok was punching him but he was a robust, well-built fellow and did not drop but simply wavered from side to side. He stood his ground and said quite calmly, "Shoot me and get it over with." We heard a shot and the man fell. Another shot rang out.

We passed by in silence. I had a bitter taste in my mouth. All the charm of the previous evening and night evaporated. We now had the village behind us and the snowy slopes ahead. Tread in the steps of the man in front of you. Isolated shots gave off strange echoes in the snowbound wood.

On and on we trudged. We seemed to have left our pursuers far behind and to be now headed for the safety of those impassable virgin forests, where our flag had once before fluttered from a tall pine tree, a target for the Italian artillery.

There was a short burst of fire somewhere to our right.

Firing broke out to our rear. We soon felt the full force of the attack. Shadowy figures were running through the wood. Were they ours or theirs? Crackle of rifle fire, interspersed with short bursts from automatics. Another noise came from beyond the ridge. I later discovered that the Germans were using dum-dum bullets which explode twice, once when they are fired and a second time when they encounter an obstacle, which need not be harder than a bud; here of course they were hitting the pine trees. It is not easy at first to distinguish the sounds of discharge and impact and troops can get the false impression of being surrounded. Yosht kept up a steady fire at those figures in the woods; somewhere a mule brayed. I wondered how my new rifle would perform.

With bullets flying all around us, I went the same way as most others. The snow was spattered with blood. We flopped to the ground, lay on the path and fired at random at some unseen target. To your feet, forward! Now the Germans attacked our flank. We clambered briskly up a ravine, waist deep in snow, grabbing the branches and hoisting ourselves higher and higher—and ran straight into a German ambush. The man in front of me clutched his chest and fell. We fled up a steep slope and through the trees. There was not so much snow on the ground here. I was surrounded by strange faces and did not see any of those I had spent the previous night with, in the farmhouse.

There was a field kitchen at the crossing of two paths. The cook ladled out a soup he had managed to rustle up. At the crump of a mortar shell the mules, tethered to low trees, started tugging at their ropes. A sack of white flour burst. A wounded man lay slumped across the back of a mule which a young fellow in plus fours was leading by. We set off for the high ground. We fell in at a plateau between tall pine trees. Someone in charge appointed me a political delegate. Once again I was posted to a unit where I knew no one. Firing broke out again.

One bullet hissed uncomfortably close. We hurried up the path. Two men cradling automatics stood by the path, puffing at whole cigarettes. "Let's have a drag," pleaded the fellow in front of me. "On your way! Move it!" said one of the pair, obviously on edge.

The whole of the forest floor hereabouts was trampled flat. Soon it would be night. Was it true the Germans packed in at dusk?

Our night march continued without end or break. Explosions were followed by yells and bursts of firing and shouts of "retreat." A patrol ran past our column.

On our way, we encountered some figures, shadows on the ground, on the path; a long line, extending maybe five hundred meters, of wounded men on stretchers, one after the other, with bearers standing by.

Downhill now. A long road through thinning woods. A ridge with a few trees. The snowflakes glimmered as the moonlight broke through the clouds. A solitary house, or was it a haystack or something? A metallic voice broke the silence: "Halt!" A burst of automatic fire. We hit the deck as a hail of bullets rained over us. We slid down a steep slope into a ravine, where the snow was slipperier. Halt, fall in! Retreat! Up the hill! More shooting. We lay behind a slight rise in the ground, firing back. "Look out, gas!" came a panic-stricken cry. Someone was not used to the smell of the explosive charge in our ammunition.

Hand grenades at the ready! Charge! We stormed forward, and encountered no opposition. Not a single German in sight.

Down along the ridge. Patrols forward. Halt.

Exposed by the light of a rocket, we were a perfect target for the machine guns. Down below on the main road, tanks were waiting in ambush and the whole valley was encircled in a ring of steel. And where was my unit? Another rocket. We were now locked in a merciless cross fire. I could no longer make out separate shots in the utter pandemonium of that night. As the bullets hissed and whined around us we dived into a cleft . . . I landed in the water . . . We hurried uphill by the bed of the stream . . . The water seeped through into my boots . . . Higher! Higher! Through the snow-covered brambles.

It was now a race for the top, with us on one side of the mountain stream and the Germans on the other, occasionally illuminated by the white and red rockets cascading overhead . . . Higher, higher still! So the Germans did not rest at night. Both ridges, split by the deep cleft of the ravine, met at the top. Who was going to make it first? Hurry, hurry! Forward! Rockets lit the night.

A fine forest road, trodden by countless feet.

We left the firing behind and on our right.

Surely we were now going back the way we had come! Where then is that famous stronghold, Mount Mokrec? And how can the Krauts keep their bearings in these woods? They have the Whites to guide them. Someone heard Croatian spoken; that means the Ustaše are with them. Another heard Russian; Vlasov's troops are here too. All the roads in the valley are completely blocked and the place is lousy with tanks. Just as well they can't get into the woods!

Day was breaking when we came to a highway through the forest but we kept to the forest edge. I was just wondering why the devil we had not taken the high road, when we heard a rumble . . . the black mass of a tank with a long gun-barrel projecting from its turret came into view! We withdrew deep into the wood.

On and on we trudged.

In an oval valley, we had a rest and a warm meal. Firing could still be heard, faint and far away.

We were here reviewed by a commissar they called Chiro. Where had we fought side by side? It had been in some brush with the Germans, but where and when? Was it yesterday? Last year? A hundred years ago? By firing very short bursts, he had carefully saved the ammunition for his old Italian automatic with the fat cooling jacket.

Chiro divided us up into companies and appointed commanders. Without any fuss, he put me in charge of one company. My own unit! I looked at their faces and they at mine. I recognized one of them, someone I had known in town. This was the usher from the Matica cinema. How often had he clipped our tickets when I had taken a girl to the cinema. He remembered me too. I recognized none of the others. I was now haunted by one thought: how would I perform when the action started?

Chiro had a short pep talk. From his manner of speaking, I deduced that he was a teacher. We must stand firm just a little longer. The Germans have been overwhelmed on the Russian front. Our forces of national liberation are destroying the enemy throughout the whole land. This offensive is the Germans' last vain endeavor. Our homeland expects us to carry out our duties in these last moments of the war. During an offensive, discipline is always a little lax. He called on his commanders to hold their units together, to maintain constant contact with headquarters and to perform all tasks. All lapses of discipline would be punished by court-martial. Anyone dropping out without proper cause would answer for it when the offensive was over. He finished by quoting some lines of the poet Gregorčič: "Our duties are determined not by rank and station, to give his all is each man's obligation."

Commanders and commissars remain for a meeting, the rest are dismissed.

The meeting was held beneath a large, shaggy pine tree. There were about ten of us sitting or crouching there.

Keep your people together! . . . (easy enough to say but rather meaningless seeing that we were ourselves scattered, like chaff from God knows how many formations). Always know where headquarters are located. Maintain contact! Otherwise we are not an army. Send out patrols! The whole business may last one or two days, but hardly three. The Germans are having heavy losses. They are transporting truckloads of corpses down to the valleys. When you are ordered to take up a position, that means you must hold it. You must talk to the men, let them know what they are fighting for, what a radiant future awaits them! And you must be on your toes against spies and infiltrators. Don't let your men slip off again. Battle will weld us into a healthy fighting force. We've already shed much of the rotten wood. Now we must go forward with a new enthusiasm. Don't forget to patrol both your front and your flanks. Keep well informed of what is happening and don't let the Germans take the initiative! Protect your service personnel and care for the wounded!

A good commander must know his men well. I got to know mine through my acquaintance, the cinema usher. He told me that there was someone else who remembered me. His name was Leon and we had been together in the Scouts, though I would not remember him as he was considerably younger. I sat chatting with them on any topic they chose and tried to see deep into their hearts. I felt particularly sorry for one of them, a sickly, olive-green youth, in clothes that were many sizes too big for him. He looked about thirteen, although he himself claimed to be almost seventeen. A man in a red checked cowboy jacket told me his brother was Petkoshek the cobbler. Yes, I remembered him. I used to take my shoes to be repaired at his workshop on Gosposka Street. "He's dead; he was picked up and shot as a hostage."

We were visited by a fellow with black teeth, a sick man obviously, who told us he was a political delegate. After checking up that we were the third company, he asked how many of us were members of the party. There were three out of thirty. "And what about you?" he asked. I shook my head. Was it so important at this moment? You don't ask questions in the army. Chiro was of the opinion that candidates could be enrolled during an offensive. Any man who proved himself could become a candidate. Peace was at the door, the hour of liberation was nigh, we would soon be marching to Ljubljana. He was hardly a gifted orator. He concluded with a clumsy phrase that went something like this: "As each man now shall make his bed, so shall he later sleep in peace." Leon, who had a sense of humor that Mussolini would have detested, burst out laughing. I changed the subject to the state of our arsenal, how much ammunition we had, whether the machine guns were in good order, how we were for hand grenades. The machine gunner did not inspire my confidence.

"What can you expect from this Breda," he complained. "It's got a nasty habit of jamming in the damp and frost. If only I had a Sten gun!"

I much preferred Yosht, who took everything as it came and was always ready to snuggle up to his old lady, as he put it. He was always cleaning it, or taking it to pieces and reassembling it. You never heard of his Breda jamming! I did not think much, either, of an elderly character with long whiskers who was forever whining about our irregular meals, although in the end, I was more sickened by the cantankerous stuttering of the agitator with the carious tusks, who delivered a political sermon to my bushy friend on the morale of the partisan combatant. I simply remarked that a lot of people had been cured of stomach ulcers while serving with the partisans and that no one had died of hunger so far.

So this was my own company! I felt little confidence as I examined those harassed faces. The lad in flapping rags, the bewhiskered moaner, some anonymous characters without a spark of life between them . . . With two or three exceptions, there was nothing resembling a soldier among them. And soon I would be marching into battle with this gang. Where are you, Hitler's crack battalions?

I reported to Chiro and found him talking to a man in a sheepskin-lined greatcoat. There were some new faces there too. I told him I needed more ammunition and hand grenades for my unit. Just at that moment we heard a sudden volley in the distance. He smiled and pointed in the direction of the firing. "There's plenty of everything down there. You'll relieve the Germans of some of that if you're worth your salt." All the same, he had a word with someone and they got a few Italian hand grenades and five or six handfuls of rifle bullets from one of the supply mules.

As the quartermaster issued these items he said, "There have been times when you'd greet any stray cartridge you found lying in the road like a lost child. Have a break, we're off at dusk . . . unless the Krauts say otherwise."

Some of the men crouched by the small fire, warming themselves and drying out, while others scraped away the snow, sat and drowsed, propped up against the trees. Whiskers was perched on his blanket roll, smoking and gazing gloomily into the distance. Of the whole lot, only our "Titch" looked alive. He told me in confidence he would like to be a machine gunner.

Advance!

We lined up and moved off on our own, along a fairly wide path through the snow, destination unknown. I walked at the rear, then advanced to the front. I picked out a couple of men and told them they would be responsible for communications in case of need. All in all, no one seemed to be very much concerned. No doubt some were thinking they would push on till the first sign of action and then slope off in the good old way. Others were halfway between slumber and consciousness; I knew that state of suspended animation. They would come back to life when the bullets started to fly and afterward revert to their weary coma. It started to snow again. Most of them covered their heads with tent flaps or blankets. The white snow-covered figures staggered through the forest, not glancing to either side but keeping their eyes on the footprints of the man in front. My earlier indifference had now given way to a nagging worry. The political preparations had been no accident and we could look forward to some nasty surprise. I decided that in case of an attack, I would keep to the side of the unit, so that I could have both front and rear in view. I was now ready for my first test at any moment.

Halt . . . halt . . . halt . . .

We stood there for a considerable time. There was nothing to lean on. Some broke ranks to get a drink of water.

Chiro and the man in the sheepskin coat walked up past the column and disappeared in the shadows ahead. No one felt much like talking. The night was passing and no one knew why we had halted, what was happening, or where we were bound. We should have been moving our legs in the damp and frost but it would have been a waste of effort. Shrouded in snow, we were gradually fusing with the white and gray of the natural scenery.

Advance . . . advance . . . advance . . .

Slowly the column shifted and stirred, as if still half frozen.

Four men were standing by the path through the snow. Chiro was one of them. We passed them.

Suddenly there came the dull echo of a fusillade ahead of us. Rifle fire. Shouted orders. Someone raced by.

First company, halt! Second company, take up your position on the left flank! Third company, to the right!

The third! That was us. I leaped into action. "Machine gunner, forward!" I called out and then corrected myself: "After me!" I clambered up the right-hand slope. They were rather slow in following me. I counted them . . . fell back to the rear again . . . there I found a slowcoach . . . or was it a malingerer? I shook him and stared straight into his face. Well, well, spots before my eyes! Come on, man! A kick up the arse, a few muttered grumbles, and he rejoined us. I raced up ahead again. We were closer to the firing now. My machine gunner, cradling his Breda in his arms, was slowly plowing through the deep untrodden snow . . . He glanced at me when I reappeared. Forward! A shot came from so close that we could see the flash from the barrel in the dark . . .

My gunner fired from the hip and the others joined in. I drew the pin of an Italian grenade, waited a little while, then lobbed it forward. After the bang, we moved forward again. We were surrounded by thick tree trunks . . . visibility was down to almost nil . . . One company had stayed behind on the path . . . Was there any danger of them opening up on us?

(Things are by no means so straightforward, and it is hard to say whether it is all happening simultaneously or in sequence . . . or whether some impression was valid or not . . . Surrounded by visions and illusions, each man reacts instinctively and adapts to his circumstances. In the mass of jumbled shapes and sounds, there is a sudden flurry as he springs into action. A soldier who is given no particular allotted task will be guided by what he finds around him, ahead or on either flank . . . while a man of senior rank tries to keep an eye on his men and help them to cope . . .)

A pile of logs at the edge of a clearing. This would give us good cover. A fine dominating position. But the firing had stopped. What was going on?

"We've just had a brush with a German patrol." Chiro was at my side. Where had he sprung from? And how did he know? He went on: "They'll soon be back with reinforcements. They didn't expect us. They'll be coming up the road. They don't attack on a broad front at night. They're setting up ambushes. We shall have to creep past the sentries . . . or fight our way through . . . but the less noise the better. Keep your eye on the higher ground all the time. Don't let anyone slip away! Advance slowly!"

He disappeared as if the earth had swallowed him up.

I inspected the company. I thought they were all present. With the machine gunner in the lead, we moved off.

I appreciated Chiro. Here was a man who issued instructions, carried out inspections and at least pretended to know what was going on. Maybe what he had said was not at all true, but in his general behavior, I found something I had missed before. I would do the same. For the time being, it was the only way.

"What the molting season is for birds—the time when they lose their
feathers—setbacks, misfortune and hard times are for us human beings . . .
Being friends, being brothers, loving, that is what opens the prison, with
supreme power, by some magic force. Without these one stays dead . . .
There may be a great fire in our soul, but no one ever comes to warm himself by it, all
that passers-by can see is a little smoke coming out of the chimney, and they walk on . . .
And people are often unable to do anything, imprisoned as they are in I don't know
what kind of terrible, terrible, oh such terrible cage . . .
I chose the kind of melancholy that hopes, that strives and that seeks, in
preference to the melancholy that despairs numbly and in distress."
Van Gogh, *Letter to Theo*, 1880

"Moreover you should also know that I do not believe . . . in God . . ."
From a play by Salacrou

". . . knowledge clarifies judgment, extirpates prejudice and gullibility, and
uproots superstition and fraud."
Fran Erjavec, 1873: *Animals in Pictures*

"They have cooked us a fine farrago; we shan't go hungry. We're in water
up to our necks; we shan't go thirsty. They are playing with fire; we shan't go cold.
Someone's looking after us."
Törne: Official announcement, 1934

4

Where you expect them, you won't find them; where you don't expect them, there they'll be. That is the first principle for the sensible partisan. He must be on the lookout all the time. You never know where you might come across Germans lurking in the undergrowth.

Chiro had hardly assured us we were through, when we heard a burst of rifle fire to our rear. Experience of nocturnal operations had taught us by now that a fusillade from automatics was not necessarily a good guide to the enemy's position, as the main ambush could be quietly concealed elsewhere. It was almost a rule that concentrated fire did not indicate a particularly hopeless position. And anyway, how could we probe and test each other without dialogue?

We tried to hold our position and opened up with both machine guns simultaneously. I was just thinking of giving the order to charge, when we were hit from our left front. Now we retreated slowly.

"Stop crouching behind that bloody tree and use your rifle, damn you!"

The dim figure beside me raised his head. It was my old friend, the cinema usher.

"I've never fired one of these things before, never in the whole of my life," he moaned. "I don't know how . . ." He pressed the trigger but there was no report. I planted my own rifle upright in the snow, grabbed his, reloaded and fired. There was nothing wrong with his weapon but, God help us, the chap did not know how to work the bolt. I flung it back at him, snatched up my own, fired another round and quickly surveyed the surrounding gloom.

"Back slowly to the footpath! Fire as you withdraw."

A local civilian, escorted by a partisan, was hurrying back to report. Where on earth had Chiro got to? We lined up. We had two casualties, one with a bullet in the arm, the other with a neck wound. One shot from the front, the other grazed from the rear. Very significant. We had no bandages but clean footcloths are just as good. Not a sign of Chiro. Where could he have got to?

"Have you noticed how jumpy the Krauts are getting? They don't like these nighttime capers in the woods. Next time we open fire, we'll give them a couple of rounds, then break through wherever I can spot a gap."

In the gloomy silence that followed, only Shorty supported me.

"Sure we'll break through," he said.

"Look here, for Heaven's sake, we've got to get out somehow, and it's going to be much harder if we leave it till daybreak, isn't it?"

"Dead right," Shorty agreed.

"Prime your grenades."

We made our way in Indian file back down the track in the snow.

Three times more we walked into an ambush that night; drifters appeared from other parts of the woods. After looking them over, I put them on the strength. Meanwhile, some of my own men disappeared but whether they had lost their way, deserted, or been killed, I had no way of knowing. Night had her own rules. Mirko, the machine gunner, was quite a good man. On the other hand, we had seen nothing, for some time now, of the party activist who had been with us by the log pile. When I met Chiro, I asked who Black Fang was. Our political supervisor? And had he disappeared? Chiro frowned. "When he shows up, send him to me. I know him. He joined a long time ago and has given good service, particularly at the start, but he's one of those convinced they're going to stop a bullet in the last five minutes of the war."

"Well, Mirko, have you ever known such a hell of a fuck up?"

Mirko agreed with me. "It's always like this when you're withdrawing. You lose some men, you pick up others. So far you're doing a good job keeping this lot together."

I had by now discovered that the character in the sheepskin coat was a battalion commander who had taken the Russian name of Mikhaylov.

I was now keeping an ever closer eye on things, scouting well ahead, returning to the unit, dropping back to the rear. A disorderly scramble was out of the question. We were covering the evacuation of a long column of severely wounded men on stretchers. I found Yerney and had a few words with him.

We came to the crossroads and stopped. Patrols were sent out along both roads. Sporadic firing could be heard from above us. The patrol returned from the lower road.

Making my way back to my men, I took a path parallel to the one the soldiers were halted on. One group were huddled together, pointing at something behind me. I looked. "A snowman," someone said. And it really looked as if a white figure were standing at the crossroads with one hand pointing down the valley. A figment of the tired brain? Or just a trick of the light, the silhouette of grass under the snow?

That was the direction we took. We halted again. "Machine gunners, forward!" Ours moved forward with the rest.

We soon arrived at a grassy ridge and were about to descend the left-hand slope when we were fired upon from higher ground. It was a brief encounter. Downhill, veer left and back uphill again!

Once again we changed direction. We were all worn out, half dead. There was no talking, only groans, occasional expletives, silence, wheezing, curses. I found Mirko. He still had his machine gun on his shoulder but had mislaid his assistant with the ammunition.

Our last ambush was the worst. It came just before dawn. We walked straight into the enemy's cross fire and there was nothing for it but a sharp dash for the steep slopes of the forest. Shorty was still with me, the usher too, and Mirko sans ammunition. I located Leon and a few others from the squad.

Dawn had almost come without most of us realizing it. The forest became thicker and our path wound steeply upward between fallen trees, over mounds and hollows. I saw a mule's hoof on the track, sliced off, trampled in the snow.

A fine mess we're in if they hit us now. I fingered the grenade I was carrying in my pocket and arranged it so that it was resting on my foul, damp handkerchief. A man always needs some prop of moral support.

I glanced at Shorty. The poor bastard could hardly drag himself along. His face was now a greenish shade of gray and he had great difficulty in keeping his eyes open. All the same, he attempted a smile, though all he could manage was a grimace.

"Can I be the machine gunner's mate now?" he asked. His lips were sticky, flaked with a dry, white froth.

"But we've got no ammo." I tried to put him off.

"We'll soon have plenty," he insisted.

On the spur of the moment, I gave him a kiss on the cheek. He did not care for that at all.

The Delphinarium at Palma Nova.

A pool with bluish water. All around us were the zoological gardens we had visited earlier. Pink roses, green netting behind them; beyond this an artificial stream and pink flamingoes. Large parrots, green and red, screeching on a rush-matting roof. Apes sunning themselves on the branches of dry trees. Flocks of brightly colored songbirds. Somewhere, a bell was ringing. Somewhere, a girl's voice was singing a passionate Spanish ballad of love and death. We went into the wine cellar. The corridor had a built-in aquarium with sea fish. Behind a large glass pane, floated the great body of a dolphin, which seemed to be smiling as it watched the people go by. "And that's what Mama Dolphin said to her son: 'Don't behave like people!'" said Joseph Bitter.

We were sitting on the steps of the grandstand, with the sun shining in our faces. A white boat with trippers moved slowly across the bay. We applauded the act of three sea lions, who returned our applause by clapping their flippers, their great flat forefeet together. Three dolphins were swimming around the pool, shooting up out of the water, impatiently awaiting the end of their rivals' act. "They just can't wait for their turn," said Mrs. Bitter.

We all know those sea creatures that weigh several hundredweights. We have already met such scenes on cinema newsreels or on the television screen without really imagining how much the roguish acrobats like to show off for the spectators. They leap, turn somersaults, propel themselves through hoops set high above the water, shoot up vertically so that only their tails remain submerged, race each other around the pool, play ball, come up to their trainer standing at the side, pretend to embrace him and kiss him. He throws three hats into the water, they dive in after them, balance them on their heads. A girl dives in, takes a ride. Her mounts circle the pool at great speed. "Incredible . . . incredible . . ." Bitter and his wife exclaimed.

We made our way back to El Arenal on the deck of a blue and white motorboat. We were sitting on a bench, with Bitter between his wife and me; she had asked for this arrangement so that she could talk to her husband. We soon stopped chatting about the prowess of those redoubtable dolphins. Bitter had less pleasant news; he had had a very bad night and his head had been aching all day. Something to do with the wind? Not really; he always suffered these headaches sometimes around the full moon. In fact, the full moon could be seen in the sunny sky. I noticed how the expression of his face would change; addressing me, he was serious, but when he turned to his wife, he tried constantly to smile and kept nodding to her gently. The steward served us with a crimson wine.

"There is something in what you said yesterday," he remarked. "Not that I enjoy war! No, believe me, I'm a normal human being after all. But it must be admitted that a man can never know himself and his environment better than in wartime. Although circumstances may recur, they are never exactly the same; meanwhile a man may perish or may develop. I gave some thought to your question. Of course one needs to imagine various types of wartime situations . . ."

He looked out at the choppy sea.

"Perhaps you conquer, overwhelm the enemy, occupy a town he has had to evacuate . . . Then you experience the sweet taste of power . . . After all, we're all human, my friend . . . And victory always goes to your head . . . I saw how the Russians behaved when things began to run more and more smoothly for them . . .

"Or maybe you're lying on your belly somewhere, and you've no idea how things are going . . . The situation has reached a stalemate . . . You take a risk . . . You play your card . . . You've paid before and you will again . . . We're only human, as I've said before . . . You can't escape the general mood . . . You take your orders and you pass them on . . . You deploy your units and weigh up the possibilities . . . You're all tensed up, in a bit of a sweat, slightly crazy . . . Yes, indeed, you couldn't stand the strain if you were not slightly crazy . . .

"Or you are retreating . . . The whole system you are accustomed to is collapsing around you . . . Nothing is as you would want it . . . You have no overall picture of the situation . . . You don't know who is where nor what the next moment will bring . . . You assemble your men . . . Some of them fill you with pride, others should be shot out of hand . . . Especially if they know the situation is hopeless . . . but nobody can admit it . . . and you must tell lies . . . if you want to save your men . . . and they lie to you . . . and the whole thing degenerates into a well concealed cover-up, mere delusion and self-deceit . . . then there comes a minute change in your circumstances . . . and the falsehood suddenly becomes true . . . You emerge wiser, more experienced . . ."

He was silent for a moment.

"No." He shook his head. "I haven't put it very well. I relived all those events last night, but in fact they occurred on three separate occasions, in three different places . . . yes, in very real places, with the people I then knew around me . . . events I can't relate to you now. It would distress my wife. I would become agitated and she would know immediately what I was talking about. I'll tell her we're discussing what Brehm has to say about dolphins . . . Just a moment."

He had a word with his wife. He really was a very good actor.

I did not feel confident enough to ask him what division he had served with in Yugoslavia. I tried in vain to steer our conversation toward this topic.

"How was it that the Germans decided to occupy so much foreign territory?" I asked him.

"Well, wasn't it the same with any army in history? Except of course, that we tend to forget it, the farther off we are in time. Do you really believe the Greeks invaded Asia Minor on account of some woman? At certain periods, there has been a flood of war that has inundated all surrounding countries. The Romans and Carthaginians. Alexander the Great too. Then the French under Napoleon. Why did the Spaniards sail to America? No one now asks the Italians, and I apologize for mentioning it, what they were doing in Africa, the Balkans, or France. We've forgotten all about the Japanese. The Russians are quietly settled in parts of Europe. And no one ever mentions those English concentration camps in South Africa, at the time of the Boer War, although it was those democrats who invented what we call the "*Vernichtungslager*," the extermination camp surrounded by an electrified barbed-wire fence, and who machine-gunned defenseless women and children."

I observed him closely. He gave no sign of anger and spoke so calmly, he might have been delivering a stock market report.

"Great powers have great armies and do not need to disguise their appetite. Do you think the Irish would not occupy England if they were more numerous? Yugoslavia would have annexed Albania and Bulgaria if Stalin had been ready to turn a blind eye. That would have made the Greeks sit up and take notice. And why do the decent, peaceful Danes still hang on to Greenland? Who ever heard of a flea owning an elephant? But just remind yourself of all those colonial wars. Compare the Portuguese mother country with her overseas possessions in Africa.

"The Americans have discovered another system. They do not occupy by force of arms but with the almighty dollar. It's more economical, it's the modern way: money, propaganda, capital, espionage. Look, the Portuguese have to serve six years in the forces, three at home and three in Africa—and no one really knows how it will all end. Germany had her colonies, Holland too. But an American makes a phone call, provides the money, has his own president assassinated—no trouble at all, promises foreign aid, withholds it, and it's all done quietly and efficiently. Like a game of chess."

"Herr Bitter, do you mind if I put a question to you?"

"By all means."

"You may find it strange but I wanted to ask whether you are of pure German descent."

He gave me a rather wry look, then broke out in peals of laughter, in which his wife also joined. She was so pleased I was having a good influence on her husband, and smiled at me gratefully.

"For Heaven's sake! You can't get a more German surname than Bitter, can you?" He stopped and chuckled. "You're not a racist, my dear sir?" The query was ponderously jocular.

When we disembarked, his wife walked on ahead.

He now turned to me and told me, in all seriousness, that his mother was Polish and came from Upper Silesia, a so-called *Wasserpolakin*.

"But how on earth did it occur to you to put the question? My father always maintained I took after my mother, you know. Well, well . . ."

The beech trees now gave way to pines. The sunlight hardly penetrated the dense foliage. We heard a rustling in the treetops but down below we were aware only of the soft breath of the south wind, which was quickly melting the snow. Heavy flakes of watery snow slipped off the branches and splashed on the ground.

The line of figures moved slowly upward, treading the sodden track with heavy steps. The only sound was the slithering of boots over snow and earth, brushwood and leaves, and the occasional rattle of a falling stone or the clang of metal on metal. No one knew where he had come from or where he was going; no one paid any attention to his surroundings; no one slept, no one was wide awake; no one ate, drank or relieved himself; they were neither dead nor alive; minutes, hours, days, years, centuries no longer made any sense; they had lost contact with the past and knew nothing of the future, aware only of this forest, this road, this march. Even these things were unreal, nothing but a strange dream. The Chinese are supposed to say about the tortoise, "Bone on the outside, flesh on the inside." If you touch the outer bone, the animal will hide its head and legs under the shell; a touch of fire from a German automatic would have the opposite effect on these bowed figures, galvanizing their heads and limbs into instant action.

The snow took on a blue tinge and immediately afterward changed to orange. I realized this was an illusion but there was nothing I could do about it. I tried hard to focus; dark blue and gold circles swam before my eyes. I sank into them and recovered. The figures in front of me were swaying to a gentle, monotonous music, like weightless puppets. Even the tree trunks danced, and my own feet became as light as air, so that I could no longer feel them . . . until I tottered and started . . . the circles before my eyes disappeared . . . the picture vanished, the music stopped . . . then everything shifted, shook, misted over . . . now all was blue . . . had night come? I reached for the snow and licked the chilly dampness. I now felt the pain in my swollen lips.

An order came down the line, "Halt, pass the word on . . . pass it on . . . pass it on . . ."

I received and passed on the order . . . It was only afterward, when I had stopped and was staring at the back of the man in front of me, that I realized the meaning of the words. No, no, night had not yet come, it was still morning . . . or maybe noon by now? I could have a look at my watch . . . of course I could . . . then I'd know the time of day . . . after all, I have a very reliable watch . . . yes, I could have a look . . . but why should I? Maybe down in the villages, the bells are now ringing . . . maybe somewhere, people are still living in houses, in rooms . . . When the snow melts, you can hear it gurgling in the gutters . . . Maybe I'm dreaming . . . But no. Look, I can open and close my eyes. A strange thing, though . . . The light is the same whether I open them or not. I was already walking again when it struck me that the word "Forward" had come down from somewhere. Someone had sent it down the line then . . . someone more wide-awake than me then . . . a better man . . . stronger . . . Just a moment, I'll soon be wide-awake myself . . . after all, I have my unit . . . Oh, my God, the unit . . . I slapped my thigh . . . I must keep my eyes open! I shall go quicker, I'll pass this man in front . . . but who is it? I don't recognize him. I must see who he is . . . I'll have a look when I draw level . . . They might start shooting at any moment! As for me, I'm fine, only my limbs don't want to obey me . . . It's like being asleep, dreaming, when you want to jump and you can't . . . My surface is as hard as a knight's armor, and I can't break out of it . . . I can only peer through the visor . . . Did I really slap my thigh? Or did I only imagine it? My hand is just not working. Only my legs are working. But now I'll make the effort and sprint past this fellow in front, then everything will be fine.

In fact I did, with a great effort, conquer my immobility, but everything within me seemed to crack and resist . . . The man in front of me was . . . Who on earth was he? I wanted to have a word with him. But he did not look at me, did not see me . . . It's the usher! Muddy, yellow and black, shrunken, shaggy. How could I recognize him? I had a closer look. He looked at me too, with vacant eyes . . . as if he was looking through me. I wanted to say something to him, to stretch my lips in a smile, but I could only produce a sort of croak.

We emerged into a gently sloping gorge. On either side full of men, crouching, sitting, and lying down. Under three enormous beech trees, a meal was being prepared. There was a fire, a cauldron, people. There was the smell of smoke and the sound of conversation. The man in front of me sat down at the foot of a tree. I sat down next to him, with Shorty beside me. There was another familiar face here. Who could it be?

Come and get it! A long, slowly moving line of men with mess tins. Gray wisps of smoke were already rising from some of them. Someone was crouching on the ground, bent low over the aluminum vessel which he was holding between his knees. How many were there of us? How many units were there here? A mule's head, chopped or cut off, lay in the snow with staring eyes and protruding tongue.

We had a rest and a smoke. The food had brought us back to life again. Mirko told me he had found a small box of ammunition and now had a new mate. Shorty gave me a sharp look, both begging and accusing. Leon was here too, and Petkoshek in his gaily colored shirt. The usher spoke, more or less to this effect: "When you shoot, you've no idea what you're aiming at, and afterward you don't know whether you've hit it."

Petkoshek waved his hand and remarked scornfully, "Fat lot of shooting you've done."

The usher felt ashamed. Our eyes met. He was terrified of me repeating what had happened a while back, that he could not work his bolt. The thought had never even occurred to me. The main thing was: here we were, talking, smoking, breathing. Shorty also tried his hand at rolling a cigarette, though he made a pretty poor job of it, with all the licking and twisting. How many of the third troop were here? Nobody was bothered. I overcame my reluctance to move, rose, and walked over.

Along the track toward me came a partisan with a bandaged head. He had a cap perched on top of the white bandage. The eyes were familiar. It was Anton. We greeted each other and fell in together. He told me he had been hit by a splinter or something, maybe a stone. It had floored him but they had picked him up and put him among the other casualties. He had soon made his getaway. He preferred to be on the move with the fighting men, he had no faith in hospitals. "Did you see it?" he asked. I did not know what he had in mind; probably the chase, the pursuit. By way of reply, I smiled at him. I gaily asserted that all was well.

It really defies description, the speed at which a human being recovers his strength. A nibble, a slurp of soup, forty winks, a cigarette, a word with the lads, and he is reborn. Maybe he still cannot see the sunlight, but soon, he is noticing minor details of his surroundings, gabbing, hoping, lying. The chase will soon be over. Victory is just around the corner.

Anton is a real character, quiet, calm, with his own opinion on every subject. His puttees are wound rather carelessly around his scraggy shins. He listens in silence while I try to amuse the men and raise their morale. I read their palms for example and forecast a bright future for everyone. I did in fact learn something about palmistry when I was still in the navy. I know in particular about the line of love and the life lines. Reading their palms, I did not actually say what was in my mind. How was it that they all had such short life lines, as if they all must already be dead. I casually checked my own. It was as long as it had always been, almost reaching up around my finger. My freckle was intact too.

"Don't give us that crap, Berk," he said. "We all know it's a load of old wives' tales." I hoped he was right. Anton gave me a meaningful look: you're doing fine, keep it up. I remembered how he had ignored me when we met at Ribnica. I had been affronted then, although in truth I had no real reason for this. I felt like reminding him of that occasion. At the same time, all that business seemed to belong to the far distant past and we were now on completely different terms.

He scratched his head. "My head's crawling with lice," he said. "There's nothing like a wound for attracting them." I agree. The stinking rag on my right hand was also alive with them.

Mikhaylov appeared. I do not know why I found that apparently heroic figure so repulsive. He said a few words—how are things, lads; have you eaten; hang on just a bit longer—then wanted to start moving. I rose and asked him quietly what the position was. I spoke coolly, calmly, casually. He looked away, repeated some bromides ("All's going well at present; let's hang on a bit longer") and left.

Our meeting with Chiro was nothing like this. You would have thought that Chiro was the commander and Mikhaylov the commissar, and not the exact opposite. Chiro said the way before us was "clear" (for once our patrols had gone far ahead) but that in such an action, you never know what may happen in the next half an hour.

"In any case, we must break through tonight," he went on. "There's a lot of movement on the road down below. The Krauts are getting reinforcements. All the villages nearby are swarming with them. If we don't get out tonight, there'll be hell to pay tomorrow." For a moment, he laid his hand on my arm. "Very well, Berk." He nodded and went off. He has some confidence in me, I thought; just as well he doesn't know the state I was in a couple of hours . . . or minutes . . . or was it centuries ago! Of course he isn't made of iron either. Who knows what he himself was going through then? He's more experienced, it's true, and this isn't the first time he's been on the run. But a yard of road is still a yard long for him too.

From time to time came the crackle of fire in the distance, both to our left and right and behind us; only the heights before us were silent.

We moved off fairly smoothly. The Krauts were groping around, somewhere on our flanks. Maybe they had even lost us. A new column joined ours, from a track on our left. What unit are you from? No answer. One of them had his hand wrapped up in a rag through which the fresh, bright-red blood was oozing.

Anton was a printer. Back in town he had worked in an illegal printing shop. Walls and a narrow room were all he had to see. Here also he had been posted to a printing unit. They were to be stationed out of the way, in some village. "No more bunkers for me," he told them, and preferred to move off with the active service units. "There, you just crouch in some hole and wait to see whether they find you or not—there's absolutely nothing you can do, except shoot yourself at the appropriate moment, if you have a weapon." He had left his stretcher and slipped away. There were too many of us, he thought, and this action was doomed to failure.

All along, I had the feeling that he had had some particular experience that he preferred not to talk about; I never felt that he was a novice in military matters. On the forest road, we saw a long column of wounded on stretchers. "You see," Anton remarked with peculiar emphasis. I did see and felt a dark foreboding. "Just as well I didn't stop a bullet in the leg." He was deadly serious.

I could never imagine the sprawling massif of Mount Mokrec. After the war, if I survive, and of course I am going to survive, I'll look it up on the map. The regular army has known the importance of maps for some time. Instead of them, we have the locals who appear and disappear like ghosts.

Why are so many men breaking ranks? There's farting in the forest. My guts are moaning too. Diarrhea. The mule's carcass had had no time to cool, that's why. Someone told the story of a whole brigade that got the shits after eating cooked beef which hadn't had time to cool first, somewhere down on the Kolpa River it had been. "The Krauts opened fire but we went on crapping like otters," he said. Good humor dictated that someone else remark, in a thick Lowland dialect, "Court-martial the fucking crappers . . . they're marking a yellow trail for the Krauts." Then he himself made a dive for the bushes. Someone was crouched close by the track. He had lean bony buttocks and the flesh on them was the bluish tinge of sour milk. I too was caught short. The thought flashed through my mind: What if the Krauts open fire now? I was still at it when Petkoshek came and crouched down beside me. We chatted.

"Have you noticed that some people have taken the badges off their sleeves?" he asked.

"Badges? Can't say I have noticed."

"They say that Mikhaylov lost his battalion on Travna Mountain; just left it and pushed off, and now we've got him."

"But Chiro's our real commander, you know."

"Now, Chiro's as cunning as a ram's horn. There were some people down at the crossroads reading German leaflets, when Chiro came by."

"What sort of leaflets?"

"Oh, the ones the Krauts drop from the air; guaranteeing safe conduct and good food to any partisan who gives himself up."

"I knew absolutely nothing about those leaflets!"

"Sure, sure, they're ordinary sheets of paper with the text in German and Slovenian. 'What are you reading,' Chiro asked. 'Cigarette paper or toilet paper, eh?' he looked each of them in the eye and said only, 'Now, now, lads.' Not a harsh word—but they dared not look him in the eye. And he simply dismissed them, directed them to different units, some here some there."

226

There were plenty of yellow marks in the snow by the track. Just as well things were quiet. Only to our right and in our rear, there was a rumble from below. It would stop for a moment and then start again. In the distance, on our left flank, there was the occasional crackle of rifle fire.

Once again, we started on our endless trek.

We emerged into a clearing, a slope with beech trees, surrounded by pine woods. A break. We sat down and talked. By now we were getting to be better acquainted. There was someone called Vili who said he was a musician with a band in Ljubljana. His feet were killing him. He had taken to the hills in a new pair of hobnailed boots and his feet were now covered in blood and blisters.

We had also been joined by Stefan, the student I had been with that night in the village, where we drank tea with brandy and Sonja sang those Hebrew songs. There was also a Highlander who swore like a trooper. He'd have rather stayed up at Jelovica, he moaned. There, he knew every rock. When they come after you there, you dig in and wait until the buggers move on. Not like here.

A girl in ski pants went by with one group. She seemed to be hardly moving, dragging a long Mannlicher after her through the snow. "Poor kid," remarked the usher.

"They ought to have some other arrangement for the women," said the Highlander.

"They should be together with the wounded," Stefan opined. "What if she starts . . .?"

"Most of them don't get their periods," Mirko explained.

That was my squad. There were a few others who did not talk. Stevo, a Croatian, a window dresser from Ljubljana. Shorty, who seemed to be all eyes, probably still feeling sick after his cigarette, with the sweat standing out on his forehead. Leon took the cigarette from his hand and threw it into the snow. The Highlander picked it up, carefully put it out, and slipped it into his breast pocket. Shorty leaned against a tree and made the biggest mistake he could in the circumstances: he closed his eyes. He jerked upright and spewed his guts out behind the tree, belching, panting, and coughing helplessly at the same time. I tried to support his forehead with my hand but he refused, he felt so ashamed. Afterward, he tried to tell us that mule meat gives some people the shits, while others have to bring it up. We heard his explanation in silence. Anton looked at each in turn but didn't say a word.

Someone in the vicinity fired his rifle by mistake. The people nearby were furious. They cursed him, railed at him, and would willingly have torn him to pieces. Someone asserted that he had done it on purpose to give the Krauts our position. I noticed my men were getting jumpy too.

Our nerves were shot to pieces.

A runner came for me. There was to be a meeting. "And isn't Paul here?" he asked.

"Who's Paul?"

"Your political delegate," he told us.

"He's on leave," said Leon.

Mikhaylov was gabbling away, without telling us anything except that we were to line up again. "And let's see some order . . . If I say first troop, that means the first troop . . . If I say second troop, that means the second . . . And let's have some discipline . . . Don't want anyone smoking on parade . . ."

Chiro realized full well that we couldn't stand Mikhaylov but he waited quietly until he'd finished. Chiro's advice was more practical: "The second troop has lost some weapons; you must look after your gear." He drew a sketch in the snow. "The Krauts have encircled Mount Mokrec and are advancing upward along the roads, setting ambushes, combing separate areas by day and retiring to key points by night; the Whites are acting as guides. Since we haven't got through to the Ljubljana-Turjak highway and broken out across the road, we shall move northward by day and creep or burst through at night. Last night, Chert's battalion broke out there without loss. A German prisoner admitted that their morale is at rock bottom . . ."

After this, he spoke about the tasks of individual units. Some ammunition would arrive during the day. "Paul is with the wounded in the rearguard," he told me. "Peter can be your political delegate." Peter, Paul; I thought the man must be joking. Chiro sent a runner to the third troop, for Peter. "Peter fought in Spain," he told me. A Spanish veteran—for me? I went over all those people in my mind. They were mostly raw recruits; there was probably some mistake. "Victor," he called. "Assemble a rearguard of older men. We must relieve those guarding the wounded."

Victor, a broad-shouldered fellow with an automatic, set off on his appointed task immediately. "Jaka, take ten or fifteen volunteers, and two machine gunners in the lead."

And who should appear but Anton! Was this Peter? Indeed it was. Anton (or Peter) was the Spanish veteran Chiro had been talking about. I did not let on that I knew.

Now we were to line up and set off. Right over the summit. We would be given the password in the evening; last night some of our men met up with Slovene-speaking Whites.

When we had lined up in the widest part of the small valley, there were twenty-eight of us in all, belonging to the third troop. Anton stood beside me, as I told the men that during the day we should be making for the point where we were going to make our breakthrough after nightfall, some units had already made it to the other side. Chert's battalion had got through without loss. I gave them no sign that I had not the faintest idea who Chert was and what battalion he commanded. "Chert again, eh!" someone chipped in. "He sure is one hell of a guy!"

Anton simply said, "Now have a good look at each other, so that you won't get mixed up with other units. Any stragglers will be left behind." He scratched his head.

We were off once again. The tracks were getting wider. How many feet trod this path in those days.

I let the unit march past me and then moved up ahead. Anton was quietly marching behind the machine gunner's mate. Small details and a few explanations regarding our road all helped to rouse new hopes, fresh expectations. The men's eyes became human again.

We had grown used to the sound of machine guns rattling somewhere on our flanks and to the boom of cannon to our rear. We had even become accustomed to the feeling that firing might break out any moment immediately in front of us, although this was not always probable. In the forest above us, about twenty meters away, I could see the patrol on our flank hurrying up the slope. There would be no firing from that quarter now. Our track widened out into a forest road. I could walk alongside Anton. He told me he had been in the Krim battalion in 1941 and that in that harsh winter, in January, 1942, he had been cut off. There was ice and the snow was knee-deep when three of them set off for Ljubljana. I could hardly hear him as he added with a smile, "We were sent back to town, as they say." Across the Moors to the Little Dyke, then every man for himself. The Italian sentry at the bridge was frozen stiff. Anton gave him some smoked sausage and the soldier let him cross the bridge into the suburbs. Of course, the partisans at that time were dressed like civilians, or even sportsmen. About a fortnight later, the Italians caught him in a raid and packed him off to the Belgian Barracks. He was locked up there for almost a month. Where the hell was that? In the old garrison prison, the one known as "the Vicarage." Snap, I said. What was your cell number? Numero otto. Bravo, I was in numero cinque.

Our path narrowed and we could no longer walk side by side. We had thick pine trees on our left and right, so high it was quite dark in their shadow. The shooting on our left seemed to be farther away, but on the right it was getting closer. We could relax a little when the track swung left, away from that unknown "Fleischmachine."

I stood beneath a pine tree, beside the track and watched the men march by. A break. I went to find Chiro. I could always learn something from him.

I found him leaning against one of the few mules we still had left. He was smoking and chatting with someone. The mule driver was leaning on the animal with his eyes closed. I paused alongside and lit a butt. "Berk! Someone mentioned to me that you were once a political delegate," Chiro said.

"Really. It's the first I've heard of it."

"Where were you recruited?"

"In town. By the K line, I have no idea why."

"The K line? You mean Culture? Did you belong to a cultural group?"

"Not really. Though it's true I did write something for the *Reporter* . . ."

"Are you a party member?"

"No."

"In what capacity did you join the Liberation Front?"

"As a Sokol. From the left wing of the Sokol movement."

"They're our best officer cadres, Berk."

"That's nice to hear, Chiro."

"Of course, they've mostly joined the party."

I gave him a piercing look. His voice became persuasive, but it had for me an altogether different ring in the peaceful, bracing air of the forest under snow.

"Liberation is approaching and with it, the takeover of power. I don't think there's any need to waste words on the revolutionary aims of the future government," he remarked. "All positive forces will unite to rectify the millennial exploitation of man by man. The party will not withdraw into itself. It is the armed fist of the working class. Of course, our present task is to break out of this encirclement; we shall do so and break out next time too; we shall capture several more positions; there will be other offensives but we shall hold out and this will transform us into finer, more devoted fighters for our just cause—you know why I'm telling you this, don't you, Berk?"

"I am ready to do what I can, Chiro."

"Very well. I think you could apply to join the party. What do you say to that? Some of us have talked it over already."

"But what do I know about politics, Chiro? In my student days, I took part in strikes, was arrested two or three times and accused of being a communist, since I found the Radical Union as objectionable as the JNS National Party, to say nothing of Ljotić . . . But what did I know about politics?"

"When did you join the Liberation Front?"

"Early. July '41, I think."

"You see."

"I haven't read a single book about the theory."

"What have you read? Do you know our publications?"

"I haven't the least talent for politics, I tell you."

"There's someone here who was interned together with you, in Italy. He says you know your way around and you're a good type, though a bit standoffish. You had a nasty argument with some Italian officer, didn't you? Quoted Cankar to him. It raised the morale of the others in your hut. Do you remember?"

Well, well. That officer had not been such a dangerous type. He had been a bank clerk in civilian life. He was not a Black Shirt.

"Why do you deem it necessary to make remarks about the Russo-German Pact and the Soviet occupation of Estonia, Latvia, and Lithuania?"

"One thinks things over . . . and remembers . . ."

"You see. You think things over . . . in your own head . . . on your own somewhere . . . and you are assailed by doubts. But if you belong to the right organization, think, and talk things over with your comrades, with people who share the same aims . . . they can help one another to dispel those doubts. The West has its 'high' politics; the Fascists have their politics of power; The Soviet Union, surrounded on all sides, has had to prepare itself for a terrible struggle. Until it was ready, it could not risk an engagement. Do you think Stalin found it congenial when, for tactical reasons, he had to deal with the Krauts? There is no revolution without revolutionary tactics and strategy. And the lead must be taken by a revolutionary party, monolithic, always on the alert, offering a dialectical explanation of events, and setting forth the objects of its activities."

231

He really wants to recruit me, I suddenly realized. I had to give an answer. A couple of sentences more and then the naked question would be put: "Yes or no?" The unhappy prospect depressed me. I forgot all about the war and our present circumstances. I carefully studied the hair on the mule's hide. There had been an occasion when I had discussed the matter with Franc. He had constantly threatened me. Chiro was penning me in with logic. Back home, the ideologists were always on about God and the nation. I had resisted their non-sense. What had I in fact read? The causes of the Russian revolution were clear to me from the writings of the nineteenth-century Russian novelists. I would never forget the accounts in Tolstoy's *Resurrection* of the convicts driven by the police to Siberia. I had been greatly impressed by a book called *Thirty New Prose Writers of Modern Russia* which I had read in German. Lidin, Ivanov, Babel, Sholokhov . . . I had decided to join the resistance, I had tried to do my bit. I had submitted to discipline, I had become one of "us," I had taken to the hills, here I was now, with the partisans, committed to a life-and-death struggle.

Why then should I not remain as I was? It was perfectly possible that I still retained some latent spark of liberalism, or even anarchy, but I would never cause any harm. I would perform all necessary duties, right up to the last day of the war. I would not join in the cheering, that was not in my nature. I would not carp, I would not intrigue, I would not gather around me people of like mind. But I would still wonder in my heart of hearts: "What more do you want of me?" I came here as a left-wing Sokol, admittedly with a completely washed-out ideology, but why can't I be left alone, as an "ex-left-wing Sokol," to play my proper part in the struggle? Just to think of Stalin's purges! That is a problem for the Russians, perhaps for you too, but it is not for me. No, no, I shall never be pro- or anti-Trotsky. What has all that got to do with me? Surely you're not going to tell me some day that your rifle fires in the service of a bet-ter future for our people, while I use mine only to protect my own backside?

He looked me full in the eye. I could tell from his piercing glance that he knew what I was thinking.

"You know I've lived a very dissolute life," I said.

An objection can be found to anything, especially when all is flight and confusion.

I met his gaze and began to repeat to myself that simple sentence, "Must make the hilltop . . . Must make the hilltop . . ." I blanketed all other thoughts with this. His eyes lost their hard look. He said a few more words, then a patrol came along to report. "Very well, Berk," he said as he dismissed me. "Think it over. Next time you can give me your answer."

I felt little confidence in myself as I left him. Gradually, the war was creeping up on me. But who had told Chiro I had my own ideas about that unfortunate pact between Hitler and Stalin?

I could not afford to tell anyone about myself, I could not talk things over with anyone. That non-aggression pact had taken me by surprise, it is true, but I did not really feel indignant about it. I found it much stranger when I observed how disappointed Joseph Vissarionovich Djugashvili Stalin was, when Hitler invaded the Soviet Union, had gone back on his given word, had breached the contract. Anyway, what was it to do with me? I think that, in general, I have my own opinion about politics. Poets survey the world around them and express their hopes and fears. Politicians project some plan of development for themselves—and whatever in the world falls in with their calculations is real, while anything that disagrees is an abominable falsehood, even though it may be true. Therefore, the only question is, can you contradict them or can't you? That is how it is with these politics now. Homo politicus, a hodgepodge of prejudices gleaned from all quarters and all periods. One thing I can admit: that a whole regiment of people like me couldn't manage a parish, never mind a country or a whole system of government.

Soon we were on the move again. Where was my unit now? Or was it still mine? Vili, the musician, whose boots were killing him, brought up the rear.

"Have you joined, Vili?"

"Sure thing. I've been in the Liberation Front since '42."

"And what about the party?" He seemed a little startled, probably thinking I was about to propose that he should join.

"That's not for me," he answered slowly. "I play in an orchestra and I know how things are."

I did not get the point. He explained. "First we get used to one conductor, then another comes along and everything which was right before is now wrong, and what was wrong before is now right. I'm reliable, I keep up my practicing, I play conscientiously, I carry out instructions, do what I can; that's all."

How had he joined the partisans? He had gone down to Dolenjska to pick up some vegetables for the winter and had stayed. His brother had taken to the hills the previous winter, at Christmas, when the Whites were arresting suspects in Ljubljana.

"They came knocking on our door too . . . 'Open up! In the name of Christ the King!' . . . Word of honor, just like that . . ." They were looking for his brother but fortunately he was not at home.

"Is your rifle in working order?"

"Yes, it's working, bugger it . . . it's working . . . Listen, is there any hope of us getting out of this mess?"

"We should manage it tonight."

"Don't tell me it's going to be like last night! I can't hold out, these boots will be the death of me. And it's not only the boots. A man gets to feel like an empty sack. My mother is religious, but my brother and I are quite different . . . We believe in having a good time. But the old lady always used to say: 'One of these days you'll be down on your knees too, Vili!' And last night I was. Not that I'm going back to the church, no. It's just like begging for something and then forgetting . . . You know those Tibetan prayer wheels, you've heard about them, haven't you? Little wheels with tapes wound around them, and on the tapes there are prayers. You turn the wheel and it's just like praying. And how long have you been in the party?"

"I'm not a member."

"What! And you a commander?"

"Well, yes, I'm just a byproduct of this foul-up."

He smiled at me, as if this was a good joke.

Occasionally, the trees thinned out and patches of sunlight appeared on the snow. Then we would be plunged into dense forest, where it was so dark you would have thought evening had come. Lack of sleep, exhaustion, monotonous motion, occasional flashes of clarity, the momentary realization of what might be just around the corner, the mind wandering as you plodded on: all this mixture made up the gray course of those days. Our vigilance was blunted, our movements became automatic. The memory would bring back some distant event with complete clarity, while being unable to recall what had happened a day or two before.

My hand stank to high heaven. Was it festering or something? At least I could move it. My boots were wet and sucked my feet. Is eternity like this? Persisting in each of us, dragging on in our limbs and brains, so that we, all together, constitute an endless line, in perpetuity, a ring around the earth's crust, a closed gray ring, where suddenly there is nothing in front, nothing behind, no present, no past, no future. Our motion is the ghostly reflection of a weary, bewildered spirit. Silently, a yellow leaf fluttered down, rode the air and gently settled on the bluish snow beside the track. The thought of a derisive spirit somewhere far beyond this world. Poets, raise a memorial to that leaf, the analog of all of us who had fallen or were to fall in those days. Maybe there was some sequence of events but we were unable to follow it. I cannot say whether the bombs first started to rain down on us or whether we had previously been the witnesses of an encounter between one of our units and the Germans in a forest clearing below us. I do remember that the bombs took us completely by surprise. We listened in amazement as the first salvo exploded. They came from above, through the treetops, like a gift from heaven. One man was hit square in the back and another full in the face. There was no knowing on which side of a tree to hide. At first we were looking at each other accusingly, as if someone had accidentally let off a hand grenade. The Krauts could not see us and the whole thing was pure chance, or so we hoped.

When the firing had broken out among the tree stumps, below us and to our left, we were just emerging into the light, from the dark slopes of a pine wood. In the distance, we could see longer lines of figures, pursuing a routed group. The pursuers were firing continually, the fugitives were dropping, and also returning the fire, or at least some of them were. Our men disappeared into the forest and the Germans poured in after them. The firing ceased. In the rear of the German pursuers, other figures were slowly advancing. One of them paused by a tree stump and aimed a big, long pistol at the ground. The shape lying there jerked at the shot. The whole action continued, somewhere farther into the woods. There were hurried bursts of fire in the distance but these gradually grew less frequent. Then once again firing broke out, this time even farther away.

Mirko was lying behind his machine gun, looking out over it. Leon was well away: "You know, I fell asleep during our march. I know I was sleeping because I dreamed that somewhere . . . far off . . . I had gone in a green tramcar . . . to visit someone . . . beside a river where someone was rowing . . . and they had a house built on a raft, just like a fairy tale . . ." he went on relating his daydreams . . . how the tram would not stop, and he should have got off long ago . . . Leon had probably told this story a number of times before. I had seen him in that pine wood and then in the narrow gully where we had our break . . . At this point, Shorty said something to Mirko the machine gunner, who shook his head and finally rebuked him: "Bloody crap, mate. You can tell that to the horse-marines!" I wanted to know what.

"This kid's telling me—me, mind you!—that a machine gun gives you the best cover. When a machine gun always draws the most fire. And they always try to wipe out a machine-gun nest first. Now he comes along trying to teach me my own business!" Shorty was so red in the face I could hardly recognize him. He usually had the greenish tinge of rotten yogurt.

Such minor quarrels would break out now and then. A few words, a curt remark, then silence once again. The nervous tension was such that anything we said seemed sharper than usual, chaotic, sometimes downright stupid, surly, and then even caustic and angry. In the circumstances, there was no reason for surprise if you trod on the heels of the man in front, when the order to halt came down the line and you did not hear it. But he might turn on you, with a furious volley of oaths, or again he might not feel anything. You might collide with him and he would lean against you, and you would have to take care that he would not fall when you moved away. At such a time, argument, teasing, and sermonizing have no point. I was astonished when Chiro gave us a pep talk during a break. He had nothing new to say. Only that we should persevere through these last exertions; which of us did not want to do so?

The evening came by fits and starts. When it was quite dark in the pine wood, it was still fairly light where the trees were thinner. We cooked a meal in the shade of hundred-year-old trees, using branches to hide the fire, which flickered like a magic flame beneath a small cauldron hanging by a chain from a bough.

The body needs food and demands it, as long as it appears at regular intervals. But in that Italian camp, hunger made some men forget their hunger, though they glowed like firebrands. In our march along some meridian, in the closed circle of the planet, our greatest desire was for that warm, damp, misty puff of steam rising from the mess tin to the face, although not even a mule's festering sores had such a horrid stench as one of the partisans' long unwashed cooking pots. The cooks, those mysterious goblins of the forest, had a whole series of trade secrets. You never knew where they disappeared to, you never knew where they sprang from, you could never guess where their supplies came from and you would never discover what seasonings they had salted away. When a cook dispensed food with that enormous ladle, he became a real foster father. He looked closely at everyone, before pouring and before adding some thick broth from the bottom of the pot, although he fully realized how ungrateful children are. Some people believe that delusions are common during an offensive and that the vision of a cook distributing food in the middle of the forest is brought on by hunger, exhaustion, and the need to eat. Not so; men are dreaming of that puff of warm air in the face, the only source of warmth in these hateful, frozen woods. When a man is frozen to the marrow of his bones, so they say, he would fly over the chimney pots to get warm. In the extremes of cold, there apparently comes a sensation of warmth, just before we freeze. In the damp and continually penetrating chill, we lose our ability to remember that heat and warmth exist. Only that steam from the mess tin reminds the benumbed body of certain wonderful things you can still perhaps find in the world: warm rooms, warm blankets, warm hearths, warm clothing, warm words about warmth, warm homes.

Shorty's face was poised over the vapor as he gazed out in front of him with wide-open, unblinking eyes. His tiny palms cupped the bulbous mess tin. I glanced from one pair of hands to another. They were all tightly clutching their warm hoard. Hands, scratched and bloody, hands with festering wounds, with filthy fingertips, with long nails, black, gray, and blue, stiff, rough, and clumsy. When I finally looked at my own, I did not recognize them; they were like black paws, with numb fingertips and swollen fingers, covered with scratches. Green pus was oozing from under the gray-black rag that was doing duty as a bandage for my right thumb.

Our forefathers, a hundred thousand years ago, probably did not suffer such hardships. They also, presumably, were no great shakes but their limbs were hardier and they fought each other with the clear intention of eating the enemy. But why, today, have we got armies, a million strong, fighting each other? I felt a violent desire to hear Anton's views on the subject. But he too was absorbed in the warmth of his pot. Come on now, dear Adolf, give us a whiff of grapeshot, for God's sake! Let's see some action.

It was past evening by the time we moved on. It was a very clear night: up above us, through the branches and treetops, we could see what is called a starry sky. In the forest, the snow became more brittle and crunched beneath our feet. We must have been pretty high up by now.

Not a sign of life from dear Adolf, apart from that distant rumble we were already accustomed to, a burst of fire, some shots, and then silence. Or the slow and persistent rattle of a German machine gun; they can afford it; they have plenty of ammunition.

I heard someone in front of me mention Ljubljana. Yes, that's our town. The castle, the river, the embankments. Then I caught sight of a pool of light, somewhere far off in the darkness, little lights winking under the stars, and something bright and tall stood out above the twinkling throng. Stefan, the student, spoke in a hoarse voice: "The skyscraper . . . there's a café there . . . That was one of our favorite haunts . . ."

The reel of internal images mixed with external impressions snapped: there was the Ljubljana skyscraper, crowned by the café with its illuminations, tables, chairs, sofas, waiters scurrying among the guests . . . There is the corner where I used to sit with Mariana. Was it in some other past life, or did I dream it all? I had different hands and feet then, I was wearing different plumage. There was a small orchestra playing in the corner. The conductor was a law student. I can hear him playing, but I do not know what. A tree obscures my view. When I was sitting there, there were other eyes gazing at us from across the moors . . . gazing at the well-lit town and the skyscraper, with its illuminated upper stories. The trees swayed before my eyes. I must be moving, then.

Stefan was saying, ". . . I used to go there in the mornings to study . . . A coffee, Srechko . . . Turkish, if you please. With the sugar separate."

The whole world is full of cafés. There are even countries where they do not know we are fighting a war. Some people read newspapers, others do not. Now I roll tobacco dust, in pages torn from old newspaper, where the Catholic worthies falsely claim that the partisan forces have been completely wiped out.

All that I saw that night was marching on and on in single file into some powerful German ambush, then back again to an ambush on the other side, then up hill and down dale, into a new trap. I remember only some quite insignificant details I encountered. A mule driver, walking behind a mule with his hand stuck up the animal's rump, pulling it out and moving over to the other side, then plunging his other hand into the animal's guts, warming himself and sleeping at the same time.

An explosion, fire, a shower of sparks, a long volley of tracer bullets. I started shooting and yelling, although I realized no one could hear me. We raced down a timber slide, slipping and riding on our rumps till we landed on a road where a crowd of our men watched us without moving. This gave us the impression we had reached safety. A shadow in the trees was moving very suspiciously. I did not know whether to fire or not, whether it was friend or foe. Then the shadow disappeared, as if the earth had swallowed it up. Two men with automatics in their hands shouted something in sharp, steely tones. I did not know those words but I understood them. They meant: "Follow me! Let's go! Charge!"

A wounded man was calling for help. Swift steps approached over the crunching snow. Forward! Forward! Why are you dawdling? Leon! What is it, Leon! Where! Without waiting for a reply I moved on. Leon was still walking, though he was bent double. Anton's face appeared just before me and then disappeared in the shadows. The snow in the forest glade was gleaming in the moonlight. A few people were standing there in a circle. Were they going to start a circle dance? A figure lay motionless on a stretcher.

My ears were throbbing with the uproar. Even before a shot was fired, I heard the sound of flying bullets and I was not bothered. I was hit on the leg and immediately afterward on the face . . . I felt faint, staggered and fell flat on my face . . . I crawled on all fours, dragging my rifle after me along the ground, wondering whether I would be able to stand. I made a mighty effort to pull myself up. I could feel my body resisting but I got up and hurried on . . . I was okay. A shout. Somebody whispered in my ear: "Breda—Belgrade . . . Breda—Belgrade." He disappeared and I dully realized that this must be the password. "Breda—Belgrade." What use was it to me?

Mirko was berating me in a hoarse voice. "Bloody hell, I've got no flaming ammunition; do something, for God's sake!"

Shorty ran along behind me without a word, one leg of his breeches hanging loose. There was firing close behind us but we were moving, slowly . . . or at least we seemed to be moving slowly . . . it was only when I lurched and banged my arm against a tree that I realized I was running.

Halt! We have a break; we are not here, we never were, and we cannot be. The Germans have had a good rest, lucky bastards. Half a day off, kipping on a baker's oven down in the village. Now they are on night duty; a little sport won't do them any harm. A night out hunting their inferiors. Wouldn't be surprised if they're buggering hedgehogs too!

Why is my right knee aching? Did I stop one, without noticing it? Water is as wet as blood. But hang on, the blood is warm. Ours isn't any more.

Petkoshek was beside me. I had to be careful to avoid showing him what a state I was in. I wanted to say something but my throat was parched and I could not speak. In any case, he looked past me without seeing me and would not have heard me. The usher was cramming snow into his mouth. Another halt and this time visibility was rather better than shortly before; perhaps it was daybreak for all I knew. Was I leading these men or were they leading me; was it really dawn or only my imagination? It was clear by now that we had not broken through. But neither had the Krauts made any significant gains, devil take them! The whole of that forest was still crawling with our men and I was a nobody in my vicinity without a gun. But what sort of crack troops were serving in the enemy's elite divisions, if they could not wipe the floor with this lad in the torn breeches or the cinema usher, who could not even reload a rifle when Hermann Göring launched his attack on us?

Sure, now I know full well why the Negroes, as I had heard, do so much shouting before they advance to the attack. And those Krauts, poor sods—this is what I'm getting at—there are a hundred of them to one of us, they have been specially trained, strained, stuffed like turkeys before slaughter, and what does it get them? ". . . a wooden cross for me . . . for me, Lili Marlene . . ."

This was the day. We were going to break through, I could feel it in my bones. Any moment now, we were going to see the cook and his pot, risen up to feed us, before disappearing once again into the bowels of the earth. Morale is not only a matter of knowing why you are afraid. There are times when that ceases to be of any importance. You must stoke up your anger, rage, and fury against the enemy, first of all, but also against yourself and the whole world. And you must also cherish a yearning, even if only for a goblin-cook: picture for yourself, in the heart of the ancient forest, a cook, a woman with golden hair in a spotless white skirt. First we'll eat, then hop and tumble into a soft bed . . . Come, my dear, you're so warm, take me, all of me. Forward! Very well, forward, damn it! All in all it could be very much worse, although this depends on whether you are dreaming of an apple strudel and suffering because you can't get your hands on it, or whether you are thinking of how the

Krauts might be skinning you alive because you refuse to reveal the location of your battalion's secret kitchen.

It was not so bad after all. The living would survive and later be quite unable to remember how it had really been. But grass does not grow for a dead donkey. We had heard that the local farmers are burying the dead. Really, we should be taking special care of kids like Shorty, who was clinging to us like a tick. Or that old woman volunteer, pale and feverish. Far off in the German rear, an enormous and growing territory had already been liberated, so they said. I was concerned about the wounded. Where were they now? During the night, we had passed by the stretchers again and again. Chert had got through with his men, Victor also apparently, but the Germans had closed the gap and the rest of us had been unable to follow them. He seems to have broken back in again if what a passing courier told us was true. It was pretty hard to believe that anybody would willingly stick his neck back in the noose.

You had to get used to the idea that at some moments, your position would seem so hopeless that you would feel like throwing yourself on a grenade, but that next thing, the whole situation might change; you were still alive, marching, eating, smoking, hoping. It was a continual sort of massage of the nerve endings. But could it be compared with life at the front, where troops lay for whole days and nights under an artillery barrage, pinned down, awaiting their fate, gazing at death and destruction, unable to stir from their poorly sheltered trenches?

It was half past six, a misty morning and all indications were that the sun would soon break through the clouds. Why had I looked at my watch after such a long time? Was it to see and know what time it was? For myself it was a pleasant surprise. Perhaps also I was heartened by the realization that those around me had a little confidence in me. This observation was based on quite insignificant impressions.

"When the Krauts open up, drop to the ground and return their fire straight away and even if your shooting's all to cock, don't for God's sake turn tail. They're only men like you. He doesn't know either, exactly what the position is, who he's facing, how many there are of us. He's got pretty good hearing, especially if something whistles past his ears . . ."

They listened with set, grimacing faces and then had their own say. I also thought it important that they should see me from time to time conferring with a courier, a patrol, or Chiro. They did not know what we were talking about, but would take it that I had now discovered why we had to press on uphill, or that I now knew what the situation was, what was cooking, where the Germans were, what was going on . . . So that we were not going around in circles. In fact, of course, I myself knew very little more than they did, but that was not the point. Occasionally, I would drop a discreet hint that would lead them to conclude that there was some sense in what we were doing and that there was even a plan of operations. Twice or three times I put on an act: the man with nerves of steel. Why had I looked at my watch?

"It's now half past six," I said. "We'll be eating in about half an hour." Pure bluff, of course. I am not a poker player for nothing. It works, it helps, it does no harm. If we do not eat, we shall say something went wrong and blame the bloody quartermaster and the flaming cooks. There is no morale without hope. And just as I had been lucky a few times before, so now too my luck held. Before an hour was up, we had joined a longish column, beside which a cooking pot was hanging from a sturdy bough.

Men were becoming more and more like each other, wet, dirty, unshaven, bowed down, losing their identity. Sometimes I had to look close at the face and eyes of someone I thought I knew, to remind myself where I had seen him before. There were some gallant fellows who stood with feet planted apart in an heroic pose, with head erect. I admired their determination to show no weakness. A staff of sorts was seated beneath the canopy of three gigantic trees. I could see commanders' and commissars' badges of rank on their sleeves as they talked and smoked. A patrol with a machine rifle moved off in some unknown direction, a courier arrived and gave a clenched fist salute before reporting. This was no robber band. The position was difficult but this would change. It was not the first time we had been so crowded and it would not be the last. Fatigue was normal but the partisan forces never heard of demoralization. It was rather harder at the moment because there were so many raw recruits. But that too would soon sort itself out. The kitchens were working a little irregularly and supplies of food were rather scanty but the whole machine was working. The wounded were being taken care of.

The Germans came into the woods and they knew where they were going. They had to drive their White guides before them at the point of a gun. We would hold out, because we had no alternative. The Krauts would not, because they did not need to. A Prussian would arrive from Paris or the Russian front and here, at the world's end, he would be dying from a partisan's bullet in the knee. He would have no idea where the chase was leading, whom he was chasing, who was firing at him. German morale was falling considerably. They had heard reports of the collapse of the Russian front, of air raids on German cities and they had bad news from home. Our brigades would reorganize in their rear and strike from that quarter at any moment. We were mining roads and railway tracks, blowing up tanks and trains. The orderly Krauts were cursing poor deliveries of arms and food supplies.

Man's development as a creature other than the animals began with his invention of speech.

Troop number three, arms inspection. The army must always be doing something so as not to decline into a civilian organization. Statement of strength. Always imagine that this march is instead of regular training. When attacking, everyone must shout "Charge!" and not only the three in front. This has an effect on the enemy and you also find it easier to advance. The man who finds the best cover is the first to get hit. Every bullet can miss. If you hear it whistle it has passed you. If you hear firing behind you, it might be the Krauts or it might only be the dumdums exploding among the branches. They are not dangerous.

I round up the groups to see who was there, how many there were of us and what the others were up to. A doctor with a handsaw was amputating one man's leg. The wounded man was conscious and a nurse was holding his head up. He was looking away, with the sweat pouring from his face, forehead, and nose. He was groaning and gritting his teeth. Splinters of bone were flying from the saw. They were giving him brandy from a flask and also pouring it over the wound.

Chiro asked, "Is your unit okay?"

"Our numbers are up to twenty-three again. Some of the original lot are missing but a few newcomers have joined us from units that have broken up. We have two Cankars and one Gubec . . ."

"I've promised Peter some rifle and machine-gun ammunition. We have to economize, we're a bit short at the moment. This afternoon the locals will be along with some food, bombs, and ammunition. We're expecting a mine thrower too, a big one," Chiro said and offered me a cigarette.

They were now carrying off the wounded to send them to hospital. I did not tell Chiro I had lost the Highlander and another man, who had gone off together to hide, as Petkoshek had hinted to me ("They've buggered off on their own").

"That Croatian in your unit is a reliable chap, he's okay. I was telling Peter about him." I registered no surprise. Mikhaylov appeared and once again began mouthing his phrases, while Chiro kept a discreet silence. ". . . discipline must hold . . . morale must improve . . . the Russians are advancing toward Berlin . . . scaremongers will be court-martialed . . . any sods who complain about the grub will be seen off."

I wandered among the men who were sitting or half lying in the snow, too lazy to break off a pine branch and lay it under their behinds. Some were leaning against the trees or against each other. A wave of nausea assailed me at the sight of their wet, death-house linen, the yellowy gray of their pants, their wool stockings stiff with sweat, their green faces and gray-blue hands. Their damp jackets clung in tight folds to arms and bodies, forming, together with the pants, a sort of half finished statue. There was a heaviness and stiffness, an air of creaking joints about every movement. Their eyes were drowsy, damp locks of hair struggled out from under their tightly fitting granny caps. Some of them had lost their headgear. They had been running and a bough had whipped them off and there had been no time to recover them. Their lips were pinched, without color, sagging at the ends, their ears were jutting out, their moustaches drooping. Rifles were either held between the knees at the ready, planted at one side, lying on the ground, or poking out in all directions. Green linen satchels of Italian make, sports or ski bags, an old Yugoslav knapsack, a great leather bag. Everything soaked, crumpled, wrinkled. Not a flash of color, not a shape to attract the eye. Silence and deadly weariness.

No one was looking at me either, as I was well aware. I was just like them, in the first stages of decay. I would not have recognized my ski boots. Once they had been dark red with white laces but now they had a gray-black hue. Material tires, material starts to disintegrate. Within our human husks, which suffer a slow and persistent decline, there is another type of decay which occurs in a state of hallucination, a sleep of conscious disgust, in the weary struggle of the instinct of self-preservation, with its occasional interruptions, when some formless but sharp and unquiet thought flashes through our minds: Home!

244

Mother! Brother! Children! Heaps of polenta. That log has the shape of a biscuit. A house! The civilians have got barrels of lard, sacks of flour, macaroni with bacon! Writing in blue on a white kitchen serviette. The hand of a girl behind a tobacconist's counter offering an elegant packet of cigarettes.

The rifle was making my shoulder ache. I had a dull pain in my side . . . that was my pack . . . didn't realize it was so heavy . . . Maybe today they were going to close in on us, firing from all sides . . . I had a pain over my eyes, a cold maybe. My fingers were numb. My fingertips were made of wood . . . The sound of firing was getting nearer and nearer . . . Probably all hell would break loose when we were getting our grub . . . Nobody could help anyone else, we were all exhausted. Whoever had something to say to his neighbor said it. Who gives a darn for me? Who needs me? Number off! Fine, fine, but who is going to count you? The slightest movement makes you ache all over. What if they capture me alive! Alive, you say? I'm half dead. I have no face of my own any more, I am just like that one or that one or that one or those over there. Close those eyes and you will see a death mask. We'll never get out of here. The only question is: how long can it go on? The best thing would be to go to sleep and never wake up again. I can't get to sleep anyway because of the noise. What is this awful ringing in my ears? I am climbing a wall, the wall is smooth, and there are very few cracks in it. I must get up to the top. If I leave to go now, if I slip . . . I'll be smashed to smithereens on the rocks below. A moment of terror: I open my eyes to see black and white spots with gold spirals creeping over them. I clench my fist: Is this a forest? Or only a delusion? No! It really is! What? Someone gripped me by the shoulders, but I could not see who it was. After all I had no one. It would be nice to have someone to take me by the shoulders because he really wanted to look me in the eye and tell me something pleasant. My friend! And I am your friend too.

Bang your head against a tree. Then you will realize how damp, chilly, blind, and stupid it all is. What does the Moon care for the Earth? There is a rustle in the treetops. What do they care? The mountain stands here. What does it care whether you fall on these slopes or move on?

Even going for a piss was a great effort and a completely idiotic exertion. Grope in your soaking rags, aim, and shoot. This was probably the only warm thing in the forest. A rusty spoon with a hole in it lay on the snow. My piss is the color of rust too. The snow was covered with black dots. I am a black dot in the snow too. Some fictitious divinity up in the clouds pissing on the earth. "O.C. troop three." Yes? "On parade when you've eaten."

Dropping, dropping, dropping, into a terrible dark pit inside yourself, a bottomless pit, then flashing up again as if propelled by a spring. And now you are happy to feel the eyes of your men focused on you. You act differently because of this affection than you would without it. Later on, someone will say, "That was the famous battle of Horse Droppings." Yes, somewhere a bright, fine future was awaiting us. The children would learn at school about the iron hearts of the heroes who stood shoulder to shoulder fighting for a better future for our country.

We ate and lined up afterward.

Mikhaylov came along and gave us some more of his nonsense. He was tongue-tied and nobody paid any attention to him. But he was mercifully short. Afterward he waved his hand. We moved to take up position. I looked at my watch. It was half past eight. Morning, I thought, and looked up at the patches of sky between the treetops. During the whole action, I had looked at my watch only two or three times, but this was the second time today. The watch was working in spite of everything. Leaving, going forward, probably even ticking. I wonder now, whether I then had a presentiment? A feeling that we were on our way to a massacre. That I should see all those men die before my eyes.

Maybe I did have that feeling. But I had many other necessary, pressing, and practical matters on my mind.

For example, the sheer mechanics of our progress to take up position, through the forest, where our way was blocked by branches and fallen trees, with hollows buried by the snow, into which we would sink right up to our crotch, and this repeated over the whole mountainside. Behind us came another troop, which Mikhaylov was bringing along.

So we advance together with Mikhaylov. Probably he had taken two troops and Chiro was now leading the two others to take up their positions. I myself was not very clear what position we were making for, or why, or with what object. Don't ask questions in the forces. Through the forest came the sound of rifle and machine-gun fire in the distance. We were used to this by now. When it was so far off we paid no attention to it.

Mechanics.

Some people are of the opinion that mechanics is the queen of all the sciences. There still exists a purely mechanical view of the world, which teaches that all events are produced by forces, that all consequences mechanically follow from causes—and that apart from this, no higher unitary aim exists. The old adherents of mechanics compared man with a mechanism which works in this way. That view may itself now belong to the past but its supporters, conscious or unconscious, are still living among us, notwithstanding all the teleologists who proclaim various kinds of higher purpose, so that in the same battle, someone would fight for the Emperor, a second for the nation, a third for the state, a fourth for an ideal, a fifth for God or for the Führer, the Revolution, liberty, world conquest.

Survival demands its own mechanics.

War also.

In a textbook, we have read that mechanics is, like physics, a science concerned with the motion of bodies and the causes of motion, of the forces which induce motion. The study of equilibrium is called statics, the study of motion, dynamics. We have the statics and dynamics of solid bodies, fluids, and gases.

An army's strength, Napoleon said, is the product of its mass and speed. So mechanics teaches us. The Blitzkrieg, as waged by the Germans, is ultimately only the latest manifestation of that principle, using modern military resources. And partisan tactics are the surprise attack and swift withdrawal; but in this chaos on Mount Mokrec, have we not forgotten some important, basic ideas? We have a lot of raw recruits; in fact there are probably too many of us on the ground, we are "as thick as Turks," and the offensive shows no signs of slackening. However, that is not my business.

Beside me walked the man who bore all the responsibility for our movement through that wood on his shoulders: the thick-set Mikhaylov. He gave us the order to halt and sent forward the second troop, which had been following us, to deploy, in the wood below us. When they had disappeared in the thickets, I felt a gentle but important change in myself: if the firing starts now, I am responsible. I glanced at my men.

A man belongs to his military unit in a special way. There can be something inborn (one comes from a military family), something acquired (from the Scouts, from sport, and from army service), something unpleasant but necessary; if the commander has not the gift of leadership, the subordinate will feel unhappy and at risk; you may be quite intelligent but when danger threatens, you cannot evade that simple but pervasive thrill. Courage? Courage is a purely relative concept for a soldier. I have seen some intrepid blockheads advancing to the charge. The first time they were scared shitless, the next time it was easier, and the third time those simpletons had decided without undue deliberation that if they had got away with it twice already, nothing was likely to happen this time either . . . and they even survived without being hit. Nothing like that for improving the morale, for keeping the chin up. An officer however, must always offer a good example. It is normal for him to show no fear. We know you, you sod, you've always got decent billets, feed on the fat of the land, never short of cigarettes; when this lot's over you'll be swaggering around, proud as a peacock, and if you've lost your horse, you'll soon find another in some stable . . . so let's see what you're worth! It is not healthy to talk about courage in the army. But there is something else which bids you, "Man, know thyself." To know what is to be done at that moment, what will save us, what may ruin us, to have an overall view of the events and the people; to have some bond with them. Our platoon consists of twenty-three men, all in a centipede with forty-six legs and one brain. If such indeed be the case, and the ideal is probably unattainable, then we have what is called a good unit. The spine which connects all the members into one whole is unseen but must be consciously felt. That platoon which went to take up position with Mikhaylov was a little larger, numbered probably over thirty. No one liked Mikhaylov—he was a poor speaker with his perpetual absurdities, he was arrogant, he did not look you in the eye—but he was now the head of our centipede and I was only his transmitter of instructions.

Once he was back, and he was already on his way, I would shed the burden of command and he would again assume full responsibility. Beside me, Anton shook his head but he did not say a single word. I knew the meaning of that headshake. Sensitive as he was, Anton realized what was passing through my mind.

"Coming events cast their shadows before."

We formed a single shadow in that baleful silence that throbbed and rumbled somewhere on the periphery. Mikhaylov came forward, surveyed the forest; none of us had any idea what his intentions were. Had he decided to remain with us? This spelled trouble.

Beside me, Anton spoke in a low voice. "The road of duty is the road to glory, the Krauts say." He said this with a perfectly casual air. He had told me, during a break in the forest, that he had read a good deal as a typesetter.

We had arrived at a more open part of the forest, where an incline sloped down to a muddy forest road. Mikhaylov stopped and looked up and down. Above us was a belt of dark pine wood. Somewhere far off, the wind was whistling in the treetops.

"Take up your positions!" Mikhaylov said. We looked at him. "Machine gun there!" Mirko moved forward, followed by his mate, and both halted, examining the place indicated by Mikhaylov. "You will have good cover there," he went on. "They will be arriving from there." From where? "From there. They'll be coming along the road." So they would be approaching from our left. The platoon slowly spread out. Mirko found a good spot for the machine gun. Anton and I were standing beside Mikhaylov, who had struck a dramatic pose, legs planted apart, automatic held at an angle and to one side, planted in the snow on a sturdy fallen tree trunk. Leaning on his gun, he gazed into the distance. When the men had moved off, he spoke swiftly. "They'll be coming along the road . . . Hold your position here . . . and when I say hold on, I mean hold on . . . We're covering the withdrawal of our wounded . . . You are the edge of the left wing. If you fall back, they'll cut through and our casualties have no other cover . . ."

I examined our surroundings with a completely different outlook than before. Mikhaylov saw that the whole affair did not inspire me with much confidence.

"To your right is the second platoon . . . in front you have Jaka . . ." It looked as if he might be about to leave us. "Stand fast, lads!"

"What if they come at us from the higher ground?" I asked.

"You'll extend your left wing higher up the slope, won't you?" He seemed rather irritated.

The men were standing in a line which extended over the hillside. They were looking at us.

One machine gun, three automatics, nineteen poor rifles, two revolvers and a few hand grenades, not even one apiece; we did not have much ammunition either. "They could come in behind us . . ."

"Post a lookout up above . . . Have I got time to start teaching you now?" Either he was angry or he was pretending to be angry. Anton and I exchanged glances. There was something going on, we agreed, something rotten in the state of Denmark.

Mikhaylov did not favor us with a parting glance as he turned around and strode off, down toward the forest road. He then turned right along the road. His figure was only just visible still through the thick foliage when we heard a volley from his automatic. Some of our men fell instinctively to the ground.

"Send a patrol after him!" I croaked. "You and you!" I pointed to a couple at the far right of our position. They rushed downhill. "The rest of you take up your positions!"

Mirko wedged his Breda between two gaps in a rock and the barrel of his gun was trained on the road to our left. Excellent, but what was that noise from our right? I sent a Cankar and a Lowlander to an observation point up on the left below the pine wood.

Anton, with a few others, moved out to our left flank. On the left, I had the other Cankar and the Gubec; they both had automatics. I settled down between Mirko and the left wing with a tree stump or some such for cover. Leon was beside me. Shorty had joined the machine gunner's mate, almost as if he really believed his own theory about the machine gun offering the best cover. Between the machine gun and me lay a miner from Zagorje. He also had an automatic and a whole bag of ammunition, or beams, as he called them. Petkoshek was a little to the left, below me. After him came the usher, the country lad, the Croatian, the student Stefan, the Lowlander with the long Austrian repeater he had got from the Whites when some village guardhouse had been destroyed; there were also some vague figures I can no longer remember.

The patrol had returned and was conferring with Anton.

Anton rose and came over to me.

He spoke softly. "It looks as if Mikhaylov discharged his Schmeisser in the air and took a powder. They know nothing of his whereabouts down at the second platoon. There's no sign of the Germans anywhere."

I gazed at him in amazement.

"If they are anywhere in the vicinity, they'll be along to see who's firing," Anton remarked gloomily.

That was the last I heard of Mikhaylov. In summer, 1944, he walked into a house in Gorjanci where I was sitting with four comrades.

"Keep in contact with the second platoon," I instructed Anton as he withdrew. I called Petkoshek and another man. "Patrol downhill to the road. Hold your fire; if you see anything, gave me a hand signal and come back up here."

I moved over to the empty ground to my left with Leon—not too far, but just far enough to give us a view of the gently sloping bank through the trees, which were thinly spaced at this point. Leon thought it was a good moment for a cigarette. We lit up. Our observers above were ensconced at the edge of the wood. Leon froze in mid movement (he was bringing the cigarette up to his lips), took my arm and pointed upward. Something was stirring in the woods. We stood there motionless, hidden behind the trees, staring out. From out of the branches one figure appeared then another, and we breathed again. Three partisans were hurrying upward. Was this patrol? Were they stragglers? We were too far away to call out to them. They disappeared in the woods above. There was no firing in their wake. Therefore there were no Germans over there either, so far. We returned to our platoon.

"You don't remember me," Leon told me quietly. "I was in the Scouts; I was a Wolf scout . . . You were my idol—you could use a lasso . . . That was at a camp near Bohinj, wasn't it? At Anvil Head. Close by the camp there were some trenches from the First World War, and remains of barbed-wire entanglements, with rusty wire. It was a warm, sunny July. We had plenty of opportunity to inspect that ancient rust and wondered what war was really like."

Leon still had the soft eyes of a civilian, of an indeterminate, rusty gray color. His voice was pleasant too, homely.

A patrol arrived from our right, from the second platoon. Two quiet, simple lads. They told us that in our rear, the wounded were being evacuated to a field hospital. That there was a long column of them. We suddenly heard a strange, dull drone. We listened. Armored cars, said one of the new arrivals. Armored cars, somewhere below us, not far away. The two hurried off back to their own unit. So Mikhaylov had not invented the casualties. But why had he fired into the air? Had he made a mistake? Impossible. Would he be back? We could forget that, it was of no importance now. Every single minute gained a couple of meters for the casualties on their stretchers. Anton was animatedly explaining something to the men with him on our right flank. He was keeping them amused, sustaining their morale, easing their tension.

I liked the miner who was lying on his side, digging in the snow; glancing back, he said in jest, "Looks as if we're going to spend the night here."

Bloody well hope not! It's only about nine o'clock now.

"And I looked, and behold a pale horse: and his name that sat on him
was Death, and Hell followed with him."
Revelation 6:8

"*Ça ira*," said Benjamin Franklin in Paris, "We're on our way."
"But where to?" Anton remarked.

"Be patient and tough; someday this pain will be useful to you."
Ovid, *Amores*

"These dialogues disclose bitter realizations. In them we see twelve lost
lives. They did not bring deliverance, as the generals expected; the lads
are still standing in the tomb. They are still standing after the third general
has gone down with his machine gun."
Account of Irwin Shaw's play, *Bury the Dead*

5

The position we had taken up was far from ideal.

In the first place, as an ambush party, we were too near the road by which the enemy could approach. Moreover, there were no real obstacles between him and us.

We had only one machine gun. We would have to use automatics for cross fire. The Breda was useless for the purpose in this damp and cold.

The fact that we were waiting for the enemy and not vice versa gave us one basic advantage. At any rate we should see him before he saw us.

The wood behind us could offer a safe retreat but on the other hand, the enemy could creep up on us from that direction.

Our left flank was open and there was so little cover that an attacker would be taking an enormous risk were he to attack from that quarter. But it would then depend on factors which we could not predict.

On our right flank was a troop with whom we were in contact.

Our men had time to find the best possible cover and consider the possibilities, clean their weapons and be ready to fire at the right time. I would open fire, that was an instruction everyone had to comply with.

There was now neither time nor opportunity to change the position of our ambush. We had to accept that. Probably very little would have been gained anyway. Below us were thickets, unsuitable for our purpose; behind us, open ground reaching back to the pine wood.

Our task was to stand our ground. For how long could not be foreseen. At any rate, we should have to make sensible use of our ammunition and hand grenades.

Crouching low, I made my rounds, from man to man, from group to group, to have a few words with each. I remember their eyes very well.

The throbbing of the engines—armored cars probably—came nearer and nearer, and then ceased, as if cut off.

I had the feeling I had now done all I could. Anton gave me a rather queer look. He knew how inexperienced I was.

I myself felt I wasn't really a soldier. Every little detail made too deep an impression on me. My heart sank when I saw the anxiety in some eyes, like a tiny flame stirring in their murky depths. I was seized with despair and a sense of my own inadequacy, when I saw in Shorty's eyes his unshakeable faith in me. He nodded agreement when I spoke to him and seemed to be all eyes, great eyes in his pinched, sea-green face. I felt some confidence in the men on the left flank. They seemed to be ready for anything, chatting amongst themselves in low voices about God knows what, looking at me in a perfectly matter-of-fact way, as if they had been through all this before. Leon gave me a pleasant surprise when he told me he would look after any casualties we might have; he had a first-aid kit with him. I had quite taken to Petkoshek and he seemed to be happy to have me around. I saw him on watch down by the road, staring now and then in my direction. I helped Vili the musician to find better cover. He said his boots were so tight it was all the same to him now, whatever happened. He still managed to come out with a facetious remark. "If we have to make run for it, so help me God and the devil himself, I'll sling my feet over my shoulders and run on my hands."

"That should give the Krauts a good laugh," said the man next to him.

"Quiet, they might hear you," a third man said.

The second retorted, "They're having a drop of the hard stuff, sipping our best plum brandy at this very moment; they'll be ready to advance when they've drained the lot."

There was an ominous silence.

I still had to visit my friend, the usher. He had his head well hidden by a tree but his heels were sticking up behind him. He would get it in the calves when the firing started. Yes indeed, a fine spot that bastard Mikhaylov had picked for our ambush! A pity the trees were so sparse. Moreover, we had no idea whether certain heaps of snow or covered rotting timber afforded any effective protection or whether they were mere foam.

Again and again, I went over our position, sometimes casting a glance down below, where Petkoshek was still on watch with another soldier, a very young lad with a girlish face, the hair only now beginning to appear, a soft down on his cheeks. Sometimes I looked up at our observers posted by the edge of the wood, a man from the Cankar brigade and a Lowlander.

Anton was on our far right, together with the fellow who had the Mannlicher. Vili the musician as well and the elderly man with the dormouse fur cap were there. Then came Mirko's machine-gun nest, his mate and Shorty lying there as well.

Our miner with the automatic; beside him a slim lad with very bandy legs. Leon.

Me.

A slight gap, vacated by the couple who were down on watch by the road.

The usher, the country lad, the Croatian, Stefan.

Out on our left flank, the other man from the Cankar brigade, our Gubec with his automatic, the chap with the Italian officer's coat (an artillery officer's probably), several sizes too big for him, and the other Lowlander.

The position we had occupied was most advantageous where it commanded the open ground on our left flank. From there, our line ran on to our weakest point on the left flank, guarded in theory by the second troop. We could direct our full firepower down on the road, either to our left or right. The automatics on our left could combine with the machine gun to provide a cross fire against assault from that quarter. We had to keep constant watch on the ridge above us and on the open ground to our left. Our best lines of retreat would not be directly to the wood behind us but along a small valley overgrown with dense thickets, in the rear of our right flank. The track which ran along the valley was well hidden by the thick vegetation, although footprints could be seen in the vicinity, footprints of our own men. A rise in the ground beside the muddy road was within bombing range.

"My God, I could eat a horse!" This came from the man with the bandy legs. It was a good sign. I had completely forgotten how hungry I was myself.

"You're obviously not a smoker," the miner said.

"I've had trouble with my lungs, mate."

At this precise moment, I saw Petkoshek waving to me and pointing to some spot down below. I signaled back that I had got the message. Our two lookouts came hurrying back to rejoin us, crouching low. They dropped to the ground, taking up their positions to my left.

Petkoshek gasped, out of breath. "They're coming . . . they're leaving the transport down below . . . there aren't so many of them . . . they're wearing black uniforms . . ."

All the men realized what this was all about. They gazed at us and then turned their attention to the road below.

The beardless youth who had been on lookout with Petkoshek added his own observation: "I can see them coming up the road . . ." We all pressed hard down against the ground and remained motionless.

This was it. *They* were coming . . . *They* were on their way . . . *They* would be here any moment now . . . *Them*! I could sense *them* physically.

After a decent rest, they had been conveyed here in their transport and were advancing up the muddy road, outwardly calm, surveying their surroundings like trained hunters, and quietly cursing to themselves all and sundry. Their heads were protected by steel helmets, their jackets clung to their shoulders, their trousers hung loosely on legs and buttocks, their boots trampled the mud. They had had a good crap before moving off. Their weapons were good, reliable; not the sort to let you down in snow and frost, mud and damp. They had plenty of ammunition. Before leaving the valley, they had eaten army bread with margarine and marmalade and washed it down with a mug of coffee. Now they were to proceed over Hill X to Hill Y. Their commanders had maps and guides, they already knew both plan and objective. The forest seemed to be empty, though there were footprints on every side. Wonder how many of the lousy bastards there are around here, enough to give us all the crabs, I'll bet. Daren't even sit down for a minute in one of their houses! Where were they bringing our casualties in from last night, so quietly and all? Why the hush-hush? Some of them were dead too. How much bloody longer have we to put up with these bandits? Looking behind trees, shooting at you, then taking to their heels. They say we're in line for a spell at the seaside after this operation. Might even be some dames there too! But first we've got to traipse over these hills, these bloody hills, and scour the flaming forests. It's eight to ten hours' hard slog, I've heard. Holy God! If I get my hands on one of those tramps, I won't waste a bullet on him! Did you see the oafish look of those characters we shot down in the village? Slavonic rabble! Pan-Slavism, my foot! But where do the bastards get all their weapons from? When do they get a chance to scoff their fodder, with us at their heels all the time? I've heard they climb the trees; you've got to keep your eyes skinned for that. If they only knew back home how these blackguards have got us on the hop! Just imagine. We've taken a firm hold on Europe, from the Atlantic Wall to the Caucasus, from Narvik to the African desert . . . and here are these communist cowboys shooting it out with the Wehrmacht. They wouldn't believe a word of it back home. But you have to be on the lookout when you're dealing with a lunatic. The idiots don't seem to care about dying. To think that only a couple of months ago I was brushing up on my Latin: mensa, mensa, mensam, mensae . . . Now the chief thing is for our backroom boys to get on with the job and produce that secret weapon as soon as possible. Once we have that, we can wipe Moscow, London, and Washington off the face of the globe in a day. Then we shan't have to waste time chasing this shower around the Balkans. The QM had a skinful of wine last night. Did you hear what he was saying? Seems someone dropped a prize clanger when we helped Lenin to get back to Russia. Himmelkreuzdonnerwetter, I can't keep my footing in this shit! If I catch one of those commie bastards, I'll have him eating the muck and liking it!

We now saw some movement down at a hump in the road. Dark shapes appeared, halted, and looked back. Then they moved forward. Three in front, behind them two, and one more makes six. Was this their advance guard or a flank patrol? From behind his Breda, Mirko glanced across at me. I shook my head. If they were going to pass, let them advance. We would first see what was behind them. They would not be walking this road, high up in the hills, by themselves. And soon the next lot came into view. They were approaching calmly. I could clearly make out their weapons and equipment. One was wearing a knee-length jacket with a fur collar and lining. The others were in greatcoats with gleaming buttons. I trained my rifle on the leader of this second group. My hands were trembled slightly. Nerves. If I opened fire too early that would spoil things. If I left it late that would be no better. I did not know which would be the right moment. Petkoshek had told me there were not so many of them. No doubt we were all holding our breath. I was afraid the Germans might even feel our silence.

Taking careful aim, I let him have it in the chest. Immediately, my ears were deafened by the din, as the machine gun rattled, the automatics chattered, and the rifles cracked. Down below, there began a strange dance of death. There was no doubt I had hit my target; he clutched his chest and lurched forward to fall on his face. The others were flailing, leaping, diving down the hillside, at the same time returning our fire. In the crackle of rifle fire, bullets were flying past, whistling about our ears. Vili, my musician, was the first to hurl a grenade. He lobbed it with his right hand in a fine long arc. Good for you, Vili! I saw the usher, with his head pressed to the ground, raising his rifle, firing at random, then drawing the weapon back again. Time and time again I aimed and fired, without checking any longer whether my shots hit or not. The Germans regrouped with amazing speed. Some of them had taken cover below the verge on the upper side of the road and were spraying us with their Schmeissers. Others had rushed down to the road and were dragging the dead or wounded off, firing at the same time. The man with the Mannlicher, beside Anton, gave a strange cry, slumped quietly to one side and lay there motionless. Anton's carbine had probably let him down; he worked the bolt furiously before firing again.

Time passed and I was no longer thinking of myself. The butterflies had stopped fluttering in my stomach. I took aim and shot whenever I saw a target. Meanwhile I surveyed the position to our left and right. A German lobbed a Stiller from the edge of the road. It landed in front of the country boy, and beside the usher; he grabbed the bomb as soon as it touched the ground and tossed it back, down toward the road. For the moment he was a sitting duck. I saw him clutch his side and spin back on to the ground. It looked as if he had stopped a volley. But there was another, louder report down below, like a shot from a cannon. The explosion of the Stiller had some effect on the Germans. They were now firing from both left and right. Mirko let them have a short burst, stopped, and waited before spraying them again; he was saving ammunition. I heard more rifle fire to our right; the second troop also had the Germans on their neck.

"Look out, to your left!" yelled the Croatian. Three figures were darting uphill through the sparse trees above the road. One of our Cankars fired at these targets, reloading his rifle furiously; then the Gubec let them have a volley from his automatic and waited a moment. The three dropped back to the road. Were they dead, alive, wounded? One and then another soon resumed firing again. The Croatian and Stefan were immediately struck in the hand by bullets from that quarter. Leon noticed Stefan's bleeding palm, crawled over to him and opened his pack. A bullet whisked off his cap but he was already sitting beside Stefan, bandaging his hand. Wild shooting now broke out on our right flank. By all appearances, that troop had come off much worse than ours. The Germans below us were rushing across the road, a little farther down, and still firing at us from the right, where the ground rose somewhat higher above the road. The road immediately below us was "clear." The first phase was over therefore. But what next? Quite mechanically, probably hankering for the evening, I glanced at my watch. Really? Was it possible? It was almost eleven. When had I got those three parallel scratches from some thorn bush?

Anton turned and looked in my direction, as if he would have liked a word with me. Speak! I tried to guess what he wanted, to read it in his eyes. "Should we withdraw?" We can't, Anton. You know what is going on somewhere in our rear. And the enemy will be back again. Now we know a little better how things are going. I can see that we would now still have time for withdrawal, but we have no idea what is coming later. And our wounded have not yet reached the safety of our camouflaged field hospitals on higher ground. You probably agree with me, don't you? What I would give to have someone else take over this responsibility. What action should we take right away? Leon is looking after our casualties. "Mirko, how are we off for ammunition? How long will it last?" Right. When it's used up, we shall withdraw immediately in that direction! Leon and the usher carried the country boy, who was severely wounded, to a hollow behind the thick trunk of a beech tree. The Croatian threw his rifle after him. Our Gubec was trying to light a thinly rolled cigarette but his matches were damp. The Germans down to our right set up a heavy machine gun, a Schwarzlose, which was now raking our position. Get your heads down! The usher was hit in the leg. They peppered us with bullets and then concentrated on our Breda. Mirko answered with a short burst. Anton lobbed a grenade forward and down. There was a loud explosion but the machine-gun fire continued. On they came again and dived for cover; the miner sprayed them with automatic fire. The elderly man, lying next to Anton, was steadily aiming and firing at the figures who were moving forward covered by the Schwarzlose. Our lookouts on higher ground, a Cankar with an automatic and a Lowlander, were still at their post; they signaled that they had nothing special to report. I sent the lad in the oversize greatcoat up to relieve the Cankar with the automatic, whom I posted on our right flank, thereby improving our firepower. I would have liked to send a patrol out to the second troop, but I could not spare the men and had not the confidence to deploy them. Meanwhile, things were heating up on our right. Probably the Germans were hoping to force their way uphill and take us from that side but they were doomed to disappointment. The Schwarzlose kept up a long and steady fusillade. The position made it easier for us: we could toss our grenades downhill, while the Germans had to hurl theirs uphill. One of them emerged slightly from his cover to be hit in the neck and breast, either by Mirko's machine gun or by the miner's automatic. But what was this? Mirko rolled his mate's body over, looked at me, and indicated that he had got a bullet in the middle of his forehead. Shorty rushed down to join Mirko and the dead man.

And so it went on and on without ceasing. We had three dead men and three or four wounded, one of them seriously. Eleven of us remained. The weather was gray and misty, the visibility about forty meters. The temperature was just above zero. There was a wind in the treetops but it was almost still at ground level.

Increased activity down below suggested the arrival of German reinforcements. On our right flank, the firing seemed to be moving higher and higher. Was the second troop retreating? There was also some movement down below to our left. They had found a way through to our left flank. The Gubec and both the Cankars were keeping an eye on that quarter. An attack was imminent; we could hear whistles and orders shouted in German.

Hand grenades exploded beneath our position, throwing up spouts of gray-black slush, and we were showered with a mixture of earth, stones, tree branches, and filthy snow. The Croatian was hit once again. Anton threw a grenade. The Germans were preparing for action; they were now racing up the hillside in threes, or so I thought. The miner was firing short volleys from his automatic. Mirko likewise, with Shorty now acting as his assistant. He really was a tough little fellow. Some Germans had ensconced themselves behind rocks on the bank below us, where they could not be observed from above. Oh, for a sack of hand grenades, no matter what make. I still did not draw my little black, segmented grenade from my pocket; worse was yet to come. Now there was even more movement down below. We would be overwhelmed. Those who had found cover on the sloping open ground to our left, in spite of all our efforts, were now peppering us with rifle fire. Stefan the student was no more; he had flapped his arms and fallen, after leaping up as if he had been thrown. In spite of his wound, the usher was attempting to crawl back to the point where Petkoshek was steadily firing away, the young lad with the down on his chin beside him. In that constant hail of bullets, it was impossible to poke your head out of shelter, but I did see Shorty on his knees, feeding Mirko with ammunition. What could I do? I could not go down there and if I yelled at him, he would not hear me. Now he was flat on his face; was he wounded? Probably not. Then came a thunderous series of explosions to our right, as if someone had thrown a stick of bombs. What on earth was that? For a moment the German attack was repulsed. Something to our advantage had occurred. Never mind what. The great thing was that the Schwarzlose had stopped chattering. That damned steady, cold, deathly tick-tock-tock had been getting on my nerves.

About six or seven meters below me I saw a German lying on his face, with his Schmeisser stuck in the snow by his right hand. What an opportunity! The temptation flashed through my mind . . . but the terrain gave no cover. Down below *they* would have a perfect view. I could not risk it, although my men could give me covering fire. And how were we doing for ammunition? I rushed over to Mirko, who had Shorty there beside him. We were down to our last stocks. "When we've used that up, we'll get the hell out of here. And you can take a rifle off one of the . . ." Understood. I did not want to say "dead." Although the fusillade had slackened, the bullets were still flying overhead. I crawled in Anton's direction; for the last few yards I flung myself on the ground and rolled down to him. I struck something sharp with the hand in which I was holding my rifle; my fingers were bleeding and chafed, though there was no longer any feeling in them.

Anton's face was gray; he had no cap and the bandage on his head was a gray-black color. Somewhere uphill on our left, not very close to us, a machine gun stuttered; then came the sound of a brisk fusillade and rifle fire. I glanced up the hill. Our look-outs, the Lowlander and the man in the outsize greatcoat, were also taken by surprise and were wondering what had happened. They themselves were not under fire. There was much movement in the forest to our right, where automatics had opened up. The man in the dormouse cap was now shooting in that direction and we followed his line of fire, trying to detect his target. Things were heating up immediately below us and on the open ground to our left. Mirko was restricting himself to bursts of two or three shots, choosing his target carefully. The figures to our right disappeared.

I looked across to see what was happening on our left. The Gubec had been hit, the miner too, more or less at the same time. That German trio were safe and well hidden behind the shelter of a jagged rock. Only a few paces separated them from us. Vili fired his rifle, without taking special aim. Our Lowlander threw a grenade at the precise moment when the trio broke cover to rush forward. He could not have timed it better. Voices were yelling orders in German. The Schwarzlose opened up again.

Was I leading these men, or were they leading me? We all lay together, the living, the wounded, and the dead, still at our post. We were getting our stint of military training and could not get over our surprise that we could put up such a prolonged resistance, although we were unused to action. No one gave any signs of uncertainty. Each of us looked about him, saw that others were firing and joined in himself; saw someone else throwing a grenade and remembered that he too had a bomb at his belt. The Germans were not immune, immortal, or iron men. In any case, we were probably not dealing with frontline troops. How many of us were still sound in wind and limb, no one could say. I could not understand why they did not try to outflank our position on the left and take us from the rear. Clearly, their tactics were also not so brilliant, so infallible, taking account of all possibilities. Or maybe they were trying to operate with quite small forces.

Things were so heated, there was no chance to discuss our position with Anton. Leon shuddered, gazed up to heaven with a look of surprise and toppled over, face down in snow-covered bilberry bushes. Beside him lay the usher, clutching his cheek. I felt I was needed over there, but hardly had I moved when there was a thunderous explosion behind me. I was showered with debris and felt a violent blow in the middle of my back—I later came to the conclusion I had been hit by a stone. I saw Anton with his hands up to his face. The man with the dormouse cap lay pressed to the ground, flat as a pancake. Vili had been flung on his back. Face covered in blood, he was staring up at the sky with wide-open, unseeing eyes. Anton was still alive, the man with the dormouse cap was hurling a grenade, Vili was lost forever.

I was now in that slightly crazed condition when some things seem clear and obvious, while others seem arcane and senseless. When the ears are deafened by the din and yet that very deafness hears what it must. When the eyes are dazzled by lights and sparks, yet know what they must see. When the body is both heavy and weightless, when a moment of great pain is immediately followed and swamped by a dullness of the senses. Different impressions of varying emotions follow each other in quick sequence, hope and despair alternating like light and dark, noise and silence, both delivering strong, sharp shocks to the head and guts, shocks that last only a moment in a long, timeless sequence of events, suspended between eternity and delirium. In a moment of hope, I could have thrown my arms around someone; in my despair, I could have wept; but I did neither, it was all bottled up inside me. I promised myself I would embrace the elderly man in the dormouse cap if we ever got out alive. Previously I had noticed only his cap, but now I couldn't wait to tell everybody what a marvelous chap he was! I had completely forgotten what Anton's face looked like. I crossed over to the cinema usher. A bullet had gone clean through his hand, which he was clutching at his blood-soaked breast. He did not seem to see me. He was gazing in fright at his own flesh and blood. He knew I was beside him, trying to help, though there was not much I could do without bandages. I could only undo my clothes and tear a strip off my shirt; that might help. He shook me off, as if I were intruding on his privacy. "I had only two clips of ammo," he said, "and now I have only one bullet left . . ." Quietly he added: "For myself." In spite of the bombardment and fusillades I heard him with unusual clarity—or was I lipreading? I took hold of Leon's hand. It was still warm. Although we were all frozen stiff and half dead, the softness of Leon's hand had for me the sensation of warmth. His shock of fair hair hung down in the snow. A vein was poking out of his neck wound, by now producing only a small trickle of blood. An important vein, obviously. I saw the snow in front of him red with blood, red and spattered with black spots.

Things were not quite like that. It was only a second or two before I was stretched out again, firing. A Kraut, well sheltered by the rocks, was firing away with gay abandon, but I had to save my ammunition. A new clip . . . was it the last? I could not afford to waste these bullets. I felt a surge of deep resentment at the thought of the enormous stocks of ammunition available to the Krauts to keep up this constant bombardment. The crackle of rifle fire grew brisker on our right. That was probably where they would break through. Three or four of us could not hold them up for long.

And now Mirko! Shorty was dragging his corpse away from the machine gun. Anton came across to join me, accompanied by the man in the dormouse cap. The bandy-legged fellow was on his own in the center, still taking aim, still firing. Petkoshek and the beardless youth exchanged a few words and glanced back at me. Yes, lads, I understand, but it's out of the question for the present. Don't worry, the time will come.

How did I know who was right? I would have liked to start yelling, but who would have heard me? Then I felt a certain slight relief, when the thought crossed my mind, that at the moment, we had no alternative to our present course of action. My right eye was closed. I felt it with my left hand and removed a lump of mud. I could see again with both eyes. At last Shorty managed to open up with the Breda again, although he had no assistant. Seeing this, the man with the dormouse cap rushed to join him. Anton took over my previous position without mishap. He had good cover there. He fired one shot and looked across in my direction. Yes, we would withdraw at the first opportunity. I felt in my pocket; the small black grenade was still there. Whistles, orders, shouts, indicated increased activity among the Germans below us.

Five, or was it ten, horrible minutes followed. Violent, arbitrary events follow their own willful course and nothing can be otherwise; we can no longer exercise any influence over things. If all water suddenly started to flow uphill, people would at first be astonished and then get used to it. Things no longer happen by chance but by necessity, without cause or consequence. Men are no longer men, nature no longer nature; there are no more thoughts, no more feelings, only the spool of memory spins on, recording, without knowing why.

They had brought up several machine guns, which now opened up at us from all sides. They broke through simultaneously on our right and left flanks, not that we had anyone on the flanks by now. The whole place was swarming with them. We were raked with bursts of automatic fire from all directions. Those of us on the left withdrew uphill, fighting desperately. The Cankar fell. The man with the dormouse cap dragged his machine gun up through the snow; Shorty was left, slumped at his post. The beardless youth also fell and Petkoshek retreated rapidly. The lookouts I had posted up above, I now saw, were also under fire and began to withdraw. The fellow in the outsize greatcoat seemed to have his legs cut from under him as he somersaulted down the slope. The Lowlander was kneeling behind a tree; the rifle had dropped from his hands. I saw some Germans racing uphill, straight at me. I just managed to strike the percussion cap of my small grenade and throw it at the right time. I did not wait to see what damage it had done but leaped over a fallen tree trunk with Anton. The man with the dormouse cap got a bullet in the back and collapsed. Now we were making for the shallow valley, which concealed a path leading up to the edge of the forest. Petkoshek shouted and I looked around. He had stopped and was holding the small of his back. He lurched sideways. Anton and I raced back and dragged him along with us, supporting him under the armpits. Bullets were whizzing past our ears and thudding into the ground behind us. Now our legs were our only hope, provided our hearts did not leap out of our throats. Petkoshek was quite a weight. He could not move his legs, but he was conscious. "Leave me here, leave me . . ." he said, "I'm done for . . ." He was moaning and groaning in pain. We were dragging him along, unable to stop long enough to lay him on our rifles, which might have made it easier to carry him. But how was it that the Germans still had not caught up with us? The snow was here no longer trampled by many feet, and gave way under our weight. At a bend in our path I looked back—strange, there were no Germans to be seen, though the bullets whistling about our ears suggested they were not far behind and only the nervous haste of our hunters would save us. We tried supporting Petkoshek on a rifle but it was too painful. "It won't work," he said. Anton swiftly took the blanket out of his pack and unwound it. We sat Petkoshek on the blanket and took hold of the ends. The operation seemed to last a lifetime. The injured man put his arms around our necks. I wrapped the end of the blanket around my rifle. This also proved very inconvenient. I slung the weapon over my shoulder and took hold of my end of the blanket with both hands. We hurried on. There were still no Germans in sight, although the bullets had not stopped flying—or was it my imagination? No, they were still firing. Three or four other partisans appeared, hurrying up another path. I did not recognize them. They were running too, I could hear them panting. They hurried past us up the path which was widening out, with the snow trampled by many feet. I even saw a mule's droppings. A blanket is terribly awkward for moving a wounded man. I could feel my fingernails being torn out. Petkoshek was groaning aloud with the pain. He removed a hand from my neck to clutch at the wound in his stomach. The bullet had struck him in the back and come out through his stomach. Anton's mouth was open and his eyes were bulging with the effort. Here and there, the snow was blood red. But what was that? A red Italian hand grenade. I picked it up and examined it.

"It has no firing pin," I said.

"Throw the bloody thing away!" Anton's voice was unusually severe. I threw it down the hill; it went off with one hell of a bang. Anton gave me a long, cool look and tried to close his dry lips. More partisans came pushing uphill behind us. We still weren't out of range of rifle fire. Anton barred the way and called out in a commanding voice, "Wait there! Lend a hand!" We handed Petkoshek over to two of the new arrivals, who didn't say a word.

Petkoshek looked at me and said, "If you see him . . . tell my brother how it was . . ." He thought we were going to abandon him. We were walking just behind the bearers. We were relieved of a great burden. I felt weightless, as if I were drifting up toward the tops of the pine trees. There were now more and more of us on the path. Some hurried past us, others gathered behind. We were all going in the same direction, without knowing where it led. Did anyone at all know? I recognized no one and we spoke to no one. Now I felt a pain in my back, as if a piece of iron was lodged close by my spine. I could neither bend nor hold myself erect. I was walking in some intermediate posture. The sound of gunfire was not far behind us, and showed no intention of leaving us.

We arrived at a crossroads. Our path through the snow ran on, wide as a cart track. A still wider path, of the breadth of a highway, well trodden, ran off to the right. Two medical orderlies, wearing Red Cross armbands, took charge of Petkoshek. "Tell my brother . . ." he repeated as they carried him away. That was a really fine black-and-red shirt he was wearing. Maybe he would pull through. Together with Anton, I joined the stream of people which continued to climb higher. Now at last I could take a good look at Anton. He was a real scarecrow. Head bare and bandaged, with one of his puttees trailing loose and bloodstained in the snow. I wondered whose blood it was. I realized that he was inspecting me too and thinking: "What a fine fellow he was, but look at him now—a real scarecrow." Many centuries earlier, we had left a certain town together, on our way to join the army. That night, we had crouched in a hedge and talked about how long this war would last.

At last the sound of firing behind us receded into the distance. Look out! Experience had taught us that in these circumstances firing might break out either ahead or on our flanks. I still had two bullets but no grenades. Nowhere did I see a face I knew. But we were all hurrying to the same destination. It was about half past three in the afternoon.

No doubt an expert account of the preceding action could be written by a military historian, who would regard it as a small item in the continuing story of a campaign fought by the German divisions to clear a certain territory from the "red rabble." The writer would have at his disposal data from both sides, would be able to check his sketch against a large-scale map and would also know the date.

The report of the commander of the third troop would have contributed nothing more than his own state, the time by his watch and his losses. He did not even know the name of the battalion to which his unit belonged, nor the date of the events, nor the numbers allotted to the hills. Therefore, names of individuals and accounts of gallantry are unimportant.

The Germans are keen on photography. Maybe one of them took a photo or two. Landscape with dead bandit. We saw a lot of such photos after the war.

What view of the battle did that small insect have, from his nook in the bark of that mossy tree trunk? Don't tell me he was a figment of my imagination.

What was the view from the Moon? The Earth was shrouded in mist.

The view from our distant past? *Plus ça change . . .*

The view from the remote future? Things were cheaper then.

The view from various standpoints, of disputing philosophers, military theorists and political attitudes? Pure chickenshit.

The memory of it decades afterward? A dull pain.

The truth about that action will never be known.

Such was the tenor of my thoughts, on a summer night in 1973, in a late-night restaurant, the Ca'n Morey "The Grotte" Barbacone Grill, in El Arenal. *Abierto toda la noche*; open all night. *Cene con ambiente musical. Essen sie mit Musik! Bibidas 25 ptas*; drinks 25 pesetas. *Especialidades. Spezialitäten!*

Perhaps man is a mere bubble in time's froth, doomed to disappear without a trace; but no one can prove this. Who can deny that within me, there still live on many men who have died, perished, vanished into thin air? For example, that fellow with the dormouse cap. The sight of him hurrying to Shorty's aid— and that child too still haunts me—is painfully printed in my memory. Or Vili the musician: how often he comes back to mind! He still lives and demands that I remember him. How many of them have come with me to the Spanish Riviera, to bathe with me, to saunter with me along the lively streets, gazing at the shop windows and their colorful displays, listening to the music of the guitars, drinking coffee on the pavements, sitting with Joseph Bitter and his wife, contemplating. *Essen sie mit Musik.* Maybe there really was an insect on the tree trunk that had his life and being in that moss and watched what those noisy people on the ground were doing. An insect has no ideology, the poor thing could not distinguish a swastika from a five-pointed star. An insect could not be expected to know that some Germans were more for Hitler and others less so. He would not know that the Liberation Front was composed of various groups, that party members, left-wing Sokols, and intellectuals were here deployed below him. Perhaps he could only distinguish between the dead and the living. He would not know that while insects die and stay dead, people do not want to die and stay dead but to go on living, roam the world, go sailing. Furthermore, they are sometimes violent. They wake you up in the middle of the night, prop you up on your elbows, and drag you out of bed, just to accompany them to that all-night restaurant, the Cuevas Ca'n Morey, where the band plays till dawn.

There is no way of telling which individuals are going to be officially declared immortal and given a monument. Take the pharaohs: they built their pyramids and whole generations of slaves toiled virtually from the cradle to the grave to raise them. On the granite peak of one of the pyramids an immortal ruler had the following lines inscribed:

> *Higher is the soul of Amenemhet than the height of Orion,*
> *and it's united with the underworld.*

Poets and men of learning cherish the hope that "in their works they shall live forever."

Dante's *Divine Comedy* immortalizes his name, Ohm has the unit of electrical resistance named after him, the Bering Strait is named after Bering. Napoleon even has a monument in Ljubljana, while hundreds of thousands of those who fell in his campaigns have earned themselves a monument to the unknown soldier. A monument was set up in Switzerland, in honor of a sagacious Saint Bernard dog, which saved several people from death in a snowstorm. Inscriptions are engraved on tombstones all the world over and the most popular is: "In Loving Memory." In Luanda, the capital of Angola, a one-time Portuguese colony in Africa, I saw a beautiful avenue named after the poet Luís de Camões. In what used to be called the Belgian Congo and is now Zaire, my knees buckled when I saw the Lumumba Memorial—erected by the man who had sent him bound with rope to his death. The world is full of memorials to perpetuate their everlasting memory. In their wills, men set aside a certain sum of money for their posthumous stone memorial. Stone is forever.

Crucero de la tarde a través de la bahía . . . Afternoon cruise around the bay . . . See the cathedral, the old city walls, the Bellver castle, the Moorish citadel . . . Stone eternal . . . Bronze cannons, giants in stone. In eternal memory of the conquerors. And the poets, please. There stands a conquistador, broad-shouldered, with cross and sword; beside him a poet, slim and pensive; both of them gazing out over the sea, into infinity.

Conejo a la brasa. Roast hare, please.

A bordo les serán servidas galletas con moscatel. No olviden su máquina de retratar! Cookies and muscatel wine will be served on board. Don't forget your camera!

A waiter, with the splendid name of Serafin, explained for my benefit why they did not have any more strikes in Spain. "Just look at England and all that strife, all those crises caused by the multi-party system. We don't have that here."

I heard the same explanation from the taxi driver who charged no more for fifteen kilometers than one of ours would take for a five-hundred-meter hop to the railway station. I wonder whether, for the fun of it, I might take an interest in Spanish affairs. I'll never forget what Anton told me at the end of that nightmare retreat. After careful consideration, he said to me, "No one should discuss Spain and the Spaniards until he's lived there a few years at least."

. . . *Un recuerdo imborrable* . . . An unforgettable memory . . .

That was shortly before his death.

We kept trudging on of course, and God knows what thoughts were passing through our heads.

We were tramping along a path through the snow, which was getting wider and wider. We had now left the enemy far behind us. But there was no telling when we were in for the next unpleasant surprise.

The Germans had made it to Stalingrad but came to a full stop there, as we often reminded ourselves during the course of this operation.

Some people maintain that life is a battle. An old partisan once told me: "Life is one eternal slog." Then there is a saying I have heard from other people and seen in print on the occasion of someone's death: "He has reached his journey's end."

Our march was becoming less disciplined. As soon as we felt more secure, hunger began to assert itself, growing stronger all the time, lowering dark curtains before the eyes. The saying that a man's sight goes dim with hunger is no old wives' tale.

Somehow or other, we got ourselves organized in single file and put an end to the overtaking and straggling. No orders were passed down the line. I have no idea who decided on our direction. You don't ask questions in the army!

I noticed, with some jealousy, a fighter not far ahead of me who had a light machine gun slung over his shoulder. We had lost ours and a whole heap of other gear too. We would preserve a discreet silence about that, Anton and I. Here we were, the commander and the commissar! But where was our unit? The captains had escaped from the sinking ship but the crew had gone down to the bottom. Blame the Krauts. How many men there were in the column, safe and sound, still marching on, while I had lost mine? I trudged on in silence. Should we have withdrawn when we had the chance? Fool, don't ask questions in the army! Look there! Snow White is cooking supper for the hard-working dwarfs. Come and get your helping, stand in line, you'll have a big ladleful to keep body and soul together. You shall eat. Warmth shall flood your veins; you can hardly wait, can you? Something will travel from your mouth to your gut, nothing in particular will happen, and yet all the world will be transformed. Why don't they get a move on, those dawdlers in front of you? In your way, aren't they? But now you're in line, it doesn't occur to you that you are in anybody's way. Like to guzzle the whole pot, wouldn't you? What a small helping you got from Snow White, the nasty, stingy greedy-guts! Now find a seat, anywhere at all, you're carrying the essence of the universe in your grimy hands. What would you do now, if someone tried to take your food, your dole of life from you? Look, that fellow beside you has sipped the last drop of brown slush, but he's still hungry. Go on, give him yours! Oh, come on now, tell him you've got the stomachache and can't

272

take any food. Just for the fun of it! He'll enter into the spirit of it: he'll take it without a word, won't even say "thank you," and why should he? You don't want to? You can't? You bag of wind and idle chatter. Eat up and belt up! Go on, get it down, you shameless guzzler! Don't look anyone else in the eye, for you would both see through to the shallow floor, where that naked worm called hunger squats, wrapped up in body tissue: how it works you don't know, but outside you have the skin, then the clothing and a whole jumble of principles. You see? A couple of spoonfuls of food and we're back to our principles again.

We move off again. Not a word of thanks. We simply move off. Withdraw into your shell and march on as if nothing has happened. Never for a moment let it enter your head that someone had to organize the serving, and someone else had to cook the meal; what do you care how he survived this day, where he got the firewood (firewood needs collecting and snow does not burn). Do you remember the cook's face? Did he have a face?

No, no; it was all a mirage. Longing. Illusion. A dream.

Now you have left the firing far behind. Hunger is not gnawing at your body. You have had a smoke. And you have realized now, of course, how exhausted you are. Like to lie on a warm stove, wouldn't you? And you might then start thinking about a woman . . . well, that's how desire feeds on desire fulfilled. Caesar intended to have himself crowned emperor, but they killed him first. That was why Napoleon was more careful and surrounded himself with police and guards.

Unexpectedly, the order came down the line: halt! So we belong to a unit, do we? Someone is leading us, someone knows where we are going. I pass the word on to Anton, who is now walking behind me. He also winced, halted, and looked beyond me somewhere in the distance. I could not have recognized his face; it was black around the eyes and otherwise without color. A black bandage around his head and black rings around his eyes, which had sunk into their sockets.

Be ye therefore wise as serpents and gentle as doves, the Old Testament teaches us somewhere. Not so; at times you should be furious with yourself and the whole world, otherwise you will not survive. Civilization? In the twentieth century! Heil Hitler! Our present trudge through this never-ending wood is the culmination of thousands and thousands of years' development of our civilization; we must not forget this! No more bowing and scraping before it and its upstart representatives! No more drumming into idiots and schoolkids the claim that man is the crown of creation! We must shatter all idols! We have more and more rights, since at any moment we may no longer have anything to lose. Life? What is that, ye prophets! We have seen human bones, pulverized meat, slit arteries, corpses, carnage; we have killed and been killed, without quite descending to cannibalism; we have marched and marched and marched, but we have not seen life anywhere! Should we now start whining, groaning, moaning, weeping, wailing, sobbing? Cursing, praying, gnashing our teeth? Celebrating the ghosts of a paradise lost? No. "Sod it" shall be our motto; sod the world and all who sail in her, ourselves included. Others before us have had the same attitude but the majority has quietly immured them in the foundations or the monuments of their culture, so that those who came along later have always had to think twice before violating the gods. Whole generations of the Slovene intelligentsia have crept devoutly into the bowels of Privy Counselor Wolfgang Goethe, who observed at close hand the doings of the German soldiery, without breathing a word about it in his writings. *Goethedämmerung*, not *Götterdämmerung*. Generations have visited Vienna, enjoyed the life of the capital, drunk in the most expensive places, and absorbed the lively spirit of German culture. Slovenes were highly regarded in Austria as conscientious officials, gendarmes, and financiers; the Highland Jocks were, along with the Bosnians, the best assault troops—with a gut full of rum, they would rush into battle for "faith, home and Emperor." A parson from Kranj and a dowager mayoress of liberal stamp stood guard over the national spirit. Faithful people. Come all ye Slavs! Then the First World Crap, followed by a match in Belgrade, to decide who knew how to serve the national interest (of course) best: the Clericals or the Liberals. Cue for the swish of rubber truncheons belaboring the backs of the shameless students of Ljubljana, sweet music dedicated to the Yugoslav National Party and the Yugoslav Radical Union, breeding grounds for the White Guard and the Blue Guard movements of the German occupation. Nothing is so systematic as an arse in a high chair. And at the same time, they buggered things up for themselves. Anyone who gets ankle-deep in shit will sink to his knees, navel, neck in it, without fail; the occupier, a master of political skills will see to that. For the high and mighty—decorations and titles, for Hinko Smrekar, the cartoonist, a bullet in a gravel pit. One reverend fire-eater preaches anticommunist sermons with a six-shooter tucked into the girdle of his vestments, while Fran Finžgar (also a cleric) figures on a list of hostages. Bishop Rosman blesses German arms, while university professors are transported to Dachau. Informers denounce our men, and we shoot them in the streets of Ljubljana. Let Slovene arses quake; the fatter they are, the more may they quake. Maybe, at rock bottom, war is not such a bad thing; if only it were not necessary to do so much foot-slogging.

Night came but brought no halt in the march. We are going to complete all the world's journeys in one lifetime. Around the world in eighty days. Tao the king, the doctrine of the right road. The Odyssey. Gulliver's travels. Through desert and wilderness. Journey to the end of night. In Christ's footsteps. A sentimental journey. *Der Weg zurück*. Karl May. In the Balkan mountains. Gagernova Cesta. Under a free sun. Genghis Khan. The Anabasis. Captain Grant's children. Journeys of exploration to the North and South Poles. Across the Gobi Desert. Voyages of the conquistadors. Cook's voyages. The Argonauts. Poe's rider on the road to Eldorado; he met a pilgrim's shade; we meet no one.

A rest at night in the forest. Anton gave me a handful of cartridges. I did not ask him where he had got them from. I gave him a cap with a star. I did not tell him I had found it beside our path through the snow and had tucked it inside my jacket. I filled my magazine; he covered his head. We were soldiers once more.

And soon we were on the move again.

So far, those in front had not encountered a German ambush. Afterward we marched back, then on once more. When Dante and Virgil visited Purgatory and Hell, the souls of the deceased were sitting or lying in circles. We were moving in circles. Dante and Virgil were sitting in the middle, with eternal, stony eyes. After the war, I would lie in a hammock slung between two trees and watch the geese going to the stream and coming back again.

Thus, our great minds used to sit in a café in the center of Ljubljana, pontificating about Thomas Mann, Goethe, and pantheism, while I was sailing in a small boat through the Bosphorus, from Istanbul to Skutari, under the impression I was journeying from one continent to another. Later, I went to hear the camel drivers calling in Alexandria. I was tempted to travel to Paris.

I went up the winding river Seine as far as Poissy. I drank coffee in Cairo. In Casablanca I found the finest whore in the world. In Brazil I got mold on my shoes and mildew in my traveling bag. In the Savannahs I did not have the price of a cigarette. I got on quite well in Spain—bought myself a silk shirt with wide sleeves. In Crete I got lost one evening in those hills; I thought I was seeing an apparition from ancient Greece when an old shepherd started playing his slender pipe. We ate roast lamb. From Venice I made my last leap back to Ljubljana. As before, the officials were still sitting in the offices of the royal ministries, the mounted police were chasing students, the schoolchildren were learning Goethe's "Prometheus" by heart, and the intelligentsia were sitting in a café in the center of Ljubljana, pontificating about Thomas Mann, Goethe, and pantheism. A drunken painter was the only person I could bring myself to confide in. I told him all about my penniless wanderings and he believed it all, or at least he pretended to, but when it came to the story of that beautiful whore, he lost his temper, claimed he knew all about women and that such a woman did not exist in this world.

Now I come to think of it, walking is the most essential part of life. We come into the world, we complete life's journey, and we depart. Then we say that someone went very far, or that another got nowhere. Wishing them both all happiness on their journey through life.

The charms of a night hike are now revealed. You are always hoping you will break out. Meanwhile, you sleep on your feet. You are hemmed in by a gentle darkness sporadically broken by flashes of light; not only your legs but your whole frame sinks into the blue chasms of oblivion. For that whore was not really a whore at all; she supported me for some time and Jorge also—a Brazilian I called George. Talk about a bed of roses! I was admitted because she liked me, Jorge because she was sorry for him, others in return for presents or money. A grocer was allowed restricted access, a mere fumble under her skirt, and the rear quarters only, at that. I never knew her name but my God, what a tail she had. I have always particularly prized that part of the female body. But before I met *her* I did not know why, and in the hundred years since, I have not found another which appealed to me. One in a hundred thousand, one in a million maybe. I am not thinking only of its form, which was perfect in every way, if anything in this world can be perfect: her legs, thighs, curvaceous buttocks, each proudly jutting so that you could almost balance a matchbox there, without it falling off; hips neither wide nor narrow, simply the silhouette of that long superb sweep, whose lines fore and aft converged in the taut unseen warmth of her crotch. When a woman like that walks along the street, other women sulk in her shadow and men burn with an inner need. And they do not realize what they are missing. They do not know the smoothness or the tautness of her skin, the echo of a smack on that masterpiece, the feel of that solid, heavy, firm flesh in their palms. Something wonderful: a man is better off if he never gets to know it. Add to all this the soft skin of her inner thighs, the down beneath her buttocks, her goat's beard fleece below a perfect flat belly, her back, her marvelous breasts, which defy description with their tips like cigarette stubs, with their perpetual swing and sway, always at odds with each other, one glancing left, the other right. The touch of the hollows below her knees is like an electric shock in a man's guts. Three other things I shall never forget: she always wore very short silk dresses, she wore nothing beneath them, and, most surprising of all, she did not realize how unique she was, that the serried bevies of Miss Worlds were riffraff by comparison. She lived with an old Berber woman, a lesbian who loved her with a dog's devotion. Instead of a door, her bungalow with the little windows had a grimy old curtain. No one ever had to force his way in; she kept open house. She was life on the prowl, life in its finest, natural colors; sweet, yet doomed to corruption. Admittedly, instead of a brain she had the thick dense kernel of a mango fruit. When you buy a mango you get the kernel along with it; afterward you throw it away on a rubbish heap, where it will not sprout. She was good as gold and as dull as lead. But would you be better off with those academic masterminds? They are not even worth a strip of peel from that mango fruit—and they do not know anything really. But whenever I approached that beauty, I only had to make contact and she took care of the rest; tossing, pressing, trembling, drawing deep and almost throwing, but never losing the rhythm. She was from a Muslim region but all the same, did not remove her body hair. She drained my marrow; we would lie, gently embracing, perfectly united at that moment, with all mental or cultural barriers removed. Nothing could better that experience. When once again I heard the sound of the water, which continually sprinkled the courtyard, I knew that all my senses were working normally again and that, for the time being, the magic spell was broken.

I returned to Ljubljana. There I found neatly dressed people sitting in a café, while one of them declaimed Goethe's pantheistic hymn:

Über allen Gipfeln
ist Ruh (comma)
in allen Wipfeln
spürest du
kaum einen Hauch (full stop)
Die Vöglein schweigen im Walde (comma)
warte nur, balde
ruhest du auch (full stop)

With flippant student wit, the last lines were amended to:

Die Armen vögeln im Walde,
warte nur, balde
—vögelst du auch.

And who should I now regale with the story of my Callipygian Venus? Who could I talk things over with in my home town? With my high-minded relatives? With the purveyors of small-time gossip and scandal? With the managing directors of banks, insurance companies, and large concerns? With municipal officials or the Episcopal ordinariate? With enquiring minds, still unconvinced the earth is round? With the lady who refused to accompany me to a dance (what would people say?), with the Scouts, with the Sokols, with the left-wingers? At least I had it from that painter that it was generally agreed in Paris that for a woman, a pear-shaped was preferable to an apple-shaped derrière, full stop.

I could find nothing but tunnels, intellectual death traps, pretension, and obscurantism, while I dodged among impressions of faces, objects, houses, hearing the soft babble of incomprehensible talk in my own language. I used to talk to Jorge and her in a mixture of Portuguese, Spanish, French, Italian, and English words and sounds. At a bathing pool in Ljubljana (the old Kolezija), I had a conversation in English with a couple of average American girls: I soon realized what my poor English was worth. I had brought back a pair of red socks I had bought somewhere. What an awful shock: a man in red socks!

From Paris, I brought the yellow shoes I was given by the young fellow who lived in a garret on the Boulevard de Clichy; these incurred the hatred of liberals, clericals, and pantheistic humanists alike. The first of these would have gladly bound me up with barbed wire and drowned me in the Sava as a traitor to the Sokol movement; the second lot would have given me a slight electric shock at St. Ulric's and murdered me under the old Slavonic lime tree in the courtyard; the third came over to us and they too are here now, tramping through the forest. I am best off with these silent fighters; together we drop, together we march, and no one loses his temper.

At the next ambush, the order was given: "Machine gunners, forward!" That action seemed to last some time. Afterward, we took another path through the snow. Anton stuck to me like a tick. I did not want to lose him either. Only the two of us could tell the full story of the previous day. And only the two of us could agree not to tell.

Now we could no longer tell east from west or north from south. The Scout's dictum that moss grows on the north side of tree trunks is sheer balderdash. The sun, the moon, and the stars had disappeared. The calendar was dead, we did not know the date; only my wristwatch was still going but it no longer mattered what time it showed. Now we measured not in kilometers, but in steps. We had no names; our features had changed beyond recognition. All individuality was lost and even our dress became uniform. Such distinctions as great and small, heavy and light, rich and poor, healthy and sick, handsome and ugly, strong and weak, smart and stupid, hairy and bald, young and old, male and female, were now beside the point. The amiable, the irritable, the dejected, the quiet, the rowdy, the taciturn, and the garrulous were all reduced to one level. No more shoe sizes, no more shirt sizes, no more addresses, no more school testimonials, no more passports, no more identity cards, no more mariner's certificates. We had forgotten our elders, our children, our brothers and sisters, the rooms and houses where we used to live or used to visit; we forgot that the world has hamlets, roads, railways, lakes, seas; we were not quite dead, not quite alive; we were no longer thinking that somewhere in the distant past there was a lost paradise and that possibly deliverance awaited us in the future, in a new paradise, either on this earth or in the next life. Also, the hope of a breakthrough flickered only at odd moments, growing fainter all the time. The question of where we should make our breakthrough became completely pointless.

When I sat down for a rest beside the track, the fearful stench of my own body hit me full in the face. When I had a smoke I had to hold the cigarette in my left hand. My right, in its filthy rag, was probably festering. It stank to high heaven, worse than that mule's putrid wound, the cooking pot, the corpse, and the drying maize all combined. Sitting in my own stench, I was assailed by two noxious gusts, one from my crotch, the other probably from my armpits. Although I had a cold, a blocked nose was no protection. The most nauseating reek came from the filthy rag I was using to wipe my nose; it was no longer recognizable as a handkerchief. I had no feeling in my toes, my fingertips were numb, I had a fire in my back which flared up at every movement. I could still sit down but getting up was not so easy. Here, I had to overcome my own natural instincts in order to summon up all my reserves of willpower, which had crumbled in my grim depression, then I felt a sharp pain in my joints as if I were on the rack and my limbs ached so much that only by odd spasms was I able to jerk my body half upright, into the shape of a question mark. I became dully conscious of all this only when I was again on the move, in a semi-lucid interval between one blackout and the next. I had forgotten Anton and was even lost to myself, bound only by some extrasensory waves to someone or something in front of me and someone or something behind. Sometimes I seemed to be moving or floating on a wave, or slipping out of control through showers of sparks in a pitch-black gloom; sometimes I heard a long and lingering sound, like the creaking of an ever-opening door. My mouth was dry, parched, and leathery, without a drop of saliva; my lips were painfully blistered; all around my nose, the skin was sore and inflamed. All this torture was both simultaneous and sequential, for as the irritation in my skin grew, the booming in my head slackened, and then my eyes began to hurt: spots and sparks chased each other till they sank in the eye fluid; blinded, I drowned in the swirling chaos of the void. That too would pass and all would be well again.

I do not know whether all this happened in the course of one night, or whether a second night followed an intervening day. I remember that on one occasion I was scared stiff. We had been ambushed and firing broke out, without either waking me up or rousing the instinct of self-preservation. The action in fact did take place some way behind me, while I was once again marching in the column. Why didn't you take the rifle off your shoulder? We'll be leaving you behind. But how do I get the thing off my shoulder?

Another coma—and another fright . . . But what am I really afraid of? The firing has stopped, hasn't it? Once again, I slid into the void . . . till suddenly we came to a pretty hamlet . . . in a forest like this, just imagine, one-story and two-story houses, real mansions . . . with music playing . . . carnival . . . a party . . . dancing . . . showers of confetti, all colors, flying through the air . . . what a pretty sight, yellow, red, green, blue, white and gold too, whole clouds of confetti . . . the man in front of me can see them too . . . as we walk this wide road through the happy hamlet . . . there is no one to be seen in the brightly lit windows . . . nothing strange really, they are all dancing . . . Well, let's drop into one of these houses . . . What does it mean? Who is taking us straight past the magnificent façade of this palace . . . I refuse, I am not going on; someone from behind gives me a push in the back, where it hurts most . . . I'd like to turn around and give him a piece of my mind . . . surely we're not going to miss such a golden opportunity . . . ignoring the place as if it didn't exist . . . Well that just shows you what sort of leaders we've got! And they say there's going to be no more exploitation! All right, if the rest of you are marching on, so am I . . . but I shan't forget . . . at the end of the village, at the end of the village, someone says . . . What a village that was! A village with mansions and palaces . . . and fine orchestras . . . What strings!

Somehow we have left the hamlet . . . we're back in the forest now . . . on a wide road through the forest, with troikas and tinkling sleigh bells . . . and a Cossack choir is singing . . . what basses . . . it must be Serge Jaroff's Don Cossack Choir . . . What a pity, they are way behind us . . . or they're way ahead of us in their troikas . . . But where have these Russians come from? Maybe they are White Russians? Émigrés? How could that be? Don't ask questions in the army. Leave that to the politicians . . . They are fine artists, that you can't deny . . . bass voices like organ pedal notes . . .

The whole forest is full of music . . . but you can't distinguish the playing of one group from the next . . . this is stupid . . . And they are playing in the dark, by ear, without their parts . . . they've got bandstands but they're all at loggerheads . . . What an unholy racket . . . let's press on . . . enough for this pandemonium . . . pity they can't sort it all out.

Did I hear firing again? . . . that's why the music's stopped . . . they've taken fright . . . the musicians are afraid the Germans might find them here in the forest . . . and think they were playing for us . . . Then they'd round them up and send them off to a concentration camp . . . If we start firing now we might hit a musician . . . But no doubt that's already taken care of . . . we're turning aside, we're on our way . . . but this isn't the right way, we should go back to the hamlet, and then not think about what will happen next . . . That's all decided beforehand.

Another breather. Have we broken through then? Lighting fires strictly forbidden. A wonderful thick, bushy pine tree, with a double root protruding out of the ground, provides a cozy nook, almost like a real seat. Lighting fires forbidden under pain of death. Who is that playing on a guitar? The melody is very familiar; I know the rhythm too . . . Of course, a minuet . . . how restful, wafting you off to other ages, to other regions of this green world. Am I sitting in snow? Yes. I scrape it out from between the twin roots and stretch up to break off a branch and sit in the embrace of the great tree which has given me such a friendly welcome. I cannot straighten up. I shall stand on tiptoe, I'll manage somehow. It's all a matter of willpower and know-how. I am all on my own under my dense canopy of branches. There are some figures by the tree to my left and others a little ahead and on my right. Behind me too. When did we scatter through the forest? Who is playing the guitar so well? He really can play. And that's a minuet in A major. The composer's name will come back to me any moment now. What luck, it's one of my special favorites! I imagine myself moving in the rhythm of the dance, very gently of course, otherwise the pain in my back would be unbearable. Well, there's no hurry. Now I'll make myself a really comfortable bed, as we used to do on our trips through the Kočevje woods, for example, when we were making our way to the sea, by the ordnance map, over hill and dale, as the crow flies. I seemed to remember it was quite a short name . . . and that it had an "o" in it . . . bog, cog, fog, hog . . . I went as far as sog . . . sop . . . sor . . . Sor: I have it. Sor, that was the name of the Spaniard who composed that minuet. Anton is probably under another tree close by. This is no time for talk however. I have enough to do here if I am to put this house in order. I have the Cossack fur cap in my pack; that should come in useful when I'm settled under my own roof. Below the spreading lower branches there were dry twigs and boughs jutting out, starved of life by those above. I broke off a small stack of these, some of them not much longer than a toothpick, and laid them beside my makeshift couch. I had plenty of time.

I lay my folded blanket against the tree and slowly lowered myself into my nest. The trunk was at exactly the right angle for me to rest the upper part of my body. I placed my pack and rifle at either side, spread my legs, scraped the twigs together between my knees, wet a finger and held it up in the air. The right side felt cool; there was a slight breeze from that direction. I made two tunnels in the snow along this line, one to my left, the other to my right, raised my knees and began to form a small pyramid from my stack of twigs, just big enough to fit between my palms. I did not see anyone lighting a cigarette but here and there a firebrand glowed. I took my matches and shielding the flame with great care I scraped the sulfur against the driest spot on the matchbox. I applied the match to my small pyramid, which began to burn with a low flame. I shielded it with my palms and blew the smoke in the direction of the tunnels. It gave off so little heat it hardly singed me, yet I felt a thrill of sheer delight at having my own fire. The ancient Greeks believed that special beings lived in fire. Prometheus stole fire from the gods and I had kindled a fire against strict orders. I had no time to dwell on that stupid line of thought, when I felt that rare joy shoot quick as pain up my arms and around to the back of my neck. This was worth dying for, worth living for too . . . why bother thinking or using one's imagination . . . when nothing else is required . . . except these blessed waves of well-being . . . Slowly I added other sticks to my little pyramid, not so much that it would burn too bright, nor so little that it might go out . . . Now a wisp of smoke rose lukewarm between my palms up toward my face. Thinking would spoil everything. Now my thighs felt that glow from the earth's core . . . My fire was such an insignificant flicker that I could hardly see it under my palms and yet it changed everything, sending out rays of well-being, bathing me more and more in its generous warmth. By now I could think of Anton. What a pity for both of us that he was not here, that I could not pass on this warmth to him . . . Obviously I was coming around. That was a good sign . . . Sitting by a fire, a man cannot remain sullen and timid like a forest beetle. One wish gives rise to another; desire fulfilled provokes unsatisfied and even impossible desires, but I had not reached this stage, or anywhere near it.

Meanwhile, during this interval which I could not measure, I managed to complete a full process of renovation.

I took off one boot, poured the water out and placed it by the glowing mound, upper side toward the warmth (Go on! Dry out! Warm up!). I peeled off the wet sock, wrung it out, and lay it beside the boot to dry. I massaged the wrinkled skin of my foot, scraped the black, greasy filth from between the toes, washed and rubbed my foot with snow, and began to dry and warm the toes, sole, heel. I rested one foot on the upturned boot and dealt with the other. When I had dried both, I took the Cossack fur cap out of my pack and turned it inside out, so that I had the black silk lining on the outside. I then tucked both my bare feet into the soft fur. I trembled with delight—they do say sheer pleasure may provoke a heart attack.

And so I carried on working to a plan, which wrote itself as I went along. I dried my filthy mug, untied the rag on my right hand and wiped off the pus and lice, which formed a black ring around the wound; on the scaly, wrinkled, bitten flesh I put a thin slice of inner tree bark and bandaged it all with my filthy but dry handkerchief, stiff with snot rind. I rubbed the old "bandage" in the snow and dried that too.

A man hardly has time to get used to unaccustomed comfort than the accompanying drawbacks of the situation become known. The lice began to attack me mercilessly, especially the insides of my legs, where I had become so pleasantly warm; then they started on my chest and under my armpits, and eventually over my whole body. I scratched, rubbed, scraped; the itch in my crotch was so unbearable I could have done myself a violent injury; with the same scorching fever on my chest, I could have leaped into the air and dived into the snow. I read somewhere that, in the Middle Ages, the schoolmen would discuss in learned dissertations the sense and purpose of Creation. They wondered why God had created fleas, lice, and bedbugs. A wise theologian found the answer: vermin see to it that man does not grow lazy, that he remains active.

I felt the pangs of hunger too. I still had some hard crusts of bread. These I toasted on my fire and then munched them, slowly, deliberately. I had my tin of sardines too, but I had no intention of touching them at the moment. Anything could happen yet. I rolled myself a long thin cigarette in newspaper and laid it on the twigs. I put my boots on and tidied myself up, then lit my cigarette with a twig from my own fire . . . I took a deep drag, so deep I could have exhaled through all the apertures of my body . . . slowly I released the smoke . . . waited a little, then inhaled again . . . I felt a wave of intoxication come over me, such a sweet, soaring sensation that I had to clutch the ground to prevent myself flinging my arms out wide. All pain was forgotten. I wedged the fur cap on my head and fell asleep, drifting into an earthly paradise, where everything was unreal, soft, safe, tortuous, fragrant, soothing, good, and true.

It is hard to say what had happened. Probably the same thing occurs with a dried-out plant when you water it. Or with a hibernating frog when the spring thaw comes. Death and birth at the same time anyway.

When the time had arrived to move on, I felt a hand on my arm. I got up, collected my gear, and joined the column which was passing by. It was only some time later that I noticed Anton close behind me. I recognized him by the bandage on his head.

We turned sharply left, off a gently rising road onto a much steeper, harder, and rockier path which led us down into a ravine. We now found less and less snow beneath our feet.

Slowly the sky grew brighter, the silhouettes of trees and branches became crisper, the rocks and stones of our path stood out more clearly, and the man in front of me now had the recognizable semblance of a human back. The thought suddenly struck me that our path was leading down to a valley, not a ravine.

Daybreak came suddenly. When we emerged from the forest beside a rocky mountain pass, we glimpsed, far below, a sparkling stream, tumbling through wild rocky country. We began the descent toward Iski Vintgar. A rocky canyon lay open before us, with rapids, waterfalls, pools, little chasms . . . all clearly visible as if on a plaster model. Our path grew steeper, rockier, more precipitous. I suddenly realized the ground was bare of snow.

On the other side of the valley, our long column was already ascending the steep hillside. While we were hopping across a narrow section of the stream, on stepping stones which jutted out of the rushing water, the sound of an airplane engine was heard overhead. We looked up. It was a small reconnaissance plane, a so-called Stork. There were two figures in it, one of whom was leaning far out, so that he must have had an excellent view of us. The plane flew off in the direction of Ljubljana. This was an unhappy omen. We had dallied far too long. We should have been across the river before dawn. The woods, rock walls, and pillars lay silent in the morning air, the only sound coming from the foaming stream, the rapids, and the waterfalls. The clouds beyond the hills at our back were now tinged with sunlight.

Over there is the path up the steep slopes of Mount Krim. We stop only to drink a handful of the swift water.

We had certainly covered some ground. But were we safe yet?

While we were resting in the forest, some unknown pathfinder had discovered a gap in the German ring and we had crept through. At last.

How many times we had camped in this gorge before the war! Somewhere, lower down, there was a pleasant meadow beside a deep pool, where we used to bathe; there were three tents pitched on the grass. The water was teeming with crayfish, greenish shrimp, and trout; chamois roamed the rocks up above. When evening came we would make pancakes, sit by the campfire, singing discreetly. The gamekeeper suspected us of poaching trout; every day, he would come quietly along the path to keep his suspicious eye on us. He did not know we had posted a lookout on much higher ground, who could give a very good imitation of a jay.

I decided that if I survived the war, I should come here again some time. Maybe I would then be able to understand things a great deal better. Then there would be no more dark forebodings alternating with bright hopes, or would there? At least I would know where I had come from, I would know the date and have a good idea what I could expect that day.

The going was much tougher on the other side of the stream. The man in front of me slipped on the steep path and was struck on the head by his own rifle. He cursed, picked himself up and took shorter steps on the rocky slope. Through the roar of the waters below, I heard Anton panting heavily.

We could now see the rocks above us, glowing in the light of the rising sun. In the circumstances, we would have preferred to shelter in the gray anonymity of mist and clouds. In warfare, beauty does not always spell advantage. A soldier interprets the landscape in terms of stronger and weaker positions.

The Germans were somewhere around. But where?

There were some who knew but they were not telling. They marched on without a word.

To our right, somewhere further down the canyon, a cannon roared. One thing I could be sure of—it was not one of ours.

Bracken, undergrowth, trees, rocks, moss. Our path crossed a somewhat easier slope, then started to climb steeply once more. The sunlight filtered through the branches. Behind me, I felt rather than heard Anton's groans in the general noise and uproar of the hurrying column, tramping, panting, slithering, coughing. I looked back. His face, pale against the murky grime of his head bandages, was twisted in a gargoyle's grimace. He was holding his left breast with both hands, as if he had been shot. He stopped for a moment and someone pushed past him and between us. Anton tried to catch my eye. That mute appeal was eloquent enough: I can't go on, my heart's letting me down. What! Now that we have the worst behind us? When we've almost reached safety? When we've broken through? When things will soon be easier? I let the man behind me pass, and tried with encouraging glances to drag Anton after me. He made a desperate effort to keep up. Heart trouble—in wartime! Who ever heard of such a thing?

Of course this road of ours led somewhere but we were hurrying after the man in front like sheep, without knowing where we were off to or, furthermore, why we were in such a hurry. Somewhere above us, well over to our right, we heard firing. The roar and sharp reports stopped long enough for us to draw breath, then opened up again in a storm of machine-gun and automatic fire . . . Meanwhile, our pace slackened and we glanced apprehensively at each other, trying to read in the faces of those nearby whether this spelled trouble for us or not. Keep moving there! Very well; on we go. Something bright, metallic, egg-shaped, came rolling down between the feet of the man in front of me. I picked it up. It was a hand grenade, a French fizzer. I looked at Anton, wondering whether this one was as dangerous as the other I had found back there. Anton's nod told me I should keep it, it was a good one. I pocketed it.

Others were passing us as Anton and I lagged behind. No one seemed to be taking any notice. Two machine gunners, shouldering their weapons, overtook us on the left of the column. One of them had two full cartridge belts, one around his waist, the other draped around his shoulder. They were followed by two men armed with automatics and some other soldiers. They pressed on uphill. We caught some of their talk, shot a few questions at them, while those who hurried to follow them also had something to say. We were splitting up into stragglers and overtakers. I was trying to support Anton but the path narrowed in places. Physically he was helpless and completely in my hands. He was relying on me to push him upward. All the same, I realized that he was keenly following all that was going on in our vicinity, listening to every word spoken in earshot and also making the logical connection between sound and sense.

"The Germans have cut us off . . . The Germans are down below in Vintgar . . . The Germans are up on the summit of Mount Krim and we must make for one of the passes . . ."

From down below us came the sound of loud reports . . . the echo of a steady fusillade . . . and from our left shrill, venomous bursts of fire . . . Why don't we turn off this path? Take cover in the rocks? What's going on? Are those just isolated pockets of enemy fire? Anton grabbed me around the shoulder and I felt the clutch of his hard, bony hand. He dragged himself up the steep path, with me as his mobile support. We were not going to get far like that; I could feel his weight in my knees and even more in my feet. He was completely absorbed in what was going on up above us, as if he was gathering information with all his senses.

Two men came hurrying up along the left of the column. One of them had a commander's badge embroidered on his sleeve and was carrying an old-fashioned German thick-barreled submachine gun in his hands. The other had a Yugoslav rifle. They were calling to the men in the column as they hurried past.

"Rifles at the ready! Prepare your grenades! Line up! What are you, soldiers or a herd of cattle? I want you in groups of ten. Right, up to here makes ten! You're in the same troop as the ten below you. What a fucking shower! Are you deaf or something?" They rushed past, out of breath, livid, hoarse. Some of us followed them, others lagged behind.

The trees thinned out, the path became less steep, the valley widened; we were approaching the pass. Only now did I see how many of us there were. Anton was almost a dead weight and my own strength was giving out. A sweet taste came to my mouth. Everyone else was racing past us; was it just my imagination or were they really so fast? I slipped and banged my right knee on the ground. Anton fell on top of me. As I struggled to lift us both up, all around us I saw stars, sheaves of fire, then clouds of black midges floating in the air, obscuring my view of the grass and trees. We were no sooner back on our feet, and the whole business probably only lasted a split second, than there was a crash from the woods to our left and figures came running down the brush-covered slope. I could not distinguish our men from those others. Who were they? I heard the man in front of me working his bolt. So he had opened fire? I myself had Anton in an awkward grip, with his rifle in my face, and was trying to stand him on his feet. By now there was an infernal racket on all sides but I had no idea who was firing and could no longer distinguish shots and shouts from the general uproar. I heard Anton say, quite distinctly, "You'd better leave me, Berk. I'm done for. Try to get through yourself!" When I did not release him, he tried to push me away. At the same time, he was gazing ahead, into the trees or right through them. Our men were still hurrying forward. We went in the same direction. I realized that the bullets were hissing about our ears. I was getting used to it by now. I strained and managed to get a grip on Anton's waist and drag him along by force. He gave up his resistance and even made an effort to help me. A strange gargling noise, like that of a bubbling liquid, came from his throat, as if he was snarling, or trying to tell me something. Our rifles were only a hindrance to us. Weighed down and clumsy, had we any hope at all? For a moment if struck me that I couldn't care less about the whole business. How could I go on like this? My legs had almost ceased to obey me. The arm around Anton's waist had gone numb. Had I still got hold of him? Or was he now holding me up? At least these figures around us are our own men. But what were we all supposed to do? We were in motion, our limbs were moving; was this some sort of strange dance? We were in a hollow, with bullets flying past us from all sides. How was it that so few of us were falling? But there go two now. And the man in front of me. A crowd came rushing down from our left. Were they ours? Yes. Heading for our valley. That fellow had clutched his belly and seemed to topple over on to his face. To our right was a steep tree-covered slope.

But those figures to our left—they looked different. They were not ours! They came running, shooting, shouting—or was that someone else shouting? We heard the crack of bullets all around us. We seemed to be under fire from every side. Three men ran up from our left, shot past us down the valley. Ahead of us too there was movement and the sound of heavy feet, as ten or so of our men came racing down the slope to our right. All this fused in a general, deafening pandemonium, so that individual movements, footsteps, leaps seemed to make no noise, as if everything were happening under water. Lines of green figures were pouring out of the woods to our right—swift, winding lines of green specters, green on green.

I do not know whether Anton and I turned around or whether we stopped and joined the crowd that was rushing back past us or whether we were simply swept up in that tide which bore us back on our tracks, down, down, clinging to each other, prized apart, holding each other again, slipping on the ground, kneeling, running on our knees, getting up, looking for each other. Someone had trodden heavily on my left hand—it must have been on the ground. Anton told me later that I had carried him on my shoulders. That I cannot believe. It would have been quite impossible. What bound us together in that long—or short—indefinable interval of time, I could not say. Whatever I said could only be imprecise, and possibly even quite wrong. There was the instinct of self-preservation, no doubt. That animated and drove not only Anton and me, but also the rest of us. Was it that we did not want to be taken alive? Maybe. But why didn't the enemy take us? We had turned tail, without even firing our rifles, when the fighting was at its worst. I had not reached for the grenade in my pocket. Scrub all thought of resistance! Only flight was left. Did Anton sense that in me lay his only hope of rescue from a diabolically dangerous situation and clung to me for that reason? But he had offered me the opportunity to leave him, to abandon him, go on without him, so that each of us would find his own salvation among the crowd, when we were at the end of our tether, when we could no longer think clearly, when the whole nervous system was no longer operating as before, when the senses were benumbed and the clouded consciousness saw without seeing happenings and surroundings, when all your actions proceeded quite automatically, in imitation of those around you, when you no longer feared the bullet, when at the back of your mind there lurked an icy dread of falling into the hands of those green figures, those specters which are not human at all but monsters swiftly moving along their own paths to their own goal, beings you could not hate any more than a tree trunk, at the moment when you see it toppling down on you from the heights; when you are not hungry and have no other desires; when frost, lice, and painful boots no longer bother you; a dull grief attacks you, envelops you, traps you with a thousand snares, so that you can no longer run, jump, realize what is happening—and you are borne along with others on a tide which sweeps you along to somewhere new, somewhere unknown.

Anton was an awful millstone around my neck, and yet—there was something else about him that I only appreciated much later. I found the key to an understanding of my desire for Anton, in a quite trivial memory from the tangled confusion of that downhill scramble. We had tripped over some rocks and fallen on our faces. We tried to reach for each other's hands but lost contact and parted. Others were jumping over us, as the crowd in flight grew continuously. I got up on my knees. There was no sign of Anton; all I could see was boots, feet, legs, narrowly missing my face. In that fraction of a moment, in that hundred-thousandth of a second, the thought flashed through my mind: "He is gone, and he should be with me, because otherwise I am quite alone in this world." Then I caught sight of him again, not beside me, but down below, crawling on all fours over steep mossy rocks surrounded by undergrowth, heading downhill, where others were hurrying; we would be quite safe down below. I rushed over to him, we picked ourselves up and hurried onward, downhill, the going much easier now than our uphill climb. We lost our separate physical and mental identity and fused into a new entity, rather like two drops of water which come close to each other and then, after a momentary tremor, leap together to form one single drop. I admit there could hardly be anything more pathetic than the thought that drops of water are bothered about life or death. There are moments when quite impossible and quite inconsequential thoughts come to mind.

We came to halt in a gravelly cave beneath a jutting rock, its entrance hidden by undergrowth. Here we lived out the rest of that day, the following night.

I have not the faintest idea when, why, and how we decided to leave the main stream and take a turn to the right toward some steep rocks, and crawl away from the rest by ourselves, in search of a refuge. It was true that we had not heard any firing on our right. But I do not know whose suggestion it was, nor could Anton throw any light on it later on. Also, we could not decide which of us had found that convenient cave. The one thing we both remember is the sound of machine guns opening up down below and rifle shots and bursts of automatic fire from the direction in which the retreat was heading. By then we were on our own among the rocks. When we were already well ensconced in our cave below the rock, we heard and even caught a cursory glimpse of men leaping down past our hiding place, accompanied by a downward rush, like a small avalanche. Our rifles were lying on the dry gravel beside us. We just listened, held our breath needlessly and did not even look at each other. Only once Anton said: "Germans!" I do not know how he could recognize them from the sound of feet outside but he certainly kept his voice down. I do not even know how I heard him and I did not look at him to try to read his lips. I do know that at a certain moment I could hear his heart beat, pulsing louder and louder; I thought it might give us away! Then the rather jerky and irregular beat grew quiet. Anton lay with his face flat against the gravel. We were both lying on our bellies. I suddenly felt a pain in the back and rested my head on my right ear in the sand. I looked at Anton's head. I was worried at the thought that he might be dead. His heartbeat could not be heard now. I could not bring myself to touch him, nor even to utter a word. I was petrified. The thought occurred to me that he was indeed better off if he was dead.

Once again a wild commotion broke out, not far from our hiding place. We both raised our heads, no more than a whisker, or perhaps a finger, above the sand, which had a smell like rotting wood. Again we had the sequence of noises far off, noises near, shooting, faint cries, distant shooting, someone leaping the rock, then wave after wave pouring down over our heads. Earlier, we had been hurrying while all around us seemed to be at peace; now the two of us were at peace and the whole area was seething with activity. Our cave was only about a foot and a half in height at the entrance but the ceiling rose to some two and a half feet; the whole cavity was well over two yards long then suddenly narrowed to a grinning black crack in the rear wall. We were not the first inhabitants of the place; by the gray-brown wall lay a rotting rag of no distinct color and beside it, a rusty, broken spoon handle. Crackle of firearms, scrape of boots, something thudding to the ground, rustle of the branches of the bush at the mouth of the cave . . . then we were alone once more, left in peace as before.

For a long time we lay like this and probably even dozed off meanwhile. At moments I did not feel the ground beneath me and once I suddenly shuddered when a strong light shone on me; fortunately it was only the light of day. It began to dawn on me that I was in a good place. I heard the sound of water dripping. Somewhere a loose pebble slid down the unseen slope outside. I was in a cave, as I attempted to explain to myself. A cave, with its floor beneath me and its ceiling above. Yet in these flashes of consciousness, there was no feeling of security; I was too imbued with the spirit of the march, the chase, the retreat. Our ancient forefathers hid in caves from wild beasts, enemy tribes, foul weather. But they would certainly have had two exits. The animals too, burrow emergency tunnels from their hides. But if a German discovered the entrance to our cave—what then? However, all was peace outside. Firing could be heard only in the remote distance. Apart from this, there was something else well worth noting: Anton was sleeping, resting, dreaming, not straining to hear what was happening outside. And Anton was a subtly sensitive instrument; he would have sensed any danger in our vicinity—I had grown used to his faculty for picking up and registering any signals from his environment. Once again there was some movement up above and again we were perfectly safe; could we continue to rely on our security? Soon night would come and then our taut nerves could have a rest. It must have been my nervous network that was jangling within me, stretched out from my skull to the ends of my intestines; I was beginning to feel it in my limbs too. Anton lay with his eyes closed and with an occasional tremor in his left eyebrow. It was still quite bright. In the greenish light which seeped into our den, the branches of the bushes made round and angular shapes. The dark silhouettes were intertwined, as if a Chinese painter had drawn them with his brush. I was as happy as a child at the spectacle. Thinking of the slender brush and a droplet of Chinese ink on the sheet, of the shrewd eye guiding the dexterous hand, of the wholesome smell of rice paper, I experienced the innocent joy of a children's fairy tale—a joy that came down, like a soothing balm, on the trembling arcs and coils of my nervous fibers. I felt my tissue drawing mysterious strength from that miniature vision. And in fact, I was at the same time beginning to feel hungry.

I had a tin of sardines in my pack. This was really the last of my stock. Tucked away in a notebook I still had one cigarette with the brand name MORAVA in green letters; I had been keeping this hidden, even from myself. I had matches. Through a crevice in the rock, water was leaking and steadily dripping down from a small stalactite. Below, there was a small patch of dampness in the gravel floor, nothing more, and there the modest trickle of cavern water sank into the ground. What more do we need, Anton? Carry on snoozing while I count our blessings. We shall eat, we shall smoke by our own fireside. I shall gather twigs for it from the bushes at our door; we shall drink the clear water; maybe we can even make tea from the leaves of the bushes. I wonder whether I shall ever tell you about the thought of a Chinese paintbrush that preceded my hunger . . . and my thirst too . . . But I no longer find it surprising that a caveman should draw and paint on the walls of his cave. I imagine he would have objected violently and thrashed anyone who told him this was elemental art. "You idiot," he would have said. "Your noble ancestor would have had a meal, a warm bed, and a good woman long before he would turn his thoughts to anything that you are accustomed to calling 'beautiful.'" I was getting hungrier all the time but the light in the cave entrance was still too bright. Anton trembled slightly, as if from an electric shock and not from a dream. He was slowly coming back to life.

We still had to take things very easy. I had no idea where we were. Perhaps we were not far from a road. Someone only had to throw a bomb in and that would have been the end of us. On the other hand, if things were to go on like this, how long could we last? But this thought was only in the mind: matter thought otherwise, matter wanted to go on living, to live forever, to be saved—clung with all its might to the faintest hope of survival, hung on to its miserable weapon and continued to resist, would hear nothing of death, of bombs, of sudden disaster. And so we decided to lie low for the time being. I remembered and would not forget how thorough the Italians had been on one of their offensives, when they had shaken every bush to make sure there was no partisan strongpoint hidden beneath it, how they had hurled grenades into every aperture, loosed off bullets into dense treetops, bayoneted bales of straw and loads of hay. Yes, they certainly went the whole hog—not that it helped them very much. They tried to propagate their two-thousand-year-old culture, killing goodness knows how many young and old people who did not understand a word of their language, shooting many peasants, cutting off cows' udders and baking them; well, what can you expect, there's a war on.

The Germans are not so thorough, in spite of the reputation they enjoy. I decided I had better not tempt fate, trouble would appear even uninvited. Better lie low and pretend you're not here. The lice were feeling hungry again and began to devour me, starting between my legs, then under my armpits, and finally on my chest, so that their tickling and nibbling seemed to cover my whole body. The little bastards had kept their heads down during the shooting! For the first time, Anton showed some discomfort, rubbing one side below the armpit with his elbow. Our eyes met. We dared not laugh but both realized we would have happily done so. Things were looking up indeed—and he still did not know I had a tin of sardines, nor did I know that Anton had some beans and a clutch of cigarette butts. The air held a promise of junketing and sweet stupor: later, whatever would be, would be. I also had needle and thread. We could do a little sewing. We could tear off strips of shirt and bandage our infected wounds. We could not possibly foresee everything else that might happen before we moved on. Snow White and the Seven Dwarfs? Well, hardly! There were two of us, each with two Tom Thumbs and eight fingers.

Slowly but surely, it was getting darker outside. There was not a sound from either the valleys or the steep mountainsides. Soon, suddenly, it would be completely dark. We had already seen that the belief that the Germans did not operate at night was not entirely justified. But, at the same time, they did not venture into the inaccessible wilderness. I was going to creep out, hoping to find that we were alone. Anton quietly approved my intention, which he could gather from my movements. My whole body felt as if it had been pounded and chopped like raw steak. After lying rigid for so long, every movement gave me so much pain that I was gasping and puffing for some time before I managed to force my upper body out into the open. The stars were shining over the darkness of the valley. Gradually, my eyes got used to the starlight. Somewhere nearby, there was a flutter of wings; I had disturbed a roosting bird. From deep below me I could hear the murmur of the stream and from high above, the distant boom of a waterfall. I crawled out, drawing my legs after me with some difficulty. I did not know what hurt most, my knees, back, hips, or feet. Slowly, I pulled myself together and got up on my feet, attempted to stretch, and inhaled deep breaths of the fresh night air. I could now make out the tops of the pine trees and the pale patches of rock face. I took a few paces to left and right but the ground was full of clefts, fissures, stones, and roots, so that I had to drop down on all fours and grope my way forward, feeling every inch of earth. By the time I returned to our cave, I was convinced we had found a good spot. I called Anton but he did not seem to be in the hole. Had he gone to sleep? Not heart failure, surely! I flattened myself on the ground and poked my head in. He was there. I thought I could see the gleam of his eyes. He did not let on. "All's well," I said. "Looks as if we're on our way," I added.

"Really?" he said quietly. "Where?"

At this, the thought occurred to me: "Of course, he's a man of great experience, fought in the Spanish Civil War, and God knows what he's been through since." Anton did not suspect I knew anything about this. It was quite possible he might never mention his Spanish experience. I had decided I myself would not raise the subject. But he had probably been told then too that things were going their way. Better wait and see. Yes.

Time to start thinking about our domestic arrangements, Anton.

There are no Indians around, the pirates are probably down below by the stream and bandits are afraid of the war. The only thing we must be careful about is to shield our small, infinitesimally tiny fire. There might be some German field glasses focused on us from the opposite side of the valley. We collected the water dripping from the stalactite in a mess tin. We met a little difficulty in opening the sardine tin without a key. Here, the broken spoon handle that some previous tenant had left in the cave came in handy.

A couple of hours passed, but what an improvement in our standard of living they brought! We had eaten the fish and drank the oil, and the best of it was that we had not been staring jealously at each other's fingers as we took our portions. We were both by nature above such trifles. We had had a drink of water. We had enjoyed a smoke in peace and quiet. We had soaked Anton's beans and would cook them a little later. Three hours' soaking was all we could afford in the circumstances; we reckoned on an hour's cooking at least. The beans were young but they would be tough eating. Not that we minded.

We also dressed each other's wounds. "What's this? Are your brains putrefying, Anton? Pus, lice, some queer old slime, all mixed up with your hair; blisters on your skin; deep, wrinkled scars. I've never seen anything so repulsive in my whole life. Does it hurt here?"

"Maybe—maybe not. I can't say," he replied.

"And what have we here? Sort of splinters of some hard material, fragments of rotting bone? You've got sand here too, even pebbles, or is this something else you've been collecting? You've got a network of sewers up here and you stink like the plague." He kept his head bent meekly. An hour must have passed before I wearily left off my rehabilitation of the surface of his skull.

By comparison with his, my own wound was quite harmless, although it too was lice-ridden, festering, and gave off a sickening stench.

"We're rotting away, Anton, no doubt of it." The rending of a piece of shirt was the only answer I got.

The water dripped very slowly. We attended to our feet. It was a real joy to taste the elegant lifestyle of salons and spas. We did a little sewing as well. Meanwhile, we either talked or kept silent and also dozed off for various short intervals during the night, but I do not think that both of us were asleep at the same time, although we made no conscious arrangement. He slept during my monologues; when he was speaking, I could hear his voice from somewhere far away but slumbered on, not understanding a word.

The beans were sweet and tasty, though rather hard. After our night meal, we had a smoke and only now exchanged some words, but what we talked about I could not say. Probably about nothing at all, just talking for the sake of talking. I cannot remember a word of our conversation, which was rather a confused jumble of sound, of mumbling inconsequential blather, no real demonstration of the human gift of speech. All our activities were prompted by unspoken inner stimuli, and they were following some particular design. In normal circumstances we would never have devoted such care, either to ourselves or to each other, but this was rebirth, a transformation. We were once again something resembling human beings; we were once again ready to march on and on, to girdle the earth. We could now distinguish wood smoke from tobacco smoke. We were now pulling faces at the rancid tang of our cave water. I inspected my rifle and saw that I had a cartridge in the barrel. I examined the hand grenade I had found. Anton was familiar with the type. He told me it packed a good charge and was activated by a handle at the side. I suddenly realized we were now talking quite naturally and understanding each other—and what had happened a few hours earlier was forgotten, had vanished like one of those dreams when you felt you are unable to move. The nightmare was over. We were soldiers again. But where were the rest of us? Yes, indeed; where could they be? Nowhere was there a voice to be heard. I was sure the Germans had not wiped them out. But there were hardly enough underground caves in the whole region for so many men. Had they broken through? And were we still encircled? Anton advised me not to worry.

He knew. He knew what he was talking about. I had come to trust him. No more worrying then, no more brooding. Should we get a little sleep? It was night.

It was already morning when I woke from a horrible dream. I started up and struck my head on our rock ceiling and collapsed on top of Anton, who woke abruptly and grabbed me with both hands. "It's nothing, nothing," I whispered. "Only a bad dream." Neither of us spoke.

We lay there gazing through the branches of the bush at the daylight. That dream, that horrible dream.

"Aim for the heights,
for the fresh blue?"

. . .

"then bend low"

. . .

"her red-black body"

. . .

"Shun the eyes of the dead."

I was standing in a dry riverbed and a long line of gray, brown, and black shapes with white horns were moving past me at a dogtrot.

"I have eaten his body and drunk his blood."

The man with the dormouse cap, Vili the musician, Mirko the machine gunner ran by.

They all ran past me. They knew I was there but did not look at me. Figures wrapped in gray, black, and brown shrouds, with white horns on their heads. Petkoshek! The usher! Cankar! Gubee! Shorty! It was awful; there were so many I could not recognize them all. The miner from Zagorje . . . Anton too was there running, stumbling, swathed in his cerements. Leon! The Croatian! All in haste, all knowing, as I did, where they were bound.

A minuet for guitar.

"We're cannibals and cannibals we shall remain."

The hordes kept coming, from far back over the sands of the river bed . . . irresistible . . . blind . . . unfeeling . . . calamitous . . .

I had to eat all those heaped-up banks of brown sand.

"Then bend low . . ."

"Her red-black body!"

We had to eat dung, putrefying skin, hair, scabs, to lap up pus, to suck the gray matter from shattered skulls . . . For we were cannibals and cannibals we would remain. This had been decided, for I no longer remembered what I ought to do.

Eat! Shun the eyes of the dead. There had been the severed head of that mule in the forest; we had eaten the rest of the animal. The guitar music was getting louder all the time . . . for now came that . . . which had to come, which would come blindly, like a dance of furious waves . . . which would engulf all else . . .

The sweat poured over me as I waited in anticipation of something evil . . . which would alter my belief in my own good fortune and obliterate it forever, engulfing all else . . .

On that occasion, back in the village, I had gone over my dream again after waking, so as not to forget it.

Now it had returned in a new guise, now I would like to forget it but could not cast it off. I belonged to it and it to me. In it lay concealed the answer to the riddle of human life.

I shuddered and looked at Anton. His eyes were fixed on me. Did he perhaps know something about my dream? He asked me quite calmly, "I suppose I was there also, wasn't I?"

Sure.

He continued: "I never believed in good luck. That's that."

A little bird perched on a bough of the bush which hid the entrance to our cave, twisted its head this way and that, until it caught sight of us and flew off in alarm. We now had clear evidence there was no one else in the vicinity.

"All those poor bastards, Anton . . . Do you think we missed our chance to withdraw?" I asked.

He stayed silent. That too was a sort of answer. But why did they have white horns?

We may say that nothing makes sense, that all ideas about the world are mere fabrications. We can curse war and deride peace. We can feign idiocy, guffaw, and dribble into our beards. We can play the conscientious official. We can submit to trial and execution for an ideal.

In our cradle, all is forgiven us. Later, they weigh us on various scales, which show different answers and employ quite different standards. They measure us with tapes, which employ completely different systems of measurement. They reach us, train us, lead us, encourage us, praise or blame us. No plant, no animal, no object, no stone, nothing except us is judged right or wrong, but we must submit to two verdicts, other people's and our own, and rarely do the two concur. Nothing, no one is as colossal, as weighty as we would like to believe. We are all guessing and no one knows for certain.

We shall stay here till the end, we shall stay here forever, Anton. All is right with us and all is wrong. What do I care what the last man says. There is no one else; just us two. That's to say, when we stop, not when we're rushing about with the others, can we manage?

"Soon it will be time to get moving," Anton said after a long silence.

We stood for a little time outside the modest den where we had spent the remarkable night. The mountainous world of that unspoiled canyon lay before us in the quiet of the morning; forest, rock walls, ravines, stone pillars, with the boom of the river from far below and a bird singing somewhere nearby. We set off across the steep slope in the direction of the river, which took us a little uphill. Without trying to remember it, I had a song running through my head that I had heard down in the valley, before the action began: ". . . with your rifle on your shoulder, into battle for your freedom and your bread . . ." Our clothes were dry, the biggest holes had been patched up, we had eaten and slept, we were rested and refreshed, ready to face a new day. I drew my belt a little tighter around my waist. It is true our joints were creaking and our legs were fairly stiff but that would pass when movement brought back the warmth to our bodies. We stepped over stones and tree roots, scaled mossy rocks, forced our way through bushes and reached the bed of a small mountain torrent. We clambered from rock to rock, waded through prickly mountain grass, and climbed up to a height beyond the hillock, from the other side of which we had heard the boom of the water down below. The transparent greenery in the heart of a dense wood was a welcome relief. I walked in front and Anton followed me like a faithful tortoise. We heard a woodpecker trimming the bark of a tree with his beak. We came to a forest path, lit by beams of sunlight struggling through thin clouds. We had to decide whether to go downhill or uphill. Following our instincts, we decided on the latter. The bandage on my wound had been changed; a mere detail at first glance, but how that grain of comfort improved my sense of well-being.

We walked on, slowly and steadily. "Not to worry," had been Anton's advice last night.

In the security of a small glen, we both felt it was time to attend to the natural functions of the gut and bladder. God knew when we would next have such an admirable opportunity. We tried to calculate on our fingertip when we had last had the pleasure. We could not agree on the date of our last crap. That would remain an unsolved puzzle in the mists and snows of mighty Mount Mokrec. In spite of some difficulty, I managed to perform; the olive oil from the sardine tin eased my task somewhat. Poor Anton suffered from hemorrhoids. He bitterly inveighed against Mother Nature who had given him carious teeth at one end of his life support tube and piles at the other. I was already sitting on a rock and smoking a tiny twist of paper with a few grains of tobacco in it, while he was still crouching and groaning, adding a string of comments that had nothing to do with the situation.

"I have never yet set the type for a book without reading it through. I was always hoping to find one of us in some book, a real authentic Slovene, you know, a bit of a bore, a bit of a wag."

I enquired what sort of a blend was that.

"On the one hand, a misery, a pen-pusher, a twerp, an ill-bred, narrow-minded boor; on the other someone completely different, though hard to characterize. But remember that, apart from the Bosnians, it was the Slovene Highland Jocks that provided the most daredevil assault troops in the Austrian army. Of course, you'll put it down to Dutch courage: give a Carniolan his fill of rum and he's ready to face the devil himself! What the hell! You can get an Itie tanked up and all he thinks of is women and song. There's no such person as Martin Krpan, the story's a mere fairy tale for pious folk, imported from abroad. Tell me anywhere else in Europe where you can find so many people murdered or stabbed on a Saturday night as here. Now Prešeren's character, Chertomir, has got many imitators. Every time there's a change of government, they line up to be baptized like him but the ceremony doesn't really mean a change of faith or heart. You'll see what it's like after the liberation. I can see the new converts lining up already." He started laughing but his laughter turned to groans when the blood began to flow. He went on rather testily. "The bailiff Yerney seeks his rights! Look, Berk, you might find me something softer. This bracken's playing hell with my hanging gardens."

I looked for some softer leaves. Above us, the birds were singing, an unusual thing for that time of year.

"All those tormented victims you meet in our books destroy any joy you might have had in reading. All that moaning, all those complaints, and nothing less. I tell you, I've seen a good bit of the world, I've seen how those people live and I know what life's like at home. Sometimes we're top dog and throw our weight around; sometimes we're at the receiving end. We have our weddings and we have our funerals, but what the hell! That's not the point . . . I can't put my finger on what's wrong. There was a Frenchman who used to insist that man was neither an angel nor a beast. I would like to see one of our writers acknowledging the fact that we Slovenes aren't all lovable dream girls or mettlesome heroes. My God, I've had enough of this, I need a bit of a rest. A crap like this takes more out of me than all your foot-slogging." He fastened his trousers, drew his shabby narrow belt tight and sat on a log, swinging his legs apart and back again to loosen the knees, stiff after all that crouching. At the same time, he went on, not paying any particular attention to me: "Martin Kachur is the most authentic Slovene character in literature. He takes to drink and flings all his ideals on the scrap heap or dunghill for his more practical neighbors to pick up, when the right time comes . . . You're going to see quite a lot of that . . ."

"Don't you mean we're going to see it? Surely you'll be there too?"

"You think so?" He said no more. We set off again.

The going was easier now and our path emerged into a narrow meadow between steep wooded slopes. We saw some figures there already.

They were partisans, some sitting about, some on their feet, some testing, some preparing a meal, some smoking and talking. In the middle, there was a group of what appeared to be staff officers, judging by their equipment, badges of rank, and revolvers at their belts. No one paid any particular attention to the pair of us, as we perched on a tree stump not far from the field kitchen. There were no familiar faces here. But once again, we belonged to some unit, troop, detachment, or what have you. Here at last, was, if not peace, at least everyday army routine. A bull-necked fellow of a puce complexion was brandishing a needle on a long thread as he sewed a button onto his jacket. I started talking to him. I learned that we had been attacked from all sides. The ambush had been laid on the old partisan way over Mount Krim. The Germans had struck from two sides and the Whites had come up from Blok to assist them . . . The Germans were by now back in Vintgar, or so it was believed. "When they had us in their grasp, they suddenly let us go. Well, that's the Germans for you. They keep to their orders." I saw patrol come in and approach the staff officers to make a formal report, judging by the saluting that was going on.

They say that a good general should have foresight. On the other hand, it is not advisable for an ordinary soldier, since he will always find everything turning out not as he had expected. No sooner does he get accustomed to a chain of events than the pattern changes completely.

We were called on parade and addressed by two speakers, one of whom dwelled on the indomitable resolve of our forces, while the other outlined our immediate tasks. The German thugs had suffered a deathblow, our own Quislings were quaking in their shoes, the people stood united, shoulder to shoulder with the National Liberation Army, which was celebrating victory on victory throughout the whole land. Our troop was to guard the approaches to the valley of Ishki Vintgar. Four of us were detailed for a reconnaissance patrol in the direction of the village of Ishka Vas. I had some difficulty in getting them to allow Anton to come with me. His bandaged head and whole appearance did not inspire confidence. The commander of our troop, a young fellow with keen gray eyes and a German automatic, a Schmeisser, appointed me leader of the patrol. We had a meal first.

Anton was chatting with some of the lads. He seemed to be in a good mood. "To be continued," he said. "It looks as if we got away with it this time, once again."

I was admiring the commander's Schmeisser, remembering with regret the one I had seen stuck in the snow, up there on Mount Mokrec, a few meters below me, with not a snowball's chance in hell of getting my hands on it. It's easy enough to say: "Go and get a weapon off the Germans." I was curious to know where the gray-eyed youngster had won that gleaming black prize, but it would have been an offense against common decency if I had gone ahead and asked. In any case, I would have gotten some jocular rebuff, such as: "Oh, I bought it from a secondhand shop" or "I found it in a pear tree, so I helped myself." I was now wise to this sort of thing.

We reached the brink of a ravine, where the four of us left the rest of the troop and set off down a cart track. Our orders were to reconnoiter the Vintgar valley. The Germans were probably still down below, with their transport, judging by the drone of car engines. We were also supposed to discover whether any nocturnal ambushes were being prepared on the high road below. If we got as far as the village, we were to report to one of the end houses called locally "The Chandler's," where we would be briefed by a Mrs. Spelca. Any stragglers were to be directed back up the valley.

There was nothing special about our two new companions, a couple of lads from some paramilitary formation. They both had Italian rifles, slung hunter-fashion over their shoulders. One had an old mountaineer's cap, the other a flat cap, pressed tight down on his ample cranium. I tried to strike up a conversation with them, to discover how they had been the previous day, but I could get no sense out of them. I do not think they wanted to lie; on the other hand, they did not trust me enough to tell me the whole truth.

The cart track ran a winding course through forest clearings. This was the road used by farmers to bring timber from the woods to the sawmill in the valley. It was wide enough for us to walk two abreast, with Anton and me in the lead. Bighead knew his way around here. He told us that, if the Germans had not killed the miller, we could get bread and brandy from him. An expanse of open grassland lay on our right. The clouds glowed with the light of the sun, which was striving in vain to burst through. This is how it is with armies on the march. One moment you find yourself in a sudden turmoil, all havoc and Armageddon, with men falling, leaping, running, killing and being killed, and then there comes a morning so peaceful you would think nothing had happened, with no sign of dead or wounded men, no traces of battle, just a pleasant, quiet cart track, meandering down to the valley. It did not matter whether we were old acquaintances. We were marching together to perform our allotted task. And so another day would pass.

"A glass of brandy wouldn't be amiss," I said to Anton, just in order to break the silence. That awful dream had partly faded away since the morning, but now and then, some detail would come back to mind, some image, like the hurrying multitude in their shrouds, or the brown sandbanks.

We came to a point where the bracken stopped and dense clumps of shrubbery encroached on the higher verge of our track, while the lower was littered with chippings; someone had been trimming logs here, before carting them down, probably some time last autumn. Obviously this area had been incorporated not too long before into our own territory, the free state of the forests. Then the Germans came along, but they had now departed and no one could foresee what the future held. Anton's advice would have been "Not to worry."

Our path now ran through an open space, the forest border withdrew some way up the bank and the cart track seemed to sink deeper and lower in the muddy ground. "How far is it to the mill?"

"Taking it easy like this, about an hour or three quarters of an hour."

We sauntered on, hands in pockets, rifles slung over our shoulders. The other two behind us mounted the verge, so that they were walking one on each side, with Anton and me between and below them. Ahead of us, the track ran into a shrubbery and vanished among the trees. We moved at an easy pace down the gentle gradient. Not a sound was heard, not even the rustle of a leaf or the chirp of a bird. This must be what they mean by peace in heaven and on Earth.

We were now approaching the shrubbery. Did I see some branches moving? I stopped automatically midpace. "Who's there?" I called.

Someone answered in Lowland dialect: "Eeh, it's only us. Come on, lads!" The other two, on the high verges of the track, whose legs were about on a level with our heads, proceeded happily on their way, but Anton and I held back for a moment.

Men suddenly sprang out of the bushes and started raking us with their Schmeissers. They were Germans, real Germans in blotchy camouflage jackets and steel helmets—I could have even sworn that I got a perfectly clear picture of the features of one of them, red-haired, rosy-cheeked, freckled, tall, thick-set, who handled his gun like an expert, soon finding his target and spraying us with bullets. Our two companions up on the verges were cut down at once, as I saw from the corner of my eye, while setting a new world record for the high jump. I leaped for the bank and landed first in a dense patch of bramble, which proved on this occasion no obstacle. I covered the hillside in swift bounds, as if I were swimming through a cornfield. Behind me the fusillade continued, an unbroken burst of fire. I was already high up and out of range when I halted, heart in my mouth and legs tangled in the thorny coils of the bramble. Occasional bullets still flew, fortunately off target; peace in Heaven and on Earth, my sacred oath! Somewhere to the left and below me, I heard the heavy thrashing of tangled feet; the happy thought flashed through my mind that Anton had got away too.

It was some time before he dragged himself up and joined me; we sat side by side in the undergrowth, with open mouths, gasping for breath. The thought struck me that I had heard no complaints about his heart from Anton on this occasion. No time to stop and think, eh? The whole thing seemed so absolutely ludicrous but I was too short of breath to enjoy a good laugh. How does that partisan song go? . . . "take your rifle in your hands . . . let the fusillade commence . . . make the enemy jump to it . . . in the final dance of death . . ."

"Life . . . is not . . . a bowl . . . of cherries . . ." I somehow managed to articulate in disjointed syllables. Anton looked at me, nodded, and delivered his own weighty judgment: "You can . . . fucking well . . . say that . . . again . . ."

"Anyone who is going to experience two wars in his lifetime should know that the second is always a disappointment by comparison with the first."
A veteran of the First World War

". . . there are some people whose tongues are tied by that dumb devil . . ."
Goriuppe, *Gospel Commentaries*

"The Spanish are one of the few people whose defects suit them."
Anton

"There is no disgust greater than that of a man forced to eat human meat if he is not used to it. But there is no disgust to which man cannot slowly be reconciled."
Shipwreck survivor

"In German dictionaries you find that 'coitus' is *Beischlaf*;
I've always thought this a great joke."
Anton

". . . *getrennt marschieren, vereint schlagen!*"
Moltke, *Feldzugpläne*

6

We had decided to cross the hill on our left and drop down to the highway in the valley to locate our friends. Quietly and calmly, we made our unhurried progress through a virgin beech wood, listening occasionally before cautiously moving on. We traversed a dense gully between two hills and arrived at a forest of tall straight pines. Here the going was much easier, because the dark floor was thickly strewn with pine needles that muffled the sound of our steps. We came down the hillside, gradually approaching the valley, assisted by the continually growing noise of the swift river somewhere below us. We were carrying our rifles in our hands. From the side, we probably looked like two birds with necks outstretched. We heard no shots, no human voice, and yet *they* were somewhere down below, not far off. The Germans did not dig trenches and did not climb trees; that was all we knew about *them* at that time.

The hillside grew steeper. We came to a halt simultaneously. Through the trunks, we could see a faint white line below us: the highway. We moved on a little farther down. The white macadam road was quite empty. On our side was the steep slope of the pine wood. On the other lay a narrow strip of grass, beyond which a stream ran between alder trees. We were perched about thirty meters above the road, on either side of a mighty trunk. We heard the sound of water in the distance but there was no other sign of life. We sat there in the semidarkness with our eyes fixed on the spot where some living creature might appear on the road and give us some idea of what the situation was. If they were still lying in ambush up in the hills, the top end of the valley must still be swarming with them, and if they were up there, it followed that they must be in communication with the lower end. There would be orders, patrols, everything as it should be on such a campaign. We sat there for about an hour. There was no sign of movement.

We had picked a good position, perched in the dark where we could not be seen. We could see through the trees to our left and right, so that no one could steal up on us unnoticed from our flank. Behind us was thick undergrowth on a precipitous slope. We had a good view of the road. A cigarette was therefore in order. We lit up, although there was more paper than tobacco in the thin tubes. Anton moved over and squatted beside me. Apropos of nothing, he observed, "A man never knows at what bend in this road of torment he is retracing his steps."

Spain again, I thought. Don't suppose you want to talk about it, though.

He looked into the distance and puffed at his cigarette. He gently refused, which could have meant "How idiotically life repeats itself" or "I don't like talking about it." Never mind.

Any idea what day it is today? November, 1943. What day of the week? It's all the same. Somewhere people are still lying in bed, stretching, wondering whether to get up and make the coffee or have another forty winks. The pine needles are as dusty as an old ants' nest. Anton would have liked to speak out, I knew, but some dumb spirit had him by the throat. He shifted position so that we could talk more easily but could not get a word out.

M em emm emme not an ant or emmet black or red in the ant's nest, only dead pine needles, my hand, and Anton's knee. All together this makes up a part of the world: the absent ants, the dead needles, a hand, and a knee; all the rest is peripheral. My eyes are peripheral; Anton's face is peripheral, so are the minerals in the earth beneath the absent ants. How silent, the operation of the cells in this scratched and filthy hand with its blue-black nails. Close your eyes and the trees disappear; open them and the towering black shapes swim in the murky green gloom, everything is submerged in the waters. Anton has lost contact with me and does not know what is happening; time, which each of us creates for himself, bears each of us with breakneck speed out to the furthermost distances, where there is only pure existence, with no cares or troubles, light-years away from the absent ants, the dead needles, a knee wrapped in gray cloth, a hand with black nails scrabbling among the needles; the circling power absorbs all, obliterating shape and struggle; entity and nonentity are an illusion, growth and decay are part of the same charade. It's nothing more than an enforced passage from one transformation to another, just a secret metamorphosis, anonymous and indefinite and for this reason there can never be any return. We are cut off, drifting somewhere in the universal, and if ever again eyes meet, they will not be ours.

Ferrocarriles de Mallorca FEVE N° 06205
Palma - Arenal - Palma
Precio (impuestos incluidos) 6 ptas.

For the ninth time, I read the ticket I was holding with two fingers. That ticket swallowed up the bus and the river of traffic hurrying past us on the asphalt road. Black letters on yellowish paper.

Consérvese el billete a disposition de cualquier empleado: keep the ticket at the disposal of any employee. Three by six centimeters of thin paper.

My eyes—the ticket—two fingers, my so-called fingers—Joseph Bitter's bony knee in his light brown lined trousers. All together this makes up a part of the world. Here I was apparently moving in the direction of Arenal–Palma, my surroundings and other particulars suggesting that I was on a certain Spanish island, that it was summer, 1973, that Joseph Bitter's wife had given him leave of absence and allowed him to take a bus trip in my company to the celebrated town of Palma. She was going to stay in bed, as she did not feel well on that windy, overcast day, so unsuitable for bathing. She would come to find us in town at six o'clock. We were to meet at such and such a place. We had drawn a plan of the market square, where there was a pleasant café. Meanwhile, the two of us were to have a look at some buildings, museums, and also the cathedral, where visits were allowed from four o'clock only. Absent ants, pine needles, my hand, Anton's knee—and the surroundings. My eyes, the ticket from Ferrocarriles, two fingers, Joseph's knee. Mere illusions of existence and environs, I was aware of the skin of this sturdily built German, rough and coarse as if it had been knit; well doused and scrubbed, aging a little, his skin contained some organism, some organic mechanism, some consciousness which had drifted far away from me. It would return when I stopped reading the inscription on the ticket. No real contact of our minds was possible. Whole countries, whole periods of history formed a barrier when our eyes met. His mind was full of a flood of particulars, while mine wandered far away to the pure motion of the tiniest particles, pulsations without matter, the natural arrangement of events in waves and particles. We could not understand, only perceive each other. Our eyes would meet when we arrived in town and stepped out along that wide avenue. Where had that new wound at the top of my palm come from? There were mornings when I noticed such a new scratch and realized that my fists had been flailing around during the night. But the bedding was soft wherever my hands had stuck and the metal frame was only down below and behind my pillow. I would never understand this. I must have been striking something hard. We are arriving. Both of us. Here we are.

Yes? Well, well. *Freilich, herrlich, gut . . . wir sind da . . . ja, ja.*

A line to get out and another line, twenty meters long, waiting to get in. People hurrying past. Stores, shop windows. Everything orderly, clear, sure. We stepped out, turned right automatically. Coffee first? Naturally. Except we both ordered a beer, as if we had changed our minds at the last moment. The table on the terrace of an elegant modern café was already waiting for us; the only one unoccupied, it was in a prime position, with a good view of the road, the busy traffic and passersby. From within the café came the sound of music, that naturally attractive but rather tempestuous Spanish music.

Dos cervezas. A coffee too, eh? Coffee? Very well. We are regaled with details about decibels, temperature, pollution of the atmosphere by exhaust fumes. *Dreher Birra.* Words, words. Written, spoken, fleeting, lost in the din and the welter of colored signs. Oleanders and myrtles in great pots. The utter idiocy of it all. Could anything be more idiotic? Tourism. You can invest absurdity with the multifarious trappings of good sense. Tourism, for example, has many sound points: it broadens the mind, it is good for the health, it is a tonic for the nervous system, it eases inner tensions, while a change of environment is in general a very good thing. It is also possible to find innumerable contradictory good points in the nonsense of war. It is only a question of externally reshuffling the details in the sense of some idea. I no longer needed to listen to what Bitter was telling me; it was enough to put in the occasional remark as an indication that I was listening. God knows whether other people too are incapable of adapting their view of the passing crowd, so as to see only what they are intended to see, or whether they shamelessly peer beneath the surface of things, like a pornographer below the clothing, like a butcher beneath the skin, like a physiologist at motion, like a metaphysicist at existence. What a relief, when finally, a really well-dressed girl comes by, with an attractive gait, a promising sway of the hips, in an ideally tailored outfit, neither tight nor loose-fitting, the sort that conceals to reveal. One in a thousand. She is always just around the corner, only a question of waiting and hoping. Then your cigarette smells better, your blood runs quicker and the light grows more pleasant.

"War can be the death of a man, even if he survives it physically," Joseph said. "I have seen colleagues of mine who have emerged from captivity like mere shades of their former selves, like living corpses. Their bodies did not die but something was lost. And since the beast in man never dies, what expired in them? All the same, war has its compensations: a greater awareness of life, a more willing acceptance of destiny, a remarkable response to one's surroundings. A man realizes what his real needs are and are not. He discovers what his real values and also his own true worth are. All this affects his environment—a whole series of positive influences. What then can it be, this thing which dies in a man when he has survived a war? His ideals? They don't even come into account. Religion? We can class that with his ideals. A man acquires a new knowledge and a new outlook; he can no longer look straight or accept the world as it is. Of course, there are also braggarts, who talk about the war later as if it had been a series of adventures, with them in the leading roles. At rock bottom, these he-men are arrant liars of limited intelligence. As for the zombies I mentioned, I shan't talk about them but you know what I mean?"

"Well, I suppose you mean a special category of people, don't you? Not those who survive and forget, not those who go on about their stupid exploits, but human beings with a body like me and you but with a corpse, or something dead, in place of a soul. Do I understand you correctly?"

"More or less. Something has affected their souls. But what that was and what part of them it has affected, it would be hard to say."

"Maybe it was some event, or some whole chain of events, that so affected them that it tore apart and destroyed some aspect of their soul?"

"The Americans are right to dedicate so much attention to the psychological and moral rehabilitation of their veterans. The best friend of my youth, Heinz let us call him, is a good example of such a zombie. He's a perfectly normal fellow, a businessman. His wartime experiences were no worse than mine, I might even say not so bad, but he can't escape from his continual spiritual crises. We can be talking, you know, on any topic at all, when he'll suddenly start gazing out into space; I know then what's up. 'How many of them are dead, Joseph,' he'll say. 'How many of our relations, schoolmates, friends, and acquaintances . . . and you carry them around everywhere with you, inside you, as if they still exist . . . alongside them, you grow old but they stay young . . .' Yet I know it's not this that is getting him down. War is another way of life, different from what a man got used to in his youth. Some men survive the war with injuries, greater or lesser, some even without injury, while others experience a complete change of personality. Heinz never got over the war, never truly returned to his family, could no longer grasp the concept of property in peacetime. You understand, I'm not talking about the moral aspect but rather about the biological or sociological!"

He gave me a piercing stare. We were standing, with a group of tourists from all over the world, in front of some old altar in the cathedral. The guide was churning out his commentary in various languages, telling us what we should particularly remember.

"You were saying something about property."

"Yes. Society is based on some concept of property. Now in wartime, and this goes for all the armies in the world, there is the same concept of personal property. You cannot imagine how important it is to have your own pocket knife, you know, a perfectly ordinary pocket knife, with possibly a tin opener and corkscrew as well. There's no point in having a house, which could be bombed at any moment by the enemy, no point in having a car, which will be commandeered by the army, no point in having an account at the bank, since the money may lose its value at any moment. The same uniform, the same weapons, the same mess tin, and a little money in your pocket, dear sir! In wartime, the concept of property goes up in smoke. At least, that's the usual pattern; we're not discussing exceptions. In wartime, the important thing is your position, your relationship to superiors, subordinates, and colleagues. A good position spells security, a weak position danger, no matter where the enemy happens to be at a given moment. Remarque can enlighten us on that. Have you read *All Quiet on the Western Front*? He celebrates a comradeship of sorts. Sure, that's it. That really is most important. The Nazis also knew it, my dear chap, but, at the basis of the idea of comradeship, lies the biology of security!"

"Don't you think there's also a little love involved?"

"Love? Probably so. Yes, of course. Sure, sure. Only—what is this thing called love, my dear sir?"

"Yes, indeed, what is it?" I wondered. We looked at each other in surprise. We were both acting. I allowed him to proceed.

"When Heinz and I were growing up, he was very fond of cockchafers and I loved green tadpoles," he put in.

Calmly I retorted: "Love for one's native land is on a par with love for calves' liver *à la crème*."

Relations are one thing: the only thing. I had him in my sights. An experienced tactician would wait for the appropriate moment, I knew. The time was approaching when we would at last join battle, that battle we had been carrying around inside us for thirty years. How would it turn out? Remarque was on my side; for Joseph Bitter, I well knew he represented only the Jewish surname Kramer in reverse. In the old-fashioned way, we would choose the place of conflict, survey the field of battle. In order to compare the last war with others, we chose a small bridge by the Italian village of Arcole.

"Do you like Napoleon?"

From one victory to another . . .

That son of a dog hastened from Corsica in 1796–97,

Montenotte, Millesimo, Dego, Mondovi, Cherasco, Lodi,

Piedmont is taken, the gates of Italy are broken,

Lodi, Lonato, Castiglione, Roveredo, Bassano . . . now a night march over the moors, across the dams on the Adige . . . and before dawn, the grenadiers reach the bridge over the moorland stream, the only possible crossing: unexpectedly the bridge is heavily defended; the cannon begin to bombard it, while Croatian battalions of the Austrian army lie in ambush on the other side.

. . . not a battle but sheer slaughter . . . The French covered the bridge with their dead. "Beneath the bridge Alpone's stream ran red with blood." The French had fallen into a trap. The first column was wiped out, the second, third, and fourth rushed on to their death. The cannon and the salvos of the defenders, like a giant's broom, swept them off the bridge. The soldiers no longer had any stomach for an attack which meant certain death.

"Napoleon seized a flag and rushed on to the bridge."

"Tolstoy and Taine both thought Napoleon Bonaparte was a coward; Stendhal did not agree with them," I meditated.

"A commander should be a good player," Joseph Bitter remarked. He knew a lot about that.

"Courage and cowardice are equally contagious," says a writer on war. "Like lighting one candle from another."

Bitter and I reflect: "A battle is disorganized chaos; everyone who takes part sees things from his own angle. Afterward, one legend or another takes shape and the eyewitnesses have the least influence on this. Legends are, for the most part, invented by cowards sitting in the security of their homes. That is why they are usually so heroic."

We went on with the legend.

"Napoleon seized a flag and rushed on to the bridge. Behind him thronged the grenadiers and commanders who were still alive.

"General Lannes protected Napoleon with his own body from the first salvo and fell dead. His commanders surrounded him. At the second salvo, Colonel Muiron collapsed on Bonaparte's breast, his blood spattering Napoleon's face. Soon they reached the end of the bridge, where the Croatians and the Jocks from Carniola attacked with cold steel and threw the Frenchmen back. In the tumult, the grenadiers bore Napoleon back and he fell from their arms into the marsh and began to sink in it, muddy and bloodstained. Once again they attacked the bridge, rescued Napoleon, no one knows how, from the marsh and brought him to the bank. They seated him on his steed."

From the above I drew the following conclusion.

"Soldiers love their commander and officers sacrifice their lives for him. Napoleon sacrificed himself for victory. The Croatians sacrificed themselves for Austria. The Austrian general, Alvinczy, loved his Croatians and the Jocks from Carniola. Napoleon loved his officers and grenadiers. The Austrians were defending their free country against the invaders. The French were bringing liberty to the country. They were all sacrificing themselves for the sake of freedom. They all loved their country, freedom, their comrades, and commanders. Two loves brought together in corrosive hatred for a life-and-death struggle. A legend of love."

Bitter got my drift. He smiled as he heard me.

"After the battle on the bridge at Arcole, the Austrians withdrew from Mantua, Verona, and the whole of Italy, and the French marched on from one victory to another, to the Egyptian Pyramids, to Marengo, Austerlitz, Jena, Friedland . . . and further. The rain at Waterloo stopped them . . . Later, a sick little man on the Island of St. Helena had plenty of time to think it over. On his deathbed, they say, he was dreaming (or raving?) about an attack on a bridge. *Tête . . . armée . . .* he whispered."

Let us examine this man who loved war. "Here, at Arcole, Napoleon was the son of the Revolution. The Republic was bringing freedom from their chains to the emperor's oppressed peoples. Happy that the Austrians had withdrawn, he wrote to the Archduke Charles after the battle on the bridge, 'As far as I am concerned, the life of a single human being is dearer than all victories.' He was fighting for peace. So he pretended. A love for the struggle for peace. Napoleon loved the Revolution, he loved the Republic and respected human life. After his coronation, he loved the Empire, put down the enemies of the monarchy. A million lives in his path meant nothing to him, said Metternich.

"He built a fearful war machine. We all know that comradeship was highly developed in Napoleon Bonaparte's French army. From Alexander the Great and Julius Caesar onward, so they say, there had been nothing but mercenary armies, without a spark of the high morale inspired by military comradeship. A real leader can develop a fine spirit of comradeship in arms. A real soldier has a blind faith in his commander.

"The Army is the soldier's family. The State is his mother. The Commander is his father. His comrades are his brothers. Love for our fatherland binds us in a ring of steel. Honor is our mistress. Our weapons are what we hold most dear.

"Crawl—move! Crawl—move! Squatting begin. One, two! One, two! Crawl! On your bellies! Move! Forward march! Left, right! Left, right!

"Napoleon seized a flag and rushed on to the bridge.

"For unity, fraternity, liberty! For the Revolution! For the Republic! For free Europe! No one says: for the capture of foreign territory."

I stopped, short of breath, and thought: "Should I be ashamed because I liked that man with the dormouse cap? It's probably stupid to talk of comradeship as a sort of love. But what do regular, mobilized troops know about the comradeship of volunteers who take the field against foreign armies of occupation?"

Joseph Bitter was thinking aloud. "From the beginning of a soldier's training, the greatest possible psychical stress is laid on one demand: that he should become completely integrated as 'one of us,' and that in the depths of his soul, he should never dare to imagine that something might be wrong, and that he should feel guilty of treachery if he should feel the slightest stirrings of doubt in himself."

I thought this over to myself. "Why, even in the regular forces where a soldier is formally recruited, trained, and sent off to the front, couldn't he still live, in spite of that sense of self-doubt? Only, what about a man who joins up as a volunteer? Or an observer? Someone who is not really engaged? Wouldn't he go out of his mind? What an existence for your homo sapiens, your normal and intelligent man, caught between a terrible enemy and the threat of court-martial?"

Bitter went on. "At rock bottom, you know, every soldier has a profound sense of the falsity of all he has been taught in a particular civilization. He realizes that relations between people are not at all as they are described in fine books. That human life is something quite different. That our lives are in the hands of blind, stupid forces, which drive us along unknown paths. Everyone feels this and the feeling grows stronger. And when two share the same feeling, that's a whole new ball game. They lack the confidence to say straight out what's on their minds, but a hint or two, a sly dig in the ribs soon leads to a secret alliance, very secret indeed, since they have the military police and the court-martial breathing down their backs, and furthermore, it's a crime against 'the common cause,' a betrayal of their comrades, who've put on blinkers so that they can carry on with no inner schism."

Each of us was delving into the past for his own purpose. Bitter said wearily, "In fact a complete disenchantment with all fairy stories sets in. There remains only the bare truth. Bare, flinty, blind, deaf, unadorned, a sense of reality that quietly, cruelly, imperceptibly but with the clean cut of an axe, kills all joy in life. There are human cells that can never be renewed."

I, on the other hand, pursued my Napoleonic theme. "'In our day, men have ceased to think of great deeds; I shall set an example.' Napoleon's own words. He later explained: 'At that time, I despised everything that did not spell glory.'"

Two spare pairs of boots in your knapsack and a new pair on your feet!

It is thirty miles from Rivoli to Mantua. Six thousand of Napoleon's men had to march at the double all night and day before hurling themselves at the enemy, who numbered sixteen thousand; yet they won. They came, fought, and won at Favorita. ("Favorita will shine forever in Napoleon's sky like a marvelous diamond.")

"'The Roman legions used to cover twenty-four miles a day, but mine cover thirty, and spend their rest periods fighting,' Napoleon wrote to the Directorate. Hitler's motorized divisions sometimes did more than one hundred kilometers a day in some sectors."

While saying this, I was thinking that I could never say how many miles I did a day, although the Germans who were pursuing us, united by the bonds of military comradeship, could have rendered an exact account.

Meanwhile, I spoke and pressed on ruthlessly. "We've heard of love for horses, for dogs, for animals, love for old people and children, love for the sun, warmth, and light, for freedom, peace, one's own work, love for travel, swimming, boating, for one's native language, for books, the theater, the cinema. A trainer loves his animals, an old lady her cat, her canary, her goldfish. We've heard of love for God, for beautiful women, for black pudding with sour cabbage. Coitus, bodily love, coexists with love for reptiles . . . But what binds us, Mr. Bitter?"

Bitter looked at me very seriously. "Faith, hope, love? Faith in what? Hope in what? Love for what? Under a blue, colorless sky. In a life torn by doubt."

Something suddenly came back to mind. "A man who dies for his country has lived long enough." Just before he was shot, our poet Rob quoted these words of Dante in the original to the Italian firing squad.

He loved, he hoped, he believed. Don't we owe him something for that? That red-haired, red-bearded, unprepossessing fellow. Never had any success with the women but was brave and intelligent all the same.

Should I feel ashamed because I cannot keep him out of my mind?

Should we admit that all his dreams of a brave new world in the future will come to nothing? What of his faith, his hopes, his love? In spite of doubts and falsehood, he explored those themes to their core.

I said in answer to my own question. "One must play one's role to the end. Every journey has its end."

The end is unknown. Faith, hope, love lead to an unknown end. At rock bottom we find the unknown, intersected by the hopes of the day and the doubts of the night. The effects of drink, waking at the dead of night, wear us out: don't worry, the day will soon be over, the night will soon pass, the sun will shine and disappear again. A human being needs love. And not only to propagate the race.

"I love my wife, of course," Bitter said, "and she loves me. We need each other too. It will be very hard when one or the other of us dies. She is seven years younger than me but you have noticed how protective and motherly she is. She brings me a sense of security and I do the same for her. Sometimes I cut loose, deceive her, lie to her. She senses it, feels it, knows it. But she isn't the military police who allow no wavering. She isn't a court-martial. She patiently educates and instructs me, knows and loves my defects, so that we have come to a certain permanent arrangement that is a mixture of conquest and enslavement on my side, and the exact opposite for her."

After which he suddenly added, out of the blue: "They tell me in the hotel you're a Yugoslav. I wonder why you didn't tell me . . ."

Oh, wide and high stands Jahor Mountain . . .

Anton and I probably did not exchange glances when, at that familiar sound somewhere below us and to our right, we were brought back to what is called the here and now. We had flown through the infinities of space, to come in on lightning tangents and land together in the forest. On the highway in the upper part of the valley, we heard the rattle and roar, the metallic clanking of tanks. No question of them being ours, of course!

We quickly dropped down the hillside to our left, where sturdy pines soared up from a steep slope. We climbed along the boughs, which here touched the bank to find ourselves four or five meters above the roots, each of us on his own tree and about four yards from each other, and eight meters over the road, which ran below us. We each pressed close against the trunk and gazed in the same direction through the pines.

Two enormous shapes loomed up, detached themselves from the greenery. The noise got louder, and we could now distinguish the clank of the broad tracks from the boom of the motor. Now the outlines of a second tank began to appear behind the first. The first had its cockpit closed, and its long cannon well oiled; it moved on with a steady, hollow pulse, its caterpillar tracks covered with patches of light-colored sand from the road. The cockpit of the second was open, and there stood a figure in a dark uniform, with a cap on his head. He did not have a helmet but stood there, calmly gazing ahead. He was hidden by the branches but I got a closer view of him through a chink in the pine needles. The tank commander. Behind him rumbled a great gray armored car.

The first tank passed by below in easy spitting distance. It was going faster than I had thought. The second arrived. I saw the badges of rank on the collar and epaulets of the man in the cockpit . . . Were I to fall now I would land on the tracks about a yard from him. The tank was working like a well-oiled machine. He had his hands in black leather gloves clenched on the rim of the cockpit; a powerful young fellow, stocky and broad-shouldered, with a smoothly shaven nape . . . then!

He then began to turn his head, looking behind and above him . . . He had felt my gaze on his nape . . . In horror I changed my line of thought . . . I was going up the hill . . . up the hill . . . must get up to the top . . . far, far away . . . he quickly scanned his surroundings . . . his glance seemed to come quite close to me . . . He could not understand what had upset him . . . but he drove on . . . Then I felt Anton's gaze, fixed on me, first astonished and reproachful, but soon relaxed again . . . The whole episode lasted only a moment. The armored car roared by, followed by trucks covered with tarpaulins . . . A close shave! A fine mess we would have been in if they had started raking the trees with machine-gun fire . . . Would they? Well, if the hunters could not think of some other amusement.

We remained for some time perched up in the trees. There was no further sign of movement on the highway. When it got dark, we started to make our way slowly down the valley, moving parallel with the road.

We approached the first house in the village. We could see a small light in the window. There was nobody about on the road.

We went through an orchard behind the second house, in which there was no sign of life. Our rendezvous was one of the last houses. Do you remember the name? Sure.

The people knew it was not wise to venture out of the houses.

We quietly proceeded, nerves on edge in the baleful silence, in which only the murmur of the water flowing somewhere close by could be heard.

I tapped gently on a window where a lamp was burning behind a curtain. For a considerable time, there was no response. Then an old face. A low whisper: "Is that you, Maria?"

"Where are the Germans?"

Who knows. They've probably moved on. Run for it, lads, run for it.

There was fear in that voice.

Finally we found the place. Two women, mother and daughter, and three children aged from four to eight, the two youngest were boys. The mother was obviously scared stiff. She sat us down at table, brought us a dish of warm milk and a pot of potatoes boiled in their skins.

"Didn't you see it? Didn't you come down the road? There are about fifteen bodies lying there at the roadside. Some of them still clutching those leaflets the planes dropped, with a guarantee of good care and safe conduct. People who surrendered. At Strahomer, there are twenty-five of them lying by the road, so an old woodcutter told me. The Germans were here again only a few hours ago. Yes, they ransacked the whole place, turned the mattresses upside down, bayoneted the bedding in the stable, drove long pitchforks into the hay. They've opened up the wardrobes, been up in the loft and there's not a corner of the whole house where they haven't poked their prying noses. Well, come on, eat up."

We were sitting at a table in the hall. The door was half open and the children were darting in and out.

Warm milk. Delicious potatoes.

We heard men's voices outside. The sound made us all shudder. The little girl rushed into the house with an excited whisper: "Germans!" We jumped up, Anton and I, and grabbed our rifles. What now? The woman seized us by the elbows, bundled us unceremoniously into the living room, and locked the door behind us. We rushed for the window, thinking we might leap out into the open but sturdy iron bars blocked our way. By now we could hear male voices in the hall and we could tell they were speaking German. I drew Anton to one side of the door and took the grenade from my pocket. The bright metal glittered in the faint light which filtered through the window. I held the firing pin. I had to be careful, not to draw either too early or too late. Wait for the door to open. Wait for them to come in, so that they would accompany us to paradise. The story of the bodies by the roadside came back to mind and I thought of those naïve conscript partisans, who had put their faith in German military honor. They had probed the bedding and the hay. Now they were back again. For another search. Why are there two bowls of milk on the table? I see. Beside me, Anton's breath was short and labored. I felt the warm, smooth, metal egg in my hands. I was relying on it alone. Where was my rifle meanwhile? No doubt hanging by its strap from my elbow. I imagined the explosion, the flash; I'd seen a few of them go off at night and knew they were hot stuff. Shapes would appear as the door opened . . . there would be a light from the hall . . . I would hear a few words of German . . . maybe: "*Du, Joseph, schau mal da hinein . . .*" And it would not be only one. There would be two or three.

I felt my belly and the sinews in my neck grow taut. I was hardly conscious of my legs. A man should go through this sort of thing once in his life . . . What? The grenade? No, what's coming I mean. Dawdling here over warm milk and tasty potatoes . . . mouth's now bone-dry and tasteless, like leather. It will rip my flesh . . . and then I'll feel no more . . . it will come like a knockout blow. No pain. Only a drunken silence. We'll fall asleep. That's all, a sudden flash, then soft darkness and rest, and anyway I'm absolutely worn out; very, very tired after my long journey. Steps outside, slow and heavy. The sound of talk, meaningless, receding. If I understand anything of this, I shall never be able to tell anyone about it. The living room was not at all dark, it was radiant with light. The door began to open but I did not draw. Something stayed my hand. The lady of the house was standing there, addressing the empty space before her. "They've gone . . ."

Now to get out of this bloody trap!

"I'll give you something to take with you," the woman said. "Some oil, flour, fried pork, potatoes, bacon. You must go to Ravbar's and cook your meal there. Little Yeritsa will show you the way. Ravbar is a good man, though his daughter is a bit of a bitch. But you'll be all right. Safer there. We're too close to the road here."

She put some articles in a basket, thrust it into my hands and we set off, the woman, little Yeritsa, Anton, and I, across the yard. "Ravbar's house is down there by the river. Tell him that I sent you. Dear God, hope it will be all right. Good night, lads."

Ravbar was a tall, slim, slightly stooping man. He told us later he had trouble with his lungs. Yeritsa said something to him when he appeared at the window, after putting the light out. The little girl said good-bye and left.

He had a good carbide lamp, which gave a strong white light. The stove was still warm. A pretty girl came out of the kitchen, barefoot, her hair loose, wearing a nightgown that fit her like a loose, white sack. She gave us a dirty look but said nothing, only pulled a face and withdrew. Ravbar sat us down at a wide table and poured us each a glass of clear cider. Just what the doctor ordered.

"The Germans were here earlier, they won't be coming during the night. They don't like straying from the beaten track." We told him how we had nearly been trapped in the other house. He shook his head and sighed. "She gave you something, I suppose." He inspected the food we had brought in the basket.

"Would you like to eat now? Have you any cigarettes? I've still got some here. I used to enjoy a smoke when I was still well." He produced a whole parcel of assorted cigarettes, some envelopes, Zetas, Moravas, Neretvas, Ibars, Dravas, and even Vardars with their gilt lettering. The future looked radiant.

"Would you like to dip your feet in a basin? Might bring a little relief, eh? Sabina! Sabina!"

There was an unpleasant response from the room at the back. "What is it now? What do you want, Dad?"

"Would you bring a basin of warm water, Sabina?"

"What for?"

"So that they can wash their feet."

"Well they can get it themselves! Bringing their crabs into a clean house!"

Ravbar went himself and brought us two basins of tepid water, throwing a handful of salt into each. Anton and I took our boots off, hid our filthy wrappings under the table and dipped our feet in the water. We gasped with relief and sat there with our trousers rolled up. Ravbar sat at the table. Now we could quietly and slowly enjoy a cigarette.

Ravbar took our food into the kitchen. We could hear him arguing there with his daughter, who would have gladly thrown us out of the house. Anton gave me an enquiring look. What now? We moved our feet about in the water. Our rifles were quite close, within arm's reach, propped up against the bench and a chair. I unbuckled my belt and put my bag and blanket on one side. Anton followed my example. Ravbar reappeared. "I've put the polenta on," he said. He looked through the window and nodded. All was quiet. "Don't worry, there's no chance of them coming back tonight." He had trouble with his daughter, they did not get on well at all. She had her own ideas and seemed to be somewhat around the bend. Like her mother. "Suffered terribly from headaches. She died in the hospital, I've no idea what of. Sabina and I have now been on our own for two years. She can be quite useful when she wants but you see what she's like when she has one of her wild spells. Here, use this to wipe your feet. I know something about route marches. In the First World War, I did my stint in Galicia, I was over in the Carpathians, I know what it's like. I'll go and see if the water's boiled."

Another altercation with Sabina, who was getting more and more irritable. "I'm going for the Germans," she screamed. Ravbar returned, very red in the face, clutching at his chest and coughing. "What a stupid, stupid bitch . . ." he gasped. "Please pretend . . . you've heard nothing . . . for my sake . . . bloody young fool hasn't a grain of sense . . ."

She came in, noisily dragged a chair away from the table, plopped down on it and glared at us, and me in particular, defiantly. Ravbar reached out his hands, as if to say, give it a rest, woman! Still wearing her loose nightgown, she struck a shameless pose, sitting there with her legs wide apart. She was not bad-looking, with full breasts and sturdy thighs. Her eyes flashed, as she told us she had a "fiancé" in the Home Guards, an officer in charge of a roadblock, not a tattered ruffian like us. On Sunday, she would put on white gloves and walk through the block like a real lady. The soldiers would salute her, just like this, and no one would ever ask to see her pass. What would they say if they knew her father knew helped such lousy scoundrels? It was a disgrace for a decent house.

At this, I rebuked her savagely. "Do you know what you're saying, you flaming trollop!" The reprimand made her angrier than ever.

"A trollop? Me? Get your boots on, scarecrow, and take yourself off, while I throw your corn mush out into the yard after you." She stood with arms akimbo, her bare feet tapping the red-painted floor. Her father tried to calm her down without success.

I addressed her with a suitable argument.

"Go on, fire!" she yelled. "Take that stolen gun of yours and fire. It's all your like are good for, shooting women and children!"

I wiped my feet and put my boots on, while she delivered a running commentary. We would never be able to afford socks. Our boots would fall to pieces.

Anton put his boots on too. Ravbar persuaded his daughter to accompany him to the kitchen. I would have liked to wash the rags that served me as socks but it was hardly possible in the situation. Anton murmured, "Damn and blast the silly cow . . . What next?"

Ravbar came back and wanted to say something but he was seized such a fit of coughing that he could hardly get a word out. His face flushed and he clutched his chest with both hands. The clatter of pots came from the kitchen. Surely she's not going to throw our food out. At this awful thought, I made for the kitchen. It was neat and tidy, there was a damask cloth on the table, a cupboard, a polished kitchen range and a box for firewood. On the wall, there were shelves for dishes and cutlery.

She blocked my way. What did I want here? She made to throw me out but no sooner had she touched me than I blew my top. I took hold of her hands and twisted them. She was soon kneeling on the ground, howling with pain. I held her over the firewood with my left hand, while I reached with my right for the long ladle on the shelf above. With an almighty crack I delivered the first blow on her taut rump. She cried out hoarsely, with a different note than before. I now rained blows down on the squirming, twitching mass of her rounded buttocks. I have no idea what provoked me but I reached for the hem of her nightgown and tugged it right up to her neck. Beneath it she was naked. My left hand was now clutching both her wrists and nightgown, and probably her hair too, while my right belabored her curving flesh, which began to glow as stripes appeared on the pink skin.

She was now gargling and sobbing, uttering muffled cries which had assumed a regular rhythm. Her resistance was steadily weakening, as if she were resigned to her fate. I felt the pulse of my own blood in my neck and temples. All my sur-roundings were glowing with a reddish hue and my guts began to churn. Her left hand had escaped from my grasp but no longer mattered. I felt her hand between my legs. Everything now happened with breakneck speed. In a flash, she opened my trousers and found me straining at the leash. She released me and squirmed toward the counter. I let her right hand go, seized her by the hips with both hands, and speared her while the ladle flew off unheeded. She rose and thrust, head buried in her hair, which she had tossed forward over her face. My first stroke into her quivering damp heat had been like an electric shock. I held her up in the air and carried on stuffing her. Suddenly, I dimly realized I was caught, enslaved, and I did not mind at all . . . I was crazy with delight . . . The meaty sphere opened and closed, until a sudden convulsion gripped our flesh and we came together. Then at last my vision cleared: Anton was standing in the doorway, gazing at us with a strange and foolish smile on his lips.

After this, we were all one big happy family. We had supper and Sabina served us. After supper we had a smoke, Sabina, Anton and I. She did not know how to inhale but tried hard to cooperate. I took her cigarette, put it out, and pocketed it "for a rainy day." She put up no resistance. Ravbar pretended that nothing had happened.

326

We were to sleep on the hay. The two of them accompanied us to the hayloft. It was a quiet, rather misty night. We climbed up the ladder into the loft. We heard the house door close on the other side. We spread our blankets and used our packs for pillows. Then I felt a bit worried. I got up and went to the end of the loft. I felt the wall. It was made of stout planks. One of them was a bit loose. I made an effort and pulled out the bottom nail, so that it was hanging by one nail, and it was now possible to slip out that way. I came back again. "Aren't you going a little too far?" Anton remarked, and we fell asleep, dead tired.

I was woken by the sound of voices. I raised my head. It was morning. My whole body froze when I realized they were speaking German. I snatched up my blanket, pack, rifle, and rushed toward the back wall. Then I looked back. Anton was sleeping with lips open, lying on his side, with that filthy bandage around his head. I had to go back. I heard a boot on the first rung of the ladder below. Talking, shouting. I grabbed Anton's mouth to gag him. He woke immediately. I whispered one word: "Germans," and we both hightailed it for the loosened plank, which saved our lives. We leaped down and started running through the misty orchard. Behind, we heard the sound of firing and bullets whizzed past our ears. There was the sound of pursuing footsteps, cries of Halt! Halt! and cursing in German. We raced on with all our might. I was holding my rifle in one hand and my pack and trailing blanket in the other. "If only the mist doesn't lift, they won't catch us . . ." We ran down to the shallow river, which at this point widened and split into two channels . . . Through the water, over a gravelly island, across the second channel, up the gravel on the far side, on to a bank, a bank covered with young pine saplings, no taller than me, but dense and hard to penetrate . . . Beside me, a little behind, Anton labored on . . . up the bank, higher, higher . . . The firing was now behind us . . . we could no longer hear the shouts . . . we panted as we pressed on through the pines . . . dropped onto the moss in a clearing as if we had fallen from heaven.

When I looked at my watch, it was almost half past six. There was a buzzing in my ears. With sudden pleasure, I heard the strings of a guitar playing a minuet. I realized it was an aural illusion but even so it was pleasant. There was plenty of brushwood about and the mist gave us good cover. I lit a small fire and we cooked the bacon skewered on sticks, nibbled our tasty bread, and finally smoked a Morava.

The sun broke through the mist at about nine o'clock. We put out the fire.

At about five o'clock, we approached the village warily.

We had spent those eight hours in a comatose state, in which vague thoughts flashed across the mind, though I cannot remember any words being spoken. I wondered whether Anton too had heard the notes of the guitar playing the minuet in that monotonous rhythm. But I could not bring myself to ask him. Some dumb devil now had me by the tongue.

Later, we saw and heard the whole story before going back up the valley.

The last of the Germans had now finally withdrawn and the valley was liberated. The drive against the partisans was over and people could walk their roads freely again. Two old women and an imbecile were standing among a heap of corpses, children shot by the roadside. We could see them laid out on the grass verge. Arms, legs, faces. Anton and I could well have been lying there with them, if the grenade had been a dud, say, or if I had not woken up at the right time. I looked, and could just imagine the two of us stretched out there, beside one of them who had his boot fastened with string. I also happened to notice one of those yellow leaflets calling on us to surrender. The German sense of humor. Traces of tank tracks could be seen on the road. The afternoon sun was sinking behind Mount Krim.

We now caught a glimpse of our first patrol coming down through the village, a couple of men with rifles slung over their shoulders, moving slowly and unconcernedly. This was the ultimate proof that the German action was over. We had a word with them. They told us there were a lot of partisans up at the mill.

We walked along the highway. Evenings were long in this valley, lasting whole hours, from sunset to night. We camped higher up, by a deep pool. The sudden realization of our complete security set my nerves tingling. Half of my left palm, together with the ring and little fingers, began to go numb as I felt an attack of pins and needles. It was time to give voice. I yelled, "Death to Fascism!"

Anton joined in with gentle mockery: "And liberty to the people!" We both started to gabble away at random. The sullen spirit had lost its power.

Yesterday, there had not been a living soul in sight, neither man nor beast. Today, cows were taken out to pasture, hens were scrabbling in the farmyards, children were racing about the roads, and even old people were venturing out. Yesterday we had been whispering and straining our ears; today we were bawling, gossiping, and even trying to laugh. Was this in fact the end of the war? "No," said Anton, the expert on such matters. "Then you won't be able to move for the crowds on the roads and everybody will go crazy. It won't be a pretty sight. They'll all be guzzling, crowding, shouting, and only really sensible people will be deep in thought and full of apprehension. A fool is always thinking about what has passed, a wise man about what is to come."

"How do you know that?" I asked.

He smiled. "I've often had to begin again," he said, then added, "but I've never brought anything to a conclusion." All his statements had some deeper meaning. And in all of this, I could sense a comparison with me and my mode of life, or his view of it. Those days had brought us so close together, there was no longer me here and you there but only the pair of us, a sort of new entity. There was something pleasant in the sensation; each of us felt himself more extended, though this too exerted an added pressure on us.

Things may appear fenced off and separated, while in reality there is a barely perceptible link between one thing and another, between both and a third, and ultimately among all things. Everything operates and moves according to fixed laws except for the individual, for man, for the knowledge of man and humanity; man tries to comprehend the natural order of things, attempts to set up natural boundaries—and teaches us to believe categories he has instituted himself. From our separate selves, Anton and I had fused a new, common self. We were smoking our Moravas, eating our dry biscuits, sipping our brandy from our flask—a gift to us from Ravbar; we were following our path; neither of us could, even for an instant, revert to himself alone, a creature with his own will and own ends. This led to quiet difficulties, an atmosphere of possessiveness and liberation, an almost imperceptible friction. We spoke our words as we understood them, sometimes in agreement, sometimes clashing and rebounding. At any rate, our freedom was also our enslavement, and this is probably what is meant by comradeship in arms. It was by no means confined to a common security. Together we had tamed Sabina and she had given us an old sheet, from which we had cut new cloths and bandages. We had shortened Anton's bandage considerably. His wound was healing and the old rag was clinging to it in places and scabs were forming. We sat by a stream, gazing at the swift current. Slowly the evening passed. If a man tried to understand only the inner chemistry of his organism, or even just part of it, for example the action of salts and metals in it, he would need to devote the whole of his life to such studies, and even then would die stupid and ignorant. We can all say whether God exists or not, we can all engage in discussions about life and death, but can we describe the function of sodium in the body?

The mill was full of partisans, sitting in the hall, the dining room, and the parlor. The miller handed out chunks of bread and poured us glasses of sour wine, while for starters, everyone got a tot of homemade gin. Everyone had plenty to talk about. Where could they have all come from? We learned there was a meeting place in a certain village called Golo. Their guns were propped up against the wall and we added ours to the line. Two jokers, already somewhat under the influence, were singing lighthearted folk songs in raucous voices. "Last year he bought her a kilo of coffee. This year she'd like a whole heifer off 'ee . . ." There was plenty of coming and going; some would be sleeping in the mill, others would be billeted on the neighbors. "Where, where, where shall I get it, where shall I get it to give to the wenches . . ." Those two were singing in the house hall, while the parlor echoed with bass voices intoning, "By the booming Adriatic . . ." Fighting songs also had their turn.

Anton and I decided to move on. We got up and reached for our rifles, but they were nowhere to be seen. We made a thorough search but ours had disappeared. When we told some characters what had happened, they smirked and sniggered, asking us why we didn't admit we'd ditched our guns instead of putting on this act! We were left without weapons. We realized the obvious. A couple of others had in fact abandoned, ditched, or lost their rifles—and quietly helped themselves to ours. In the general hubbub, no one had noticed. We asked the miller if he had any weapons. "You're too late; I had three hidden under the floorboards but handed them over to the partisans this morning." We walked off with our hands in our pockets. We could have screamed with fury. However, Anton thought we would probably pick up something the following day. "Meanwhile, we're traveling light," he said, I knew he wasn't really unconcerned. Imagine a soldier returning from battle unarmed. Who would believe our story?

It was a bright night. The clear moon forecast fine weather.

We spotted a small litter bin by the road and decided we could spend the night there.

We lay on the leaves but could not get to sleep for a long time. We now exposed another fallacy. People say lice and ticks cannot abide each other, that fleas will not attack anyone who is lousy. But a hungry tick is in no mood for such theories. For days afterward, we were still discovering strangers we had picked up in that pile of leaves, bugs that had dug deep into the skin around our testicles. It was over a week later when I located a prize specimen parked under my armpit, plump as a bean seed. Anton had once set the type for a textbook of physiology, so he did know something about the composition of human tissue. We had decided that there was no problem, as far as the existence of God was concerned. Something does exist beyond man, above man; in a hundred years, people will have ceased to argue what this should be called. Strange to think that man is his own god. God or nature, Spinoza said. "Anyway, it is something that is unconcerned about man and his fate," Anton remarked. Man has no guardian angel. On the other hand, he has no crawling devils to molest him. That thought is worse than any concept of hell. Man on his own, left to the mercy of himself and his human society, with no forces of evil or good, no eye in a triangle watching over him! Throughout every civilization, he invents myth after myth, and later unmasks them one after another, yet is unwilling to believe that good and evil exist exclusively in him.

We lay on our backs in the strong-smelling leaves while the moon cast a silvery light on our feet. At such a moment, you could believe yourself conscious of each individual leaf below you, of your own separate cells and of everything up to the distant galaxies, while at the same time understanding remarkably little. We have too much intelligence to be dull, happy automata, and too little to raise ourselves above the quest for happiness . . . and why should we? A man hopes all his life that he will discover something so important that his whole life will change and a most difficult problem will cease torturing his brain. In fact there is no solution. He would have to go back on himself to his infancy, or even to a purely animal stage with normal, natural organs for observation of the world.

At this point in our deliberations, we fell silent and each tried to get to sleep.

It was hours before I fell into a fitful sleep. The debate continued in my dreams; I woke up and would have liked to get up and go for a walk around this hovel. When once again I fell asleep, it seemed to me that in my slumbers I had at last discovered some exciting secret.

For surely these two propositions cannot be both true at the same time: I am fully conscious, I know what exists and what is happening, I remember the past, I anticipate the future, I have the faculty of logical thinking, that something exists and something else will follow as a consequence, I live, I mature, I develop, I wither and die; and yet, at the same time, I know nothing of what is happening to me, nothing of its cause or purpose, nothing of what exists beyond me or above me, and all my notions of the relations between man and matter seem degenerate. And here you are, still at war.

Judging by his gentle snore, Anton was asleep. Would I be able to tell him the next day what I had discovered this night?

We were both up well before the sunlight penetrated the Ishka canyon. We lit a fire and cooked up our corn mush. We ate and had a quiet smoke, drank some hard spring water, and then set off. We no longer felt disposed to unravel our mental Gordian knots. Morning gave the lie to night. How could we go on living otherwise?

We were crossing the stream by the stepping stones when it struck us we ought to wash our pricks. We stood with legs planted apart, each on its own stone. I washed mine with river water. Anton used his urine, rinsing it down later with water.

"I learned that trick in Spain," he said. "Urine is the best cleanser. It's good for wounds too."

It was the first time he had mentioned Spain.

"Just look how the cheese collects behind the skin . . . Nature always keeps the tool well oiled . . . expects us to be constantly on the job . . . not just pissing . . . I myself haven't overworked it. I started late and finished early—moreover, I never found a single woman who really suited me . . . You wouldn't have looked twice at any of them . . . and it was always so strained . . . I never had anything of my own. When I got back from France in 1940 I couldn't even retrieve the five or six books I'd left with one of my friends."

He laughed without even the slightest shade of self-pity. That was something I especially prized in him. He continued without the least hint of reproach and even with approval: "You meet a woman, take her, make her, then drop her the next minute. And I've absolutely no idea, I haven't the knack, I don't even know how to start . . ." With something near enthusiasm he went on, "Some screw, *me cago en tu leche*! My old man enjoyed it too." He chuckled at the thought of that spectacle. Meanwhile I was washing my buttocks. "Did you force her?" He spoke facetiously but with a peculiar catch in his voice.

"Not at all," I retorted. "That's the joke. She raped me!" Like school kids sharing a naughty joke, we burst out in peals of uncontrollable laughter.

A man should always count his blessings. Here we were for example, with no worries about eating, since we had enough food in hand, or about drinking, since we had an almost full flask of brandy; we could return to the village and enjoy a glass of wine in convivial company; we could visit the now submissive, compliant, gentle Sabina. We could even take leave if we felt so inclined. We had a smoke when we felt like it, we had everything except for arms. Here we had only our grenades left. But we were completely relaxed and each of us had someone to talk to, someone to hear him out. We had no farther needs. Our ablutions proceeded in stages. Next it was off with our jackets and shirts. The cool water of a swift mountain stream has its own unfailing magic. Was any army in the world better off than we were? Everywhere else, even in the most trivial matter, a soldier had to ask an N.C.O., go down on his knees to the man on duty, bamboozle his own sentries. We imagined what it was like for the Germans, Russians, Americans, Japanese, English. Field regulations, military police, courts-martial. Or those poor oppressed civilians in the towns. Or the famished P.O.W.s in their camps. Or the prisoners in jail.

A man should appreciate how well off he is.

"All the same, the Second World War is a constant disappointment by comparison with the First," Anton told me. He had heard this from a veteran of the First, who had completely lost his way this time.

"So is this war of ours a disappointment by comparison with the Spanish Civil War?" I asked. "You lost that one but we're going to win this time."

"Ah, España!" A note of nostalgia crept into Anton's voice. "Five years ago it would be, roughly at this time of year, we'd had it. We were all wondering whether France would take us in or not. Would they lock us up or not? You remember Christ's words on the cross: 'Lord, Lord, why have you forsaken me?' It's hard for a human being to accept that no one cares what happens to him, no one gives a brass farthing, no one is either for him or against him. Who is concerned that the Hungarians are landlocked? I had hardly managed to extricate myself from the French internment camps and get a job in a printing shop before the Germans arrived from another quarter . . . Someone denounced me to the Gestapo, one of my own countrymen, mark you, and once again I got away by the skin of my teeth. Then the Germans followed me to Ljubljana, so that they've been chasing me all over Europe. If you hadn't loosened that nail in the plank, we'd have said good-bye in the hayloft yesterday. When the same pattern keeps recurring, you get fed up with it. It should be enough for a man to realize, once and for all, how useless his thoughts and emotions are. The revelation comes but does the consequence follow? Not at all. You recognize the truth, then somehow you are forced to forget it, you see it again, and forget it again, and so it goes on. And there is nowhere on the Earth's surface for you to settle down; your pursuers drive you round and round in a circle. You are hunted by those ideological enemies of all classes, always well armed, always well informed. Your own people are suspicious because they never know exactly what is going through your mind. In the end, you begin to have your own doubts. Then perhaps you end up on the winning side but your body is maimed and your spirit warped—and it all starts once more over again."

"A Spanish veteran!" I said with a quiet sigh.

"A Spanish veteran? What does that mean? Take a close look at me, friend. A man without a name. I no longer know whether I am Peter, Pedro, Juanito, Antonio, or Anton, and my surname is gone forever, I'm just one of the thirty thousand, from all over the world, who gathered together without arms or equipment to oppose a Fascist army a hundred thousand strong, that landed fully equipped and armed with the most sophisticated modern weapons. There were a hundred thousand Blackshirts from Italy alone. The Germans sent tanks, artillery, and aircraft, with well trained crews. Whether by accident or design, who knows, no one seemed to be in a great hurry. They were all testing their weapons and schooling their officers in a blueprint of the next war."

"What about the Russians?"

"The Russians? Stalin is following a realistic policy; his model is Peter the Great. Not Lenin. Stalin is going to set Russia on its feet, even if for the time being he has to bury the world revolution. Some people were astounded by his pact with Hitler. Others think that the Russians are not well informed about our 'heroic struggle,' since they show no particular enthusiasm for us. We've been through all that before and survived. Franco had technical difficulties in landing his supplies and we defended ourselves with promises. Just as well we didn't know much of what was going on. It was general anarchy that defeated us, Stalinists against Trotskyites. Communists and anarchists at each other's throats. The Catalonians were moved by local patriotism, the French sympathized with us in secret, the Russians sent us some political agents, tanks, and aircraft, propaganda leaflets, and booklets. Franco's siege of Madrid lasted two and a half years. All that time, we were relying on Joseph Vissarionovich to send us the arms we needed, either tomorrow or the day after. You can imagine my feelings these days, when I hear our wise experts explaining how immense aid from Russia is on its way to Yugoslavia and will arrive any day now. Such is the simple faith that comes from a reading of *A Short History of the Bolshevik Communist Party*." He abbreviated the book's title to its initial letters.

"Are you a Trotskyite, Anton?"

"No. I'm an orphan of the storm with no name or other rights. Trotsky claimed that Stalin had betrayed the world revolution. I only say that Stalin is a realist. He knew that the Russians then had nothing to gain in that part of Europe, and that in any case, the whole affair was only a curtain-raiser before the main production. I was nothing but a dumb extra in that prelude. I kept my eyes and ears open, not that it did me much good. 'The crows will peck your eyes out if you see too much in life,' to quote François Villon. Be happy you're a political illiterate. Am I a Trotskyite indeed! Don't you know the wrong answer means a bullet? You can be a Christian, a Pan-Slavist, a Social Democrat, a liberal, a Catholic, a pantheist, a bourgeois, anything you like—but not a Trotskyite, by God, by Marx, by Stalin! In the Middle Ages, is wasn't heathens they burned at the stake but heretics, not Turks but Franciscans. I can hardly wait to get back to some underground press and sit things out there till the next manhunt. There's nothing more revolting in this world than to be a disenchanted revolutionary; circumstances will never allow you to retire from politics. You can go for a ride on a tiger but you can't dismount. The whole business cannot have a happy ending. You can't change into a beetle or an ant. You're tossed on waves of suspicion and doubt from one untenable position to another, even more untenable. This has been one of the rare moments of happiness in my life. It will soon be over."

He washed himself with slow movements and gazed into the distance, upstream between the trees. He spoke as if he had a vision.

"The horsemen of the Apocalypse have had their day . . . war, famine, plague, and death . . . In the new versions of the Apocalypse, instead of the plague, we have suspicion and doubt, both the result of dishonesty . . . Dishonesty, falsehood have always been with us, even before reaching the accolade of an ideology. War, famine, suspicion, doubt, and death . . . there are times without war, famine, and death . . . but there are none without suspicion and doubt . . . We're all the same today. We have no family but belong to some nation, state, ideology, organization, international movement . . . It's a real question of who is the worst off: the fighting men, those on the run, those locked up in jail, the slaves in the concentration camp, people pulled in for questioning. What's going on all over the world at this moment? Everywhere, the civilian population has the brutish soldiery on its neck, and has to endure bombs, police, speeches, the press, unrelieved mental stress . . . Pan-Germanism, Pan-Slavism, Pan-Islamism, the Roman Church, Freemasonry, secret societies, capitalist cartels, the Mafia underworld organizations, and the struggles seen and unseen, religious or ideological, between these . . . And you cannot trust appearances. Each man doubts himself and suspects his neighbor . . . in a war against peace and well-being . . . the great contest of hidden forces . . . in which little men doubt themselves and are therefore suspected of treason. Each individual can fall under the galloping hooves of doubt and suspicion. The best sport is the hunt for your ideological opponent. After the drama of the chase and capture, you have time to decide what to do with him. You can destroy him and have one enemy less. Or you may break him and convert him into your best agent. Then you can turn him loose among his old, fellow thinkers. One hell of a sport, eh?

"Generally there's no sense in talking. Why bother lying? And what's the point of speaking the truth if it's only going to land you in trouble? It's a good idea to let off steam occasionally and then you can keep it all bottled up for another six months or a year, or even longer."

We got dressed and set off along a path which wound slowly upward through the forest. We felt lighter, cleaner, brighter. The happiness of that moment persisted, since we had not spoiled it with any lies.

"You know how sometimes you have a whole flood of memories of people you once knew?" Anton spoke in a hushed voice. "Last night Žarko suddenly came back to me. It was in Guadalajara. A sort of Till Eulenspiegel, an eternal prankster. He fell in the last days of the Phalangist offensive, sometime around New Year's, 1939, it must have been. I heard his voice again. He had his own way of talking. If you didn't know him well, you could never understand what he was on about. For example, if you or I wanted to have some potatoes we'd say, 'I'd like some of those roast spuds.' But not him. He'd say, 'I wouldn't eat those bleeding spuds for all the tea in China—though I might make an exception this time.' You see? Or he'd say, for example, 'There are no better diplomats than the Russians. They always deliver late but take promptly.' Get it? 'I hate the Spaniards,' he'd say, 'they're rogues and bandits, just like me, with no time for anything but guzzling, drinking, and chasing the women, incapable of taking anything seriously except for those ceremonies of theirs.' But no one loved the Spaniards more than he did, you know. He'd spend whole nights listening to a guitar player."

"Did you hear the sound of a guitar last night?" I asked him.

"Yes, did you too?"

"Yes."

"You see, he was haunting you too." We both laughed. "The dead are very powerful," he remarked. "They are the most numerous race in the world."

I heard all about his sheepskin jacket. He fell more or less as our own Petkoshek, with a bullet in the back which went right through him. His mates carried him along with them and handed him over to the stretcher-bearers, after which no more was heard of him.

"Do you think we'll ever hear anything more about Petkoshek?" I asked, with a sudden sense of foreboding. He looked at me, most annoyed. A good mood can only last till the first false note. I nodded and we skipped the momentary mental block. Žarko had been in great pain but even in that uproar, he kept his own style. "See you in the next war," he had said—his parting words. Here Anton snorted, "And see. He did."

Groups of partisans were walking up and down the valley road. The trees stood motionless in the soft sunlight.

There was a celebration in the first farmhouse we came to; the farmer's wife had given birth to a son that night. The women had baked pastries and the men set up drinks on the table. An old man in a battered hat was playing an out-of-tune accordion. We were plied with food and drink. We had to inspect the baby's red, wrinkled face and say what a sweet bonny boy. If we had arrived a couple of hours earlier, we might have had to assist at the birth of this new inhabitant of the globe. Out of curiosity we asked what the baby had been named, and we were told Miha, after his father and grandfather. Miha! Not without surprise, I noticed that Anton was inspecting him with genuine interest and addressing him with a gentle note in his voice: "Well, well, you little bandit!"

There were about five of us partisans sitting in the room, three farmers, a few older women, and a crowd of children. I had a word with an elderly farmer about the possibility of picking up a couple of guns somewhere.

He took us down a deep cart track into the forest, groped among the clods and roots and pulled out a long bundle: three French rifles of unknown provenance wrapped up in shiny yellow paper, each with a magazine of three bullets. Anton and I took one each. They were well greased and properly cared for but hung down almost to our heels.

We went back to the party in the farmhouse. It was almost as if the war was over. No hunger, no thirst, no death. A new life bawling in its large basket. Miha by name. An old man was playing old-time polkas on an accordion. I joined in the dance with a buxom partner; a healthy, bouncing, rural spinster who fairly squealed with delight as I spun her around. She was still pretty nimble on her feet, in spite of her double chin. She had clear sky-blue eyes and teeth as white as a turnip. Anton was leaning on the strange new weapon, which he gripped like a long pole between his knees. He was watching me with a satisfied smile. I realized I reminded him of Žarko. See you in the next war!

"Yes, Herr Bitter, I'm from Yugoslavia, from Ljubljana."

"*Ich vermute, dass sie bei den Partisanen waren?*" (I suppose you were in the Partisans?)

"*Bei den Banditen?*"

"*Bei den Partisanen, hab' ich g'sagt.*"

After so many years, the front still ran between us; on one side the well-run German army machine, on the other a lousy Communist. On one side a mobilized regular army, on the other a band of volunteers. There the swastika, here the red five-pointed star. There the dramatic conquest of the world, here the Bolshevik crimes against humanity. There the pure Aryan race, here a Jewish conspiracy. On one side the Krauts, the invaders, the Fascist criminals with their lackeys, on the other the freedom-loving people. On one side a foul monster, on the other heroes. There hell, here paradise. Between these concepts there is a constant hostility and any compromise is a betrayal of your own camp, of you yourself. Now it was my shot.

"Ich vermute, dass sie ein Mitglied der N.S.D.A.P. waren?" (I suppose you were a member of the German National Socialist Party?)

"Ein Mitglied der blutigen Hitler-Partei?"

"Ein Mitglied der N.S.D.A.P., hab' ich g'sagt."

"Nein, mein Herr, das war ich nicht."

"Did you vote for Hitler?"

"Yes. In the year 1934, when he won the election with ninety-nine and a half percent of the votes; need I say more?"

"But those elections were followed by a number of fateful measures: rearmament, rejection of the Versailles peace treaty, the anti-Semitic laws, the annexation of the Rhineland, the Anschluss, the occupation of Czechoslovakia, and so on."

"You won't find my name on any list of war criminals, though you might find millions of others."

"And I don't figure on any list of their victims, though you can count them in tens of millions, often anonymous."

"Somewhere at bottom we have remained enemies, haven't we?" he asked politely. "Have you seen that film, *The Four Horsemen of the Apocalypse*? No? That's a pity. One branch of a German family is for Hitler, the other is against him. Calamity strikes both of them. That's how it was with us. That's why I know these matters from both sides. Uncle Guenther on my mother's side was in Spain with the International Brigades. Uncle Johannes on my father's side was in the S.S. Guenther died in a concentration camp at Oranienburg. Johannes was captured and shot by the Russians in Berlin. Please continue, I shall understand."

"If it's true that every seven years all the cells in the human body are replaced, we've already had four complete metamorphoses since the war, and we still fundamentally don't know what really happened then. One side won, the other lost, but that's not the whole story. You know, the war never really ended, did it? I'm not only thinking now about the wars in the Pacific, in Korea, in Vietnam, in the Middle East. I'm not only thinking about the Cold War, smoldering all the time and ready at any moment to flare up into the worst conflagration. The war lives on and continues to thrive in each of us, renewing itself all the time, ready to flare up at any moment. We're not prepared to accept the world as it is; and in this we are fully justified. Old wars are constantly begetting new ones, whether we like it or not, and meanwhile, we have absolutely no idea what has happened and what is happening, till one fine day we find ourselves part of an armed multitude, breathing hellfire and locked in a life-and-death combat. At heart, we are still old enemies, as you said, but we have also bred a new enmity. We have not lost our allegiance to our old armies, but in some mysterious way we belong to armies of the future, even though we have watched the degeneration of our ideals, even though our rosy spectacles are smashed, and we should logically stand aside as embittered witnesses of events."

The discussion had excited both of us. We both felt we would be unable to express our ideas fully. We would approach the truth, then recede from it. A lot of what we said was beside the point and our true meaning was buried much deeper. We could not comprehend what the driving force was behind this unending discussion. We both felt the desire for a new, integral understanding of those ancient problems. The air around us sometimes throbbed with a mixture of oaths, like the frenzied buzzing of a swarm of wasps, oaths not of our invention but those same curses that turned the air blue on both sides during the last war. If we had not exercised some self-control, we would have come to blows. And the next moment, we were linked by a common feeling for human life, both of us trying at the same time to explain, to state something fundamental, then breaking off, as we realized we could not find the right words. Bitter sensed this in a different way from me. He was a man of systems and considered that we ought to present our arguments in an orderly fashion, while I was driven by a passion for picturesque metaphors. As long as Bitter was sitting in the company of others like him, he could not get excited; they were either no longer interested in the last war or were too much in agreement with him. He needed an interlocutor of my stamp, someone he could regard as an adversary. The way I skipped from one figure of speech to another puzzled and perplexed, but also roused him. He was accustomed to everyday conversation, in which everything has its own proper dimension and proper place, while I was darting from man to universe and from universe to microcosm. In our Milky Way alone, there are millions of solar systems, many of them greater than ours. The hydrogen atom is one hundred millionth of a centimeter in size. At that very moment, some coolie was running through the streets of Hong Kong—and his inner constitution was no different from Bitter's or mine, as we played the tourist in Spain. In the Yacht Club, there

Jackie Onassis vied with Liz Burton, who had just been presented with a prize diamond by her boyfriend; Ari and Dicky followed with straining pride the flaunting combat. Some idiot destroyed a precious work of art, just in order to get his name in the newspapers. The superpowers, so it was said, were organizing new spy systems based on extrasensory perception. Overpopulation of the Earth. Conquest of the cosmos. Pollution of the atmosphere and the water. The struggle for peace. The possibility of a new war, since we have still not settled old accounts. Thirty years old. Three hundred. Three thousand. Three hundred thousand. Africa awakes. South America in ferment. Asia looking toward Europe. The American way of life, the consumer society, the rat race. "Have you read Arthur Koestler's *Darkness at Noon*? Or Orwell's *Animal Farm*? Or Artur London's *The Confession*? Or Solzhenitsyn's *A Day in the Life of Ivan Denisovich*? I have. I've also read Henry Miller's *Black Spring*. I've read things, I've seen things, I've thought things over. I've traveled the west coast of Africa from Morocco to the land of apartheid; I've looked and I've seen and I've thought for myself. I was steeling myself for combat but could not find an adversary; perhaps my opponent dwells within me."

"You're an unhappy man, aren't you?" said Bitter.

This made me really furious. "Look, I have only one life. Would you like me to live it like an imbecile, looking only for my own happiness? That's not my idea. I want to raise, if only for a moment, this head of mine above the ideological blizzard that besets this world. To see beyond the technological projects that are ruining our environment. Beyond the redemptory ideologies that result in nothing but new disasters. Sometimes, at night, I succeed in laying them all out for mental inspection. I examine them, exposed to view on a silver platter, and by their effects recognize their true nature and influence. Then morning comes, and night loses her truth; I must start again. I must go back millennia, centuries, decades. For no one is ever guilty. I can't forget the Nuremberg trials of war criminals. A feeling of black horror comes over me at the thought. That was a defeat for all humanity, no matter of what age or nation, and yet we've still learned nothing. We've quietly watched the constant growth of political crime and even its technical perfection. Nuremberg drew the last veil and we glimpsed the sight of homo politicus, at work in his confidential cubbyholes. But we soon let the curtain drop again, consoling ourselves with the execution of some stupid fall guys.

"Now it's no longer a legend. The death industry is with us.

"An enormous amplifier would give the instructions: 'Strip naked, hand over your false teeth, artificial limbs, spectacles, and everything else. Surrender your valuables at the special window. Carefully fasten your shoes in pairs.'

"So they went through the avenue of trees, all naked, men, women, children, invalids without their artificial limbs, mothers with babies at the breast, tiny children. Most of them knew what was coming. The stench itself forecast their doom.

"Seven or eight hundred people, cooped up in a space of forty-five square meters.

"Closely packed, in death they stand; there is no room for them to fall . . .

"Corpses damp with sweat and urine, filthy with excrement, legs dripping with menstrual blood, are cleared out of the gas chamber. Children's bodies are flung through the air . . . Gold teeth and crowns are removed with hammers and tongs . . . Bowels and genitals are searched for hidden gold, diamonds, or other valuables.

"The stench fills the hot August air far and wide, like the plague and the whole place swarms with millions of flies.

"Day after day, the witnesses at Nuremberg spoke of their experiences. Among the material evidence presented by the prosecution, there were even films, some of them the personal property of S.S. officers, others taken by Allied cameramen after the end of the war. The data of the death industry were most precise.

"There was a comprehensive program of experiments on human beings from which death was the only release.

"Particularly painful and lingering, was the death of those victims of research whose legs were injected with gas, or arteries with cancer cells, or those who were shot in the thighs with poisoned bullets.

"At Buchenwald, tattooed prisoners were killed and flayed. Their skin was treated and used in the manufacture of lampshades and various souvenirs.

"Hitler published, in 1941, his 'Nacht und Nebel Erlass,' which was signed ('checked and approved'), by a soldier, Field Marshal von Keitel. That was an edict of cruelty, a plan of ruthlessness and atrocity, an order that enemies should perish in night and fog, without trace. That was the charter for the industry of torment and death. Resolution! So it's not only a matter of war as such, Herr Bitter. And it is also true that not all wars are the same.

"Summer and autumn in Nuremberg. The jails, the trial, the allowances and traveling expenses of the allies, hopes for the international validity of the Nuremberg laws.

"At the Nuremberg trials, the explicit principle was registered that 'crimes are committed by human beings and not by abstractions.' But the draft remained a draft and never became a convention.

"It's a foul lie, that granny was eaten by the wolf; every single honest citizen knows she was gobbled up by the forest administration.

"Why should the great powers tie their own hands? Why should they let anyone come poking around among their secret plans, their night and fog?"

"The menu, please."

> Ox tongue
> Pig's head
> Calf's breast
> Heart in gravy
> Brains with eggs
> Finally a sweet
> surprise.

"We're idiots, idiots, a herd of idiots, the whole lot of us who believe in civilization and good breeding, in science, progress, God, and lucky black cats; a jibbering rabble, smitten with hysteria.

"The only sensible people are those who turn our simplicity to their advantage. Men of sense hold the world's armies and police forces in their control.

"Poets, get off home and write your verses; don't interfere where men of sense have work to do! Or have you still not learned your lesson?

"Waiter, the bill, please."

Mrs. Bitter was about a quarter of an hour late. She was well rested and in fine spirits. She stopped when she spotted us at our table in the crowded Spanish café.

"What's wrong? Don't you feel well, Joseph?" She then looked at me. "And you look a bit down too. Well, what's wrong?" She was quite ready to accept our explanation that we were almost half dead after so much walking around the museums and art galleries. She even found it amusing. We had to describe the paintings on the cathedral altars for her.

343

"The crack of a rifle cannot be recorded in words. Neither can love or
hatred be described. No one can say what tomorrow means. And yet we
have been ruined by the very thing that separates us from the beasts—speech."
Giannini

"Rare are the moments at the root of all things."
From a wartime notebook

"Yes, my dear friend, I do indeed despise nature, precisely because I know it so well."
Marquis de Sade

Adolf Hitler (instructions to the Commanders-in-Chief of Army Groups, the O.K.W.)
"Even if Yugoslavia offers declarations of loyalty, she must still be regarded
as an enemy and therefore smashed as speedily as possible . . ."
27 March, 1941

"Furthermore, we must realize that human life in the territories concerned has no value
and that we can intimidate the whole population only with extraordinary cruelty."
16 September, 1941

". . . the army is therefore both justified and obliged . . . to use any means, without
restraint, even against women and children, provided this leads us to our goal . . ."
26 December, 1941

"Stepan: Nothing that can serve our cause should be ruled out.
Kaliayev: I am ready to shed blood, so as to overthrow the present despotism.
But, behind your words, I see the threat of another despotism."
Albert Camus, *The Just Assassins*

Three poets in 1973:
"I am what I lack."
Tahar Ben Jelloun, a Moroccan

"How I would like to be a sandwich and die on my feet."
Paul Vincensini, a Corsican

"I quail to think that I exist."
Claude Esteban, a Basque

"One fine day we discovered we were alive—and now we cannot forget it."
Giannini

7

Meta was the name of the girl I was dancing with, putting on a show for Anton, an enthusiastic and encouraging spectator. Meta, by the way, means "target" in Serbian. The peasants told us they had been out since dawn burying the dead. The newborn infant was bawling with all the power of his lungs. When the old fellow in the battered hat gave us a loud and lively polka on his accordion, the window panes rattled in their frames.

Somewhere near this place, a well-known author had passed away. In the war diary of a certain soldier, I had found the following sentence: "We forget the battles, since they are so much like each other, but we remember the eating, drinking, the music, the women we knew in between."

Life is fine, great, of infinite variety; it is at its best, greatest, most infinite, when crammed into one thrilling moment. It is not good for a man to be on his own. Appetite grows with eating. Nothing lasts forever but there are moments when we taste eternity. Tra-la-la, tra-la-la, carnival's coming, last year I'd nought to do, this year I'm busy . . . I cannot really say the first sight of Meta delighted me and when she first took the floor with me, I did not find her very attractive. She was not one of those women who turn you to jelly with a glance. She needed to be thawed, warmed, given an extra injection of vitality, spurred on to idle fancies, kneaded, shaken, turned into pure sound and rhythm, strummed on with the fingertips . . . In the meantime, I myself would undergo a change. Anton believed in me. I had to live for the sake of all those who now lived on in me. I have eaten your flesh and drunk your blood. And you have eaten my flesh and drunk my blood. The ancient Egyptians believed that each man has a double walking the earth. It is perfectly true. My double is stamping his heels on this solid farmhouse floor. He is telling Meta things she has never heard before and will never hear again.

Anton's double was there too, watching with great joy the transformation which was taking place among these people in that festive uproar, with everyone happy that the celebration of Miha's arrival in the world was such a great success. Afterward, we had something to eat and drink, talked in loud voices, sang, then danced once more. My double was a devil of a fellow, soon had a toothless old lady doubled up with laughter; she pressed her palm to her mouth but could not smother her giggles. A careful exploration of Meta's body with fingernails and fingertips revealed that she was wearing only a slip beneath her dress. Black worn-out shoes went well with her sturdy limbs. I was surprised at her quick response to my advances, but women always have a sixth sense about those things. She ought to have realized I was only joking, but how could she guess that the whole show was put on for Anton's benefit? She looked fat but her flesh was firm, young, tight. She was one of the women the painter had in mind when he observed that the best models sometimes look like sluts when they are fully dressed. Anyway, just imagine the Venus de Milo in a suburban lady's Sunday best, or picture those Rubensesque beauties wearing folk costume. Their beauty lies in the hip line, in the curve from the waist down to the knee, in the motion of their rounded buttocks, in the glowing tips of their breasts, in the dimples around the navel, in the mysterious shifting of their thighs, in the frame of the shoulders, in the line that runs down from the nape of the neck to the parting of the ways at the base of the spine. What generous largesse! What bold exposure! The flesh glows with an inner magic. The skin beguiles and every detail offers something more . . . But it cannot all be taken in at once and breaks up into parts, parts which fuse again into a new whole, and all is in continual motion, ebbing and flowing in changing patterns.

Meta's hair smells of the open country. Her perspiration excites me. Her eyes cloud over and clear again. She would like to plant her teeth in my flesh. Pity she has rough hands; love is not her vocation. Come on, let me kiss your ear. Why are you squealing? Life is not reality, reality admits no daydreams, no ghosts. There are two roads from your knee; one goes down, down, and disappears, the other climbs up and up, a warm and smooth path to nirvana . . . but resist me, put up a good fight in our life-and-death struggle . . . which will leave us both victors, both vanquished . . . most intriguing is that hollow below your kneee . . . a mere detail, and yet there is something marvelous about it . . . something no one has yet defined . . . When women still had to keep their knees covered and carefully hidden, that point just below the knee was the first stage on the road to paradise . . . The ancient Greek sculptors hewed such women in stone . . . beautiful, cold . . . of finest stock . . . I was once in a certain art gallery when they started to put the lights on . . . Walking around a marble figure, I suddenly noticed the hollows below her knees . . . for a split second, while the lights were coming on, I half closed my eyes . . . the stone came alive and I felt the sudden warmth of a Mediterranean sun on my skin and flesh . . . I just had to embrace her . . . why on earth did I do it? I felt like her, both dead and alive at the same time.

Anton's eyes were now glowing like a cat's in the dark. The best of it was that, although I wanted to live for him, I was now so carried away I was thinking only of myself. Some people in this world have families, build houses, buy plots of land, cultivate gardens, sink wells, breed domestic animals, and so on. Others like collecting mushrooms. Others again rule their fellows, wage wars. Some cure the sick, others plan holdups. But I have been walking and walking, until at last I have reached here and found my destination, and I have no intention of stirring from here, since a man cannot travel on after he reaches his goal, or can he? You are Meta, the target, the goal. Like an arrow, shot from an unseen, distant bow, I have landed headfirst, plumb in the center of the black and white rings, your black and white rings, the rings of your skin, your tresses, your teeth, limbs, your hair, your breasts, your laughter, your screams.

"You two will be getting hitched," said the accordion player. Yes, Anton and I will marry Meta. Kiss Anton, Meta. He is part of me and I am part of him. Kiss him here, by his bandage. Anton smells of Spanish guitars, Anton is a minuet for guitar. Let's drink from two glasses! Three mouths and two glasses in four-four time; play on, accordion, but play the accompaniment, not the melody. Listen, old chap, it goes like this . . . Tram-ta-ta-tam . . . ta-ta . . . Got it? Right, play. We'll all play. We're all taut as bowstrings in the air of the valleys. Here is the first stage on the road to paradise. Paradise is surrounded by a high wall with no gates. You need to know how to get in. And no one can tell you how. Just think, Adolf said: "Make this land German for me." The English say he's a queer, but he isn't. He's a globe-shagger, he loves every square inch of this planet. The English are queers. They don't believe in paradise. They believe only in the Empire. Paradise will remain, the Empire will fall. The Big Three have decided that after the war they will hunt down war criminals. Great sport for them. We shall be looking for those gates to paradise. You draw close, you're almost there, but rough hands reject you . . . and once again you're spinning through the endless void. Why the panic? Surely we're at attention. What better moment? This is the only banner raised on the road to paradise, a blind and cunning device. This year, we have managed to survive all the seasons, spring, summer, autumn, and winter, and now we have the fifth season, meant for those who have no trees to prune, no houses with roofs to repair, but only a night of dreams. You must shed your burdens on the road to paradise; only when you have nothing can you scale the walls of paradise . . . Throw it all away. Property is bondage. Power is misery. A crown is a hat it rains on, said Frederick the Great. Glory is froth. Dress is the invention of ugly people. Fate is an idea of cowards. Money was invented by thieves who could not remove cities. That almond cake is delightful. Why don't you want to take your shoes off? The war is over. Can you bear the Alps breathing in the center of Europe? The poacher again sets off to hunt the chamois. He smears his face with soot, so that the gamekeeper won't spot him. The negro smears his face with chalk. Now we're going to have a quite different dance, my darling. We're going to dance the minuet. Soon, you'll see the grace of those noble movements and gentle steps. No one can say what he knows, no one can say what is lurking in him, waiting for a chance to get out. We're not going to live like vegetables, like rotten potatoes, oh no! We're going to live the life of a river wave, a wave that races into the distance and at the same time remains in place, for it's all the same whether wave or river moves on; all is both here and at the same time in the boundless distance. No one has the right to take that thought from me. Masterly, is it not, Anton? My double walks around a German concentration camp with shaven skull and downcast eyes; they beat him, kick him, but he feels no pain, for he has nothing to say. But he knows it all, sees it all, and will remember. The last flicker of resistance in the prisoner's spirit must be doused, the camp psychologist instructs the jailers. He must crawl like a dog on all fours, bark, and wag his tail, all to order. And how well that cuckoo trick came off. They had to climb up a tree and call out, "Cuckoo, cuckoo!" all day long. All is simultaneously here and far away in the boundless distance. No one can seize my thoughts with his hand. But I can grab you, Meta. Go on, scream! And scream again! All is simultaneously here and far away in the boundless distance.

All is here and far away in the boundless distance.

Anton and I got up while the rest of them were still asleep. We quietly set off up the road, while the morning mist still lay on the empty grassy slopes and the trees. In such a dawn, a man is far removed from and untrue to himself. What had risen from sleep and trod the hard boards was a mere robot called Berk. Nothing is happening and there is no existence. I think, I know why religious people say their morning prayers. In the same way, a wise driver warms up his engine before taking to the road. In spite of everything I must think, feel, survey the countryside, know that I am alive. The dead of the past few days have not yet started to decompose. I shall remember the new arrival, Miha, for the next ten or twelve years. Eat and crap, Miha. Does anyone know when the morning begins? This morning presumably began at dawn. Or did it?

We arrived at the village when the first sunlight was beginning to break through the mist. The hens were already scrabbling in the yard of the modest homestead. The mules were standing by with drooping heads. How could so many have survived the retreat? A horse already saddled. The early morning bustle of partisans in and out of the houses. A child in a heel-length nightshirt, apparently male. A sheaf of straw. Doves. A hen with her brood of chickens. A lad with a machine gun. A peasant woman with a pail of water. For God's sake! Is it going to begin again? Anything you like but no repetition of the things we already know, please. A cock on a rooftop. How did he get up there? He stretches his neck and crows. This must be the beginning of the new day. Where is the meeting place? Fine, thanks. Maybe, some time after the war, I shall be walking up and down the terrace of a strange house, without belonging to any organization, without having to remember where I am to report, without wondering where I am going to be posted; maybe. We reported, then went to a hay shed, where we bedded down on a heap of hay, first arranging a comfortable depression and a pillow, then gazing up at the underside of the timbers of the loft; the roof tiles were loose in places and the sun shone in through the fissures. Dare we doze off? Hunger would waken us. Our only worry was that we might miss the mealtime call. Or maybe it was not so important; after all, we knew potato and maize flour was to be had from the houses, perhaps even milk and bacon too. "*Nel mezzo del cammin di nostra vita . . .*"—midway upon the journey of our life: the opening phrase of Dante's *Divine Comedy*. Thirty years of age, they say it means. By the lines on my palms I estimate I still have long to live. God knows where and how I shall spend my thirtieth birthday . . . "*Mi ritrovai per una selva oscura . . ."*—I found myself within a forest dark . . . And I am falling into the abyss, into the depths of the void; but why have I also a pain in my gut? I listen to a dull echo of an inner question: what, at that moment, caused me such pain? I thought of that long, long road before me. I would be always groping for the meaning of things, always deceived, always having a feeling that I could not put into words, that I could never tell others of: I exist . . . I am . . . but I do not know why, how, or for what; I do not know where I came from nor where I am bound; I do not know what rules my bodily organs. I cannot imagine why I am sometimes depressed and sometimes full of enthusiasm; I do not even know what lies beneath the soles of my feet. A planet? Minerals? There are a thousand answers—and none. I rise from the abyss with all my nerves jangling. Slowly I calm down and possibly even doze off.

Next day, Anton and I parted for a year and some months. We met again on the morning of the day he died.

Toward evening, we attended a meeting and afterward had a drink in a farmer's house with four ideologists.

Everything was going smoothly and no one felt like hurrying. The faint light of the sunset forecast worse weather to come. When Anton and I took our seats at the meeting, I still did not know I had a twenty-eight-hour journey through the rain in front of me.

A meeting is a good way to boost the morale of civilians and troops and also serves to bring together both partners in the struggle and weld them into one whole. A partisan army canot operate without the close cooperation of the local population. The chief speaker was the commissar, Dolnichar, a schoolmaster by profession. After his speech he sat next to us. We sipped brandy from our flask and smoked Dolnichar's cigarettes. While it was still light, large clouds began to drift across the sky, while down below there were occasional gusts of wind that tossed the curtains on the makeshift stage. The small village, half demolished, was crammed with people. Ages ago, settlers from the valley had taken refuge here and built their homes. In the paradise to come, their descendants would go down again into the valley. A hundred years back, a hundred years on— what did this day mean to me? I seemed to be floating in a timeless vacuum. Not so long since, there had been a lake in the Ljubljana basin and at its edge the lake-dwellers had their huts on piles driven into the mud. Then the lake receded and Maria Theresa started to drain the moorland. And I could now see what that plain would look like tomorrow or the day after; with no difficulty I could see and realize what had been and what was to be. It was harder for me to grasp what was happening at that precise moment. Incidents, sensations, scenes, words—all fused into a steady, simultaneous ebb and flow within me.

Dolnichar was a good speaker. He spoke loudly and clearly, composed good sentences, knew where to lay emphasis, a pretty rare thing among us.

"Once again the enemy has shattered his teeth and claws in this land of ours . . ." The invader had come with rumbling tanks and armored cars, withdrawing divisions of crack troops from distant battlefields, supporting them with artillery and aircraft . . . and what had he achieved? Our resistance was firmer than ever, our troops had gained valuable experience from this latest action, and the link between the people's army and the populace is stronger than ever before . . . "We shall smite the invader at his every step, and his lackeys too . . . until at last the day of victory dawns . . . The army of national liberation has grown from its units, detachments, and battalions into a well-organized regular army, the shock troops of our downtrodden populace; its corps, divisions, and brigades incessantly harry the foe, demolishing the roads and railways which serve to transport the enemy's men and materials to the front; the whole country is a hornet's nest of furious resistance. The victorious Red Army is driving the enemy back on Berlin. The serpent is in his death throes. Death to Fascism!" In response, his hearers roared: "Liberty to the people!"

An accordionist now began to play, with a guitar accompaniment; both the musicians were partisans. Some distance away, large bonfires were blazing, with men and children collecting wood from all sides. A large tricolor with a red star at its center was hanging from the hay frame, tossed and fluttering in the breeze from the mountaintops. Horses stood under the trees, gazing with bright eyes into the flames.

Did the uncertainty about my future movements spoil that evening for me perhaps? What is it about a human being's make-up that suddenly turns him, for no apparent reason, from a talkative extrovert into a taciturn introvert? What is it that snuffs out his joyful high spirits? What dark premonitions beset his soul? Suddenly, he finds that nothing is going right. What was said half an hour ago comes back again to mind but what had then been full of life is now dull and lifeless.

Anton's early account of Spain came back to me again, much clearer now than when I had first heard it. The Spanish are one of those peoples whose particular faults suit them very well. They can sing of death so eloquently that you fall in love with it. They have invented a manner of fighting fear, though they are so much in love with life. Those ceremonies of theirs are nothing other than a yearning to preserve life. They turn everything into a ceremony, though they are, at heart, a most simple people. The Germans by their nature take courage for granted and for them, so-called heroism is almost a duty. The Spaniards have their own virility rite, which is simply a fight against fear. They love animals. If you say they torment and murder bulls, I will tell you that I would not mind being a Spanish bull destined for death in the arena. At least I would know what was awaiting me. And when I am slain in the arena, every gesture has its name, every movement its technical term, and the deathblow is the coup de grâce. Elsewhere, they rhapsodize about mankind, but no bands play when you are led to the slaughter. You disappear without fuss. A bull is reared, tended, has his great aim in life. But as for us . . .

In Spain, no one would steal your rifle. A Spaniard propped his gun against the wall of the trench and went home to his wife and children. He had something to eat, something to drink, sang a song, beat up his wife, came back again—and there was his rifle waiting in the same spot where he had left it. Blood, death, love, curses, prayers, it is all there tied up in the same sack with a Gordian knot; cruelty, tenderness, pity, ecstasy, love and hate, idleness and industry, all bound up inextricably. What methods of torturing prisoners (on both sides)—and what respect for family, forefathers, children! How they manage to talk of the past, have the present day in view and put everything off till tomorrow! Those devils are bored. They lie with such style they believe themselves; that mixture of Moors and Latins has produced something other nations find it hard to understand. Here we like things plain, like a new string with no knots in it.

Why then did you fall in love with Spain, Anton?

What? Do you think I fell in love? With that writing with knots on old string? After all I've seen and read about, from the conquistadors to the last century? What should I fall in love with? With the sultry Madrid summer . . . when weeks and weeks pass without a breath of air . . . when you go to sleep with your hand in this position and wake up to find a palm print in sweat?

With that awful retreat across the Pyrenees? With their architecture—in war-time you have as little interest in it as in the landscape. With their songs? With the stench of my own body? It's true that I always wanted to see Spain . . . but with my present vision. Have you seen Ljubljana, down there below us?

As if you could almost touch those lights with your hand . . .

A town like any other town in the world but you've spent part of your life there. I think that Spain is something similar for us, although its sounds and atmosphere are different. Even the horses there have a different snort.

I know; my girl's not like the others—she smells different, sounds different? Same thing, isn't it?

I was sitting there in a wee courtyard, matchbox-size stone, an old olive tree, a vine and some roses, and a small well. Jacinto was playing some stringed instrument with only three strings, we were drinking sweet wine, a canary was fluttering in a cage hung up in the olive tree, there was a lamp . . . really, it all didn't amount to much . . . we were eating bread and cheese. Žarko said he would take the whole place away in his kit bag as a souvenir. It was very much the same there as here—the war had passed us by, had receded into the background. But Spain is such a large country, I said I've seen such extensive olive groves; why do they build themselves such poky little courtyards? Our gentry have fine, large gardens around their villas, but you never see them sitting under the trees. That's the secret. That and the weather, the rocky country, and the rest of it . . . You can melt away in those Spanish nights . . . and afterward they follow you. You don't know how little a human being requires.

I do.

You don't, not yet. But you'll find out, willy-nilly.

On the program of the meeting, we had verbal reports of the news: two partisans and a girl sat at a small table and read from sheets of paper.

The Red Army had liberated Kharkov on August twenty-second and was now continuing its unstoppable drive westward. The effects of the German defeat at Stalingrad were ruinous for Hitler's war machine. There is a rising in Poland. Soviet partisans are harrying the retreating Germans.

The voices were blurred. And hasn't Kiev fallen yet; the question flashed through my mind. Where had I already heard something about Kiev?

The Allies who had landed in Sicily, Calabria, and Salerno, were continuing their advance through Italy. Air raids were being carried out on Germany.

The Moscow declaration about war criminals.

Destructive fury of the Germans in the occupied territories.

"Do you know where Kharkov is?" asked Anton.

Our partisan units are beating at the gates of Ljubljana, our divisions are on the attack throughout the whole country, the Whites are attempting to reorganize under German leadership. The invader has drawn the mask from their face.

This was followed by a sketch, a one-act play. A farmer in a hat wandered about the stage, leaning on his stick and wiping the sweat off his brow. He suddenly spotted something, peered out again under his raised palm, and could not believe his eyes: he had actually seen a partisan. "Are you alive or a ghost?" he asked, and, still unconvinced, touched and felt the other, repeating time and again, "Yes, you don't look like a ghost to me . . ." "What's up, old fellow?" asked the partisan. The farmer was still as surprised as before but went on to explain that the Germans had announced after their last offensive that there was not a single partisan left alive, that the forests had been cleared and the whole partisan movement wiped out. The young soldier told him in a loud voice and in sentences of impeccable literary style that this was an arrant lie and that the forces of national liberation were now more numerous and more powerful than ever before and that they would soon deal a deathblow to the invader and his lackeys.

This was followed by music and a partisan song.

A young, neatly dressed partisan now took the stage. Obviously a trained speaker, he began to declaim Prešeren's "Toast."

After him, we had three songs from the choir. The first was a Slovene army song.

> Make all haste, you brave battalions,
> Send white rats and black dogs packing,
> Smite the enemy in his lair;
> In the free air of our forests
> Let one chilling voice resound,
> As the sten-gun greets
> The invaders of our land . . .

Then came a Russian seamen's song: "*I nad parakhodom a krasnymi buk-vami krasnyy flot napisano . . .*"

The choir's performance met with general applause. The wind blew stronger and the first flash of lightning seared the sky. A late autumn storm was on the way.

During the folk song "Where are those paths that once I knew . . ." it began to rain without us taking much notice of it.

Recital in chorus of a sad poem about hostages.

The musicians struck up a waltz and some couples took the floor. The rain began to fall more heavily and we took shelter beneath the hay frame. Thunder and lightning. The bonfires flared in the quickening gusts of wind. The horses became fretful. In the shelter of a jutting roof, the accordionist played on and the guitar player accompanied him.

There were six of us sitting at the maplewood table in the farmhouse, Dolnichar with three of his comrades, Anton, and I. There was a jug of grape juice on the table and a loaf of maize bread. An old man was sitting by the oven. Two women sat beside him. Three children, bedded down on the oven, moved uneasily in their sleep and the oldest kept looking over at us. A red wool blanket was spread on the bed. The votive lamp by the holy pictures in a corner of the room had been put out. Dolnichar talked on in his booming voice which brooked no contradiction. For a long time, the others contented themselves with putting in an odd word here and here, without really having anything to say. Anton was almost devoutly nibbling a crust of bread.

"Drink up, friends; your health!" Dolnichar told us all about the battle of Stalingrad. We all knew a great deal about it already; after all, we had been listening to Radio Moscow and the BBC back in town. We could have added a couple of our own footnotes. We knew how von Paulus had signed the document of surrender, we knew how Hitler had raged and ranted at the news; we knew about the house-to-house, floor-to-floor and even room-to-room fighting; but Dolnichar didn't give anyone else a chance to speak. In any case, why so much talking on that topic? At this moment, we certainly didn't require a morale boost.

Greatly to Anton's disapproval, I now began to quarrel with the speaker. Anton watched me as if I were a weak pupil who was getting everything wrong. I felt I was in the right—and there was not a hope of me changing my position. Dolnichar's trio joined in support. And what was it all about? The three of them maintained that the Germans had already lost the war, while I said we could expect more hard fighting before the end came. I said this, really to offer some objection to the self-confident know-it-all who was getting on my nerves. I was astonished to find Anton in agreement with the other camp. After all, I knew exactly what he thought about the progress of the war; that had been our first conversation together. The discussion degenerated into an ill-natured wrangle with the five others against me. Then, out of the blue Dolnichar accused me of fainthearted-ness and defeatism. This made me particularly furious, for I knew what such a re-proach could mean in the army, something a little short of a court-martial; those nightly arguments with Depolo in Ribnica came back to mind. However, my fondness for dispute sucked me deeper into the maelstrom. Anton observed me with eyes wide open, shaking his head at my crass stupidity. We simply spewed theory and no one spoke about what had happened during the operation or what we had gone through in the past few days. It was unbearable, unnatural, an insult to our intelligence. It was not a debate but the mere assertion of authority. As our discussion grew more and more incoherent, certain key words were dropped, everyone appropriated what he needed and pursued his own line of argument, each of us outtalking the other. Nino, Yerkovich, Dolnichar, Pochkar—a journal-ist, a failed student, a teacher, and a building technician respectively, as I heard later. From Stalingrad we progressed to art, and then to jazz, then to Buddha and Confucius, to Freud, education and humor, finally ending with Marx and Cub-ism. Meanwhile, the farmer's family sat patiently waiting for us to stop through sheer exhaustion, so that they could go to bed. Realism is the only valid form of art, all the rest's a sham. Art is what the majority like; the masses decide. Art is a class phenomenon. Jazz: pros and cons. Where does jazz come from? Buddha, Confucius; did Christ really live? Freud was a Marxist. Without pedagogy there could be no enlightenment and without enlightenment there could be no cul-ture, which was also necessary. Even a worker should have flowers in his window. Humor is the diversion of the people; ages ago, the serf joked with the noble. Cubism is a capitalist invention. Marx valued real art highly. Lenin was a great lover of the theater. And of the film. Stalin was the best educated of all his con-temporaries; he was the teacher of nations. Until the advent of Marxism, it was not possible to answer all the problems which beset man and society. After the war, revolution would engulf the whole world, America included. Capitalism was already in its death throes. Those who thought otherwise probably wished otherwise. Freud taught atheism. When we marched into Ljubljana, a happy golden age would dawn for the Slovenes, the age that Cankar and all the finest spirits in our country's history dreamed of. Russia would take all small nations under her wing, cherish them, and bring them to a happier future.

When at last we broke up, Anton and I set off through the drizzle for our hay shed. He stopped. "Have you any idea who you were quarreling with?" he asked. "You don't know, and it's just as well you don't know, otherwise your blood would freeze. You're beyond help. You weren't meant for the forces. Your head will roll, if it hasn't rolled already."

"Well, you're a fine one, siding with them," I complained bitterly. He clutched his bandaged head.

"Can't you get it into your thick head," he groaned, "that in this world, it's not a matter of what you say, nor of what you hear, nor of whether you are right or not, and especially during a revolution? The only point is what they decide to do with you. I shudder to think how you love to bandy words." His face twisted in a grimace.

"Are you a Trotskyite, Anton? Do you know what is meant by anarchism? Of course not. It's a word you've picked up in the cafés of Ljubljana. You never lay in the streets of Barcelona, shooting it out with the anarchists."

He was angry and disappointed with me, he castigated me without mercy and read me a lecture, trying to put everything in the simplest terms, so that once and for all I should learn the lesson and, with a bit of luck, survive the war.

"Count yourself lucky you're not in the party, otherwise you wouldn't be quietly kipping down in the hay. But you are a partisan, a member of a revolutionary army that's preparing to seize power and must therefore sweep away all obstacles in its path. It's not a matter of knowledge or ignorance, superficiality or profundity; discipline's the thing. And now you've been filed away in a small drawer, where I wouldn't wish to join you. Bourgeois anarchoid? Prating liberal? And someone may ask whether this is only a mask, with a committed class enemy hiding behind it? Do you know what the naturalist Erjavec has to say about snakes? Man is the adder's worst enemy. He kills it ruthlessly, and not only the adder, but any snake that might be related to it. He will kill ten grass snakes because they resemble poisonous reptiles. It is better to kill ten innocents, than to let one guilty go. But you have to come along and play silly buggers with a member of the Politburo! It's just as well we're each going our separate ways tomorrow! A political illiterate like you simply spells trouble. A fine pair we'd make: a Spanish Trotskyite and a Slovene anarchist, the Don Quixote and Sancho Panza of the National Liberation Army! We survive a manhunt, then pitch into the Politburo! Madonna! Who ever heard of such a thing! Švejk just isn't in your league!"

He paused for breath, then probably recalled some particularly choice passage from the dialogue at the maplewood table, for he folded his arms and gazed up to high heaven. "And what was it all about? Some stale bloody rabbit's bollocks!"

We lay down on the hay.

"So you believe those old fairy tales about democracy, do you?"

I was now long past caring, and merely gave a despairing sigh.

"Now look here. Do you really imagine there was ever a democracy on the face of this earth? All right, so slave-owning, property-owning ancient Athens was a democracy, only for whom? We are all equal, we're none of us slaves, only some of us are more equal than others. We'll soon see Socrates off, then all will be well. Or maybe ancient Rome? Or Renaissance Florence? Or Paris? There has always been democracy for those who control the army and the police, while the others have had the right to repeat the words of the prefect of police. Why should it be different today? Why should you want to demonstrate that Dolnichar had never read a single page of Freud's writings? If you do survive this war, it will be a clear proof that our movement was truly democratic."

Calmer now, he continued the lecture.

"Perhaps democracy can prevail among us when we are on our own. But as soon as you take your place in society, you are on a ladder of seniority; that's inevitable.

"Have you heard how the knights dealt with insubordinate peasants?

"Have you read anything about the French Revolution?

"Have you read about the workers at the barricades?

"All history speaks of the struggle for freedom, for liberation, for democracy, for unity, brotherhood, justice. And who writes history? Who controls the printing presses? Who holds the censor's shears? Ideas are the industrial raw material of the ruling classes. You have joined the National Liberation Army and, whether you like it or not, you have also joined a revolution. At present you have a military dictatorship. Later you'll have the dictatorship of the proletariat. Basta! You will never be a judge of what is right and what is wrong. You will never have any influence on who will make the decisions, or what or how he will decide. The only decision you will have to make is whether to agree or not. And if you don't agree, others will decide what is to become of you. No one will ever engage in debate with you. Now you know. You'll never be able to complain that you weren't told. Whatever happens to you will be your own fault."

Here I quietly mused aloud: "What about that long line of people who disagreed with the great ones of their time? Socrates, Christ, Spartacus, Giordano Bruno, and a whole host of dissenters burned at the stake . . ."

"Sure, sure," Anton broke in, "We'll compile a list seventeen tomes long. Come off it, Berk! Don't you see it's not a question of the quality of life, but of sheer survival? Better get some sleep. You'll have plenty of chance, many opportunities, to reflect on my words. When you grow up."

We lay silent, but awake still. We were both dead tired. But Anton could not control himself.

"Look, this Dolnichar has another Dolnichar over him and that one has another, and that a fourth, and that a fifth, and so on, and so on, right up to Stalin, who is the supreme Dolnichar."

I raised myself on my elbows. "And have we to accept this as accomplished fact?"

"We must accept it as fact, and necessity," Anton asserted. "If Stalin were not a Dolnichar, he couldn't stay in power. In politics, your only concern is to hold on to your position. Truth, justice, honesty—justice, honesty—such concepts have nothing to do with politics. In his own way Hitler is one of the most honest of politicians, since time and again in his instructions, he's stressed, without fear of history's judgment, that any steps that lead to success are justified. He went to war to conquer the world; could you imagine him deterred by the small print of some agreement or by scruples regarding his treatment of his enemies? If we win, he said, everything will be decided according to the instructions we shall dictate. If we don't win, it can all go to the devil. This was Napoleon's way of thinking too. All 'strong-armed' politicians think in this way. Beside them democrats are amateurs. And the day of the amateur has not yet dawned."

He saw the world before him, then he recalled something from the past.

"I had similar difficulties with Žarko in Spain. Of course, we had all guessed for some time that the war was already lost, unless some miracle intervened. There was no point in talking about it. But he just had to dwell on it, bringing the subject up at every other opportunity, whereas the official line demanded confidence in the victory of our arms.

"Do you know what I heard from the orderlies who bandaged my head? The Germans found our wounded. They didn't shoot them but beat them with their own rifles. They shattered their skulls, some were battered like steaks, had their rib cages stove in and their limbs broken. The snow was literally red for a breadth of twenty meters. Afterward, they shattered the rifles against the pine trees and tossed them back among the corpses. Such poor weapons were not for them."

"And Petkoshek?"

"He was there.

"The Germans completed their operation on the day and at the hour decided beforehand. They have now swung west toward Primorska."

"And what's going to happen now?"

"How do you mean? We shall see how the situation develops. You will go on marching and I'll be immured in some printing press. It's a long way from Kharkov to Berlin."

When I was awakened next morning by the sound of horses' hooves near the hay shed, it was already daylight. Anton was no longer there beside me. I wanted to get up, to go and see where he had gone, but I noticed a gray spiral on my rifle: a sheet of newspaper with two Morava cigarettes wrapped up inside. I knew then there was no point in looking for him: he had gone off without a word.

Cinq Siecles de Guitare en Espagne.

Narciso Yepes was playing the guitar.

I was sitting alone by the jukebox in the small buffet where I went for breakfast. Joseph Bitter and his wife had left that morning. The previous evening, we had ceremonially said good-bye. As a parting gift, he had presented me with a book by Egon Friedell with the title *Aufklärung und Revolution (aus "Kulturgeschichte der Neuzeit")*. The author had jumped to his death through a window when, in March, 1938, Hitler marched into Vienna. Serafim brought me a mixture of sea foods, mussels, fish, and lobster tails with a cold sauce all in a neat white dish shaped like a small boat, and a fruit aperitif in a tall, slim glass.

Narciso Yepes was playing Fernando Sor's *Minuet in A Major*. Josep Ferran Sorts i Muntades drew his inspiration from Mozart. Here we were, sitting, standing, or hanging in the air, the man with the dormouse fur cap, the poet Rob, Anton, Miha, Meta, Joseph Bitter and his wife, Friedell, Mozart and Ferdinando Sor, Narciso Yepes, Serafim. The second-youngest was Miha, who any moment now would reach the age of thirty. The oldest was Mozart, who would soon be two hundred and eighteen years old, if my calculations were correct. He perished in an outbreak of the plague. At any rate, Serafim was our youngest one, only twenty-four years old.

"Won't the other gentleman be here today, sir?" No, Joseph had left once and for all; he would not be back again. He was present now, only in the lines he had traced in the book, so that he could still tell me something after his departure.

"Do you know German, Serafim? It says here: 'In the first place, it is the feet of our soldiers that brings us victory, and only in the second place their bayonets,' to quote Napoleon. On another page it says: 'I beat the Austrians by my marches alone.' *Märsche* . . . that means marches . . . foot-slogging, Serafim. Wars consist of nothing but marches."

"Was the German gentleman a soldier?"

"Yes, yes, he was, Serafim, though you might not think so at first glance."

"Was he a general?"

"Something of the sort, yes. I speak in jest, Serafim. Don't you know that every grown-up German is a warrior at heart? In his childhood he plays soldiers, in his old age he relives his battles. They have developed the theory of war like a game of chess. Do you play chess, Serafim?"

"Yes, sometimes I have a game."

"You see, the Germans develop the theory to a fine art, then every so often, a bungler from some other nation pops up in a corner and turns all their tactical and strategic dogmas upside down. Napoleon, for example. And later, they have to slave away once more and use all their ingenuity in order to unleash another war. When there have been great new strides in technology."

"War's a bad thing," Serafim said.

"Why? How do you know?"

"From old people who have been through it."

"But war is also a dance, Serafim. The war dance had begun, they say. A minuet. Accompanied by a twenty-five-shot guitar."

Serafim laughed. "You do like your little joke, sir." His worries were of a completely different kind.

"Is the slim lass with the long hair your girlfriend, Serafim, the one who was here before?"

"Mm." He confirmed the fact with a brisk nod.

"Now there's a pleasant battleground, Serafim."

Bitter's wife had probably once been a really wonderful woman. Before supper the previous evening, I spent some time with her. Joseph had gone to change some money. I tried to imagine what that face looked like in her youth. Beneath the present dignity and decorum, there still flickered the spark of some distant warmth, a glow in the ashes. She looked much younger in a black silk blouse with a gold brooch, her face made up, after an appointment with the hairdresser (that was the reason Joseph and I had spent the afternoon alone together, while she got ready for the evening). One only needed to forget the sight of her flesh and skin when she was sunbathing on the beach. And her face when she was tired. She had decided that this evening she would carry off her first triumph for a long time. I was perfectly prepared to regard her with half closed eyes that see better and to forget all that I previously knew about her appearance. After all, this was how the Impressionists painted their pictures. The lady was particularly fond of Spain, for young people from all over the world were so quiet, happy, and well-behaved here. In Germany, they had whole mobs of rockers and other aggressive gangs, some parts of town were very dangerous even in daytime, and some places were inaccessible, you know. "But here they walk around, dance, smile, enjoy themselves, and all through the night you hear no quarrels, and no voices raised in anger, no scuffles. As if you were visiting El Dorado. And what is it like in Yugoslavia?"

"Well, our young people like to imitate the west. Not all of them, but the ones that make the most noise."

"The Russians are very hard on hooligans, aren't they?"

"Yes, they crack down on them very hard, I believe."

"I wonder how the Spaniards have managed to deal with the problem."

"Perhaps you're right. Joseph says that the Spaniards suffered more than the others on the Russian front."

"I can just imagine."

"He writes about it in his memoirs. Did he tell you he has written his memoirs of the war?"

"He did say something about it, I think.

"At first he started writing to amuse himself but then he got carried away. How can it happen that a perfectly normal, orderly human being becomes the exact opposite. He was so obsessed by the problem that his old headaches started to recur. Those memories were making him ill. Look, lad, I said, are we going to live in the here and now, or in the nightmares of the past? Six million Germans have their names on the lists of war criminals but you, Joseph, though you've seen service in many countries, on many fronts, were not registered there, I told him. Why should you now present the account? Or pay with your nerves, your health, and your own private peace of mind for what others have done? You're neither a politician nor a writer; no one will try to understand you. And eventually I was able to persuade him to give up. You see how he's since improved? He's positively blooming, I think. A man must live in the present, not the past, nor should he overindulge in speculations about the future. And above all, he must not wonder what might have been, if things had been different . . . and take on himself the guilt of others. Submit himself to vivisection, no less. For whom? To what purpose? He was in a certain Yugoslav town where the Germans shot thousands of inhabitants in a single day. Even whole classes of schoolchildren, together with their teachers . . . It was horrible, really horrible . . . It was a town called . . . something beginning with K . . . Kra-, Kra-, Kra . . ."

"Kragujevac?"

"Yes, yes, Kragulevatz . . . Did he mention it to you? No? He couldn't bring himself to. I thought that was what you had been talking about that last time in Palma. You both looked so down when I found you in the café where we had agreed to meet . . . I was quite shocked. Did he tell you that in our family we went through all the ups and downs of the last war? That he himself had been under investigation? He didn't mention that? It was about the time of the attempted assassination of Hitler. Something he had said in company. There was some doubt as to whether he had said the Führer was stupid, or the war was a stupid venture. In German, we have a word, *irrsinnig*, which can be understood in various, quite different ways. Rather like 'mad'. You could be madly in love, madly well off, Hitler was mad, the war was mad, anything could be mad. He was acquitted but posted to a spearhead assault unit. His life was at stake and he got away by the skin of his teeth. *Dieser Krieg war ein Teufelsfleischmachine.* Joseph is as simple as a child. But he took to you straight away. You must visit us when you come to Germany. He says his discussions with you are as refreshing as a cold shower. He particularly liked your talk about Napoleon."

After the three of us had dined in a manner fitting our last evening together, the lady made her excuses and went to bed, leaving us free to order a little more liquid refreshment. We both sensed that it would be difficult to crown our discussions with an adequate conclusion. The result was we talked a load of rubbish, to nobody's satisfaction.

"What do you think of Spain?"

"Oh, a country just like any other, neither better nor worse."

"Here, in the past, one hundred poets celebrated a stairway made of white marble."

"During the Civil War, they constructed special cells, hard for us to imagine. They were built entirely of sharp concrete teeth, painted black and white in violent contrast, bathed in the glare of the searchlights. They would throw a prisoner in and switch on a recording of savagely wailing sirens. In the confined space, that would break down the healthiest nerves. But for the life of me, I cannot remember whether it was Franco's side or the Republicans that had those cells."

"Man is really an animal," said Bitter.

"You are wrong, Herr Bitter; an animal would not build cells like that. I know the saying 'Man is a wolf to man'; that's a hoary old misconception which arose in ancient days—surviving through Thomas Hobbes and others, to the present; more recently, Freud gave it a new lease of life. But just think back to the war you survived. And other things too. All those characteristics that link man closest to the animals, from whom of course he wishes to distinguish himself, all those activities he has elevated to the status of a rite. A beast, we say, is in heat, man celebrates love and holy matrimony, an animal devours its food when it is hungry, man dines, holds luncheons and banquets, farewell dinners; an animal dies, but man passes away and usually has a funeral and obituary notice; an animal drops its young, man begets his descendants;

a herd of animals is led by the strongest and most intelligent male, human society is run by shortsighted, corpulent, complex-ridden old humbugs. A man-eating animal makes the headlines over the whole world but we human beings go on quietly, day after day, eating animals, even at farewell dinners. Wild beasts—my last example—maul and savage each other, man marches heroically to war. But that is not all, Herr Bitter. When one animal attacks another, it is driven by hunger and eats its victim. Animals of the same species fight only during the mating season—that's nature practicing eugenics—or to establish hierarchy within the herd, and sometimes in deciding the boundaries of hunting territories. The zoologists tell us that serious wounding rarely takes place in such combats and death is virtually unheard of. If you want to know what an animal would not do—take the frightful list enumerating crimes and punishments in the penal code, or the prosecution's case at the Nuremberg trials. No, man is no animal. He has raised himself above the animals, sought a connection with God, made himself a god, deserted nature and attempted to subjugate her, created a world of his own, a world of man—and now, here we are, sitting here, my dear sir, dressed in our ready-made suits, with our bellies full of beef, observing each other . . ."

We really were watching each other, until at last Bitter started laughing, at first quaking spasmodically, then bursting out in peals of uncontrollable merriment, so infectious that I joined in myself, though a quiet inner smile is more my style.

"You've raised my morale," he said at last. "All is not lost . . ."

Again he found it hard to suppress a second gale of laughter. "What country was your suit made in?" he asked.

"Homemade."

"Sure enough, it's just like one of ours."

It took him a little longer before he simmered down.

"And there we were chasing one another over the Balkan peninsula . . ." He was quite relaxed, but my military instincts resented this fraternizing with the enemy.

"And we were both wearing German uniforms," I remarked.

He became very solemn.

"Did you . . . strip it off yourself?"

"Yes. It wasn't too hard; rigor mortis hadn't set in yet."

I found another passage underlined in Friedell: "In our minds, we think we no longer believe in a whole set of things, but our organism still believes in them, and that is always stronger than the mind."

The past within us will not die, the future is always other than we expect it to be, and the present is only a moving point in time.

I sat there, listening to the music of the jukebox and watching the face of a Spanish minister on the television screen. I had turned the sound all the way down. The aged head opened its lips, raised its bushy eyebrows, and gazed at me, convinced it was speaking great words of wisdom.

Who mended Videk's shirt? There was once a poor widow woman who had seven children, each of them smaller than the other . . . they had a shirt which was bequeathed from the first to the second and so on . . . until it reached the youngest child, whose name was Videk. The shirt was by now so thin, the sunlight shone through it onto his skin. A sheep gave him wool, a bush carded it for him, a spider spun and wove for him the best, the finest cloth, a crab cut out a shirt for the child and a bird sewed it. Videk looked at his reflection in the stream and cried out happily, "Oh, now I've got a fine, new shirt." (So sings Fran Levstik.) Long live our Videk, the child in the white shirt.

I do not know why I suddenly felt like weeping to the music of that jukebox. The minister was watching me from the screen. Serafim had his eyes on a couple who were leaning against the bar. At this time, all the politicians in the world, professionals and amateurs, were addressing crowds or commissions, on the radio or television and in the newspapers: all of them honoring the rights of their citizens, all believing in the arts and sciences, all regarding human life as the greatest of all values, all shaping the future, all knowing exactly what they believed in and what they rejected; all expecting the majority of people to agree with them, since "things cannot be other than they are." I myself see all and see nothing; I am aware of the laments of officials, the power of the military, the secrecy of the police, the pressing needs of workers, farmers, doctors, the risks taken by speculators. It all makes sense, but I don't. Everything has its origin, dwells in its peculiar circumstances, and has its own aim and purpose, except me. I have rejected what all others know; I have renounced my culture, my own milieu, my origins, and my foundations. And here I am, gone to earth in a poky little buffet, and no one gives a hoot whether I stay here or not. I've seen too many cartoon pictures and I have myself become a cartoon. In an avant-garde show, I once saw an act entitled "Death of a Carp." A fish was swimming in a great bowl; a man took it out and threw it onto a white cloth, where it flapped and panted, tossed, and died before our eyes. The man then drank water from the fish tank, spewed it up, and went on drinking and spewing. I grieved at the demise of the acrostic sonnet. There is no proof that God exists, nor that he does not exist; no proof that man has an immortal soul, nor that he has not; no proof man is free to make his own decisions, nor that free will does not exist. The one thing clear to me is that consciousness belongs to the individual and at the same time, the individual cannot exist without human society. Music is degenerating into sound, painting into blobs, literature into dots and dashes; philosophy doubts the existence of the world; science doubts its own validity and purpose. Never before has the past receded so far from the present. The Greeks and Romans are decades or millennia away, a century has become a millennium, a decade has become a century, a new generation no longer understands its predecessor, a fifteen-year-old will tell a twenty-year-old graybeard who still knows Latin and Greek that he is a zombie from an ancient graveyard. Meanwhile, our perspective of the future is growing more and more restricted. It is all as if nothing had existed before. In that distant war against Hitler's divisions, centuries ago, forests were changed into battlegrounds, and now scientists are measuring the extent of pollution on the leaves of the trees, on the high mountains and in the air of the forests. The ranging colored beams of great projectors in a hall full of smoke represent art and threaten to erase all memories of the old masters. Logic has forever lost its right to speak. Nations have become accustomed to mental schism, to doubt and suspicion, to double-talk. The simplistic realpolitik of the amateur has yielded to the cunning and duplicity of the professional directors of large and powerful organizations. Paranoid politics rule the schizophrenic world. Any moment now, the world will explode, the graves will open and out will pour, not the dead, but seething masses of tourists. All night long in El Arenal, the footsteps never cease, padding, slithering, tramping, while singers and bands sing, hum, and strum in the outdoor discos, to the sound of chatter and laughter. People cross over the asphalt road in their bathing costumes, on their way to the sandy beaches. Cars drive away into the night. The crowds drink beer, sweet wine, espresso coffee, and cherry brandy that tastes of prussic acid. On and on they walk and talk, the Germans, the Dutch, the Danes, the Norwegians, the Swedes, the Germans, the Germans, the Germans, the English, the French, the Americans, the Italians, the Greeks, the Turks, the North Africans, and the Germans. On a street corner by the shoe shop stands a hirsute, bearded prophet from America, informing the couples who pass by, in his American brand of English, that man will be ruined in three ways; he strikes his head and says "in body and mind," his breast with the words "in body and spirit," his belly with the words "in body and desire." From five in the morning till seven, the streets lie empty, as if submerged in a transparent fluid; then there are no voices, no sounds to be heard, except for the fresh morning breeze blowing in from the sea, driving the long rollers that make no more noise than the crumpling of a piece of paper. Then the older tourists start to rise and take their dogs for their morning walk, till eventually the Spaniards also appear to open up their shops at nine o'clock.

Who mended Videk's shirt?

Yours is a pleasant battlefield, Serafim. You'll be home any moment now, Joseph Bitter.

Morava cigarettes aren't as good as they were, Anton, I've gone over to Filter 57.

Soon it will be time for me to depart for Ljubljana; I don't know why. There may be a hidden design in all this. Wherever I travel, I always go back to Ljubljana when the time comes. Some day I shall ask the mayor what he thinks, as a Marxist, of the instincts of migratory birds.

Many of the conversations I had had with Anton kept coming back to mind when, along with ten others, I was trudging on and on through the cold rain on our way from Mount Krim to Suha Krajina; time and again, I could not separate his words from mine, since we shared a common quest, a common anxiety, a common delight in the fleeting thoughts of those days in the forests, when we still had before us a settled purpose: victory, liberation, the end of the war. Seven of us were wounded, the others were Snow Whites. One had been hit in the hand, another in the shoulder, a third in the head. Worst off was a fair-haired lad. A bullet had hit him near the navel but a little to the side and it had come out at his back. They had patched him up somehow and he did a twenty-eight-hour march with us, to show the truth of the saying, "A man can stand more than a horse." An empty gut saved his life. Hunger also has its uses.

"There are only two possibilities," Anton said. I could just see him leaning against a tree. "Either the end justifies the means, as Europe believes, or only the way is important and the end less so, as the Asians think. No one talks about it aloud; these are secret beliefs."

"Everything is boundless, in every way, although we set its boundaries. Everything operates, lives, moves according to laws beyond individuality, beyond man, beyond human knowledge; man tries to interfere with the natural order of things and later complains after some calamity."

"In the midst of the tempests of war an old woman lived on her own in a dainty little house. The modest cottage was built to suit her tiny, slender frame; it was just like a fairy tale. The old woman and her cottage remained intact. She gave me a piece of bread, a slice of bacon, and a little onion. When we parted, she said pointedly, 'After the war, you must let it be known that I am very pleased to receive guests; a German officer also promised me he would do so.'"

We arrived at division.

I made every possible mistake and I enabled all others to do the same. However, they did not kill me.

From division I went to brigade. From brigade to battalion. From battalion to company. Zgornji Korinj, Hinje, Polom. We moved in Indian file toward the road that leads to Rijeka. From there we went to Ogulin and afterward back to Loški Potok and Ribnica; fourteen months later, we went to Trieste, from Trieste to Ajdovščina, and arrived, on a sunny morning on the ninth of May, via the Vhrnika road, in Ljubljana. Hundreds of kilometers.

We marched through deep snow to Mrzla Vodica. We met a number of politicians, including some people I knew from university. Here were the leaders of our movement.

There was a bitter frost at Mrzla Vodica. The farmers' wives and children were collecting the last of the potato crop, though the ground was as hard as ice. That evening, I was invited to partake of sweet baked potatoes, really tiny ones, the size of chestnuts, but delicious, warm, a rare treat. I slept, lousy as I was, in soft eiderdowns, filled with goose down, actually. I tended to the bleeding blisters on my feet; the snow had often been red where I had trodden. But a human being recovers quickly. A German cannon bombarded our sentry posts with great accuracy, scoring a direct hit on our cooking pot. It was obvious that someone had betrayed our position. What could you expect; the women were smuggling contraband in and out of Rijeka and knew the paths through the thickets. Among them, there was one who carried a letter sewn up in her skirt.

Fog on the road to Gornje Jelenje; the Germans captured, without firing a shot, the commander of the second company. They took him alive. An attack on an airfield surrounded by bunkers. Encounter with Germans among the rocks, in fog, now and again dispersed by the wind. At one moment we were all, the Germans and us, shrouded in mist thick as milk, and the next moment, we had a visibility of several meters. You can't see a German soldier's physiognomy under one of those steel helmets. He had a nose red with the frost, just like me.

I was caused some embarrassment by Lieutenant Vagelj, an ex-Sokol and reserve officer, chief of the battalion staff. One fine day, he disappeared and I heard he had deserted and made for Rijeka. And I had been happily meeting him for English conversation, solely in order to get some practice in the language.

One night, at a place where the road had been dug up, four of us came under fire from unknown assailants as we were casually walking along the muddy embankment.

In the village of Homer, I visited an old farmer for a glass of brandy and to hear the radio. He told me how the Germans had buried a partisan courier alive, in a field close by his house. An officer had observed him through field glasses from the other side of the valley as he walked along a path. They sent out an ambush and captured him without firing. They beat him up and interrogated him, and them forced him to dig a hole in the field and jump into it; some of the villagers saw this. They filled the hole in and covered him but he still tried to lift his head clear of the soil. They covered him completely but the soil continued to move. Then they stamped it down with their jackboots, till at last the earth lay quiet under their soles.

From a good position on a hill, we pissed on a German limousine and an armored car down on the road, just as the armored car was approaching a bridge. The limousine soon caught fire but the Germans were out of those vehicles like bats out of hell and took cover down below the bridge. They fired back at us. They were saved by the dark.

Someone told me how he had met a German on Travna Mountain. Plechek his name was. He was walking through the forest, with his hands in his pockets, when he suddenly froze in his tracks. There was a German on the edge of a clearing, in a camouflage smock, holding an automatic which was trained on the advancing partisan. They were close enough to distinguish all the lines on each other's faces. They stood there, watching each other. Then Plechek started slowly to retreat backward, turned on his heel and withdrew step by step, till at last he looked back. The German was still standing there like a graven image. He waited for a shot but none came, so he suddenly took to his heels and ran like the clappers. No shot came.

In the village of Stari Laz, we were attacked by the Ustaše Black Legion. The village lay in a narrow valley surrounded by hills. We were fired on from all sides. We sent a patrol rushing up the hillside to take them in the flank, while we returned their fire from the village. The action only lasted about half an hour. There was not a single male person in any of the houses, only women and children.

At a weakly attended meeting, I heard how many railway tracks we had blown up.

Some of our men captured an old man who was supposed to be someone high up in the Ustaše. He was interrogated by staff officers. The local partisan authorities requested that we hand him over. Apparently an exchange of prisoners was already in operation.

The Ustaše were killing and torturing, torturing and killing people in a camp at Jasenovac on the river Sava. They were throwing the corpses into the river. Some of the torturers and executioners had taken baleful-sounding names. Their favorite method was pounding to death with a sledgehammer.

In Dolenjska, there were battles between partisans and the Home Guard, who had reorganized. There were shootings by the Germans every morning at Begunje. Before execution, the condemned men were bound to the stake.

I had no idea what a strange country I lived in. Along the road, there were villages, Catholic and Orthodox alternating, all the way to Ogulin. The Catholic villages were on the side of the Ustaše, the Orthodox on the side of the Chetniks; the two forces were engaged in an internecine struggle. We came along as a third force. We were received sullenly in the Croatian villages, with interest in the Serbian. We learned how the Ustaše "rechristened," with fire and sword, the Orthodox Serbs. Not far from Klek, there's a pit into which the Ustaše hurled so many people that the earlier bodies cushioned the fall of the last; for a whole week, groans and cries for help could be heard from that chasm forty meters deep. I do not know what must happen to quell that deadly hatred, religious and nationalistic, which the Germans cleverly exploit and incite as much as they can.

I celebrated my birthday in Vitunj, a Serbian village in the Ogulin valley. I arrived at a house where an old woman dressed in black folded her arms and said, "My son!" Apparently I resembled her son, who had recently died. Therefore she sent her daughters as much as thirty kilometers away to bring meat and drink for a celebration of my birthday. At about eleven o'clock in the evening, at the height of the celebrations, the Ustaše opened fire on the village with machine guns. An hour later the festivities were again in full swing. Milica, who had served in Zagreb, put on for that occasion black silk stockings, high-heeled shoes, and black silk panties trimmed with white lace—enough to drive a man crazy.

In a little place called Turković, we found one of the Ustaše in hiding. He had not managed to get away in time. A very puzzled young man. Who mended Videk's shirt? Are you going to tell us? His mother pleaded for him: he was still so young, they had taken him off to Ogulin, he had to go with them, and now he had deserted simply to see his mother and sister again. His sister had been very badly treated by a German. He had threatened her with a gun and she had to strip naked. He picked up her clothes and pushed her in there, behind the byre . . . "I came along . . . and saw what was happening," she went on. "I saw our Marija as naked as the day she was born . . . and that German following her with her clothes and his Schmeisser in his hand . . . I started screaming and wringing my hands, moaning and begging him . . . Well, he dropped her clothes on the ground, took fright, left us alone . . ." The girl, a trim figure in a loose dress, was standing there, hiding her face in her hands. Her brother leaped up, tried to escape. He got a volley from an automatic in the middle of his back. The mother flung herself on him. The man who had fired checked his gun. The rules of the game are well known.

Es lo mismo, es lo mismo, Señor!

"It's all the same, all the same, sir," said the old retainer who had cleared a clogged drain in my shower. I asked him whether Spain would become a monarchy again. "The chief thing is to keep the foreigners out."

"What foreigners?"

374

"Oh, Italians, Germans, Russians . . . No, thanks. I don't smoke Ducados, they scorch my gums. This is the brand I prefer: Extra, *cigarillos con filtro*."

"Would you like one of our cigarettes?"

"Where are you from?"

"Yugoslavia."

"Thanks, I'll smoke it later. I've got a lot of jobs waiting for me. It's the shoddy workmanship, you know. Are your plumbers left-handed bunglers like ours?"

"Yes." I saw we were not going to have much of a conversation.

Soon I shall be leaving. How shall I pass the few remaining days I have to spend in this hotel; I must stay here, for that is in the plan, it is already decided, it cannot be otherwise. A good starting point for a meditation of free will.

I undressed and went into the shower to wash the sea salt off my skull; and that was in the plan, had already been decided, could not be otherwise. I adjusted the hot and cold taps to get the lukewarm blend I wanted, exercising my free will. From then to eternity, I still had some possible decisions to make: should I dress and go for a walk along the noisy streets, or sit in the café or terrace, among the hosts of tourists, watching the passersby in their glad rags; or I could take a fiacre and drive up and down the esplanade; the scraggy horse would trot along the warm asphalt, tossing the hat perched on his head, and just waiting for evening, when he would go home to the stable, where he would slake his thirst and munch the straw in his trough; what if I were a horse? I could just imagine the pain of every crack of the whip on my flanks. Perhaps I should book a seat for the new flamenco show, or take a trip to Palma. I could do all these things; but I could not go home yet, because certain matters still awaited completion.

I chose the most habitual course of action. I put on my bathrobe and sat in a deckchair on my veranda, overlooking the disco club where the music blared out twenty hours a day, with a silent interval from five in the morning till nine. I looked up at the sky, which promised a calm, warm night, and then turned my attention to my very own slip-ons of yellow Spanish leather. Not according to the plan, but by a new decision of my free will; everything could be otherwise.

This reminded me of how, over Ogulin, I had sat on the grass, almost thirty years ago, contemplating my hobnailed boots of Russian leather. Except that, in wartime, your awareness is never exclusively concentrated on one point, your senses are always on the lookout for the unexpected, which may occur at any moment. In war, everything follows the course of an unknown plan, everything is decided somewhere else, everything must be just so and not otherwise. Of course free will is at work all the time but only choosing the best way to execute the allotted task. A friendly old cobbler in Mrkopalj had mended those boots for me. My puttees were a gift from a New Zealander we were escorting to the coast to be picked up by an English submarine. I had a black German uniform. And a Yugoslav greatcoat. I had one powerful segmented Kragujevac grenade and a small Italian one. I had an Italian pack made of green canvas and one of brown leather, probably German, that I had picked up in some house or other. I now had a really fine weapon, a Mauser I could rely on, and adequate reserves of ammunition in my pack. I had a gray German army blanket. A Swiss watch. Cigarettes from Zagreb, from the Ustaše's Independent State of Croatia. My lighter was a gift from our cook, who enjoyed my jokes. But I was well shod, and that was the most important thing. Wars are won by marching feet, it's true. What use is a superb engine if the car's wheels don't work? I had used one grenade, a fizzer, during the action in the rocks in the fog. Everything changes and constantly develops, both man and his equipment. I had never felt particularly comfortable in those shorter German jackboots, and long riding boots of soft leather suited me better; after the war, I could not get used to ordinary trousers flapping around my ankles like a woman's skirts. I had an American bush shirt from one of their pilots. He told me he was from Texas and gave me his address; I even wrote to him once after the war, for a joke, and my letter came back a few months later, bearing the words: unknown at this address. A pair of trousers from an English parachute drop, which I had made into riding breeches. A jacket from the same source, which was really a shortened greatcoat. An American belt of white canvas, thickly woven. A German Mauser-Reitpistole Parabellum, with an extension that turned the pistol into an automatic. A Belgian F.N. pistol. A khaki shirt. A Siberian fur jacket, abandoned by a member of the Austrian mission that flew in from Moscow. In the last months of the war, I acquired an American automatic. I never had anything from Japan.

Somewhere near the Kolpa River we ate roast wild duck.

Hermina came straight from Ljubljana, a sight for sore eyes, happy to get away from that inferno, a well cut skirt on her shapely hips. Confidentially, she told me that people were still going to the restaurants and cafés, in spite of the raids. A house split in two by a bomb from a German aircraft still afforded us pleasant shelter.

The battalion staff raised the alarm that night by letting off their automatics. We rushed out of the houses, by no means grateful for the surprise. Next night the Ustaše did come. We had to make a frenzied dash for the hillside, because of the time we lost dawdling, suspecting another stupid practical joke. At a complaints session, I criticized the commander and the commissar, asking why they had fled with the service unit. I got another black mark to add to those I already had.

The second-in-command of the brigade walked calmly and unperturbed, automatic in hand, through a hail of bullets that were clipping the grass at his feet, and emerged unscathed. Fusillades from the Ustaše's bunkers, a clearing with rising ground on either side. I often remembered that man later. A miner with his own peculiar sense of humor.

At a session of self-criticism, I heard my comrades one after the other admitting their faults. When my turn came, I declared I was a swell guy with no faults at all. I was told this was a pretty poor joke.

Notice of promotions had come through. Where on earth were we going to get all that gold braid for our sleeves? Perhaps the church would step into the breach? All the same, I could not forget the partisan who was condemned to death and publicly executed in one village because he had fired at a crucifix in a farmer's house. Private interference in religious and church affairs was called sectarianism and was punishable by court-martial.

The Slovene partisans were forbidden, under pain of death from "scrounging" in Croatian villages. "I never go scrounging," Milosh used to say. "I go into a house and demand food for three fighters of the National Army."

The Allies had landed at Anzio and Nettuno. The Germans were withdrawing from the Crimea. There was fighting at Monte Cassino. An unsuccessful German attack on Drvar. The glorious Red Army had reached Minsk and Kiev. The Allies in Rome; in Paris. Each day brought us great news. The end of the war was rapidly approaching, getting nearer and nearer, but not yet in sight. Stalin's orders of the day. English parachute drops with containers of arms and clothing. Our brigades were transformed. On Marshal Konev's front . . . on Marshal Zhukov's front . . . Heavy Russian automatics on revolving platforms.

Light English Bren guns. Two battalions of Whites fighting each other in the fog; we picked up the deserters and strays. Battles in Dolenjska. An early-morning attack by the Home Guards who had adopted the partisan tactic of night marches and surprise raids in the enemy rear. Air-raid warnings. Our staff mounted on horseback. The Marxist "circle." A flood of propaganda; our presses were constantly improving their output. We were ambushed. I got a real old Colt 45 from an American airman. The first elections in the field; well, well, how will they turn out? Meetings. Improved mine throwers. A commission for the institution of people's power. This is London speaking. Moscow speaking. A rush for the mountain. Polenta in a mill by the Kolpa River. Already Marx has said . . . Bathing in the river. Choir singing the Internationale. Women's blouses sewn from parachute silk, in red, green, and yellow; the material does not breathe, people sweat in it. Player's Navy Cut, Camel cigarettes. Liberators flying north to Germany and coming back after dropping their loads of bombs. A limping Flying Fortress, slowly following the rest of the formation. A German fighter plane patrolling up and down the Kolpa valley, flying low, seeking fresh prey. It zooms down on a stricken Liberator. Two English Spitfires appear from nowhere. A dogfight. The Messerschmidt is shot down and plunges, a mass of fire and smoke, to the ground. Interrogation of German prisoners. A lieutenant says he knows what to expect. Delousing. We bathe and wash off our scabs with a solution of sulfur. Wounded men. Our troops sing the Russian song, "*Vintovachka, bjej, bjej, vintovachka bjej, krasnaja vintovachka fashista ne zhalej . . .*" As Lenin has already taught us . . . Charge! The end of the war was rapidly approaching, getting nearer and nearer, but not yet in sight. We could hardly believe that Belgrade was now liberated. Low-level strafing by a light aircraft called a "stork." The air was buzzing with new abbreviations: SNOUB, IOOF, ROF, SKOJ, AVNOJ, OZNA, NOV and POS, SNOS, NOO . . . An attack by Vlasov's forces. Riding breeches with red and green stripes. They herded the women into a building and raped the lot. Even an old woman who ended up, because of them, in our hospital. Her granddaughter said, "I wouldn't have believed it if Grandma hadn't told me herself what happened." American units in Aachen. Productions of Chekhov and Molière by the partisans' theater company; costumes from parachute material by courtesy of the Allies. American tinned bacon. A Russian battalion of Uzbeks who surrendered to us. The head of the Russian mission could not understand why we did not shoot the lot: "In the end you'd have everybody saving his skin." We formed an Austrian battalion from Austrian prisoners of war. They fought the Germans like lions; they knew what was in store for them if they were captured. A mission from the Allies. English and Americans. The Partisan Choir. A call to the Home Guard to give themselves up. Germans withdrawing from Greece via Yugoslavia. Front-line theater. Partisan workshops. Issue of vouchers, our first currency. Would we still need money after the war? A letter arrived from Ljubljana, sewn up in an article of clothing; a perfectly ordinary private missive, written on a scrap of material. A Gypsy woman, pestering us for a piece of parachute. Tonight a woman made pancakes for us; a sure sign that the end of the war is approaching, getting nearer and nearer; God knows whether some day we shall not in fact see the dawn of liberation. From a nation of lackeys to a nation of heroes. Award of decorations. Advancements, commendations, reprimands. No taxes after the war. Art is a class phenomenon. To quote Stalin . . . The masses must be educated. People's power is firmly anchored in the masses. Death to fascism. Slogans. Executions. Speeches. The day of liberation is getting nearer and nearer. German offensive in the Ardennes. We're going to have a hard winter, said a farmer, with ice and heavy snowfalls. A man's guts draped on a tree. Someone had stepped on a mine. There was no end to these flashbacks; in spite of all the hustle and bustle, things moved at a leisurely pace. Memories in my ears, eyes, legs, palms. I go on learning and learning but it is quite possible I am on the wrong road. We are all leading each other into greater and greater error. Man learns all his life and dies stupid, says the proverb. There is much pride in my character, much greed, anger, vanity: surely this represents some advance! I float on a tide of prejudice, though bound to my environment and contemporary trends. You have no idea, my son, how little wisdom you need to rule the world, said an old statesman to his son. The nearer freedom comes, the more we are pressed into molds, which we produce in special commissions, and which also arise by themselves. One quiet night, a member of the Austrian Central Committee, who arrived from Russia wearing a Russian uniform, told me how in one of Stalin's purges, his wife was arrested and killed in prison. The members of the Czech mission addressed us in high-flown platitudes; they did not trust us. A company scout of the Croatian Home Guard reported that they had assurances from the English that the partisans would never come to power in Slovenia. Allied aircraft were maintaining the link between Bari and our airfield. The end was rapidly approaching and we were still marching on; we would march to the very end. Legs are the most important part of a soldier. Next comes his food, and then tobacco. In a farmer's house, I had a game of chess with an architect and we both had a good drink of rather powerful brandy. He told me that after the end of the war, the Russians and the Americans would come to blows; and what would become of us? "Here we are, caught in the draft between East and West, between North and South. The Slovenes chose to settle in a most exposed position." Modern architecture had no chance. We were now going to construct concrete wedding cakes on the Russian model. The heroic age was upon us. Man with a capital letter, as Gorky said. Before the Prophet, Arabian poets sang of life and death, love and wine; later, heroes and the righteous life were their only themes. Art in the service of the liberated populace. Best get used to it as soon as possible. Tonchka told me confidentially, between the sheets, that our intelligence service regarded me with suspicion because I was always shooting my mouth off; this boded ill for me. I went drinking with a lieutenant from the Russian mission. He was well on his way when he told me, "All you partisans have a rather simpleminded attitude to revolution." What did he mean by that? Was there something about us he did not like? An American pilot whom we had saved from the Germans taught me the song, "Home, home on the range, where the deer and the antelope play . . ." A couple of days later he was off to his base in Italy. Off? Sure. The end was getting nearer and nearer. Our liberated territories continued to grow. What was happening was not perfectly clear to me. And yet it was all following some plan. Everywhere, there were notices to be seen. The whole country was being organized. Each town, each region had its command. Local authorities. Liaison between the army and these officials. The courier network was working normally. Newspapers were coming out. Supplies were being distributed, equipment, uniforms, weapons; our brigades were taking on a more uniform look thanks to the arms and equipment from heaven. The massive machine of the organization was working well, without confusion or ambiguity. At a theatrical performance, the first row was occupied by eminent soldiers and politicians; behind them sat the army men, and behind them the civilians. An Englishman said we were something unique in history: there, a few kilometers away, were the Germans, and here was our state, in the middle of Europe. In previous wars, this sort of thing was unthinkable. One Russian used to drink brandy from a shotglass, while nibbling cubes of fat bacon without any bread. He told us he had once seen Uncle Joe in the distance. Marichka was going to knit me a pullover. The Red Army in Warsaw. Red Army on the Oder. Americans will make the Rhine crossing any time now. The end was very rapidly approaching. Many a man would stop a bullet in the last hour of the war. One of the bullets would be the last to score a hit. Any one of us was a candidate for it. Our oldest fighters were terrified at the thought of the last bullet. From the mists of memory, faces appeared, spoke, and receded. Sun and rain. Wind. A macadam road raked by a German machine gun, which raised little puffs of white sand in the air. Night in a mill when our vehicle had broken down. The thighs of a country girl. White flights of Liberators in the sky. How many places can a man be in at the same time? A dead man beside the road. A company singing on the march, with a banner and accordion at their head. Birds reawakening to spring . . . and it won't be long now. The last wartime spring, and that's for sure. For the end is near. Soon we shall be marching to Ljubljana. Ljubljana, our journey's end. Berlin for the Russians and Americans, Ljubljana for us. I guess I'll survive. I went shooting frogs by the river. After all the chaos I'd been through, I would be pretty bewildered when I got back to Ljubljana; how would I settle down? Could we believe this was really the end? And if it was? I got my dose of scabies from the Gypsy girl, I now realized. The butcher slipped us some liver. The man who was now town commander ordered the execution of a whole Gypsy encampment a year ago. They were supposed to have betrayed the whereabouts of some partisans. The Whites captured our major and cut out a red star on his cheeks before killing him. We found one of our girls raped and murdered by the Home Guards. I could not understand why, in wreaking their fury on her, they had tugged out her pubic pair with pincers. They would get their deserts, the end was approaching. They will have nowhere to hide. Death to fascism. Flaring hatred. Lust for life. Lawns have no further use. The lunacy of expecting miracles. Fatigue of tissue, human tissue. Not muscles or limbs but spirits, which drift on the south winds of February. It is no longer important what is true and what is not, nor what is just and what is not. The speakers' voices boom but I might as well be deaf. We had a drink in a farmhouse and shot our bullets at the rafters. For the end was coming. Drink up, Marian, Dushan, and Tone. If they were not around, there were others. Marching. Talking. Sleeping. Dreaming something marvelous was happening; the war was over, the bands were playing, hordes of civilians crowding the streets. A road exploded, bits of road flew up into the air and fell untidily back to earth. No one will ever restore the jigsaw to the resemblance of a road.

A civilian in an outsize black greatcoat flying through the air. Germans marching in serried ranks, singing an army song. Peasant hanged on a tree. Cossack rapes girl. Where could I get ammo for a .25? Parachute panties are no good, they don't let the air through. Americans land on Iwo Jima. Is the Pope a war criminal? The problem of God and Marx is solved. Whites on parade in Ljubljana. Two Indians, Gurkhas serving with the British Army, made their way from a German P.O.W. camp to Slovenia, reached us by the couriers' routes and were now off to Italy by plane; they only asked us in which direction India lay, so that they could face there as they worshipped and prayed. Reality invades dreams and dreams intrude on daily reality, so that nothing is any longer true.

The civilian in the outsize black greatcoat—was it perhaps an advertisement for some merchandise, painted on a house wall? When, after such a long interval, I at last stepped into a kitchen and found a mirror, it was a strange face that looked out at me. Maybe it would be possible to forget oneself completely, to pretend I am no longer me, to ignore and escape from this unknown identity. Did I myself choose this face? These hands? This body? This sex? This manner of thinking and feeling? I chose hardly anything myself. Who or what chose this external appearance for me? Who or what sent me into this world and chose precisely Ljubljana? And this time precisely? And traced my path for me? Led me into the forest, brought me to the partisans, guided my every step along the long road? Or was it something else, someone else? And now I bore all responsibility for what I was and where I was. And I had to belong somewhere, if I did not want to go crazy. The fact that I could be killed by my own side, or the Germans, the Whites, the Blues, the Ustaše, Vlasov's men, the Hungarians, the Nedich, or the Ljotich party, the Bulgarians, or anyone else, was a consideration of no importance whatever. And if everyone was rebuking me for being wrong, making mistakes, cracking poor jokes, "when we all know this just won't do"—I am afraid it was all the same to me! And if I myself felt there was something wrong? I had to make a speech at a meeting!

Me make a speech! A speech full of hoary clichés. On the one hand stands the invader, with his lackeys who have betrayed their nation, on the other hand the nation's fighters, and in between, the stealthy malevolent forces of reaction, prepared at any time to betray the national interests. There was certainly more than a grain of truth in all this. There was the invader, what else? And those who served him were his lackeys, what else? We were fighting for freedom and at the same time for revolution, though we didn't make a song and dance about it, because the Russians wouldn't like that, or at least, so we were led to believe. Every age brings its own terminology, its own forms of expression; every political movement has its own nomenclature for trends and problems—it is a well known fact. Rousseau sang during the French Revolution; Marx and Lenin are the songsters now. I write down certain questions in my notebook, but there isn't a living soul I can discuss them with. Sometimes I rush blindly ahead, without looking either right or left; sometimes I have a brainstorm and lapse into a morbid dejection without knowing precisely why; sometimes I get roaring drunk and crack off-key jokes; I resort to a female being with a body, etc., and cast a spell over both of us, changing us both into something else; but I must always come back to myself, to my own place, to my real skin to find my true face; I cannot afford to miss any sight or sound; even the scents stay with me, and so does every touch, every sunset. A little Bosnian horse lying by the roadside, ribs covered with weals, nostrils full of black flies; I sense the tragedy of that life. I have become more severe in my dealings with people, more insensitive, more sarcastic. The lieutenant from the Russian mission forecast a sad end for me, on the morning after an all-night booze-up when we had drunk everyone else under the table. Why do I strive to cram into my memory all the details of these days? Do I think there may, some time, be a need to relate all this? To whom? Why? The purpose of our own actions is hidden deep within them. Those German Tiger tanks which suddenly drove up the village street. We fled in all directions. One of them turned aside, finding the garden wall no obstacle, crushing a summerhouse beneath its tracks as if it were made of paper; it drove into an open field where two of our men were running through the grass and raked them with machine-gun fire. One got a volley full in the back, staggered, and fell. The other was hit in the legs. Around him, grass was flying through the air as he tried to drag himself forward, clutching the turf. The tank came to a halt beside him, the commander got out and planted a bullet in his head at point-blank range. He took a closer look at the other dead man and returned to the tank. He slipped his pistol back into its holster and crawled up into the iron turret. The vehicle made a hundred-and-eighty-degree turn, almost on its own axis, and returned to the road, demolishing the wall at another point. Their side riding, our side foot-slogging. Under the same sky. What is the basic significance of all this? The Party leads our righteous struggle, Hitler directs their heinous crimes. The leaders of the Whites are ideologists of 'the church militant' and out-and-out traitors. The French are fighting against the occupation. Apparently the Italians are also beginning to stir. The Russians were invaded and are now getting their own back, tit for tat, and meanwhile extending the domains of revolution. But what are the English and Americans afraid of? Of the Russians reaching the Atlantic? Surely the time has passed when men believed in self-sacrifice for humanitarian ideals? Millions of us have been engaged in a life-and-death struggle, all of us with right on our side; anyone who doubts this must face a court-martial; so it has been since time immemorial. The Germans threw sixteen villagers into blazing houses and they were burned alive. "Could you call that funny?" That was Vadnal's retort, when I was saying that basically war is something ridiculous. I tried to imagine myself one of those German soldiers, and could not. It is that blasted opera of Hitler's, that must of necessity be drama and tragedy. The end of the war is getting nearer and nearer, but we are taking an increasingly superficial view of it and not probing deeper for its true significance.

A cat walks along the wall of a building opposite my hotel in Spain, looking around on every side, listening to every sound, watching every movement. Once upon a time a cat was crossing a yard in Ribnica. Thirty years ago. A cat must know every movement in its vicinity, so that it can decide whether the way ahead is safe or not. For no other reason. A cat does not take part in warfare. And no one can force it to. But I have mounted the tiger of war and cannot now dismount. I cannot help thinking but I can tell no one the trend of my thoughts. My deliberations are of no interest to anyone and of no benefit either, least of all to me. Am I a sick man, maybe? I don't think so. At this very moment, the police somewhere are torturing a political prisoner, who perhaps shares my views but cannot say so. And things are going to get worse. Brave men are embarrassed by their bravery. It is the cowards who most love writing about war, and they are the ones who will foul up any possibility of true understanding with their lofty notions. Only sorrow remains for us; humor is unseemly. We cannot turn into cats. Like our folk songs, we must be muted, for there is too much harsh reality about us. Don't take it badly if I give the next war a miss: I'll send my excuses. I'd happily get off this progress express if I didn't have to take along a minuet for a twenty-five-shot guitar.

Es lo mismo, es lo mismo, Señor. Whether Cain slew Abel, or Abel Cain. If we are far enough away, we can view the whole thing as a ballet. When I was hit in the hand, I did not notice it at first but probably pulled a very funny face when I realized what had happened. That was no doubt a fine leap and pirouette I pulled off when I got a bullet in the leg. Oh, the hilarious knockabout of that winter hike with blisters bleeding, when I could not decide which of my feet gave me the most pain. And the supreme drollness, the cream of the jest, that the distance I marched was already determined when I told Dolnichar Freud was not a Marxist. In all, a comic ballet, to the accompaniment of twenty-five-shot guitars . . . I see them . . . I hear them . . . I dance to their sound like a clown . . . where am I! I must have dozed off. I was in the army, wasn't I? Why can a man not express in words that profound understanding which is revealed to him in the moments between waking and sleeping? I walked the long-drawn-out, elastic, muddy road . . . somewhere near the town of Ogulin . . . one tepid January . . . from the brushwood we came to a clearing . . . a grassy expanse . . . littered with corpses.

I lie here—and that unending road runs on within me . . . once the road lay still and I moved along it on these soles . . . but really and truly it's all the same, *es lo mismo,* all the same whether the Earth goes around the Sun, or the Sun around the Earth. It requires the same effort.

"When I go over them again in my memory [the strange events of his
life] I sometimes wonder whether it was not a dream."
Anatole France

"Reason demands that the bitter lessons of the bloody history of the last war
must not be forgotten."
V. Chuikov, *The End of the Third Reich*

"How do we convey information? We convey information by means of
signs, living speech, written articles, printed articles, and pictures which
may be motionless or moving."
D. P. Mrvoš, *Propaganda, Advertising*

"Paper serves various purposes. We are interested first of all in how paper
can be used in printing, or writing, or drawing."
Ibidem

"I, Herodotus of Halicarnassus, am here setting forth my history, that time
may not draw the color from what man has brought into being . . ."
Herodotus, *Histories*

"One of the peculiarities of modern civilization is our awareness of time."
Lewis Mumford

"He dozed off and slept soundly, a happy sleep with no wild dreams or
consciousness, like that of children in their cradle, just men and the dead."
J. Jučič, *The Flower and the Garden*

"Let us say that Betelgeuse, the great star in the constellation of Orion,
explodes on the seventeenth of March in the year 2000. Three hundred years will pass
before the light from the explosion reaches the Earth."
G. J. Whitrow

8

A wide amphitheater of gentle hills, vineyards, cottages, vine-covered slopes, ripening cherries, apricots, apples, roads, cart tracks, footpaths, trellises, homesteads, birds singing in the newborn morning when the earth's fragrance rises to greet the first warmth of the sky: Bela Krajina's casual drift into spring. The war often comes to a halt, like an enormous broken-down machine and then suddenly surprises the combatants with one of its steely, callous jokes. Now, however, we had our lookouts posted all around, in Gorjanci and on the Kolpa River, and there would be no more rude surprises. We were having a long, pleasant spell of blue skies and warm weather. Green of succulent young growth, brown and red of the dry soil between the earthed-up rows of vines, gray of old wood in the fields. Two little white clouds against the pure blue of the sky. The air throbs with the steady drone of bumblebees in the foliage. Titmice were building their nests in a wild cherry tree with small yellow-green fruit. A blackbird was perched high up in a tall old cherry tree on the bank, warbling his notes as loud and clear as if they were coming through an amplifier. Jays, thrushes. New vine shoots winding about an old stock. A squirrel in the one and only pine tree. Spring in Bela Krajina. A name with a pleasant ring: Bela Krajina, le Pays Blanc, Paese Bianco, the White Country, das Weisse Land, País Blanco. Here, a couple of weeks earlier, all the hillsides had been white with cherry blossoms. There were four of us making our way two abreast uphill. I had Tilen beside me. He was talking about the state of hostilities, hardly a topic for such a fine morning. Hitler had given orders for the complete destruction of Germany. A fat lot I cared what tragedies were running in the German homeland. They certainly do not have a land like this; that is why they have been pushing south ever since Roman times. We shall meet at the crossroads. I leaned against an old wooden crucifix and surveyed the valley spread out below us. Rocks, bushes, red earth, drone of bees and insects, chirping of birds. In a building somewhere above us, voices were singing a song popular during the Spanish Civil War: "Where are you going, my swarthy senorita?" On the silvery gray wood of the crucifix a man stripped, nailed to the crossed beams, hangs dead and bleeding, with what appears to be a smile on his face. A strident tenor was singing in broken Spanish: "*Di me, donde vas, morena . . . di me, donde vas, solada . . . di me, donde vas nelas tres de la mañana?*" He had an Italian accent. "*Vado en career de Sevilla . . .*" INRI. None of the occupying forces had set foot here since the Italian surrender, though the Whites had made one short-lived attack on Črnomelj. This was our own liberated territory, our provisional government. Between Gorjanci and the Kolpa River. Here was the General Staff of the Army of National Liberation and the partisan forces of Slovenia. Here was the Executive Committee of the Liberation Front. Here was the Council for the National Liberation of Slovenia. The Central Committee of the Communist Party. The party's agitprop committee. The Slovene National Theater. Workers producing scenery and costumes for their productions. The Liberation Front Radio. A training school for officers. A choir of disabled veterans. Allied missions. Transit points for allied airmen and prisoners of war who had broken out of the German camps. Storekeepers. An economic commission. The OZNA—national defense units. Hospitals. An airfield. Printing presses. The Austrian mission. The Czech mission. Courses. Schools. A commission for religious affairs. Another for the institution of a people's government. Slovenia's future ministries in embryo. Local headquarters. Headquarters of the Bela Krajina district. Somewhere hereabouts were the strictly guarded secrets of state and war, concrete bunkers in well concealed locations, buildings under constant guard, centers of police, intelligence, and counterintelligence work. The supervisory commission. Whole units came here on leave. S.K.O.J., N.K.O.J. Courses in first aid and nursing. Places where artists could produce paintings or woodcuts, where writers and poets could compose poems or one-act plays, speeches for meetings, articles for periodicals or radio programs. The presses were turning out songbooks, sketches, linocuts, newspapers, announcements, reports. Musicians were writing songs, both solo and choral. Choirs were rehearsing for concerts. Dispatch riders, communications with Styria, Gorenjska, Carinthia, Primorje, Italy, France, Austria and the south of Yugoslavia. English, American, and, later, Russian aircraft were flying in arms and ammunition. The English were also supplying food, uniforms, and cigarettes. The whole territory of the infant state was a hive of unseen activity, an ant's nest of politics, schemes, intrigue, entertainment, sessions, meetings, celebrations, training of cadres, experimentation, tax raising, and the solution of present and future problems. Here at least, the end of hostilities was already in the air.

But the war was only approaching its culmination. Anton once put it like this: "When, during a war, you have the feeling that there is no distinction between eternity and a moment of time, between a drop of water and the ocean, between a whirlwind and a sigh, that large and small no longer exist, when there is an atmosphere of spontaneous general expectation, then the day is coming when we can say that the war is over. On that one single day, you should sense that consummation. What an event in the fantastic dreams of every individual! Later, the bitter reality brings us back to earth. For in the end, absolutely nothing has changed. The barriers are down but there is still no access."

Titmice. Crickets. A cloud of midges. Heat of the sun.

Down below, there was a road running alongside the river. A bridge had been upended by an explosion which had left it erect like a tower on the bank. Someone was playing an accordion in the farmhouse above us.

Our talk was dull and boring as we made our way upward.

We found several partisans milling around the house.

It was built on such a steep hillside that, while it stood three stories on the lower slope, its rear entrance came in at the top floor. Benches and tables stood in front of the cellar downstairs. Here, the man with the accordion was sitting and playing. The partisans were wearing English uniforms. Some of them had had the trousers restyled as riding-breeches. On the table stood a great wine jar and a glass that circulated among the drinkers. After draining his glass, each man refilled it for his neighbor in accordance with local custom. There were a few farm girls from the valley. The lady of the house was standing in the open doorway of the cellar. My three companions relaxed on a bench and I walked on through the crowded courtyard with its fine view of the vine-covered slopes. Partisans were approaching along another path. We were all by this time wearing more or less the same uniform. One group rose and left. Others around the accordionist were singing: "Up beyond the lake . . . past the village green . . . my old home once stood . . ."

391

Some clumsy idiot gave me a poke in the ribs and I turned around to give him a piece of my mind but to my surprise and delight found Anton facing me. He was in an English uniform, with a Bren gun slung over his shoulder. His boots were new and he was wearing white wool socks. He had a new forage cap and a large leather kit bag. His manner was jaunty and bantering as he examined me closely. "Well, we're both in slightly better shape than the last time I saw you!" He had put on quite a bit of weight and acquired a healthy tan. As for myself, I was simply glad to be alive. The high building, a cross between a prehistoric cave and a bird's nest, towered above us. Neither of us was in any hurry. In a few days, the war would be over, and we had survived. Although a year and a half had passed since we were last together, we felt as if we had parted only yesterday. He told me he had been doing a lot of walking, a lot of sitting too. Now he was getting dental treatment in Črnomelj. He had had four granulomas. We were beginning to get each other's flavor again: Anton had the tang of tough, bitter chicory.

There were six of us sitting in a room on the top floor, chatting in pairs. The landlord, an acquaintance of Anton's, had been particularly generous to us. He brought a capacious earthenware dish to the table with pigs' shoulders smoked and boiled and carved in great slices. Like cannibals, we bit into the tasty meat. We also had a loaf of bread on a wooden platter. Our friendly Belukrainian host brought a full wine jar to set beside the one we had already half emptied.

What a room! What a climax to our visit! Were we in a house or a ship's cabin? The walls were faced with a dark timber that glowed black in the brilliant light from the long, low window. Those down below were singing, talking, and generally kicking up a din. The window gave us an extensive panorama of the lower slopes and valley. The yellow wine in the glass reflected ceiling and windows in dim and bright distortions. So the war was over. We were all penniless but rich. We were short of nothing, though we might not realize it. There were some unpleasant rumors but what did they amount to anyway? Drink up and forget it. After what we had been through, we could surely face up to anything.

But what if it came to a conflict between Russia and America? Then we'd be really up the creek. "It's out of the question, at least for the time being," Anton said. "The Americans have too much on their plate with the Japanese in the

Pacific and the Russians must first bring order to the enormous territories they have occupied. A new age will come and it won't be pleasant. Both sides are too strong to make peace and at the moment too weak to make war."

A bee flew in at the open window and settled on the bread. For her, life was easy. Her kind survived without progress. But periods of conflict still awaited us. Our line of development had taken us from proto-communism to the slave-owning system, then to feudalism, then bourgeois society, which had outgrown itself to become high capitalism, but a revolutionary leap forward had brought us to socialism, which would develop into the classless society, into communism, in other words back to our beginnings. In Anton's words, the quest for paradise lost.

Tengo miedo. I'm afraid.

Once upon a time fear stalked the earth.

From down below comes the sound of a popular song: *Muchachita de Madrid.* For tourists from all over the world. Tourists of the world, unite!

Once upon a time fear stalked the earth. Fear of ice and frost, fear of hunger, of dinosaurs, of enormous beasts, fear of your cannibal neighbor. Then came fear of the slavemaster with his whip. Ghosts, gods, natural hazards, passionate prejudices and cunning of rulers: all this merged into an awe of the Creator. Fear of the man who will oppress, rob, and kill you, who will burn you as a heretic at the stake. God put on the garb of the nation and state, bringing fear of the man who will hang, shoot, or behead you as a traitor, fear of the man who will imprison you, torment you in jail, and slowly dispose of you. Fear of the man who will denounce you. And in the last apocalypse of our overcrowded planet, there will come fear of hunger, of suffocation in the poisoned air; then property will be of no account but all will try to live longer, to last that little bit longer. Some old folk have seen a number of wars. But no one knows what sort of a war is being cooked up by the experts who have mastered atomic physics. Fear of unknown destruction. The last shudder of horror.

The great ones of the Earth are still going on blabbing about progress. After them the deluge! In our schools, they are still reciting the fairy tale about Videk and the good spider who wove a shirt for him. The great ones of the Earth bid us be optimists. What if their millions of slaves suddenly realized the position their planet was in! What greater fear could there be? Millions of slaves refusing to obey! No longer willing to build yachts and palaces, or produce toys for the pampered scions of the great, no longer browbeaten by the police, but alive to the cosmic terror and mutinously defying authority. Look, if it doesn't suit you, go and swell the ranks of the flower people! Take LSD! Join in the orgies! Go to jail! But don't think such thoughts and don't spread them around! Flesh, slave, serf, rebel, proletarian, political prisoner of socialism! Drop this quest for the true face of history! Don't engage in dialectics! Ignore the discrepancy between theoretical slogans and everyday practice! Write hermetic poems, paint incomprehensible pictures, don the mantle of the sage, practice double-think, and search, Fido, search for your bone . . . He who seeks shall find. He who digs a pit for his neighbor is the master of his own destiny. Eat, drink, screw away, forget the rest, live for today!

I have come to my senses now, as I gaze at the tips of my yellow slip-ons of Spanish leather. Down below they are singing "*Guantanamera, Guantanamera . . .*" In the Hungarian revolt, the inhabitants recognized members of the secret police by their yellow shoes. The Russian tanks soon settled that affair. In Berlin, they fired at workers in the name of the revolution of the proletariat. They occupied Czechoslovakia. Has the whole world gone topsy-turvy? The Americans were happy to have the world's attention diverted from Vietnam. America, the factory of still-unexploded dreams, dreads two things only: revolution (something in theory inadmissible, since "no one is as content as the American worker") and a fall in the international value of the dollar. The East fears one thing only: the dialectic of continuous revolution; as far as the currency is concerned, we wage a constant struggle against inflation and we learn from our mistakes.

An ancient Roman writer divided mankind's tools into three categories: dumb tools (of wood or iron); tools that moo, bleat, and neigh; and talking tools, or slaves. The dumb tools have found their voice, the whole world throbs with their din: streets, cities, factories, seas, and sky are filled with the roar of machines. How many decibels can a man stand without going mad? The animal type is on the way out and artificial cows, horses, and sheep are taking over. Only the talking tools survive, though no one dare address them as such. The mobilized talking tools move in on Vietnam or Czechoslovakia. And the common concern of all is the liberation of mankind. Anyone who doubts this will soon lose his own freedom.

For the third time I hear them down below singing "*Cuando calienta el sol.*" Something should be done, but how?

What did Leibniz gain in his last hour, from his innocent faith in the orderliness of this world? At any rate, my cat is happier than him. And what am I getting from this senseless brooding? Only a silent dread that all is competely disorganized; only I dare not tell anyone, for I would just cause them harm. What should I say to that fine cat, Florian, when he is insistently demanding his ration of pluck? "Guzzling, idling, rutting, that's all you think of, you feline beast!" And it's true. Florian is a cat who walks by himself, not a tool for the blind forces of the universe. What about a dog? Well, we could call him a guard of sorts, a kind of home defense, trained to growl and bark at the enemy, probably more loyal than the garbage that passed for our staff in 1941. And what can a cat do in a house where there are no mice? Love me or love me not? Stupid question. It needs me. And because it needs me I like it. We are all glad when someone needs us. But we cannot help hating what we need. I need money and I hate it because I can't live without it. A child needs me and I love him, but what about him? Deep down? Sooner or later? No, no, I don't care. I exist, I don't exist, I dream, I think, I see. When the time comes for your dying dose of exhaustion after your long road, you think you are arriving at your goal. Music can only express itself in sound. A tango, "*A media luz...*" in the semidarkness. Order comes in squares of scattered streets. The blossoming cherries have disappeared. Caesar is coming. Balding, with legions of tourists at his shoulder. Well-trained game dogs marching to fight for the holy word, professionals, a pretty sight... *A media luz*... Calm benevolence, fitters singing Anton in fur cap, guitars firing... statues in stone in bronze in ivory black cap with death's head I found it let's have a bit of peace a living fair-haired doll the atom *noche de estrellas* Anton for years and years careening after a fur cap a yellow ring he isn't scared of it we have eaten death big-uddered goddess of the chase a drop a soup a cat worry teaches flowers invention of yellow ice Istria Bitter has taken off for other planets they will all come for other planets all for departure to Ljubljana... now I'm flying over the Rhône estuary, the yellow-gray waters of the polluted river cutting into the clear blue of the Mediterranean... river branches in the Camargue delta... green islands... the Côte d'Azur... a highway choked with cars... fish and bird have taken off for other planets... Africa isn't really too far away... Someone is waiting for me at the crossroads, but who is in such a hurry . . .? Neither of us . . . but the road between us cannot wait. He dies at the crossroads with a smile on his lips.

It is dark inside the vineyard cottage with a brilliant blinding light in the windows. Down below we can hear the tedious drone of a choir

> . . . the waters in heaven are chafing
> as they wait to be poured into a jug . . .
> somewhere a bright star is waiting . . .
> to be hung up again in the sky . . .
> again in the sky-y-y-y . . .

Each man drank and poured a glass from the wine jug to place before his neighbor, as is the custom. I watched Anton's hand with a Camel cigarette, describing slow circles as an accompaniment to the conversation, all its movements addressed to the listeners. He was running out of words but I did not realize it. A wasp settled on the rim of the glass and sipped the wine; it would soon be fuddled with drink . . . and life would never be the same again. The end of the war was in sight; there would be an end to that folly. The titmice were holding a meeting high up in a cherry tree. Somewhere in the vineyards of Bela Krajina. One sort of enemy would perish. But we need enemies. Without them there is no struggle. Stalin's purges were no mere accident. When the revolution has destroyed the enemy outside, it starts to look within. If it can find no other, it becomes its own enemy. Revolution breeds revolution as the plant grows from seed, the ear from the plant to scatter seed that is other and different from that which gave it being; here is the secret of the dialectic. Human society is not like that of the bees, ants, or termites; they are established and do not develop. But man has invented speech and with it conserves experience. Experience enables him to change his environment, to assault nature; speech has liberated man from nature. Poets often do not realize this. Yet they fear hubris and superficiality. The Russians killed Tukhachevsky, the Germans killed Rommel. The troops do not brood about this. Our forces are blocking the German retreat. The Chetniks are fleeing northward, hoping to escape to Italy. And what about the Home Guard? They cannot get away. Now they are really up the creek, what with betraying Allied airmen to the Germans, or even murdering them themselves. How many days to go? You don't ask questions in the army. Others are in a hurry now. Anton has his joke: "At least this time I'll be on the winning side." Old memories come back, memories of the retreat from Spain to France. "Then Žarko said, 'See you in the next war!' There was something special about that fellow. He was intelligent, a deep thinker but a bit of a show-off too; some people thought he was altogether too high-and-mighty. He would start brooding, hatching up some idea purely his own, and you would feel he had his own peculiar view of everything. Then he would suddenly come out with the most unmitigated rot. Tall he was, slim, well-built, and moved like a cat. The women couldn't leave him alone; they were like wasps around a jam pot. He would gaze into the distance . . . far into the distance . . . right through the question . . . then he would come back to earth again, always with a laugh, always blurting out some inappropriate remark. I couldn't describe him . . . he was like a willow branch you couldn't break, a chord of music you couldn't catch . . . but he shed his own inner glow on all those around him. Believe it or not, I can never bring myself to think of him as dead; in his own way he still lives on."

Meanwhile death had already laid a new snare.

Only a few more seconds and that most brilliant day would yield to night.

The words flowed, the songs rang out, the bees hummed, the sunlight fell in a glowing golden oblong on the wooden floorboards, trying to sear through them. The whole world was gathering strength for a new life. The trees had shed their blossoms and were beginning to make fruit. Words would ring out. The songs would take off for Ljubljana. Let's drink one glass more. Like a chord of music.

He was lying there on the bench where we had laid him, clinically dead, dead beyond recall, killed, shot. People crowded around him. His glass lay overturned on the table in a transparent pool of wine. His cigarette still smoldered on the edge of the table.

Slowly, I withdrew from the room to a patio cut out of the hillside behind the house. I wandered aimlessly, drawn higher and higher up the cart track between the vineyards in the warm sunlight.

On and on I went.

Up above the vineyards, in a grassy clearing among the trees, I found a house with its doors open wide. There were no panes in the window frames. I went in. There was no one there. The hall was empty, the rooms were empty, there was no furniture, all the doors were either wide open or taken off their hinges and laid against the walls. My footsteps echoed hollowly in the airy living room; the back door had also disappeared. Through the bare window frames came the sound of birds twittering and a greenish light filtered through the trees into the house. And all the walls were covered with pictures, all of them painted on glass, with sunny chrome yellow the dominant hue, here and there flecked with orange or lemon tints, paler in places and elsewhere like burnished gold, with saints of amiable countenance in glowing haloes, land-scapes lit by mighty suns, violet and blue sheen of birds' plumage on the yel-low background, red and brown and yellow rings, in a tidily kept house with scrubbed floors and whitewashed ceilings, and on the chalk-white walls, the ebb and flow of yellow surfaces, spheres and rings, sheaves and stacks, of green belts, of red and blue cockerels in the bright green-yellow light reflected from outside; on all the walls, nothing but pictures, all of them painted on glass, brown smiling faces, yellow solar orbs, shining rings, waves of green, from one room to the next nothing but pictures on the walls, all of them painted on glass, one single green-yellow melody, people and landscapes and suns and hillsides and glowing haloes, one painting after another in an unending line, an eternity of circumambulation, a yellow minuet for guitar in twenty-five shots. Through the yawning doorways I wandered around from room to room, unable to change the direction of this monotonous circuit. On and on I walked, and the day seemed to have no end. Now the last word had been spoken, now there was no further danger lurking and no promises could be made. Now everyone had departed for distant parts. Now the past was behind us and the future was yet to come. Now the sunlight fused with the humming of the bees and the warbling of the birds in a transparent fluid that bore the body onward on its long, steady, circling waves.

He was in mid-sentence when his body stiffened as if he were about to take wing. He looked at me with a bright, curious, astonished gaze, then slumped down. I took hold of him, without understanding what was going on. It was not like him to play such strange tricks.

Later on, we discovered that one of a group of partisans sitting in the room below had banged his old Italian automatic on the floor, releasing a volley of bullets, a whole magazine, that had shot up past his head into the ceiling. Penetrating the wooden ceiling, the stream of bullets had accidentally lodged in a certain body. The body was Anton's. It's these automatics, you can't trust them, you know.

He still lived a few minutes. He did not let anyone undress him and examine his wounds; he realized perfectly well there was nothing that could be done. He was quite calm and collected and even tried to smile when the end came. The man whose gun had caused the trouble came up in despair but he was not allowed to speak. No explanations were necessary now, words could alter nothing. We laid the wounded man on a bench. He looked at me and I heard his inner voice: "Well, this is my lot; you can see how it is. You remember what I told you about the bulls of Andalusia who live for one great day? What a good thing we met today, that you saw it all, that you're here."

He had one arm stretched out along his side and the other pressed tight against his breast.

When at the end he tried to laugh, he managed to say only, "See . . ." But I knew he wanted to repeat that wisecrack, "See you in the next war!" Someone closed his eyelids. I have no idea why.

I am waiting for my departure to Ljubljana.

But where from, where from? Certainly not from the house with the paintings of glass. There, I am still going around in circles from room to room.

I am leaving El Arenal, I shall be off quite soon.

Even now I can hardly stand the endless repetition of that song *"Cuando calienta el sol."*

Now I remember exactly what he was saying when he met his end.

With the capitulation of Italy, he could once again, after long months walk the streets in broad daylight. He felt as if he had come back to the planet after a long absence. He gazed in wonder at the trees, the green branches, the hurrying crowds, the houses and their window boxes.

Obviously, their Italian and German brothers had inherited the records and dossiers of the Yugoslav police. For them, Anton with his lurid past would have been a prize catch. But he went to ground in his illegal printing shop. He turned out articles and war slogans and listened to noises while hiding in that cellar where he could not tell night from day. Then something began to wither in him, something that had to die if he was to survive. He began to grow into something else, something monotonous, something vegetable; an animal was slowly transformed into a vegetable. Vegetables do not walk the streets. The man did not realize what was happening to him. Only when he felt the warm breath of the city street on his forehead again did he tremble and begin to wonder. Quite slowly he started to recover his old self, for now he no longer needed to live that underground, vegetable life. All his dead emotional tissue began to revive; it itched, it hurt, it gave no peace. How hard it had been to quiet emotion, and how much greater effort was now needed to restore it! Was it really possible to grasp a fresh green leaf? To rub the rough bark? To address a passing stranger? Are those clouds in the sky real? Maybe they are a dream—or perhaps that anonymous existence was a dream, an illusion. Moments come all the time when a man pinches himself and asks, am I really alive? He fades and revives at every step of his journey. Some things must happen so that he can understand others. Sunset will come, the sun goes down . . . and the moon is already up. Footsteps. Talk. People have families. They have cats and dogs. They drink coffee. They do not know I am still only half alive. The body avoids sudden change. It wants to live the life it is accustomed to. It resists this sort of dual existence.

"Well, shortly after that, we were both leaving Ljubljana together."

In 2010, the Slovenian Book Agency took a bold step toward solving the problem of how few literary works are now translated into English, initiating a program to provide financial support for a series dedicated to Slovenian literature at Dalkey Archive Press. Partially evolving from a relationship that Dalkey Archive and the Vilenica International Literary Festival had developed a few years previously, this program will go on to ensure that both classic and contemporary works from Slovenian are brought into English, while allowing the Press to undertake marketing efforts far exceeding what publishers can normally provide for works in translation.

Slovenia has always held a great reverence for literature, with the Slovenian national identity being forged through its fiction and poetry long before the foundation of the contemporary Republic: "It is precisely literature that has in some profound, subtle sense safeguarded the Slovenian community from the imperialistic appetites of stronger and more expansive nations in the region," writes critic Andrej Inkret. Never insular, Slovenian writing has long been in dialogue with the great movements of world literature, from the romantic to the experimental, seeing the literary not as distinct from the world, but as an integral means of perceiving and even amending it.

VITOMIL ZUPAN was born in Ljubljana in 1914, and is considered one of the greatest Slovenian writers of the latter half of the twentieth century. With a career spanning more than forty years and including prose, poetry, essays, drama, and screenplays, Zupan's importance to Slovenian letters cannot be underestimated. He died in 1987.

HARRY LEEMING (1920–2004) was a philologist focusing on Slavonic languages and a translator of numerous works from Slovenia.

PETROS ABATZOGLOU, *What Does Mrs. Freeman Want?*
MICHAL AJVAZ, *The Golden Age.*
The Other City.
PIERRE ALBERT-BIROT, *Grabinoulor.*
YUZ ALESHKOVSKY, *Kangaroo.*
FELIPE ALFAU, *Chromos.*
Locos.
JOÃO ALMINO, *The Book of Emotions.*
IVAN ÂNGELO, *The Celebration.*
The Tower of Glass.
DAVID ANTIN, *Talking.*
ANTÓNIO LOBO ANTUNES,
Knowledge of Hell.
The Splendor of Portugal.
ALAIN ARIAS-MISSON, *Theatre of Incest.*
IFTIKHAR ARIF AND WAQAS KHWAJA, EDS.,
Modern Poetry of Pakistan.
JOHN ASHBERY AND JAMES SCHUYLER,
A Nest of Ninnies.
ROBERT ASHLEY, *Perfect Lives.*
GABRIELA AVIGUR-ROTEM, *Heatwave and Crazy Birds.*
HEIMRAD BÄCKER, *transcript.*
DJUNA BARNES, *Ladies Almanack.*
Ryder.
JOHN BARTH, *LETTERS.*
Sabbatical.
DONALD BARTHELME, *The King.*
Paradise.
SVETISLAV BASARA, *Chinese Letter.*
RENÉ BELLETTO, *Dying.*
MARK BINELLI, *Sacco and Vanzetti Must Die!*
ANDREI BITOV, *Pushkin House.*
ANDREJ BLATNIK, *You Do Understand.*
LOUIS PAUL BOON, *Chapel Road.*
My Little War.
Summer in Termuren.
ROGER BOYLAN, *Killoyle.*
IGNÁCIO DE LOYOLA BRANDÃO,
Anonymous Celebrity.
The Good-Bye Angel.
Teeth under the Sun.
Zero.
BONNIE BREMSER,
Troia: Mexican Memoirs.
CHRISTINE BROOKE-ROSE, *Amalgamemnon.*
BRIGID BROPHY, *In Transit.*
MEREDITH BROSNAN, *Mr. Dynamite.*
GERALD L. BRUNS, *Modern Poetry and the Idea of Language.*
EVGENY BUNIMOVICH AND J. KATES, EDS.,
Contemporary Russian Poetry: An Anthology.
GABRIELLE BURTON, *Heartbreak Hotel.*
MICHEL BUTOR, *Degrees.*
Mobile.
Portrait of the Artist as a Young Ape.
G. CABRERA INFANTE, *Infante's Inferno.*
Three Trapped Tigers.
JULIETA CAMPOS,
The Fear of Losing Eurydice.
ANNE CARSON, *Eros the Bittersweet.*
ORLY CASTEL-BLOOM, *Dolly City.*
CAMILO JOSÉ CELA, *Christ versus Arizona.*
The Family of Pascual Duarte.
The Hive.
LOUIS-FERDINAND CÉLINE, *Castle to Castle.*
Conversations with Professor Y.
London Bridge.

Normance.
North.
Rigadoon.
HUGO CHARTERIS, *The Tide Is Right.*
JEROME CHARYN, *The Tar Baby.*
ERIC CHEVILLARD, *Demolishing Nisard.*
MARC CHOLODENKO, *Mordechai Schamz.*
JOSHUA COHEN, *Witz.*
EMILY HOLMES COLEMAN, *The Shutter of Snow.*
ROBERT COOVER, *A Night at the Movies.*
STANLEY CRAWFORD, *Log of the S.S. The Mrs Unguentine.*
Some Instructions to My Wife.
ROBERT CREELEY, *Collected Prose.*
RENÉ CREVEL, *Putting My Foot in It.*
RALPH CUSACK, *Cadenza.*
SUSAN DAITCH, *L.C.*
Storytown.
NICHOLAS DELBANCO,
The Count of Concord.
Sherbrookes.
NIGEL DENNIS, *Cards of Identity.*
PETER DIMOCK, *A Short Rhetoric for Leaving the Family.*
ARIEL DORFMAN, *Konfidenz.*
COLEMAN DOWELL,
The Houses of Children.
Island People.
Too Much Flesh and Jabez.
ARKADII DRAGOMOSHCHENKO, *Dust.*
RIKKI DUCORNET, *The Complete Butcher's Tales.*
The Fountains of Neptune.
The Jade Cabinet.
The One Marvelous Thing.
Phosphor in Dreamland.
The Stain.
The Word "Desire."
WILLIAM EASTLAKE, *The Bamboo Bed.*
Castle Keep.
Lyric of the Circle Heart.
JEAN ECHENOZ, *Chopin's Move.*
STANLEY ELKIN, *A Bad Man.*
Boswell: A Modern Comedy.
Criers and Kibitzers, Kibitzers and Criers.
The Dick Gibson Show.
The Franchiser.
George Mills.
The Living End.
The MacGuffin.
The Magic Kingdom.
Mrs. Ted Bliss.
The Rabbi of Lud.
Van Gogh's Room at Arles.
FRANÇOIS EMMANUEL, *Invitation to a Voyage.*
ANNIE ERNAUX, *Cleaned Out.*
LAUREN FAIRBANKS, *Muzzle Thyself.*
Sister Carrie.
LESLIE A. FIEDLER, *Love and Death in the American Novel.*
JUAN FILLOY, *Op Oloop.*
GUSTAVE FLAUBERT, *Bouvard and Pécuchet.*
KASS FLEISHER, *Talking out of School.*
FORD MADOX FORD,
The March of Literature.
JON FOSSE, *Aliss at the Fire.*
Melancholy.
MAX FRISCH, *I'm Not Stiller.*

SELECTED DALKEY ARCHIVE PAPERBACKS

FOR A FULL LIST OF PUBLICATIONS, VISIT:
www.dalkeyarchive.com

◨

SELECTED DALKEY ARCHIVE PAPERBACKS

PETROS ABATZOGLOU, *What Does Mrs. Freeman Want?*
MICHAL AJVAZ, *The Golden Age.*
The Other City.
PIERRE ALBERT-BIROT, *Grabinoulor.*
YUZ ALESHKOVSKY, *Kangaroo.*
FELIPE ALFAU, *Chromos.*
Locos.
JOÃO ALMINO, *The Book of Emotions.*
IVAN ÂNGELO, *The Celebration.*
The Tower of Glass.
DAVID ANTIN, *Talking.*
ANTÓNIO LOBO ANTUNES,
Knowledge of Hell.
The Splendor of Portugal.
ALAIN ARIAS-MISSON, *Theatre of Incest.*
IFTIKHAR ARIF AND WAQAS KHWAJA, EDS.,
Modern Poetry of Pakistan.
JOHN ASHBERY AND JAMES SCHUYLER,
A Nest of Ninnies.
ROBERT ASHLEY, *Perfect Lives.*
GABRIELA AVIGUR-ROTEM, *Heatwave and Crazy Birds.*
HEIMRAD BÄCKER, *transcript.*
DJUNA BARNES, *Ladies Almanack.*
Ryder.
JOHN BARTH, *LETTERS.*
Sabbatical.
DONALD BARTHELME, *The King.*
Paradise.
SVETISLAV BASARA, *Chinese Letter.*
RENÉ BELLETTO, *Dying.*
MARK BINELLI, *Sacco and Vanzetti Must Die!*
ANDREI BITOV, *Pushkin House.*
ANDREJ BLATNIK, *You Do Understand.*
LOUIS PAUL BOON, *Chapel Road.*
My Little War.
Summer in Termuren.
ROGER BOYLAN, *Killoyle.*
IGNÁCIO DE LOYOLA BRANDÃO,
Anonymous Celebrity.
The Good-Bye Angel.
Teeth under the Sun.
Zero.
BONNIE BREMSER,
Troia: Mexican Memoirs.
CHRISTINE BROOKE-ROSE, *Amalgamemnon.*
BRIGID BROPHY, *In Transit.*
MEREDITH BROSNAN, *Mr. Dynamite.*
GERALD L. BRUNS, *Modern Poetry and the Idea of Language.*
EVGENY BUNIMOVICH AND J. KATES, EDS.,
Contemporary Russian Poetry: An Anthology.
GABRIELLE BURTON, *Heartbreak Hotel.*
MICHEL BUTOR, *Degrees.*
Mobile.
Portrait of the Artist as a Young Ape.
G. CABRERA INFANTE, *Infante's Inferno.*
Three Trapped Tigers.
JULIETA CAMPOS,
The Fear of Losing Eurydice.
ANNE CARSON, *Eros the Bittersweet.*
ORLY CASTEL-BLOOM, *Dolly City.*
CAMILO JOSÉ CELA, *Christ versus Arizona.*
The Family of Pascual Duarte.
The Hive.
LOUIS-FERDINAND CÉLINE, *Castle to Castle.*
Conversations with Professor Y.
London Bridge.

Normance.
North.
Rigadoon.
HUGO CHARTERIS, *The Tide Is Right.*
JEROME CHARYN, *The Tar Baby.*
ERIC CHEVILLARD, *Demolishing Nisard.*
MARC CHOLODENKO, *Mordechai Schamz.*
JOSHUA COHEN, *Witz.*
EMILY HOLMES COLEMAN, *The Shutter of Snow.*
ROBERT COOVER, *A Night at the Movies.*
STANLEY CRAWFORD, *Log of the S.S. The Mrs Unguentine.*
Some Instructions to My Wife.
ROBERT CREELEY, *Collected Prose.*
RENÉ CREVEL, *Putting My Foot in It.*
RALPH CUSACK, *Cadenza.*
SUSAN DAITCH, *L.C.*
Storytown.
NICHOLAS DELBANCO,
The Count of Concord.
Sherbrookes.
NIGEL DENNIS, *Cards of Identity.*
PETER DIMOCK, *A Short Rhetoric for Leaving the Family.*
ARIEL DORFMAN, *Konfidenz.*
COLEMAN DOWELL,
The Houses of Children.
Island People.
Too Much Flesh and Jabez.
ARKADII DRAGOMOSHCHENKO, *Dust.*
RIKKI DUCORNET, *The Complete Butcher's Tales.*
The Fountains of Neptune.
The Jade Cabinet.
The One Marvelous Thing.
Phosphor in Dreamland.
The Stain.
The Word "Desire."
WILLIAM EASTLAKE, *The Bamboo Bed.*
Castle Keep.
Lyric of the Circle Heart.
JEAN ECHENOZ, *Chopin's Move.*
STANLEY ELKIN, *A Bad Man.*
Boswell: A Modern Comedy.
Criers and Kibitzers, Kibitzers and Criers.
The Dick Gibson Show.
The Franchiser.
George Mills.
The Living End.
The MacGuffin.
The Magic Kingdom.
Mrs. Ted Bliss.
The Rabbi of Lud.
Van Gogh's Room at Arles.
FRANÇOIS EMMANUEL, *Invitation to a Voyage.*
ANNIE ERNAUX, *Cleaned Out.*
LAUREN FAIRBANKS, *Muzzle Thyself.*
Sister Carrie.
LESLIE A. FIEDLER, *Love and Death in the American Novel.*
JUAN FILLOY, *Op Oloop.*
GUSTAVE FLAUBERT, *Bouvard and Pécuchet.*
KASS FLEISHER, *Talking out of School.*
FORD MADOX FORD,
The March of Literature.
JON FOSSE, *Aliss at the Fire.*
Melancholy.
MAX FRISCH, *I'm Not Stiller.*

FOR A FULL LIST OF PUBLICATIONS, VISIT:
www.dalkeyarchive.com

Man in the Holocene.
CARLOS FUENTES, *Christopher Unborn.*
Distant Relations.
Terra Nostra.
Where the Air Is Clear.
WILLIAM GADDIS, *J R.*
The Recognitions.
JANICE GALLOWAY, *Foreign Parts.*
The Trick Is to Keep Breathing.
WILLIAM H. GASS, *Cartesian Sonata*
and Other Novellas.
Finding a Form.
A Temple of Texts.
The Tunnel.
Willie Masters' Lonesome Wife.
GÉRARD GAVARRY, *Hoppla! 1 2 3.*
Making a Novel.
ETIENNE GILSON,
The Arts of the Beautiful.
Forms and Substances in the Arts.
C. S. GISCOMBE, *Giscome Road.*
Here.
Prairie Style.
DOUGLAS GLOVER, *Bad News of the Heart.*
The Enamoured Knight.
WITOLD GOMBROWICZ,
A Kind of Testament.
KAREN ELIZABETH GORDON,
The Red Shoes.
GEORGI GOSPODINOV, *Natural Novel.*
JUAN GOYTISOLO, *Count Julian.*
Exiled from Almost Everywhere.
Juan the Landless.
Makbara.
Marks of Identity.
PATRICK GRAINVILLE, *The Cave of Heaven.*
HENRY GREEN, *Back.*
Blindness.
Concluding.
Doting.
Nothing.
JACK GREEN, *Fire the Bastards!*
JIŘÍ GRUŠA, *The Questionnaire.*
GABRIEL GUDDING,
Rhode Island Notebook.
MELA HARTWIG, *Am I a Redundant*
Human Being?
JOHN HAWKES, *The Passion Artist.*
Whistlejacket.
ALEKSANDAR HEMON, ED.,
Best European Fiction.
AIDAN HIGGINS, *A Bestiary.*
Balcony of Europe.
Bornholm Night-Ferry.
Darkling Plain: Texts for the Air.
Flotsam and Jetsam.
Langrishe, Go Down.
Scenes from a Receding Past.
Windy Arbours.
KEIZO HINO, *Isle of Dreams.*
KAZUSHI HOSAKA, *Plainsong.*
ALDOUS HUXLEY, *Antic Hay.*
Crome Yellow.
Point Counter Point.
Those Barren Leaves.
Time Must Have a Stop.
NAOYUKI II, *The Shadow of a Blue Cat.*
MIKHAIL IOSSEL AND JEFF PARKER, EDS.,
Amerika: Russian Writers View the
United States.
DRAGO JANČAR, *The Galley Slave.*
GERT JONKE, *The Distant Sound.*

Geometric Regional Novel.
Homage to Czerny.
The System of Vienna.
JACQUES JOUET, *Mountain R.*
Savage.
Upstaged.
CHARLES JULIET, *Conversations with*
Samuel Beckett and Bram van
Velde.
MIEKO KANAI, *The Word Book.*
YORAM KANIUK, *Life on Sandpaper.*
HUGH KENNER, *The Counterfeiters.*
Flaubert, Joyce and Beckett:
The Stoic Comedians.
Joyce's Voices.
DANILO KIŠ, *Garden, Ashes.*
A Tomb for Boris Davidovich.
ANITA KONKKA, *A Fool's Paradise.*
GEORGE KONRÁD, *The City Builder.*
TADEUSZ KONWICKI, *A Minor Apocalypse.*
The Polish Complex.
MENIS KOUMANDAREAS, *Koula.*
ELAINE KRAF, *The Princess of 72nd Street.*
JIM KRUSOE, *Iceland.*
EWA KURYLUK, *Century 21.*
EMILIO LASCANO TEGUI, *On Elegance*
While Sleeping.
ERIC LAURRENT, *Do Not Touch.*
HERVÉ LE TELLIER, *The Sextine Chapel.*
A Thousand Pearls (for a Thousand
Pennies)
VIOLETTE LEDUC, *La Bâtarde.*
EDOUARD LEVÉ, *Autoportrait.*
Suicide.
SUZANNE JILL LEVINE, *The Subversive*
Scribe: Translating Latin
American Fiction.
DEBORAH LEVY, *Billy and Girl.*
Pillow Talk in Europe and Other
Places.
JOSÉ LEZAMA LIMA, *Paradiso.*
ROSA LIKSOM, *Dark Paradise.*
OSMAN LINS, *Avalovara.*
The Queen of the Prisons of Greece.
ALF MAC LOCHLAINN,
The Corpus in the Library.
Out of Focus.
RON LOEWINSOHN, *Magnetic Field(s).*
MINA LOY, *Stories and Essays of Mina Loy.*
BRIAN LYNCH, *The Winner of Sorrow.*
D. KEITH MANO, *Take Five.*
MICHELINE AHARONIAN MARCOM,
The Mirror in the Well.
BEN MARCUS,
The Age of Wire and String.
WALLACE MARKFIELD,
Teitlebaum's Window.
To an Early Grave.
DAVID MARKSON, *Reader's Block.*
Springer's Progress.
Wittgenstein's Mistress.
CAROLE MASO, *AVA.*
LADISLAV MATEJKA AND KRYSTYNA
POMORSKA, EDS.,
Readings in Russian Poetics:
Formalist and Structuralist Views.
HARRY MATHEWS,
The Case of the Persevering Maltese:
Collected Essays.
Cigarettes.
The Conversions.
The Human Country: New and

FOR A FULL LIST OF PUBLICATIONS, VISIT:
www.dalkeyarchive.com

Collected Stories.
The Journalist.
My Life in CIA.
Singular Pleasures.
The Sinking of the Odradek
  Stadium.
Tlooth.
20 Lines a Day.
JOSEPH MCELROY,
  Night Soul and Other Stories.
THOMAS MCGONIGLE,
  Going to Patchogue.
ROBERT L. MCLAUGHLIN, ED., Innovations:
  An Anthology of
  Modern & Contemporary Fiction.
ABDELWAHAB MEDDEB, Talismano.
GERHARD MEIER, Isle of the Dead.
HERMAN MELVILLE, The Confidence-Man.
AMANDA MICHALOPOULOU, I'd Like.
STEVEN MILLHAUSER,
  The Barnum Museum.
  In the Penny Arcade.
RALPH J. MILLS, JR.,
  Essays on Poetry.
MOMUS, The Book of Jokes.
CHRISTINE MONTALBETTI, Western.
OLIVE MOORE, Spleen.
NICHOLAS MOSLEY, Accident.
  Assassins.
  Catastrophe Practice.
  Children of Darkness and Light.
  Experience and Religion.
  God's Hazard.
  The Hesperides Tree.
  Hopeful Monsters.
  Imago Bird.
  Impossible Object.
  Inventing God.
  Judith.
  Look at the Dark.
  Natalie Natalia.
  Paradoxes of Peace.
  Serpent.
  Time at War.
  The Uses of Slime Mould:
    Essays of Four Decades.
WARREN MOTTE,
  Fables of the Novel: French Fiction
    since 1990.
  Fiction Now: The French Novel in
    the 21st Century.
  Oulipo: A Primer of Potential
    Literature.
GERALD MURNANE, Barley Patch.
YVES NAVARRE, Our Share of Time.
  Sweet Tooth.
DOROTHY NELSON, In Night's City.
  Tar and Feathers.
ESHKOL NEVO, Homesick.
WILFRIDO D. NOLLEDO, But for the Lovers.
FLANN O'BRIEN,
  At Swim-Two-Birds.
  At War.
  The Best of Myles.
  The Dalkey Archive.
  Further Cuttings.
  The Hard Life.
  The Poor Mouth.
  The Third Policeman.
CLAUDE OLLIER, The Mise-en-Scène.
  Wert and the Life Without End.
PATRIK OUŘEDNÍK, Europeana.

The Opportune Moment, 1855.
BORIS PAHOR, Necropolis.
FERNANDO DEL PASO,
  News from the Empire.
  Palinuro of Mexico.
ROBERT PINGET, The Inquisitory.
  Mahu or The Material.
  Trio.
A. G. PORTA, The No World Concerto.
MANUEL PUIG,
  Betrayed by Rita Hayworth.
  The Buenos Aires Affair.
  Heartbreak Tango.
RAYMOND QUENEAU, The Last Days.
  Odile.
  Pierrot Mon Ami.
  Saint Glinglin.
ANN QUIN, Berg.
  Passages.
  Three.
  Tripticks.
ISHMAEL REED,
  The Free-Lance Pallbearers.
  The Last Days of Louisiana Red.
  Ishmael Reed: The Plays.
  Juice!
  Reckless Eyeballing.
  The Terrible Threes.
  The Terrible Twos.
  Yellow Back Radio Broke-Down.
JOÃO UBALDO RIBEIRO, House of the
    Fortunate Buddhas.
JEAN RICARDOU, Place Names.
RAINER MARIA RILKE, The Notebooks of
    Malte Laurids Brigge.
JULIÁN RÍOS, The House of Ulysses.
  Larva: A Midsummer Night's Babel.
  Poundemonium.
  Procession of Shadows.
AUGUSTO ROA BASTOS, I the Supreme.
DANIËL ROBBERECHTS,
  Arriving in Avignon.
JEAN ROLIN, The Explosion of the
    Radiator Hose.
OLIVIER ROLIN, Hotel Crystal.
ALIX CLEO ROUBAUD, Alix's Journal.
JACQUES ROUBAUD, The Form of a
    City Changes Faster, Alas, Than
    the Human Heart.
  The Great Fire of London.
  Hortense in Exile.
  Hortense Is Abducted.
  The Loop.
  Mathématique:
  The Plurality of Worlds of Lewis.
  The Princess Hoppy.
  Some Thing Black.
LEON S. ROUDIEZ, French Fiction Revisited.
RAYMOND ROUSSEL, Impressions of Africa.
VEDRANA RUDAN, Night.
STIG SÆTERBAKKEN, Siamese.
LYDIE SALVAYRE, The Company of Ghosts.
  Everyday Life.
  The Lecture.
  Portrait of the Writer as a
    Domesticated Animal.
  The Power of Flies.
LUIS RAFAEL SÁNCHEZ,
  Macho Camacho's Beat.
SEVERO SARDUY, Cobra & Maitreya.
NATHALIE SARRAUTE,
  Do You Hear Them?

FOR A FULL LIST OF PUBLICATIONS, VISIT:
www.dalkeyarchive.com

Martereau.
The Planetarium.
ARNO SCHMIDT, *Collected Novellas.*
Collected Stories.
Nobodaddy's Children.
Two Novels.
ASAF SCHURR, *Motti.*
CHRISTINE SCHUTT, *Nightwork.*
GAIL SCOTT, *My Paris.*
DAMION SEARLS, *What We Were Doing*
and Where We Were Going.
JUNE AKERS SEESE,
Is This What Other Women Feel Too?
What Waiting Really Means.
BERNARD SHARE, *Inish.*
Transit.
AURELIE SHEEHAN,
Jack Kerouac Is Pregnant.
VIKTOR SHKLOVSKY, *Bowstring.*
Knight's Move.
A Sentimental Journey:
Memoirs 1917–1922.
Energy of Delusion: A Book on Plot.
Literature and Cinematography.
Theory of Prose.
Third Factory.
Zoo, or Letters Not about Love.
CLAUDE SIMON, *The Invitation.*
PIERRE SINIAC, *The Collaborators.*
KJERSTI A. SKOMSVOLD, *The Faster I Walk,*
the Smaller I Am.
JOSEF ŠKVORECKÝ, *The Engineer of*
Human Souls.
GILBERT SORRENTINO,
Aberration of Starlight.
Blue Pastoral.
Crystal Vision.
Imaginative Qualities of Actual
Things.
Mulligan Stew.
Pack of Lies.
Red the Fiend.
The Sky Changes.
Something Said.
Splendide-Hôtel.
Steelwork.
Under the Shadow.
W. M. SPACKMAN,
The Complete Fiction.
ANDRZEJ STASIUK, *Dukla.*
Fado.
GERTRUDE STEIN,
Lucy Church Amiably.
The Making of Americans.
A Novel of Thank You.
LARS SVENDSEN, *A Philosophy of Evil.*
PIOTR SZEWC, *Annihilation.*
GONÇALO M. TAVARES, *Jerusalem.*
Joseph Walser's Machine.
Learning to Pray in the Age of
Technique.
LUCIAN DAN TEODOROVICI,
Our Circus Presents . . .
NIKANOR TERATOLOGEN, *Assisted Living.*
STEFAN THEMERSON, *Hobson's Island.*
The Mystery of the Sardine.
Tom Harris.
JOHN TOOMEY, *Sleepwalker.*
JEAN-PHILIPPE TOUSSAINT,
The Bathroom.
Camera.
Monsieur.

Running Away.
Self-Portrait Abroad.
Television.
The Truth about Marie.
DUMITRU TSEPENEAG,
Hotel Europa.
The Necessary Marriage.
Pigeon Post.
Vain Art of the Fugue.
ESTHER TUSQUETS, *Stranded.*
DUBRAVKA UGRESIC,
Lend Me Your Character.
Thank You for Not Reading.
MATI UNT, *Brecht at Night.*
Diary of a Blood Donor.
Things in the Night.
ÁLVARO URIBE AND OLIVIA SEARS, EDS.,
Best of Contemporary Mexican
Fiction.
ELOY URROZ, *Friction.*
The Obstacles.
LUISA VALENZUELA, *Dark Desires and*
the Others.
He Who Searches.
MARJA-LIISA VARTIO,
The Parson's Widow.
PAUL VERHAEGHEN, *Omega Minor.*
AGLAJA VETERANYI, *Why the Child Is*
Cooking in the Polenta.
BORIS VIAN, *Heartsnatcher.*
LLORENÇ VILLALONGA, *The Dolls' Room.*
ORNELA VORPSI, *The Country Where No*
One Ever Dies.
AUSTRYN WAINHOUSE, *Hedyphagetica.*
PAUL WEST,
Words for a Deaf Daughter & Gala.
CURTIS WHITE,
America's Magic Mountain.
The Idea of Home.
Memories of My Father Watching TV.
Monstrous Possibility: An Invitation
to Literary Politics.
Requiem.
DIANE WILLIAMS, *Excitability:*
Selected Stories.
Romancer Erector.
DOUGLAS WOOLF, *Wall to Wall.*
Ya! & John-Juan.
JAY WRIGHT, *Polynomials and Pollen.*
The Presentable Art of Reading
Absence.
PHILIP WYLIE, *Generation of Vipers.*
MARGUERITE YOUNG, *Angel in the Forest.*
Miss MacIntosh, My Darling.
REYOUNG, *Unbabbling.*
VLADO ŽABOT, *The Succubus.*
ZORAN ŽIVKOVIĆ, *Hidden Camera.*
LOUIS ZUKOFSKY, *Collected Fiction.*
VITOMIL ZUPAN, *Minuet for Guitar.*
SCOTT ZWIREN, *God Head.*